BURLEY CROSS POSTBOX THEFT

By Nicola Barker

BURLEY CROSS POSTBOX THEFT

NICOLA BARKER

FOURTH ESTATE · *London*

First published in Great Britain by
Fourth Estate
A division of HarperCollins*Publishers*
77–85 Fulham Palace Road
London W6 8JB
www.4thestate.co.uk

A catalogue record for this book is available from the British Library

ISBN 978-0-00-735500-6

Typeset by Birdy Book Design

Printed in Great Britain by Clays Ltd, St Ives plc

Mixed Sources
Product group from well-managed
forests and other controlled sources
www.fsc.org Cert no. SW-COC-001806
© 1996 Forest Stewardship Council

FSC is a non-profit international organisation established to promote the
responsible management of the world's forests. Products carrying the FSC
label are independently certified to assure consumers that they come
from forests that are managed to meet the social, economic and
ecological needs of present and future generations

Find out more about HarperCollins and the environment at
www.harpercollins.co.uk/green

For Michael Crosby-Jones, Margot Prew, Alfred the Pungent,
and all in their exalted circle

(*Package and covering letter sent by internal mail*)

For attn PC Roger Topping, Ilkley

CONFIDENTIAL

Great news, Rog, *great* news –

At last all those long, incalculably boring, soul-destroying hours
of trudging and waiting and moping and cussing have finally
paid off, and the career-making case you've been yearning for
(stuck out there on your lonesome, all stiff and cross and
swollen – with that haunting, blue tinge around your gills – like
a huge, neglected gouty toe; a beached whale; a dour, over-
sized funeral director with no funeral to direct; a bad joke; a
lazy error; a missed train; a dropped stitch; an unsightly stain
on the perfect, white napkin of West Yorkshire's tea-cake and
charity-shop capital) is about to land – not the *cake*, you dope –
with a lovely, resounding *plop*! right in the middle of your
capacious lap.

Oh, and it's a good one, Rog, it's a choice one! It's
something that's going to frustrate and perplex that razor-sharp
intellect of yours for many, many years to come. It's going to
haunt your dreams, Rog, and dominate your every waking
moment. It's going to confound and enrage you, Rog. It's going
to challenge you in ways you never imagined, ways you never
even thought possible.

Put plainly, Rog: it's going to take over your miserable,
pointless little existence and turn it upside down in exactly the
same way it took over (and turned over) mine (which is slightly

less miserable and pointless than yours, admittedly. No, considerably less, Rog – *considerably* less – if you don't mind my saying so).

It's a Red Letter Day, Rog, so thump the tub! Whoop it up! Blow off the lid! Because your time has finally come! And it's an important time, Rog, a vital time, a time to cast aside 'compromise' and 'waffle' and 'pragmatism', and re-embrace all those old-fashioned principles of your gilded youth – ideas like … like 'truth' and 'honour', like 'pride' and 'justice'. (Don't think 'mortgage', Rog. Never think 'mortgage'. Great men never think 'mortgage'. And while we're on the subject, don't think 'bun'. And try not to think 'steak pie' or 'battered sausage'. I know how partial you are to those.)

In short, this is no time for beating around the bush, Rog. It's a time for plain speaking, a time for speaking your mind, a time for speaking as you find; a time for barking out orders, for slamming doors, for shoving your way, brutishly, into tiny, tightly packed rooms, squeezing your big, meaty hand into a powerful fist and banging it down, forcefully – again and again and again and *again* – on to desks and tables and other hard surfaces.

It's not a time for idle prattle and mooching about and eye-rolling and clock-watching (although, God only knows, there *has* been time for that in the past, Rog – and, God willing, still plenty more of it yet to come).

It's time to step up to the plate, Rog (and I don't mean your dinner plate, lad), a time to gird your loins – if loins you still have (Sandy, my gorgeous wife – your ex – once told me how you liked to shed them, every autumn, the way a stag sheds its antlers. But darling Sandy – as we have both discovered, to our mutual cost – can sometimes be a little bit 'creative' with the truth, eh, Rog?).

It's A Time to *Dance*, Rog – as I believe the bestselling author, Melvyn Bragg, once so poetically exhorted us. Although if you *do* decide to break into a spontaneous

quickstep – or a foxtrot, or a samba – please be sure to wear
your head-brace, your shoe-supports and your corset (or else –
dollars to doughnuts, Rog – those moronic jobsworths from
Health and Safety will be sniffing around us, yet again, like a
feral pack of constipated hyenas).

Let's throw caution to the wind, Rog! This is no time to
shilly-shally, no time to test the water and teeter, nervously, on
the brink. (Ah yes, I still fondly remember those compulsory
school swimming lessons at Thornhill Baths: me, clowning
around on the high diving board – to wildly cacophonous
cheers from the boys, hysterical screams of terror from the girls
– and then suddenly, with no warning, clicking into 'The
Zone', striding calmly to its furthest tip, bouncing once,
bouncing twice, and then performing – to assembled gasps – a
near-as-dammit-perfect back-flip, barely disturbing the surface
of the pool with so much as a ripple as I entered it.
Incredible!

And you, Rog? *You?* Far down below, Rog, crammed into an
under-size pair of brown nylon/viscose-mix regulation trunks,
your soft belly bulging over the waistband like a generous slick
of extra-thick UHT cream, the voluminous skin of your upper
torso pulsing translucently – ghastly and white as a portion of
uncooked tripe – your chest heaving, uncontrollably, as you
shivered and whimpered and clutched on to your towel,
blinking, uneasily, into the blurry half-light.

You had good reason to feel apprehensive, Rog, having just
– a few moments earlier – taken the very sensible precaution of
removing your glasses: you were vulnerable, Rog. You were
hamstrung. You were tragically incapacitated.

Yet how could you have possibly *known*, Rog – except with
the aid of *very basic common sense* – that your every move was
being carefully scrutinized, from above, by a mischievous
young prankster, svelte and bendy as a cat, in a pair of tight,
bright red Speedos, who thought it would be a hoot, Rog – a
veritable *hoot*, Rog – when the opportunity arose, to steal those

3

precious glasses of yours and then conceal them – in an act of rare daring and audacity – behind the lifeguard's chair?

How could you have possibly *known*, Rog? *How*, Rog? *Eh?*

And the *moral* of this insignificant little tale, Rog – if moral there be, at all …?

GROW A PAIR, ROG!!
GROW A BLOODY PAIR!!

WHO *CARES* WHAT THE TEMPERATURE OF THE WATER IS, ROG?! JUMP IN, YOU FOOL, *JUMP IN!!*

It's time to grab the damn world by the scruff of its neck and *shake* it, Rog. SHAKE IT!!
YOU HEAR?!)

Because I'll make no bones about it, Rog: this case is a hard taskmaster. Remember Mr Philton, Rog? *Dr* Philton? With his heavy, dark green serge jackets, his Advanced Motorist badge and his chronic halitosis? Who made you wet yourself, Rog, *piss* yourself, Rog, in front of the *entire class* during Double Latin, after you forgot how to conjugate the Latin verb 'to touch'?

Pardon, Rog? Was that a 'yes', I just heard you mutter there? Was that a 'yes', Rog, accompanied by a nervous cough and a sheepish little nod of the head? It was? So you *do* remember, Rog? You *do* actually remember?

Oh.
Good.

Well, for your information, Rog, this case – this remarkable case, this *extraordinary* case – is every inch as exacting and fastidious as crusty old Philton was; every inch as unsparing and punctilious (with an impressive line in put-downs, Rog, just like that old bastard had).

This case is a cruel mistress, Rog – the *cruellest* mistress. It's a savage, top-dollar dominatrix; a natural red-head in thigh-high, black leather boots and matching corset. Wonderfully well-equipped, Rog (*astonishingly* well-equipped), with her regulation whip, her paddle, her rack, her cleats, her strap-on, and – *naturellement!* – that inevitable – almost prosaic – pair of stainless-steel nipple-clamps.

She won't take any prisoners, Rog (well, perhaps the odd one – but only with the general assurance of firmly established protocols, full legal consent, and an accepted release word).

Much as you might expect, Rog, she pays precious little heed to society's mores (that mundane index of 'accepted niceties' we all so love to depend upon). She'll just sweep into your life, Rog, *barge* into your life, Rog, demand to know *exactly* how much you're earning (to the last pound, per annum, up front), deliver a couple of devastatingly acute and haughty pronouncements (like: 'You think you're very funny, very *witty*, don't you? You think you're quite the card, but I can assure you that you're not,' or 'I noticed a little earlier, when we were leaving the restaurant, that you're going ever so slightly bald on top …'), then shoot you a disdainful smile, shove you into a chair, push up her skirt, calmly straddle your lap and promptly take over.

KA-*BAM!*

Quick as a flash!

Just like that!

Can you *see* her, yet, Rog? Can you *smell* her?

Hmmn!

She smells of dirty musk and aniseed balls and cheap vodka, and that oddly persistent aroma from inside a moist, well-used Marigold washing-up glove. A *wonderful* smell, Rog, a heady, heaving, steamy aroma. Just close your eyes for a moment, Rog, and inhale it. Go on … just … *yes* …

Inhale!

Lovely, deep breath, Rog, *lovely* deep …

Ahhhhhhh!

Let it waft over you, Rog. Let it wash, gently, over you. Let it tip-toe around you and then creep – softly, so *insidiously* – inside your head. Let it calm your fevered mind, Rog, tickle your aching sinuses, and tingle on your tongue … Don't stiffen, Rog! No need to stiffen! It means you no harm, Rog. Just allow yourself to *trust* it, Rog. Just give it your *permission*, Rog. Just hold out your *hand*, Rog, and welcome it in … That's right! *Much* better! You're doing well, Rog! You're doing *brilliantly*! Feels really good, doesn't it?

Another breath now, Rog, deep, *deep* breath, now, Rog … *Ahhhhhhh!*
Perfect, Rog. See how easy that was? Relax those shoulders, now, Rog, lower those shoulders … Great work! Now the face. Let's relax the face, Rog, starting with the mouth. No more tension around the mouth. Feel the lips falling slightly apart … Excellent, Rog!

Now the eyes, Rog. Relax the eyes. Feel them rolling back in your head … Good boy! Well done!

And finally, the forehead. Release that frown, Rog. Feel all your pent-up stress and anxiety just slipping away, Rog, just lifting off you, Rog, just floating away from you … Wave bye-bye to all that nasty tension, Rog – *Bye-bye* tension! – and then make welcome, in its stead, this beautiful, almost *overwhelming* sense of peace and contentment …

How *calm* you feel, Rog! How quiet! How serene! *Embrace* that sensation, Rog, *embrace* that warm feeling of safety and tranquillity … Just let everything *go*, Rog, just let …

OI!!

WAKE UP!!

WAKE *UP*, ROG!!!

LOOK *SHARP*, YOU BIG PUDDING-HEAD!!
You've taken your mind off the ball, Rog (what were you

thinking, Rog?!) and she is striding towards you, at speed, her heels sounding like gunshots on the ceramic tiles – *QUICK, ROG! QUICK! TUCK IN YOUR SHIRT!*

She is shouting something at you, Rog, as she cracks her whip – *instructions* of some kind, *demands* of some kind, but because of the blood pumping in your ears (tinnitus still a problem, Rog?) you can't actually make them out …

What's she saying, Rog? What's she …?

OW!

That *hurt!*

OW!

That hurt!

My *God* – just look at her, Rog, *look* at her! What an astonishing spectacle she creates! What Babylonian splendour! What brilliancy! What brazenness! What filth! What grandeur!

And what a *figure* she has, Rog! What curves! What lines! What definition! Check out those legs, Rog! Longer than Joey Barton's arrest record! And that stomach, Rog! That six-pack! Tight as the Pope's prophylactic allowance! And let's not forget those *buttocks*, Rog; those fragrant *buns*! Harder than a pit-bull's forehead!

Uh-*oh* …

Hang on a second, Rog … Something's not quite right here. Something's wrong. Just call it instinct, Rog, but something's definitely amiss … What's that she's holding behind her back, Rog? What is it? A length of hose? A *bat*?! Well, whatever it is, one thing's for certain: this girl is VERY, VERY *ANGRY*, Rog! She's absolutely LIVID! She's SPITTING TACKS! She is *FURIOUS*, Rog! Her rage is absolute, it's all-consuming, it's DOWNRIGHT, BLOODY *MAGNIFICENT*! (No. *No*. Put your *badge* away, Rog! You're embarrassing yourself, now. Get a grip on yourself, lad! That type of buttoned-up behaviour simply won't wash in this environment.)

Oh dear. Oh *dear*. Just a fraction too late, Rog. She saw the badge (worse still, she sensed the attitude) and she didn't *like* it,

Rog. Not one bit. Her red lips are tangling into an ugly snarl. Her mean, green eyes are flashing and glinting like nasty slithers of candied angelica.

BEWARE, ROG!! NO SUDDEN MOVES, ROG! BACK OFF, ROG! *TAKE CARE*!!! Because this girl will eat you up and spit you out! She'll beat you to a pulp! She'll drip hot candle-wax into your nostrils and stamp her stiletto-heeled boot into your prodigious gut. She'll make you kneel and crawl and grovel, Rog. She'll make you fawn and cower and snivel. She'll make you ask nicely for every stupid little thing ('Please, Miss, if you don't mind, Miss …') and then refuse you, point-blank.

She'll make you wish you were never born, Rog! She'll make you bleat like a lamb! She'll dress you up in a nappy – taunt you and tease you – demand that you pee yourself, then slap you, red-raw, when you do. She'll make you greet and shudder and *howl*, Rog. I *know* she will, Rog, I *know* she will, because I'VE ALREADY *BEEN* THERE, Rog! I've bought the ticket, Rog! I've taken the tour, Rog! I've used all the facilities, Rog (and left them scrupulously clean, Rog, I can assure you)!

OH, ROG! HOW I'VE *SUFFERED* AT HER HANDS! How I've bucked and gasped and *strained* at her ungodly demands! I've been her *slave*, Rog, her *worm*, her *hack*, her *grub*, her *fag*! I've been her fool, Rog, her *fool*!

And how has she repaid me, Rog (for all my loyalty and patience, my stoicism and forbearance)? What has she deigned to give me in return, Rog? By way of *fair exchange*, Rog?

Nothing!

NOTHING, Rog!

Not a *damn* thing, Rog!

Look at me, Rog! Just *look* at me! My manhood is in *shreds*! My dignity is in *tatters*! My life is in *chaos*! My pride is in *ruins*! AND ALL FOR *WHAT*, ROG? FOR *WHAT*?!

I'm no longer afraid to confess, Rog, that over the past few months this case – this damnable case, this infernal case – has pretty much taken all I've had to give. It's squeezed me dry,

Rog. It's drained me. It's very nearly had the best of me: *fact*.

It's been a heavy burden, Rog. It's been a heavier burden than – at times – it was possible for one, lone man (even a powerfully built man, well-preserved, with all his original features still intact) to bear. In truth (and in all humility, Rog), I sometimes thought this case might break me. At points I thought it *had* broken me. I was like a badly made, reproduction Staffordshire shepherdess (are you still collecting the Staffordshire figures, Rog?) after a bumpy ride down the A59 in the back of a stolen Ford Transit.

My paint – once so pristine – has been scuffed and chipped by this case, Rog. My shiny veneer has been irreparably clouded. At one point – I'll openly admit – I was even in imminent danger of losing my crook.

Oh yes, I was very nearly shattered by this case, Rog. I say again: very. nearly. *shattered*. by. this. case. Rog.

Thank heaven for Bostik.

My hands tremble a little as I write to you today, Rog – I don't doubt that your well-trained eye has already detected the slight wobble (which is precisely why the force holds you in such high esteem, Rog, and a major reason why they decided to ship you – lock, stock and barrel, at the very peak of your powers, without any kind of warning or consultation – from the bustling, crime-ridden metropolis of Leeds, to the sedate, country town of Ilkley, where you now employ your prodigious portfolio of detective skills in overseeing school fetes, book fairs and minor traffic infractions, while maintaining a standard of service which <u>no other qualified recruit on the modern force today would knowingly dare to replicate.</u>

You've got huge guts, Rog, *huge* guts. Let no man presume to tell you otherwise – or any woman, either, if one ever gets within spitting distance).

But enough of my inconsequential witterings, Rog (For what do they matter now? I am yesterday's news, Rog. My battle with this case is over), let's just grasp the nettle, Rog, *together*,

Rog, and press on, shall we? Because it's all about *you*, now, Rog. This is *your* moment. So *take* it, Rog, *grab* it, Rog (the *moment*, Rog, not the nettle, you idiot), with those huge, flabby mitts of yours, and hold on fast, kid. Prepare yourself for the ride of your life! It's sure as hell going to be a bumpy one!

Buckle yourself in tightly, Rog (I took the precaution of asking them – in advance – to enlarge and reinforce the safety-belt. They were surprisingly cooperative, Rog, and they assured me – after doing their sums – that they were at least 37 per cent sure that the stitching would hold in the advent of a sudden stop. *Eh voilà*, Rog – *Les jeux sont faits!*).

Because whatever happens, Rog (and which of us may know what the future holds?), it's going to be a crazy, hazy cavalcade, Rog: a blur of light and speed and blood and lust and heat and spunk and fire (but no biscuits, Rog. No digestives or ginger snaps or HobNobs. Possibly an outside chance of the odd Garibaldi … but then … well … possibly not).

Draw a deep breath and pinch yourself, Rog (more than an inch, Rog? Yeah. I thought as much), because what you're holding between your eight fat fingers (and two still fatter thumbs) is the *Wacky Races* of all cases. This is the Top Banana, Rog. This is THE BIG ONE! And it's all yours, now, Rog. It's completely and utterly *yours*, now, Rog.

Blink back the tears, Rog, because this case – this extraordinary case – this astonishing case – this case, which has foiled, baffled and dumbfounded some of the country's greatest living detective minds … Although … actually … no. On second thoughts, it was only *my* great, living, detective mind (as you are probably already aware, my faithful colleague, PC Hill, has been off sick for the past month after misaligning his spine – and nobody else ever really gave a tinker's cuss … A quick word to the wise, Rog, while we're on the subject: never attempt to learn t'ai chi from a stuttering Bulgarian bricklayer with one ear).

So here it is, Rog, here it is. My stomach loops and contracts

as I hand it over (dodgy prawn sandwich at lunch, perhaps?).
I am full of relief and awe and gratitude – a little humble, a
little proud. .

Here it is, Rog. It is yours. It was *meant* for you, Rog (and I
say that with all sincerity). It was preordained, Rog. It was
written in the stars, Rog. It was fated.

It's your destiny, Rog. It was *always* your destiny.

Because there have been other cases, Rog, and other officers,
but there has never been *this* case, Rog, and *this* officer. There
has never been PC Roger Topping and (my teeth tingle as I
prepare to write these words) the case of THE BURLEY
CROSS POSTBOX THEFT. Or does it sound better the
other way around? THE BURLEY CROSS POSTBOX
THEFT case? I'm not entirely sure, Rog. Perhaps the second
way is best. Or perhaps the first. Yes. The first. Perhaps the
first has more punch, Rog, more attack, more *gravitas*.

Right. Good. I'm glad we've sorted that out. So let's get
down to business now, shall we?

The package, you will observe (if you double-check the
contents back against the enclosed inventory – which, of
course, you will; I would expect nothing less of you, Rog), is
thirty-seven documents short of the initial haul. These
consisted of twenty-two Christmas cards (from four original
sources, all of which contained only the most perfunctory of
messages), nine responses to a private advert in the local press
about a foolproof, non-invasive remedy for unreliable erectile
function (it's an ageing population, Rog), three applications to
take part in a government-funded solar water-heating scheme
(environmentalist poppycock), a £212 cheque bound for an
Egyptian donkey sanctuary near Cairo (raised by Wincey
Hawkes at The Old Oak during the village's monthly bridge
night), another of £425 (bound for a clock repair specialist
from Harrogate), and a third of £2,838 (heading for the Burley
Cross Auction of Promises account at the Cooperative Bank,
Ilkley), all of which I have duly returned to Wincey, by hand,

on Tuesday (on the understanding that she may well have cancelled them during the intervening period).

I took the difficult decision to dispose of the remaining thirty-four documents as I saw fit (i.e. got Mary on the Front Desk to reseal them with Sellotape last Friday and bang them back into the post), because they couldn't be crammed inside the Jiffy bag (this was the only bag in the building, Rog, and it's *my* bag. There's been a bust-up with Supplies. The wife of the tiny dick in charge recently delivered twins – one in breech – and word on the street is that a whole twelve weeks later, she's still staunchly refusing to put out. So now we're *all* paying the price, Rog; it's well over a fortnight since I've so much as laid eyes on a paperclip).

Don't be overly concerned by the green staining on the bag – it formerly contained my monthly delivery of organic kelp powder (amazing stuff – absolutely amazing. It's worked wonders for my lazy bowel. I'm now regular as a station-clock, chiming twice daily: once at ten, and once at eight, on the dot).

Ever the consummate professional, I have seen fit to contact Messrs Thorndyke, Endive Jr, and Augustine personally (by email, at www.hystericaltosspots.com) to inform them of the fact that this case is now being passed on to the Ilkley Constabulary. I don't doubt that you will be hearing from them very shortly. In fact you have probably heard from them already. In fact you are probably hearing from them right now, if the phone in your office is ringing …

Is it ringing, Rog? Thought so. Did you answer it, Rog? You did. And was it Mr Thorndyke's solicitor, Rog, 'keeping up to speed' on things, while jabbering away, inanely, about heaven only knows what?
Of course it was.

Since I have a few minutes to spare before tea-time (who tip-toes ever closer on her sweet, icing-sugared feet) and because I consider you 'an old mucker', Rog, I'll give you a quick *précis* of my activities in relation to this case over the past six weeks (although, if you prefer, there's always the enclosed file: a whole 474 pages-worth of completely pointless paperwork, duplicated thricely, as regulations stipulate).

Credit where credit's due, Rog: PC Hill actually did much of the early legwork. His initial visit to the crime scene was on the morning *after* the theft (on the evening of the 21st – the night of the crime – we were all somewhat preoccupied in Skipton, as I'm sure you will recall, by my televised appearance on the National Bravery Awards – live, from the Café de Paris in London – following those tragic incidents surrounding the blaze at Tilton Mill; the fascinating *denouement* of which has been closely followed – and faithfully recorded, with accompanying photos and lengthy panegyrics from a grateful public – in the local and national press. Although, as I said at the time, Rog, 'The label of "hero" sits uncomfortably on me. I'm just a typical, northern copper doing an extremely difficult – and often dangerous – job to the very best of my *blah, blah, blah* …').

We have reason to believe that the break-in took place at approximately 21.00 hrs. The local vicar assured PC Hill that he posted a letter (case letter 15) at about 20.55 that evening, when everything appeared 'just as normal – in fact, if anything, *more* normal than normal'. (PC Hill comments in his accompanying notes that he found this '*more* normal than normal' statement, 'slightly odd', but that he didn't press the reverend any further on the point because 'he had just started a nose bleed and only had one tissue'.)

The crime was reported to us (with almost *indecent* alacrity, Rog) at 21.12, by Susan Trott – of Black Grouse Cottage – who had been, I quote: 'out looking for hedgehogs when I was horrified to notice the postbox door had fallen off and was just lying there, on the ground'.

The report PC Hill submitted was, to put it generously, a tad perfunctory (you will notice that some of his 'extra thoughts' were jotted down on to torn shreds of chip paper – that fool in Supplies has so much to answer for!).

No serious attempt was made to dust the crime scene for fingerprints because – as you can read for yourself – it had been 'bucketing down with rain all morning'.

His search for any kind of tool or instrument which might've been used to engineer the break-in was limited to 'a quick peek in a nearby hedge', where he was surprised to discover 'a rusty, old biscuit-tin containing two slightly mildewed pornographic magazines: *Trumpet for Boys* (Issue 13, June 1998), and *Golden Horns* (Issue 4, December 2002)'. As you can probably detect from the titles, Rog, they were directed towards the specialist brass band enthusiast's market, and aren't currently included in the body of evidence because PC Hill took them home for 'further detailed scrutiny' (he plays a wind instrument himself; possibly the clarinet), and has yet to bring them back.

While it obviously pains me to level criticism at an officer from my own division, Rog, I don't believe, in all candour, that PC Hill initially appreciated the true gravity of the Burley Cross Postbox Theft scenario – a serious schoolboy error for a young bobby of his obvious talent and considerable potential (and talking of errors, Rog, I think you'll agree that he really *does* need to learn the correct spellings of 'necessary' and 'instigated').

Even so, there's a perfectly passable description of the condition of the box itself. ('Overall, the thing's in a pretty terrible state. I'm surprised it's still functional. It's falling to pieces … There's a bit of botched-up paintwork covering several inches of rust around the base, and another bit around the door's hinges … To break into it, all you'd've really needed to do was jab at it for a while with a flat screwdriver or a putty knife …')

You will doubtless already be aware of the backstory re the postbox, Rog. The Royal Mail – or Consignia (or whatever jumped-up moniker they're giving themselves nowadays) – have been trying to replace it with a modern box for the past three years and have been repeatedly foiled in their attempts by a shadowy – but nevertheless deeply influential – pressure group in the village called The Burley Cross Preservation Corps.

The Corps is controlled by Independent local borough councillor (and gibbering idiot) Baxter Thorndyke. Thorndyke is also a staunch mainstay of both The Burley Cross Public Toilet Watch (est. 2005), and The Burley Cross Road Safety Committee, a group whose chief aim is to encourage motorists to stick to the busy A road that bypasses the village, rather than taking the – admittedly, rather tempting – short-cut straight through the heart of it (they have their own luminous, faux-military uniform and functioning speed gun – which they bought on the internet – and spend many a pleasant hour each week pointing it at random drivers and intimidating them with it).

You will know yourself, Rog, that the postbox at issue is actually situated in Ilkley Constabulary's policing territory (I rue the day some pea-brain on Wharfedale Council found themselves with a spare half-hour to waste before lunch one morning, and saw fit to spend it cheerfully reallocating the police boundary for Burley Cross, dividing it, haphazardly, between our two adjacent forces. For the record, I still don't know who's responsible for the barn and outbuildings at Deep Fell or the small housing estate on Hollow Nook Farm … So far as I am aware, they currently police themselves).

The girl at the call pool who registered (and then allocated) Susan Trott's emergency call (Cindy Withers. Are you familiar with Cindy, Rog? Incorrigible shrew. Terrible chip on her shoulder – probably acquired from lugging that phenomenal pair of Double-D cups around everywhere with her) still stridently maintains, in her own defence, that while she appreciated the fact that the box was on *your* watch, the caller – Susan Trott – phoned from a land-line inside her home, which is directly *adjacent* to the box, and therefore on ours.

A bag of evidence being unearthed in the back alleys of Skipton – a mere ten hours thereafter – was also considered pertinent to where the case ultimately ended up.

Of course the people in charge of these life-and-death decisions (hard to believe they actually have a whole *department* dedicated to this kind of guff, Rog, manned entirely by the idiot sons and daughters of Police Commissioners, I don't doubt), always reserve the right to change what we laughably call 'their minds' (thereby effortlessly generating yet another skip-load of paperwork), and have apparently resolved to do so in this instance (I honestly don't know why this might be, or what they can possibly hope to gain by it, Rog, I just try my damnedest to keep my head down, and take all their stupid, petty, pointless – not to mention hugely disruptive – subterranean political manoeuvrings with a very, very generous pinch of salt).

Returning, if I may, to the issue of the theft itself; it might interest you to discover (and this is not something PC Hill made an official note of, but he happened to mention it to me, afterwards) that during his cursory, five-minute perusal of the postbox, he was approached and engaged in conversation/ loudly interrogated/helpfully advised/subtly lampooned/openly insulted (take your pick, Rog) by *at least* twelve different individuals, including the aforementioned Thorndyke (don't these crackpots have *jobs* to go to, Rog? Or lives to lead? Or hedges to trim? Or Raku classes to attend?), who was wearing a T-shirt bearing the legend 'Your Vehicle is a Loaded Weapon!' on one side and 'Watch out World – I'm a Highwayman!' on the other.

PC Hill said Mr Thorndyke became 'quite hysterical' during their brief exchange, and at one point virtually screamed, 'This is *exactly* what they wanted! Are you *blind*?! Can't you see?! This is *exactly* what they wanted! If you actually have *any serious intention* of investigating this crime – and *catching* the cowardly vandal who committed this atrocity – then stop dawdling around here like a wet weekend, stuffing your face with battered cod, and go and speak to the man behind it! Talk to Trevor Woods! Talk to their *henchman*, if

you've got the balls! He's up to his scrawny neck in all of this!'
(I feel I must just briefly note, in passing, that there have been
no actual road fatalities in Burley Cross since 1917, when,
according to town records, 'an inebriated flower-seller – of poor
repute – slipped on some filthy cobbles, fell under the wheels of
a cart and was instantly killed.'

It should also be noted that Cllr Thorndyke was wearing a
T-shirt – and *only* a T-shirt, in temperatures of 20 degrees and
under – during his exchange with PC Hill. PC Hill said, 'His
teeth were chattering as he spoke. It was actually quite difficult
to decipher what he was saying at some points. I don't know
why he didn't just go home and put his coat on.')

A short while later, as he was climbing into his patrol car, PC
Hill apprehended the aforementioned Mr Woods (the source of
all this unbridled hysteria), driving up to the box in his postal
van. PC Hill said he was 'to all intents and purposes a broken
man, skulking around the place like a beaten dog ...'

On being questioned about the theft, Woods was quoted as
saying, 'They can't pay me enough to do the collection here,
mate. They're nutters. They should have me on *danger* money.
They're all sodding *lunatics*.'

Suffice to say, following PC Hill's initial investigation of the
crime scene (and following the discovery of the refuse sack of
letters found dumped in a back alley in Skipton – a mere two
doors down from the bijou residence of notorious local petty
criminal, Timmy Dickson), I contacted all those individuals
whose letters now form a part of the official evidence,
informing them that their post couldn't be returned – or
forwarded on – until it had been formally declassified as such.

Next, I initiated an official mail-out to the entire village (also
enclosed, Rog, translated into the obligatory three languages –
I chose Portuguese, Mandarin and Xhosa) to try and discover
if anyone had posted a letter on the evening of Dec. 21st,
which had *not* – for some reason – been retrieved in the
Skipton cache.

Nobody had, although Rita Bramwell couldn't be entirely certain. She said she *thought* she might have sent something, but that she wasn't sure what it was, or to whom it was addressed (she's several wires short of the full radio, Rog). As it transpired, she *had* actually sent something (case letter 13).

When I then asked her if she had received my earlier communication (informing her that exactly such a letter was being held by us, as evidence), she hotly denied that I had sent her one – although her husband, Peter Bramwell, later found it stuffed down the back of a chaise longue, and was kind enough to apologize to me for his wife's behaviour.

I subsequently sent Mrs Bramwell a photocopy of her own letter (in an attempt to dispel her confusion). Her response was not at all as I had expected it to be. She hotly denied having sent it – in a long and erratic email – making a series of wild, unsubstantiated claims and accusations – one of which was that it had been 'forged', and that I myself was 'in the frame' as one of the suspects for the crime (we all had a good chuckle at that in the staff canteen)!

Several people were, you will be *stunned* to discover, Rog, a little peeved by the news that their post would not be immediately returned to them (you may have seen the bilious squall of angry letters in the local rag, Rog), but this *is* Burley Cross, after all: a tiny, ridiculously affluent, ludicrously puffed-up moor-side village, stuffed to capacity with spoilt second-home owners, southerners, the strange, the 'artistic', the eccentric and the retired (most of them tick all of the above boxes, Rog, and several more besides – although I'm sure I don't have the natural intelligence, fine vocabulary or social acuity to do them all justice here ... Matt Endive (Sr) – case letter 4 – who perfectly exemplifies those latent, Burley Cross characteristics of tragic retard and unalloyed fat-head combined, called me a 'bumped-up little northern grammar-school oik', only yesterday on the phone, and then, when I laughed him off, said I was 'tragically out of my depth' and

'riddled with contumely'. I responded – quick as a flash, Rog.
I said, 'Are you sure you don't mean "contumacy", Mr Endive
– from the Latin *com* = intense + *tumere* = to swell?'

A long silence followed, Rog, and I don't mind admitting
that I enjoyed every damn second of it – although, in
retrospect, I think he probably *did* mean contumely).

Of course you know better than anybody, Rog, what kind
of problems we're up against here: to say Burley Cross is
'Little England writ large', would be like saying Stilton is 'a
dairy product with blue bits running through it' (i.e. an
understatement, Rog, and a *considerable* understatement at
that).

This is, after all, the same place where the local council's
decision *not* to install a speed-bump last year caused a mini-
riot on Pancake Day which was later 'Recorded for Posterity,
that Future Generations Might Read and Weep', in a seven-
hundred-line epic poem, (still pinned up on the notice
board outside the local shop, with copies available for sale
inside):

> *The butcher got the worst of it, when spade and axe did fall,*
> *The baker put up quite a fight, when caught up in the brawl …*

(Ironically, there *is* no baker in Burley Cross, Rog, and never
has been, either, so far as I am aware.)

Before I finally wind up, Rog, here's a little something extra
that might just pique your interest: while nobody was willing to
admit to having had a letter stolen during the theft, two people
were determined to make it publicly known that the letters
written in their names were *not* penned by their own hands
(the first, Rita Bramwell, as mentioned previously; the second,
Tom Augustine, whose letter about a little incident at the
public toilets I found especially informative, Rog – if deeply
unedifying).

A final, brief aside, Rog: I couldn't help remarking on how

many letters had been sent on the day of the robbery. The number seemed unusually high in these text- and email-friendly times (even taking into consideration the pre-Christmas rush). I was about to launch some half-cocked investigations re The Royal Mail (Consignia, *et al.*) when PC Hill happily set my mind at rest on the issue.

It transpires that an extremely attractive, young lady – Nina Springhill – has recently started work in the post office, and, since her employment there, the volume of post being sent from the village has significantly increased (not only that, but an unprecedented number of pensioners – all male – have reverted to the traditional way of receiving their bi-monthly pay-outs: at the counter, as opposed to having it paid directly into their bank accounts).

I was only too happy to check the veracity of this tip-off myself, Rog, a week or so back, when I dropped into the PO to buy a book of stamps (in fact I bought three – two more on successive visits) which Sandy later came across – on wash day – while going through my pockets.

When I staggered home from work that night, there they all were, formally arranged on the kitchen table, like pieces of evidence – in fact I think there may have been five of them, in total – and Sandy standing next to them, pointing, with a face like thunder, demanding to know *who* I was planning to write to, and *why*.

(I mean all this fuss and nonsense over seven little books of stamps, Rog! Whatever next, *eh*?!)

So that's pretty much the sum of it, Rog. I do hope my paltry insights have proved moderately useful as I step graciously aside – severing the spell-binding umbilical of this case once and for all – and redirect my energies to solving Skipton's ever increasing backlog of run-of-the-mill murders, arsons, rapes, indecent assaults *etc.* (and, of course, in case I ever get too smug and complacent: the perennially fascinating mystery of Mrs Compton-Rees's nomadic recycling bin; they found it in Hurston on Friday, then, on Sunday, a bemused call from the Laundromat in New Leasey ...).

Hush, my boy! *Hush*! What's that I hear? Is it the trusty rattle of Mrs Spokes's tea trolley?

Before it arrives, Rog, I should probably alert you to the fact that Timmy Dickson, our main suspect for the crime (this type of activity is right up his street, Rog – or should I say 'right up his *back alley*', Rog? *Arf! Arf!*), has a perfect alibi. He was bedridden in hospital in Leeds that week, after his electronic tagging device rubbed up against the delicate flesh of his calf, generated a blister, and provoked a nasty case of cellulitis (transpires he's allergic to penicillin, Rog, and blew up like a balloon when they pumped him full of the stuff!).

Fishing Saturday week, Rog? It's been too long! How are your shifts? I'm free in the p.m. from one, if that's any good to you. The following week I'm thinking of heading off to Royal Dornoch for a round or two (they say it has the same latitude as Moscow!) with Richard Usbourne (always useful to have a shrink handy on the links, eh, Rog? Although in your case, a pathologist might be more in order!).

I do think I've earned it, Rog, all things considered. PC Hill's little problem put the kibosh on me joining Sandy on her annual pilgrimage to County Wicklow to lay flowers on her father's grave (I was planning to join her for the first time this year – possibly taking the opportunity of popping in on Druid's Glen, afterwards, on the sly!). Sandy's still bearing quite a grudge after making the trip on her own.

When I mentioned that I might be heading off to Royal Dornoch over breakfast this morning (which, for the record, I made myself – there's still quite an atmosphere of rancour in the house over the 'stamps issue'), Sandy suggested that I might enjoy 'taking a short trip up my own backside', instead, then added, as a vague afterthought, 'Although that might be a

little difficult, Laurence. I'm not sure if you've actually returned from the last one yet.'
Ho ho!

The truths we speak in jest, eh, Rog?

All the best,
Sergeant Laurence Everill

PS To *touch*, Rog: *tango, tangis, tangit, tangimus, tangitis, tangunt* …

PPS *Hmmn*. A lovely warm slice of Treacle Spice Tray-bake and a steaming mug of tea! Yes. That'll do nicely, thanks.

[letter 1]

For the exclusive attn of
Ms Linda Withycombe –
Environmental Health Technician,
Wharfedale District Council

The Retreat
Saxonby Manor
Burley Cross

21.12.2006

Dear Ms Withycombe[1],

Here is the information as requested by yourself on Friday,
December 19, during our brief conversation after the public
meeting re 'the proposal for the erection of *at least* [my itals]
two new mobile phone masts in the vicinity of Wharfedale'.
(I don't think it would be needlessly optimistic of me to say
that the 'nay's definitely seemed to have the best of things
that day[2] – so let's just hope those foolish mules[3] at the phone
company finally have the basic common sense to sit down and
rethink what is patently a reckless, environmentally destructive
and fundamentally ill-conceived strategy, eh?)
    Might I just add (while we're on the subject of the meeting
itself) that I sincerely hope you did not take to heart any of the
unhelpful – and in some cases extremely offensive – comments
and observations made by the deranged and – quite frankly –

1 Are you one of the Cirencester-based Withycombes? If so, then I was extremely
privileged to serve with the Royal Air Force in Burma (1961–63) alongside your late
maternal grandfather, Major Cyril Withycombe (although – on further reflection –
Cyril may well have been a Withycoombe).
2 Hurrah!
3 Sic.

tragic subject of this letter: Mrs Tirza Parry, widow[4] (as she persists in signing herself in all of our correspondence; although on one occasion she signed herself Mrs Tirza Parry, wi*n*dow, by mistake, which certainly provided we long-suffering residents of The Retreat with no small measure of innocent amusement, I can tell you).

Because of her petite stature, advanced years and charmingly 'bohemian' appearance (I use the word bohemian not only in the sense of 'unconventional' – the white plastic cowboy boots, the heavy, sometimes rather coarse-seeming[5], pagan-style jewellery, clumsily moulded from what looks like unfired clay[6], the pop-socks, the paisley headscarves – but also with a tacit nod towards Mrs Parry's famously 'exotic' roots, although, as a point of accuracy, I believe her parents were Turks or Greeks rather than Slovaks, Tirza being a derivation of 'Theresa', commonly celebrated as the Catholic saint of information which, under the circumstances, strikes me – and may well strike you – as remarkably ironic. *NB I am just about to close this scandalously long bracket, and apologize, in advance, for the rambling – possibly even inconsequential – nature of this lengthy aside. Pressure of time – as I'm sure you'll understand – prohibits me from rewriting/restructuring the previous paragraph, so it may well behove you to reread the first half of the original sentence in order to make sense of the second. Thanks*), Mrs Parry has it within her reach to create, if not a favourable, then at least a diverting first impression during fledgling social encounters (I remember falling prey to such an impression myself, and would by no means blame you if such had been your own). There is no denying the woman's extraordinary dynamism (it's only a

---

4 Transparency is definitely not one of Mrs Parry's main characteristics.
5 I'll make no bones about it, dear: *phallic*.
6 Norma Spoot works part-time at the local butcher's, and told me – in between hysterical gales of laughter – of how she overheard Mrs Parry boasting (while she was having a chicken deboned last Tuesday) that her jewellery 'sells like hot cakes' on the internet.

shame, I suppose, that all this highly laudable energy and enthusiasm is being so horribly – one might almost say *dangerously* – misdirected in this particular instance).

I've often remarked on how wonderfully blue and piercing Tirza Parry's eyes are; my dear wife, Shoshana, calls them 'lavender eyes', which I think describes them most excellently (although, as she has also remarked, and very tellingly, I think, a 'blueing' of the eyes can often signify the onset of Alzheimer's, dementia and other sundry ailments related to the loss of memory/reason in old age. I mean nothing derogatory by this statement – none of us is getting any younger, after all![7]).

You will doubtless remember Shoshana (from the aforementioned meeting) as that fearless, flame-haired dominatrix (with the tightly bound arm – more of which, anon) who was acting as temporary secretary that day[8], Wallace Simms, who usually fills this role[9], having been bedridden by yet another severe bout of his recurrent sciatica.

It briefly occurs to me – by the by – that it may prove helpful at this point (especially in light of some of the wild accusations being thrown around by TP[10] herself in the course of said meeting) if I provide you with a short précis of some of the complex, logistical issues currently being employed by that cunning creature as a pathetic smokescreen to obfuscate the real – the critical – subject at the dark heart of this letter. If you – like Mandy Williamson, your charming predecessor[11] – are already fully convinced of my impartiality as a witness/ informant on this delicate – and rather distasteful – matter then

---

7 I do not mean to include you in this sweeping statement. That would obviously be ridiculous.

8 People refuse to believe that she actually became eligible for a free bus pass last February.

9 And then some! The poor chap's tall as a door handle but weighs in at over seventeen stone!

10 I'll abbreviate Mrs Parry from this point onwards, if it's all the same to you.

11 Did she have it yet? Was it – as I predicted – a bonny little chap with a bright tuft of ginger hair on top?

feel free to skip the next section of this letter and rejoin the narrative in two pages' time (I have taken the trouble to mark the exact spot with a tiny sticker of a Bolivian tree frog).

The Retreat (please see first document enclosed, labelled Doc. 1) is a charming – although rather Lilliputian – residence situated just inside the extensive grounds of Saxonby Manor (I have circled the residence, and its small garden, on the map provided with a fluorescent yellow marker).

My dear, late wife (Emily Baverstock, *née* Morrison) inherited said property over seventeen years ago from her great-aunt – the esteemed Lady Beatrix Morrison – who was then resident full-time at Saxonby (although she generally preferred to overwinter in the south of France, where she kept an immaculate, art deco-style penthouse flat in the heart of Biarritz).

When The Retreat was initially built (in the late 1920s) the property's principal use was as a summer house/changing room (situated, as it was, directly adjacent to a fabulous, heated, Olympic-sized swimming pool – now long gone, alas). It was constructed with all mod cons (i.e. toilet, shower etc.; see second document – Doc. 2 – a photocopy of the original architectural plans) and although undisputedly *bijou*, The Retreat was always intended to be more than a mere 'adjunct'. As early as 1933 they added a small kitchen and a bedroom to allow guests to stay there overnight in greater luxury, and it was eventually inhabited – full-time – by a displaced family (the Pringles, I believe[12]) for the duration of WWII.

After the war it became the home of Saxonby's gardener, the infamous Samuel Tuggs (he sang and played the washboard with local folk sensations The Thrupenny Bits[13]), who was

12 The youngest child's initials are still scratched into the bark of our old apple tree.
13 His voice ranged over several octaves – although my late wife used to say that while he might reach a note with all apparent ease, he could never actually succeed in holding one for any extended period. I used to tell her that this was simply 'the rustic style' (I'm fairly well informed on the subject), but she refused to be convinced.

subsequently implicated in the mysterious disappearance of his wife's fifteen-year-old niece, Moira (1974) and – rather sadly for Lady Morrison[14] – while he was never formally tried for the crime[15], an atmosphere of intense social pressure eventually obliged him to flee the area.

The Retreat's already fascinating history[16] was consolidated further when it was rented out (1981–90) to a writer of books about the science of code-breaking (a fascinating old chap called John Hinty Crew – 'Hinty' to his pals – a promiscuous homosexual whose real claim to fame was his inflammatory adolescent correspondence with Anthony Blunt[17]).

Up until this point the cottage possessed no formal/legal rights as an 'independent dwelling'. Lady Morrison had – quite naturally – never felt the need to apply for any, and my late wife's ownership of the property was only ever made explicit by dint of a short caveat in the old lady's will which forbade the sale of the Manor at any future date without a prior agreement that The Retreat (and its tiny garden) were to remain exclusively in the hands of the Morrison family. Rights of access were, of course, a necessary part of this simple arrangement.

It is, I'm afraid, this worryingly fluid and vague 'rights of access' issue that is the source of all our current heartache.

---

14 The topiary was never as good after he left.
15 I call it 'a crime' although a corpse was never discovered (there were signs of a struggle and several suspicious spots of blood, however).
16 Bertrand Russell, the famous philosopher and coward, apparently stayed there on several occasions.
17 In the early 1990s these letters were adapted into a play called My Dear Hinty ... I can't remember, off-hand, who starred in it – possibly that game young lad who used to ride his bicycle up and down those steep, cobbled streets in the old Hovis adverts. Either way, a dear school friend of mine – Hortensia Sandle, an RE teacher, charming lass, who lived in the Smoke and had a penchant for the theatre – was persuaded to attend the opening night (I'd been given free tickets by Hinty himself, but was a martyr to chronic piles at the time so found it difficult to remain seated for extended periods). I still don't know for sure what she actually made of the production (one review I read said the direction was 'all over the shop'), because – for some inexplicable reason – she refused to ever speak to me again afterwards. Very odd.

As you will no doubt have already observed on the map provided, The Retreat was actually constructed within a short walking distance of an arched, medieval gate in the outer wall of the larger estate, and this gate has always been used as an entrance/exit (into the village of Burley Cross beyond) by the inhabitants of said dwelling (rather than the main entrance to the Manor, which lies approximately 500 yards – again, see Doc. 1 – to its right[18]).

It goes without saying that many times over the years my wife(s) and I have applied for some kind of permanent, formal, *legal* right of way, if only to establish the property as an independent dwelling (so that we might pay rates, raise a mortgage, or even consider selling[19] at some future date, perhaps).

Unfortunately, the current owners of the Manor (the Jonty Weiss-Quinns[20]) have never been keen to support this application. The chief plank in their Crusoe-esque-style raft of objections[21] is that the land that lies between The Retreat and

18 To use the main entrance would actually involve cutting through a yew hedge and then swimming across a large Japanese pond full of ornamental carp.
19 The Morrison line ended with Emily. We had no children of our own – though certainly not through want of trying! Rumour has it that an inappropriate liaison between two first cousins in 1810 caused a genetic weakness in the Morrison gene pool which rendered all subsequent issue physically and reproductively flawed. Aside from her infecundity, Emily had the added distinction of a third nipple. In poor light it could be mistaken for a large mole, but she was very self-conscious about it and always wore a robe whilst lounging by the pool. Once, on holiday in Kenya, she allowed her guard (and the robe) to fall and the mark was spotted by a sharp-eyed cocktail waiter. We were subsequently evicted, unceremoniously, from the hotel. To protect Emily's feelings I determined to keep the real reason for our eviction hidden from her (and was relatively successful, to boot). She always naively believed that we were turfed out because I queried the bar bill (and gave me no end of stick about it, too!).
20 Who have always been extremely genial landlords and have never sought to interfere with our ready access to the property – although they did kick up quite a stink two years ago when we built our conservatory or 'sunroom'. Apparently the light reflects quite sharply off its glass roof and can be seen very clearly from the window of their dining room (an added complication is that this small but precious 'space' was added to the property with the intention of creating a safe/therapeutic environment for Shoshana to sunbathe, au naturel. The poor creature is prone to seasonal attacks of chronic eczema and constant exposure to gentle sunlight really is the best possible cure).
21 Which I won't bore you with here.

the gate was once the site of an old monastery (see Doc. 1 –
I have used a pink pencil to shade in the area) which is
considered by – among others – the National Trust[22] and
English Nature to be 'an important heritage site'.[23]

Were you to come along – in person – and take a good look
at what actually remains of this 'Old Monastery', I think you
would be astonished (as, indeed, are we[24]) that so much fuss
could be generated by what basically amounts to a scruffy pile
of broken stones (approx. three feet in diameter – aka the 'Old
Cloister') and a slight dip or indentation in the ground (just to
the left of the gate) which is apparently all that's now left of the
'Old Monk's Latrine'(!).

As I'm sure you can imagine, Shoshana and I have grown
rather depressed and frustrated by this unsatisfactory legal
situation, not least because our non-payment of council tax has
allowed less sympathetic/imaginative members of the Burley
Cross community[25] to accuse us of tight-fistedness and a lack
of social/fiscal responsibility[26]. Much of this unnecessary
hostility (as you are probably no doubt already fully aware)
centres around the disposal/collection of rubbish.

The situation has recently developed to such a pitch of
silliness and pettiness[27] that the local bin men have been
persuaded[28] to ignore the black bin bags deposited outside our

22 Little Hitlers. It beggars belief that these people actually have the right to claim
'charitable status'.
23 I am considering trying to claim this same status myself – I'll be seventy-three in
February!
24 And you could hardly call us philistines – Shoshana is actually treasurer of our local
History Club!
25 A marvellous, generous, open-minded bunch of individuals (with the odd, notable
exception).
26 Last April Shoshana single-handedly staged and organized a charitable quiz night
(in conjunction with Radio Wharfedale DJ Mark Sweet) to raise money for repairs to
the church organ (which she plays – very competently – whenever the resident organist
is away on holiday).
27 Encouraged, in no minor part, by the poison tongue of you know who.
28 Money changed hands. It definitely changed hands. I'm almost 100 per cent sure
of it.

gate. This means that we are now obliged to skulk around like criminals at dawn on collection day, furtively distributing our bags among those piles belonging to other – marginally more sympathetic – properties in the local vicinity. Worse still, many of these sympathetic individuals – while perfectly happy to help us out – must live in constant terror of incurring the (not inconsiderable) wrath of TP, who has tried her utmost to transform this mundane issue into what she loves to call a 'point of principle'.

As I'm sure you can now understand more fully, this complex situation re the disposal/collection of our rubbish feeds directly into the severe problems the village is currently experiencing with TP and her borderline obsessive interest in matters surrounding dog fouling.

You mentioned (during our brief exchange after the meeting) that I might benefit from reading the latest pamphlet on this subject published by EnCams: *Dog Fouling and the Law: a guide for the public*) which your department usually distributes free to interested parties (although due to recent budget cuts you regretted that you had yet to acquire any for general distribution – or even, you confessed, to become better acquainted with the finer details of said document yourself). I didn't get a chance to tell you at the time that I already possess several copies of this useful booklet (and have – as you will doubtless have already noticed[29] – taken the liberty of enclosing one for your own, personal use[30]).

Among the more fascinating details contained therein are the extraordinary statistics that (p. 2) the UK's population of

---

29 The cover photo of a booted foot suspended above a huge pile of steaming excrement is certainly eye-catching. Shoshana is very squeamish and will not allow me to keep my copies in the house (even wrong-side-up!) so I have been obliged to resort to storing them – and all correspondence relating to this issue – on a shallow back shelf inside our tiny garden shed.
30 No need to return it. The yellow marks on the back cover are nothing more sinister than grass stains (from where it accidentally fell into my lawnmower's clippings bin on retrieval).

approximately 7.4 million dogs produces, on average, around 1,000 tonnes of excrement/day.

Burley Cross (human population: 210; dog population: 33; cat population: 47)[31] certainly produces its fair share of the above, but, thanks to a – by and large – very responsible, slightly older[32] population, the provision of two special poop-scoop bins within the heart of the village and the wonderful, wide expanses of surrounding heath and moorland lying beyond, the matter had never – until TP's sudden arrival in our midst[33] – become an issue of serious public concern.[34]

I confess that I have walked[35] Shoshana's pedigree spitz, Samson[36], morning and evening, regular as clockwork, for almost five years now[37], and during that time have rarely – if ever – had my excursions sullied by the unwelcome apprehension of a superfluity of dog mess. If Samson – in common with most other sensible dogs I know – feels the urge to 'do his business', then he is usually more than happy to 'perform' some short distance off the path (his modesty happily preserved by delicate fronds of feathery bracken) on the wild expanses of our local moor. Here, dog faeces – along with other animal faeces, including those of the moorland sheep, fox and badger – are able to decompose naturally (usually within – on average – a ten-day period, depending, of course, on the specific climatic conditions). If Samson is 'caught short' and needs to 'go' in a less convenient location then I automatically

---

31 Although felines – very helpfully, but with the odd exception – bury their own.
32 The average age of your Burley Cross resident is fifty-nine (this is a quotable statistic – feel free to use it – I researched it myself).
33 Approximately eighteen months ago.
34 That said, I was utterly appalled by the filth I encountered on a day trip to Haworth in 'Brontë country' recently.
35 And not without occasional resistance – especially on icy winter mornings!
36 Shoshana's family have a tradition of naming their dogs after biblical characters.
37 Samson actually turns eight this year – he was a rescue dog and three years old when we got him. But before Samson I regularly walked Shoshana's beloved Highland terrier, Hezekiah (or 'Zeke'), although we were not resident full-time in Burley Cross at that stage.

pick up his 'business' and dispose of it accordingly.

Further to a series of in-depth discussions with a significant number of the dog owners in this village (and its local environs), I think it would be fair to say that the model I follow with Samson is the model that most other reasonable people also adhere to, i.e. the collection of dog mess is <u>only</u> appropriate within an 'urban/residential' setting, in public parks (where people are liable to picnic, stroll, relax, and children play) and finally – under very special circumstances – where your animal might be perceived to have 'despoiled' a well-used moorland path to the detriment of other walkers' enjoyment of it (although this last requirement is not legally binding but simply a question of community spirit).

I believe I am correct in saying that all of the above criteria tally perfectly with the procedures formally established by local government, and that – up until TP chanced to throw her very large (very filthy!) spanner into the works – these procedures were generally held to be not only just, but successful, necessary and universally beneficial.

With the arrival of TP, however, this fragile consensus was attacked, savagely mauled and rent asunder.[38] TP, as you may well know, owns four large German shepherds and prefers – rather eccentrically – to take them on long walks on the moor in the moonlight (I say 'them', although so far as I am aware she only ever walks one dog at any given time[39]). These four large dogs are usually kept confined inside a concrete 'compound'[40] in the back garden of Hursley End – her dilapidated bungalow on Lamb's Green.

---

38 Like an innocent young rabbit cruelly disembowelled by a savage fox (and this is an entirely pointless killing: the cruel fox is not hungry; it does not pause to eat the rabbit – it has already killed and consumed the mother – so attacks the young one purely for 'sport').

39 Pathetic creature. Hugely overweight. And I'm pretty convinced that it's always the same dog she walks; it seems to be lame in one of its back legs, although I've never had the chance to meet it – and so identify it – in daylight.

40 No judgement whatsoever is involved in my use of this word.

It was initially – she insists – due to the difficulties she experienced in negotiating/avoiding random dog faeces during these night-time hikes that her bizarre habit of bagging other people's dogs' faeces and leaving them deposited on branches, walls and fence posts – apparently as a warning/admonishment to others less responsible than herself – commenced.[41] This activity continued for upwards of six months before anyone either commented on it publicly or felt the urge to root out/apprehend the strange individual in our midst who had inexplicably chosen to enact this 'special service' on our behalf.[42]

Given the idiosyncratic nature of the bags employed (TP prefers a small, pink-tinged, transparent bag[43] – probably better adapted for household use, i.e. freezing meat[44] – instead of the usual, custom-made, matt-black kind[45]) it was easy, from very early on, to understand that the person bagging up and 'displaying' these faeces was not only happy, but almost *keen* to leave some kind of 'signature' behind.

When the bags were eventually identified as belonging to none other than TP (and she was calmly – very *sensitively* – confronted with her crimes), rather than apologizing, quietly retreating, or putting a summary halt to her bizarre activities, she responded – somewhat perversely – by actively *redoubling* her poop-gathering efforts! In fact she went *still one stage further*! She began to present herself in public[46] as a wronged party, as a necessary – if chronically undervalued – environmental watchdog, as a doughty, cruelly misunderstood

---

41 Although one really has to wonder at her facility to locate these random faeces in order to bag them up when it's apparently so difficult for her to avoid stepping in them in the first place!
42 I'm guessing that this is because the habit took a while to become properly established and then suddenly snowballed after the first few months.
43 The contents are, therefore, always fully visible.
44 Chops, perhaps, or liver/kidney/tongue and other smaller cuts.
45 To be purchased at any large supermarket or pet shop.
46 Quite belligerently.

moral crusader, standing alone and defenceless – clutching her trademark, transparent poo-bag to her heaving chest – against the freely defecating heathen marauder!

And it gets worse! She then went on the offensive (see Docs. 3+4 – copies of letters sent to the local press), angrily accusing the general body of responsible dog owners in Burley Cross of actively destroying the picturesque and historic moor by encouraging our animals to 'evacuate'[47] there.

One occasion, in particular, stands out in my mind. I met her – quite by chance – on a sunny afternoon, overburdened by shopping from the village store[48]. I offered to take her bags for her and during the walk back to her home took some pains to explain to her that there was *no actual legal requirement* for dog owners to collect their dog's faeces from the surrounding farm and moorland (The Dogs Fouling of Land Act, 1996). Her reaction to this news was to blush to the roots of her hair, spit out the word 'justifier!', roughly snatch her bags from me[49] and then quote, at length, like a thing possessed (as if reciting some ancient biblical proverb[50]) from the (aforementioned) EnCams publication on the subject.[51]

To return to this useful document for just a moment, in *Dog Fouling and the Law*, EnCams provide an invaluable 'profile of a dog fouler' (p. 4 – when you read it for yourself you will discover that it is an extremely thorough and thought-provoking piece of analysis). Apparently the average 'fouler' enjoys watching TV and attending the cinema but has a profound mistrust of soap opera, around half of them have internet access – mainly at home – but 'are not particularly confident in its usage', and they are most likely to read the *Sun*

---

47 Her word.
48 God only knows what she had in those damn bags – they weighed a tonne!
49 Lucky for TP we were only fifty or so yards from her front door at this stage.
50 And quite incorrectly, it later transpired.
51 I had yet to come across this valuable little booklet and so was, as you can imagine, somewhat confused and nonplussed by this attack.

and *Mirror* (but very rarely the *Daily Mail* or the *Financial Times*).[52]

EnCams have invented their own broad label to describe these irresponsible individuals: they call them 'justifiers', i.e. they justify their behaviour on the grounds of a) *Ignorance* ('I didn't realize it was a problem …' 'But nobody has ever mentioned this to me before …' etc.) and b) *Laziness* ('But nobody else ever picks it up, so why should I?').

EnCams insist that these 'justifiers' will only ever openly admit that they allow their dog to foul in public when placed under extreme duress. Their fundamental instinct is to simply pretend it hasn't happened or to lie about it.

Although I cannot deny that this profile is both interesting and – I don't doubt – perfectly valid in many – if not *most* – instances, TP was nevertheless entirely wrong to try and label me – of all people – with this wildly inappropriate nomenclature: I am neither ignorant, lazy nor in denial. Quite the opposite, in fact. I am informed, proactive and socially aware. And although I do dislike soaps,[53] I very rarely go to the cinema,[54] and my computer skills are – as this letter itself, I hope, will attest – universally acknowledged to be tip-top.

Since my acquisition of the EnCams document I have tried – countless times – to explain to TP (see Doc. 5 + Doc. 6: some valuable examples of our early correspondence) that not only am I a keen advocate of poop-scooping in residential areas and public parks, but that it shows *absolutely no moral or intellectual inconsistency on my part* to hold that allowing excrement to decompose naturally on the moor is infinitely more environmental than bagging it up and adding it, quite unthinkingly, to this small island's already chronically over-extended quantities of landfill. I have also told her that by

52 We get the Sunday Express at The Retreat, but only for the sudoku.
53 Shoshana, I must confess, is an avid Corrie fan.
54 The last film I saw was The Full Monty, and I only went to that because my late wife convinced me it was all about El Alamein.

simply bagging up the faeces she finds and then dumping them, willy-nilly, she is only serving to exacerbate the 'problem'[55] because the excrement cannot be expected to decompose inside its plastic skin. Rather than helping matters she is actually making them infinitely worse – once bagged, the excrement is there forever: a tawdry bauble – a permanent, sordid testament to the involuntary act of physical evacuation!

As you will no doubt be aware, around two months ago Wharfedale's dog warden – the 'criminally over-subscribed'[56] Trevor Horsmith – was persuaded[57] to start to take an interest in the problems being generated by TP's activities on the moor. It will probably strike you as intensely ironic that *TP herself* was one of the main instigators in finally involving Trevor in this little local 'mess' of ours.[58]

After familiarizing himself with the consequences of TP's 'work' (on the moor and beyond[59]) Horsmith announced (I'm paraphrasing here[60]) that while he fully condoned – even admired![61] – TP's desire to keep the moor clean, it was still perfectly legitimate for dog owners to allow their pets to defecate there, and that while excrement could not, in all conscience, be calibrated as 'litter' (it decomposes for heaven's sake! Same as an apple core!) once it has been placed inside

55 Although, as I've already emphasized, there wasn't a problem before TP arrived on the scene – TP is the problem!
56 I won't bore you with the details here as I am sure Mr Horsmith will already have bored you with them himself.
57 His words, not mine. Shoshana once observed – very wittily – that Mr Horsmith makes Alice in Wonderland's Dormouse seem hyperactive!
58 By a flurry of phone calls, emails and at least half a dozen letters to the local press (two of which mentioned him by name).
59 Three of her bags were recently discovered in Lowsley Edge – over seven miles away as the crow flies!
60 His letter was full of the most appalling grammatical errors.
61 This struck me as an astonishingly irresponsible thing to say given the deranged nature of the character we are dealing with here. As I said to Horsmith myself (on one of the rare occasions he actually made a visit to the village), by encouraging TP to think that she's got moral right on her side he's only sharpening a stick for her to beat him (and the rest of us) up with.

plastic (no matter how laudable the motivation[62]) then it *must necessarily* be considered so.[63]

Horsmith's pronouncement on this issue was obviously the most devastating blow for TP (and her cause), yet it by no means prompted her to desist from her antisocial behaviour. By way of an excuse for (partial explanation of/attempt to distract attention from) her strange, nocturnal activities, she suddenly changed tack and began claiming (see Doc. 6 again, last three paras) that – for the most part – whenever she goes on walks she generally bags up the vast majority of the faeces she finds and disposes of them herself ('double-wrapped', she writes – somewhat primly – inside her dustbin, at home[64]) and that on the rare occasions when she leaves the bags behind it is either because a) the 'problem' (as she perceives it) is so severe that she feels a strong, public statement needs to be made to other dog owners, b) the sheer volume of excrement is such that it is simply too much for her to carry home all in one go (while managing a large dog at the same time), and c) that she is sometimes prey to the sudden onset of acute arthritic 'spasms' in her fingers, which mean that she is unable to grip the bags properly and so is compelled to leave them *in situ*, while harbouring 'every earthly intention' of returning to collect them at a later date.

I am not – of course – in any way convinced by this pathetic, half-cocked hodge-podge of explanations. In answer to a) I say that other dog owners are <u>completely within their rights</u> to allow their dogs to defecate responsibly on the moor. They have the <u>law</u> on their side. It is a perfectly <u>legitimate</u> and <u>natural</u> way to proceed. In answer to b) I say that the <u>volume</u> of excrement on the moor is rarely, if ever – in my extensive experience of these matters – excessive (especially given the general rate of decomposition etc.). In answer to c) I say that it

---

62 Ye gads!
63 A point I made myself to Mr Horsmith – but to no avail – over six long months before!
64 I will return to this important detail a little later!

strikes me as rather <u>odd</u> that the same person who can apparently manage to 'bag up' huge quantities of excrement when their fingers are – *ahem* – 'spasming'[65] is somehow unable to perform that superficially <u>much less arduous</u> act of transporting it back home with them![66]

Many of TP's bags lie around on the moor for months on end and no visible attempt is made to move them. Last Thursday, for example, I counted over forty-two bags of excrement dotted randomly about the place on my morning stroll. Sometimes I come across a bag displayed in the most extraordinary of places. Yesterday I found one dangling up high in the midst of a thorny bush. It was very obvious that not only would the person who hung the bag there have been forced to sustain some kind of injury in its display (unless they wore a thick pair of protective gloves), but that so would the poor soul (and *here's* the rub!) who felt duty-bound to retrieve it and dispose of it.[67] This was, in effect, a piece of purely spiteful behaviour – little less, in fact, than an act of social/environmental terrorism.

Shoshana and I have both become so sickened, angered and dismayed by the awful mess TP has made of our local area (I mean who is to judge when an activity such as this passes from being 'in the public interest'[68] to a plain and simple public nuisance?[69]) that, in sheer desperation, we have begun to gather up the rotten bags ourselves.

On Friday, two weeks back[70], Shoshana gathered up over thirty-six bags. On her way home – exhausted – from the

65 A fiddly process at the best of times!
66 Let alone manufacture fashionable clay jewellery in such prodigious quantities!
67 I.e. yours truly!
68 Which it never was, quite frankly.
69 This is intended as a purely rhetorical question – although, on further consideration, I suppose the person who might possibly be expected to make that vital judgement could very well turn out to be you, Linda.
70 There was a large convention of Girl Guides from Manchester and Leeds travelling to the moor for an orienteering weekend. Shoshana couldn't bear the idea of these lovely creatures being exposed to TP's vile 'handiwork'.

village's poop-scoop bins[71] she tripped on a crack in the pavement, fell heavily, sprained her wrist and dislocated her collarbone.[72] I will not say that we blame TP *entirely* for this calamity, but we do hold her at least partially responsible.[73]

After Shoshana's 'accident' I marched over to TP's bungalow, fully intent on having it out with her,[74] but TP (rather fortuitously) was nowhere to be found. It was then – as I stood impotently in her front garden, seething with frustration – that I resolved[75] to take the opportunity to do a little private investigation of my own. If you remember,[76] TP had claimed that many – if not most – of the bags of excrement she retrieved from the moor, she automatically carried back home with her (only leaving the unmanageable excess behind) and placed them, double-wrapped, into her dustbin (alongside what I imagine would be the considerable quantities of excrement collected from her *own* four, chronically obese dogs which – as you know – she keeps penned up, 24/7,[77] inside that criminally small and claustrophobic, purpose-built concrete compound[78]).

The day I visited Hursley End was a Monday, which is the day directly *before* refuse is collected in the village. I decided – God only knows why, it was just a random urge, I suppose – to peek inside her dustbin (literally deafened as I did so by the hysterical barks and howls of her four frantic German shepherds). By my calculation, I estimated that there would

71 Which could barely contain the sheer volume involved – amounting to almost 3,000 grams. If you have some difficulty imagining this weight in real terms, then it would be comparable to around twelve pats of best butter.
72 I have sent another letter to your colleague – Giles Monson – on this subject, along with directions from our lawyer.
73 Shoshana an angry 70 per cent, me, a more reasoned 59 per cent (a broad, general majority, in other words).
74 Uncharacteristically hot-headed behaviour on my part.
75 Quite spontaneously. This was in no way premeditated.
76 But of course you do!
77 As the Yanks are wont to say.
78 Once again, I emphasize that absolutely no judgement is implied by my use of these words.

need to be *at least* forty-two dog faeces – from her own four animals – stored away inside there.[79] In addition to these I also envisaged a *considerable* number of stools collected from her nightly hikes on the 'filthy' moor.[80]

Once I'd made these quick calculations I steeled myself, drew a deep breath, grabbed the lid, lifted it high and peered querulously inside. Imagine my great surprise when I found *not a single trace of excrement within*! The bin was all but empty! I say again: the bin – *TP's* bin – was all but empty!! I quickly pulled on a pair of disposable gloves[81] and then gingerly withdrew the bin's other contents, piece by piece (just so as to be absolutely certain of my facts). I removed two large, empty Johnnie Walker bottles,[82] four family-size Marks and Spencer coleslaw containers, three packets of mint and one packet of hazelnut-flavoured Cadbury's Snaps biscuit wrappers, and the stinking remnants of two boil-in-the-bag fish dinners (Iceland) and one, ready-made, prawn biryani meal (from Tesco's excellent Finest range).

I stared blankly into that bin for several minutes, utterly confounded, struggling to make any sense of what I'd discovered. It then slowly dawned on me that TP might actually have *two* bins – one of which was specifically to be used for the storing of excrement. Bearing this in mind, I set about searching the untended grounds of her property[83] with a fine-tooth comb,[84] even going so far as to climb on to an

79 This figure was reached by estimating that, on average, each of TP's four dogs would be expected to defecate 1.5 times on any given day (an extremely conservative estimate, in actual fact).
80 Her word, obviously.
81 Which I just happened to have with me.
82 Not much of a recycler, then, our TP?!
83 TP is currently in the midst of having some major renovation work done to the external walls of her bungalow. If the rumours I hear about town are correct, she is trying to sue the former owners, Louise and Timothy Hamm, for some unspecified kind of 'negligence' – even though Timothy, an ex-GP and a truly inspirational human being, is in the final stages of Parkinson's and now lives in full-time residential care.
84 So to speak.

upturned bucket and peer, trepidatiously, into the tiny concrete compound to the rear, where TP's four German shepherds barked and raced around – like a group of hairy, overweight banshees – frantic with what seemed to be a poignant combination of terror and excitement.[85]

No matter how hard I hunted, a second bin could not be found. I eventually abandoned my search on realizing how late it had grown;[86] Shoshana would definitely be worried, I thought, and if I tarried any longer I could be in serious danger of missing *Countdown*.[87] I left Hursley End, depressed and confused, only turning – with a helpless half-shrug – to peer back over towards the property once I'd reached the relative safety of the road beyond. It was then, in a blinding flash, that I had what I now refer to – somewhat vaingloriously, I'll admit – as my 'Moment of Epiphany'.[88]

As I looked back at TP's property from a greater distance, I was able – with the benefit of perspective – to observe that recent renovation works to the bungalow had resulted in the temporary removal of large sections of the external fascia,[89] so that all that now remained of the property's original structure was the roof, the window frames and a series of basic, internal walls and supports, many of which had been copiously wrapped in thick layers of protective plastic (to safeguard the

---

85 Probably thinking I was an animal-rights activist intent on releasing them from their hellish penury.
86 I'd been there for almost an hour!
87 I didn't miss it, which was most fortuitous as it was an especially good episode. One of the contestants came up with the high-scoring word 'toxocara', a term that refers to a type of roundworm which is responsible for generating the dangerous infection/disease called toxocariasis. This disease is produced when the toxocara roundworm's eggs are left to fester in the excrement of a dog for a period of two/three weeks after the faeces have been deposited. I was absolutely stunned when this word came up, and honestly believe it was some kind of message from 'The Beyond'!
88 Although Shoshana will insist on calling it my 'episcopy', the silly moo!
89 Many of the more modest properties in this village – built within a particular time frame – were constructed out of a special, aluminium-based concrete which, while it poses only limited health risks to the residents, can, in certain instances, make it extremely difficult to raise a mortgage.

---

property against the worst of the weather, I suppose). By dint of this expedient, I suddenly realized with a sharp gasp, TP's home had lately been transformed (voluntarily or otherwise) into a giant simulacrum of a *monstrous, semi-transparent poo-bag*![90]

As this – admittedly strange and somewhat hysterical – thought caught a hold of me, a second thought,[91] running almost in tandem with it, quickly overtook my mind: if no evidence of excrement could be found in TP's garden – not even faeces from her *own four dogs* – then where on God's earth might it actually be …?

What?!

I suddenly froze.

'*MARY, MOTHER OF JESUS!*' I bellowed, then quickly covered my mouth with my hand.[92] But wasn't it *obvious*?! Hadn't the simple answer to this most perplexing of questions been staring me in the face *all along*?!

The moor!

Our beautiful, unbesmirched, virgin moor!

TP had *not* – as she'd always emphatically maintained – been piously and dutifully collecting/bagging excrement left by other, irresponsible dog owners, during those long, dark, nightly hikes of hers. Oh no! Quite the opposite, in fact! TP had actually been carefully bagging prodigious quantities of HER OWN FOUR DOGS' EXCREMENT and then CHEERFULLY FESTOONING THE LOCAL FOOTPATHS WITH IT!!!

---

90 With TP – I hate to have to say it, but say it I must – representing the steaming turd of festering excrement within.

91 Remember that – in my own defence – I was still in somewhat of a state after Shoshana's tragic fall.

92 For fear of attracting the unwanted attentions of TP's neighbours, one of whom, a Mrs Janine Loose, has grown extraordinarily jumpy and paranoid of late, since a canny gang of local schoolchildren appropriated the disused greenhouse at the bottom of her garden and secretly cultivated marijuana plants in it. Their illegal activities were only brought to light after Mrs Loose discovered two boys spreadeagled on her lawn, 'completely monged', when she went to hang out her washing one blustery autumn afternoon.

'Good *Lord*!' I can almost hear you howl, your smooth, firm cheeks flushed pink with rage and indignation. 'But … but *why?*'

I'm afraid that this is a question which – for all of my age and experience – I cannot answer. I can only imagine that TP must derive some sick and perverse feeling of excitement/gratification from performing this debased act. Perhaps it is an entirely <u>sexual</u> impulse, or maybe she has some deep yet inexplicable <u>grudge</u> against the people of Burley Cross which she is '<u>acting out</u>' through this strange and depraved pastime. Or perhaps the good people of this village have unwittingly come to '<u>represent</u>' something (or someone) to TP from her <u>tragic past</u> and she feels the uncontrollable urge to punish/insult/degrade us all as a consequence of that. Or maybe – just maybe – a whole host of entirely *different* impulses are at play here. Shoshana had the fascinating idea that as a small child TP might've developed '<u>issues</u>' during her <u>anal phase</u>[93] brought on by an overly strict and prohibitive <u>potty-training regimen</u>. She discussed this idea with a neighbour of ours who might properly be called an 'expert' in the field, and they explained to her – at some length – how as children we have an innocent, perfectly natural conception of our own faeces as a kind of 'gift'[94] which we generously share with our parents.

Shoshana wondered whether TP's emotional/psychological development as a child was halted/blocked at this critical stage, leading to an unusual fixation with faeces in adult life, which, many decades later, still gives TP the childlike compulsion to 'share' this 'precious' substance with all of her friends and neighbours.[95]

---

93 Who started – but never completed – a child psychology correspondence course a few years back (then swapped to aromatherapy).
94 Apparently – according to Ms Sissy Logan, an old Bluebell dancing girl turned colonic irrigation practitioner – Carl Gustav Jung has written quite extensively on this peculiar subject.
95 Lucky old us, eh?!

Whatever the real reasons for TP's extraordinary behaviour, the hard fact remains that she is currently posing a serious threat to the health and safety of the general public and must be stopped as a matter of some urgency. To this end I sent a lengthy email to Trevor Horsmith, insisting that he take some kind of positive action to deter TP from her foul and aberrant path.

Horsmith,[96] while professing himself to be 'very interested' in my theories, calmly informed me that unless he was able to catch TP red-handed (transporting faeces from her home and depositing them on the moor) then he would be unable to take any kind of prohibitive action against her. Given that TP prefers to walk only after dark and Trevor Horsmith's working hours finish promptly at five, the likelihood of this ever happening is – at best, I feel – extremely limited. Horsmith also went on to discourage me – and in no uncertain terms,[97] either – from taking any kind of independent action myself, claiming that a matter this sensitive was – I quote – 'always better left in the hands of qualified professionals'.[98]

So there you have it, Ms Withycombe: a detailed summary of the complex web of problems our small – but perfectly formed – village is currently struggling to grapple with. Call me a foolish old optimist (if you must!), but I have a strong presentiment that your input in this matter will prove most beneficial, and am keenly looking forward to bashing out some kind of joint plan of action with you at the start of the New Year.

---

96 As he will no doubt have informed you.

97 I found his insinuations extremely hurtful. As I told you after the meeting, nine out of the ten charges were dropped through lack of evidence, and in the tenth instance a credible witness was able to verify that I had merely asked the girl for directions to the nearest Tesco Metro. I have visited Leeds for many years and know the town well, but the rejuvenation of the riverside area and recent changes to the one-way system are liable to catch even a seasoned old pro like myself on the hop.

98 Although I remain a little confused as to what his 'professional' status might actually be.

Yours, in eager anticipation,

Jeremy – aka Jez – Baverstock

PS Merry Christmas! (I almost forgot!!)

PPS You will probably have noticed that I have taken the great liberty of enclosing a small, festive gift for your private enjoyment over the holiday season: an – as yet – unpublished book[99] I once wrote about my nefarious activities as a reconnoitrer, black hat and mole inside the Royal Horticultural Society of Great Britain.[100]

XXJ

---

99 This edition is limited to only thirty copies. Shoshana is wholly responsible for the wonderful, colourful, internal artwork.
100 An organization that has – over recent years – fallen prey to rank corruption, chronic inefficiency and levels of bovine complacency the like of which you can hardly dare to imagine. My lack of an independent publisher is, I believe, at least partly down to the fact that members of this powerful institution are currently rife within all – and I mean all – areas of the national media. It may shock you to discover that the Duchess of Windsor, Peter Sissons, and that queer little chap who owns Sainsbury's – or possibly ASDA – were former members and dabbled, quite seriously, in the organization for a while.

[letter 2]

3, The Mead
Denby Lane
Fallow Hill
(nr Burley Cross)

20 December, 2006

Hold on to your hat, Jess ...

And yell *HALLELUJAH*! Because <u>*MEREDITH HAS*</u> <u>*FOUND HER JESUS*</u>! She's finally *found* him! I wrung it out of her while we were stacking away the chairs, straight after you left. You were *completely* right! It was *exactly* as you said! She'd known for literally *weeks* and was just keeping the information back (out of caution? Mischief? *Spite*?!). You said you didn't trust her, Jess, and you were spot-on. *Spot-on*!

SHE'S FOUND HIM, JESS! And we're officially *THE FIRST TWO PEOPLE IN THE WHOLE WORLD TO KNOW ABOUT IT*! (Well, apart from her, obviously, and ratty little Sebastian – her loyal henchman – who was glowering at her, *furiously*, across the hall, as she told me! Oh. And probably the rev – they're thick as thieves, those two. *But who cares? WHO CARES*?! We've dragged it out of them! We've *bludgeoned* it out of them!)

I don't mind admitting that I'm feeling rather *proud* of myself right now, Jess – a tad *smug*, even. My cheeks are still flushed with victory as I sit at the kitchen table and scribble all this down (sorry about the paper – it's from that expensive batch Duncan had printed up with the old address *directly* before we moved – but it was all I could lay my hands on at such short notice).

Oh, Jess, if only you could've *been* there! You would've been AMAZED at what I put her through! Appalled! I was

completely and utterly *relentless*!! I was like an attack dog! A
Rottweiler!! I kept following her around the hall and worrying
at her and worrying at her until she simply couldn't stand it any
more and just blurted it out!

'For heaven's sake, Emily!' she shrieked (both her cheeks the
colour of boiled beetroot). 'I've *found* a Jesus. He's called
Kieren Knowles, if you *must* know. He's a professional actor
and he lives in Hebden Bridge. Now just *leave me alone*, will
you?!'

Hebden Bridge, Jess! Of course I would've rung you on the
spot and blabbed, but my dratted mobile's out of commission
(and Duncan – the old misery – has a strict moratorium on
phone calls at home after ten).

You said you'd be heading off to your mother's first thing, so
I thought I should probably just jot down all the gory details
and include them (while they're still fresh!) along with the
earring, which I wrapped up, very carefully, in a tiny piece of
lilac tissue paper.

I *do* hope I scribbled down the address correctly. You were
in such a rush – such a panic – that I honestly couldn't tell if it
was 27 Elmdon Lane, Marston Green, Birmingham, or 27
Elendon Lane, Marston Green, Birmingham (I've taken a lucky
punt). Please, please, *please* don't accidentally tip it out of the
envelope and lose the damn thing all over again (you silly
goose!).

I must confess that it was little short of a miracle that Peter
found it (Peter Bramwell – the First Shepherd – tall, grey-
haired chappie with the lazy eye who Lilian kept hectoring all
night for cracking his knuckles. I *do* think Lilian was slightly out
of line, there – and I could tell you did, too, by the way you
kept sighing and rolling your eyes every time she opened her
mouth – but I don't know *why* he persists in doing it, I really
don't. It's perfectly *maddening*. Is it any wonder Rita's losing
her marbles?! I mean wouldn't *you* under the circumstances?!).

He said it was lying in the middle of the rubber karate mat, directly in front of one of the needlework exhibits; not 'Our Feathered Friends', but 'Burley Cross Entwined', the large display detailing the complex – and somewhat tumultuous – relationship between Burley Cross and our French twin, Olonzac (it's an awfully good title, don't you think? In-*twine*-d/ en-*twin*-ed? Of course we have Shoshana Baverstock to thank for that; it's nice to know she's getting *something* constructive done as she lounges around, completely starkers, in that fancy 'sunroom' of hers all day long, eh?!).

The earring looks a bit wonky, now, I'm afraid. I'm not sure if Peter didn't accidentally step on it before he picked it up. I've done my best to wrangle it back into position, and I don't think I've done *too* bad a job …

As luck would have it, gold is one of the earth's most malleable metals (or so Peter informed me as he passed it over. It seems he used to be a metallurgist! *Imagine*?! When he told me I said, 'Oh! A *metallurgist*! Congratulations!' – I was still dizzy with the Jesus news. He just scowled and barked, 'It's nothing you need to congratulate me for!' then stalked off [?!]).

In fact – now I come to ponder on it – I remember passing you that apron to wear while you were standing and inspecting the exhibit before we handed out the teas (Sally Trident's pit pony *did* look like a Stegosaurus! I told her <u>exactly</u> the same thing myself!). I can only imagine it popped out when you dragged it on over your head.

OH *MY GOD*, Jess! I *CAN'T BELIEVE* SHE'S FOUND HIM!! As soon as Duncan gets off the internet (he's doing some last-minute research for his OU thesis on the primitive fabric dyes they used in the Bayeux tapestry) I'm going straight online to try and find his MySpace page! 'Kieren Knowles: professional actor!'
I LITERALLY CAN'T WAIT!!!!

And the look on Meredith's *face*, Jess! It was a *classic*! An absolute *picture*! I just kept going on and on and *on* at her! I came at her from all angles. Will he be a blond Christ,

Meredith, or a brunette, because I *know* brunette Christs are all the vogue these days – and very P.C. – but I can't help thinking a blond would be so incredibly *romantic* …

What age will he be, Meredith? Jesus died at thirty-three, but will you be strict and insist on *absolute* numerical parity?

By the end I was just babbling any old nonsense at her: 'Will he have his own teeth, Meredith? Won't he mind dreadfully working with a bunch of amateurs? Will he be tall? Over six three? Will he speak with a northern accent? What if he has a tattoo? Must he be a believer? Will he be circumcised?'

Turns out (and this was a <u>total</u> bolt from the blue): HE'S PLAYED JESUS BEFORE!!

Meredith was just starting to fill me in on all the finer details (his hair is brown, almost black, his eyes are 'a fine, cornflower blue' …) when Seb came barrelling over. 'Of course he's played Jesus *before*,' he says, all droll and self-satisfied. 'He's quite the *pro*, apparently – he just has "the Jesus look".'

Well, my jaw literally *dropped*!

'*THE JESUS LOOK*!?'

As I'm sure you can imagine, I was absolutely desperate to pursue this line of enquiry still further (I could've followed it to the ends of the earth, quite frankly!) but I was suddenly overwhelmed by a strong – almost violent – urge to find out something *even more pressing*, i.e.: DID TAMMY THORNDYKE KNOW YET???

I just yelled it at them. I just screamed it. I lost all sense of self-control.

'*DOES SHE KNOW*?! *DOES TAMMY KNOW*?!'

(Then I got rather short of breath and started to cough, and had to rummage around in my bag for my asthma inhaler.)

'Nobody knows,' Meredith snapped. 'I really didn't want to tell anyone until we'd sorted out the finer details of his contract.'

(Good heavens, Jess! *Get her*! What a terrible, old sourpuss!)

At this point Sebastian butted in again and started

congratulating Meredith on how she conducted the night's warm-up. He said, 'I always find the trust exercises you use so extraordinarily *liberating*, Meredith. And it's not just the exercises themselves, it's how you *approach* them, how you *time* them. So much skill! Such finesse! In fact I rarely finish one of your sessions without feeling this wild *surge* of emotion. I often get quite tearful! It's rather embarrassing! They're just so … so potent, so "connecting", so … so empowering.'

(Well, it's no great mystery how *he* managed to wrangle himself The Disciple Jesus Loved Best, then!)

Of course *I* wasn't going to be outdone (even if I *don't* currently have a speaking role!). I heartily agreed with him. I said, 'When Tom Augustine touched my forehead and whispered, "You are alive, Emily! You are utterly free! Take your freedom, now, and celebrate the world with it!" I honestly thought I was going to *wet* myself! His hand was so cold! It was like being prodded by a frozen chicken leg!' (In fact I seriously thought I *had* wet myself, Jess. That's why I seemed so distracted when you were asking me whether the wigs were still kept on the top of the prop box.)

I then went on to say how I thought the improvisational exercises tonight had been *absolutely priceless* (weren't they, though?!)! I said, 'My favourite moment was when Arthur Wolf was "being an egg", Sally Trident broke him into a frying-pan and then Jess [you!] yelled, "Oh *no*! Look! You've gone and broken his yolk!"' (I mean that *was* hilarious! *And* utterly spontaneous, to boot!)

I'd barely finished speaking when Seb turned and delivered me THE MOST *FILTHY* LOOK!!!

'Yes,' he says, snidely, 'Jess is *quite* the little comedian!' (?!?!?)

With the benefit of hindsight, Jess, I think you were *right* to be suspicious of him. I think he *does* have it in for you. And it's not only because you aren't officially 'one of us', i.e. not currently resident in the village, but because he's jealous of your talent – pure and simple! He's still stewing over the fact that your audition for Angel of the Lord went down so well. People were talking about it for weeks! Pammy Stevens got palpitations! The way you worked with the light towards the end – turned to face it, dumbly, *questingly*, then extended out your arms and slowly, dramatically, dropped your chin on to your chest …

Beautiful!

There was such an incredible atmosphere – you could've heard a *pin* drop in that hall.

WHY MEREDITH DIDN'T GIVE YOU THE ROLE *I WILL NEVER, NEVER UNDERSTAND*!!

I mean all that hogwash she came up with afterwards about the cast 'not being about individual egos, only about The Collective Will', and 'really needing to find the right kind of balance' (it's an amateur production of *The Passion*, Jess, not a Soviet-era-style, group gymnastics display)! And that interminable speech about things being 'real', and then 'moving into fast-forward', and then 'suddenly becoming hyper-real' – but 'not acting, *never* acting', just 'being', just 'believing in the moment', just 'cherishing the moment', just 'making the moment true …' (what on earth does that even *mean*, Jess? 'Making the moment true'?).

If Meredith is – as she claims – such a staunch advocate of the truth (what's her other favourite catchphrase? 'Be sincere, be here' – with a pious little pat on her heart?!) then how on earth can she possibly justify casting Tammy Thorndyke as *St Martha*?!

St Martha!

Tammy Thorndyke's converted to Buddhism! I swear to God, if I have to hear another *syllable* about that infernal trip she and Baxter took to Tibet last year, and how she got altitude sickness halfway up a mountain and collapsed, and then, when she came to, how she felt 'an incredible warmth in her throat chakra' which slowly spread throughout her entire body, making her feel like 'a glowing bottle of preserved ginger' I honestly think I shall spontaneously combust!

As I said to Jill Harpington the other day (while we were picketing Wharfedale Council about those awful, new recycling bins), 'Isn't it unfortunate that Tammy's recent "conversion" doesn't appear to be offering any kind of formal impediment to her singing lead soprano in the church choir?!'
(*Ouch*! Climb back into the knife drawer, Emily!)

But that awful, piercing vibrato, Jess! It's more than my shattered nerves can bear! Drew Cullen – on the organ – even turns off his hearing aid, and he's *deaf as a dodo*!

I actually conducted an informal survey with the help of Gillian Reed last year (Gill's the blowsy, buck-toothed piano tuner's wife who polishes the church pews etc.) after she mentioned to me, in passing, that the bats were defecating at almost *twice* their usual volume on the days when the choir either rehearsed or performed.

With a little casual investigation it became increasingly clear (I can show you the graphs if you like – in fact I'll dig one out for you, right now) that the more music we sang in a <u>higher register</u>, the more guano the bats produced – often (like when we were rehearsing 'Jerusalem', for example) defecating over *three times* as much!

Then – and this was the *real* eye-opener, Jess – when Tammy was off for a month in August (nursing her youngest daughter through a botched nose-job down in Guildford) the overall quantities produced fell by *almost two-thirds*! OVERNIGHT! Right across the scale! *I SWEAR*!

Utterly fascinating (I know), but I suppose we're trespassing a little off the subject here, because let's face it, Jess (as I said earlier this evening), if 'the truth' really is Meredith's main priority, then why does she persist in ignoring what's so patently true about St Martha, i.e. that it's not a glamorous role at all!

Martha's a <u>work-horse</u>, Jess! She spends virtually *all* of her time throughout the Gospels *JUST DOING THE WASHING-UP*!!

That's why Jesus gets into a row with her when she tells Mary Magdalen to stop hanging around with the boys all night and give her a quick hand with the kitchen chores! Jesus gets into quite a bate about it. He tells her that Mary is much better off where she is (just sitting on the floor, staring at his 'Godhead'), and that Martha's eternal soul would be far better served by doing the same thing herself!

(Well, that's all fine and dandy, Jess, but if Martha hadn't done the chores, what in heaven's name would The Twelve have eaten for dinner? How could Jesus have hosted The Last Supper? And what would Michelangelo have painted on the ceiling of the Sistine Chapel, all those years later? A dozen hungry people arguing over a raw turnip?! Hardly an appropriate subject matter for such a prominent art work I'd've thought!)

It's *ridiculous*, Jess! Pure hokum!

I mean Tammy Thorndyke has a *dishwasher*, for heaven's sake! And she has a *char* (if it's socially acceptable to describe dear Susan Trott in those terms)! And she gets all her dinner parties professionally catered by the sister of that haughty besom who runs Pinenuts (the Swiss tea-house in Ilkley). D'you know her? The Dutch girl with the strange eyebrows who Duncan calls 'The Exclamation Mark', because she always persists in looking alarmed (no matter how conservatively he orders).

Honestly, Jess, it's just a *joke*!
The 'real' and the 'hyper-real' and all that 'fast-forwarding'! What's she trying to do, turn us all digital?!

Anyhow – to get back to our little spat – I was still recoiling from the 'comedian' comment, when Meredith suddenly started throwing in her *own* two-pence-worth, saying how she didn't think you and I were 'a terribly good influence on each other, and, by extension, on the group'.

You and me, Jess? Not a good influence? What on earth can she possibly *mean*?! The bare-faced *gall* of the woman! The pure, unalloyed *cheek* of it! I just felt like grabbing her by her bony shoulders and shaking her and *shaking* her! I just felt like *screaming* into her horsey, self-satisfied face: 'I'm a sixty-seven-year-old grandmother of five, Meredith! How *dare* you stand there in your awful, gold-braided, ethnic pantaloons and scold me like I'm a seven-year-old child!'

But I just bit down hard on my tongue, Jess, and tried to rise above. Let it go, Emily, let it go, I thought. Do as the Good Lord would've done.

(It wasn't having all that much effect, I'm afraid, and then that thing *you're* always saying popped into my head: 'They only hate us because we're beautiful!'
I repeated it to myself, three times. It was *extremely* helpful.)

Yet even *that* wasn't to be the end of it, Jess! Worse was still to come! Seb then interrupts Meredith to say how 'disruptive' he'd found our contributions in Group Discussion!

I must've looked simply *stunned* by this (I think I probably started wheezing again – with the shock – and then staggered back, supporting myself, faintly, with a trembling hand, against the wall) because Meredith quickly butted in to say how much they appreciated our input, overall, and that she couldn't deny we'd invested a great deal of effort. (Remember our special DVD night, Jess? *The Name of the Rose, The Omen, The Da Vinci Code, Nacho Libre* and *The Passion of The Christ*, all in one go?)

Seb wasn't to be put off, though. He started muttering under his breath about how 'unhelpful' he'd found your views on the Catholic Church turning Mary Magdalen into a whore because 'they all feared the vagina'.

Obviously I leapt straight to your defence! I said *I'd* told you that because I'd read it on the internet.

'Oh! On the internet, Emily!' Seb snorts. 'Well, that speaks *volumes*, doesn't it?!'

Then, before I can even open my mouth to respond, he continues, 'And how about when you said Jesus "hated his own family", and "thought Buddhism was a big pile of mumbo-jumbo"? Were these shining little gems *also* mined online?'

Well, that was *it*, Jess!
WAR!!
I drew myself up to my full height (5′3″, in heels) and said (in my best Ice Queen voice), 'If you want to take issue with *those* views, Sebastian, then I'm afraid you'll need to take issue with the Holy Bible itself!'

Meredith gazed at me for a second, perfectly astonished. 'It says Jesus *hated* his own family in the Bible?' she demanded (plainly shaken to the core).

'I believe there's a fairly memorable moment in the Gospel of St Matthew,' I loftily enlightened her, 'when Mary and Jesus's brothers arrive, unannounced, to pay him a visit. A disciple comes to tell him (he's preaching a sermon at the time) and Jesus refuses – point-blank – to interrupt what he's doing to give them an audience. He simply asks, "Who is my mother, and who are my brothers?" Then, later on, he justifies this slightly high-handed treatment by saying, "Whoever does the will of my Father in heaven is my brother and sister and mother," i.e. Jesus doesn't play favourites ...' (I deliver Meredith an <u>especially</u> stern look at this juncture.) 'We are *all* his kith and kin.'

'Poppycock!' Seb scoffs. 'That doesn't mean he *hates* his family!'

'You can chose to interpret it any way you like,' I sigh, turning to look at him with an expression of infinite sadness (and of infinite pity. And of infinite patience – it was a highly complex and abstruse expression, very Sphinx-like – as I'm sure you can imagine). 'But haven't *you* hated your family sometimes, Seb?' I continued, swinging out my arm, rather dramatically. 'I mean haven't we *all*? Just as our Sweet Lord did?'

Everybody was (quite naturally) rendered dumb for a couple of seconds by my infallible logic, but then Meredith started muttering something about 'Tammy being very hurt, very *injured*, by the mumbo-jumbo comments'.

'Matthew 6: 7,' I announced, crisply. '"And when you pray, do not keep on babbling like pagans, for they think they will be heard because of their many worms."'

I meant to say 'words', obviously (I don't really know where the 'worms' part came from), but, as luck would have it, I was saved from possible ridicule by the sudden arrival of Peter Bramwell (the metallurgist) who came to inform Meredith that the bulb had just blown in the storeroom (which meant he was unable to locate a ladder – I'm not entirely sure *why* a ladder was required at this juncture).

I decided that this timely interruption presented an opportune moment to beat a hasty (if still perfectly dignified) retreat. (Always quit while you're ahead, eh?!)

Phew!

So I think that's pretty much the sum of it, Jess. Sorry if I've run on a bit. My fingers are all cramping up – I feel like I've been writing this for *hours* (Crikey! Look at the time! It's five after twelve and Duncan's not even had his Bournville yet! He'll have committed hara-kiri by now!).

I *do* hope the earring is still intact by the time it reaches you. I'm not entirely sure why you were so desperate to have it back over the festive season – I was under the strong (if possibly erroneous) impression that your mother's proclivities (fashion-related and otherwise) bordered somewhat on the conservative. If this *is* the case, then you should definitely think twice about wearing it again until you've broken your other piece of 'Big News'. Let's hope she takes it a little better than your father did!

I'm very confident (as I said earlier) that he'll have cooled down enough by now to let you drive at least some of the way to Birmingham.

When's your test? Jan 5th?
We'll definitely speak before then –

Happy Christmas, my Gorgeous Boy!

Give 'em hell, eh?!

XXXXXX

Em

PS <u>KIEREN KNOWLES</u>!!!!
'Professional actor!!'
VA-VA-VA-VA-*VOOM*!!

PPS Always remember: They only hate us because …
Oh! You know!!
XX

[letter 3]

Threadbare Cottage
'The Calls'
Burley Cross

20th December 2006

Oh Donovan,

How ghastly! Green ink! I'm terribly sorry – it wasn't
planned, I can assure you. In fact it's given me quite a turn!
The pen's an old favourite of mine which I haven't used in ages
because you can no longer buy the cartridges. Then I found
one – this very morning – at the bottom of the pine dresser,
while I was hunting down that photograph I'd promised to send
you (aren't you just beautiful in your christening robe? Plump
as a plum pudding, cheeks like little apples, huge, gummy grin!
And then that brilliantly incongruous black eye – like a
miniature Billy Bunter!).

It looked perfectly uncontentious as I popped it in (the
cartridge, I mean), the address went off without a hitch, the
first half of the date was fine, but then as soon as I hit the year,
this terrible green colour exploded from the nib (I say 'terrible',
although in truth I actually quite like the green myself – in the
abstract – it's just all those unfortunate connotations …).

I'd have started over (of course), but this is Rhona's best
paper (handmade – manufactured *in situ*, no less – from
recycled egg boxes, which makes it ludicrously absorbent and
fractionally stiff). There'd be hell to pay if I wasted a piece.

Enough of my waffling, though (I know how much you hate
my waffling – my 'pointless flummery' as I believe you once
called it!). Can I just say how broken up we all still are about
your mother? We miss her horribly. Chester's inconsolable
(although he stole – and devoured – a whole partridge earlier. It
was sitting on the sideboard, covered with a tea towel, resting,

after I'd plucked it. I didn't think he could get up there – he's still huge; over three stone, but somehow he contrived to. It'll be tomato omelettes, all round, for dinner again tonight, I fear). The parrot still won't speak (and his chest is now completely bare). Even Rhona (who isn't, as you may recall, much given to emotional displays) was heard to mutter over her salted oats at breakfast how much she 'missed the silly old trout'.

Of course I don't mind in the slightest that you didn't respond to my last letter (although there was the nagging doubt that it might've gone astray, but then Mr Baquir, your lawyer, kindly told me that this was not the case. I really appreciated that. And he seems a very charming man, Mr Baquir. He and Rhona spent some considerable time on the phone reminiscing about Egypt. It seems he was growing up in the outskirts of Cairo during the late 1960s at almost exactly the same time she was working as a volunteer there with Christian Aid).

It's only natural that you would feel angry, Donovan. And, of course, you feel hurt – even betrayed. Anyone would. In fact we were all perfectly miserable when we found out about the funeral – especially Rhona, who sets great store (well, greater store than I do) by these formal occasions. 'We have an inalienable right to say goodbye,' she harrumphed, 'and now she's snatched that away from us. It just doesn't seem fair.'

Fair or no – I imagine it must be hard for you to get any real sense of closure. If it helps at all, William Dunkley (the funeral director) told me, in strictest confidence, how he took it upon himself to say a little prayer over the coffin (and recited a Psalm, I think, although I'm not sure which one). He had been strictly prohibited by Glenys – on pain of death (or worse, he said!) – from doing so, but that didn't deter him.

I spoke to him on Tuesday at the Christmas Fair. He was quite shame-faced about the whole mess, but I assured him that we bore no grudges (although I didn't absolve him on your behalf, obviously. It would hardly be my place to do so).

He was only fulfilling her wishes, I suppose. He said she had made all the arrangements in mid-2005 (after her main diagnosis), and then had rung him up – twice, on subsequent occasions – to stress the finer details. It wasn't a fly-by-night decision, in other words. She had insisted on perfect secrecy and he had decided – with some serious pangs of conscience – that it was his professional duty to respect that last request.

Bill was very fond of Glenys himself (I don't know if you remember him well – he's quite a few years younger than we are – the nephew of Arthur and Polly). He said she beat him black and blue as a boy after he released her dog – Trumpet – from the special hook outside the shop and he ran riot on the main street, then careered up on to the moor where he savaged a moorland sheep and was shot (this was a while after you'd left home, I think, and some time before Rhona and I arrived at Threadbare, but I know she doted on that dog – he sounds extraordinarily unlovable! – and often referred to the incident in barbed tones).

I asked about the ashes. Bill said they'd been scattered 'locally'. I tried to press him further on the point but he wouldn't budge. I'm guessing it was on the moor, near the war memorial (what better place than where your father's plane went down?). She hadn't been up there herself since the mid-eighties, when her thyroid first became an issue (and her weight ballooned), but she asked me to take a bouquet most weeks, and I was always happy to oblige her. It was never any trouble.

I have continued to take the bouquets since her death. In fact Rhona has actually accompanied me on several occasions (straight after our morning swim, although she finds the last stages of the hike a little difficult because of the problem with her knee joints). I know your mother truly loved that place.

We were standing up there only the other day, squinting over towards the power station (it was an especially beautiful, crisp, clear winter's morning) and laughing together about our early experiences with Glenys after we first arrived at Threadbare. She was always a rather singular creature!

We remembered her throwing that brick through our kitchen window – and we'd barely been ensconced a week – because we trimmed the ash hedge between the two properties without seeking her permission first (we honestly didn't realize that the hedge was 'hers'; it didn't look like it had been trimmed in years!). She'd been perfectly charming up until that point – even brought us a basket of greengages from her garden on the day we arrived (although it later transpired that she'd stolen the fruit from our greengage bush the week before; they were a little soft. I always wondered why the crop was so thin that year!).

We were quite distraught about it, as I recall (the brick, not the greengages! The windows were original – that marvellous, dimply, slightly imperfect old glass which Rhona's so passionate about), and as I said at the time (you'll probably remember – we've rabbited on about it enough, since!), 'If only she'd just come outside and said something – shared what was on her mind – we'd have stopped what we were doing without so much as a squeak of protest.'

But that wasn't Glenys's nature. She was never a big one for speaking out. She'd rather dwell on things, brood on things. She knew it was a fault in her. She even admitted as much, herself.

I was convinced she and Rhona would never make it up. Rhona – as you've discovered, to your cost – has an impressively short fuse. Although I think Glenys is the only person I've ever known (and I include our own, dear Dad in this select little group) who could actually make Rhona quake.

I think they probably recognized something in each other, something wild and uncontrollable, and realized – as lethal predators are wont to do – that some kind of compromise needed to be reached, quickly, as a matter of urgency; it had to be, or all hell would break loose. And so was.

Rhona bit her tongue from that time onwards. She bit it, and she bit it (sometimes I feared she might almost sever it!). 'It's good for my soul,' she'd mutter, or else, 'What doesn't kill you makes you stronger.'

Over time the relationship with Glenys undoubtedly improved. She learned to trust us, and even (I like to think) to rely on us a little. But you still couldn't take anything for granted. There was never any predicting when she might blow, or what might provoke her. It was like having a rumbling Vesuvius on your doorstep! You'd think everything was proceeding along equitably (no real clouds on the horizon), and then suddenly there'd be this tremendous outburst. A cataclysm!

Her rage was all-consuming – like a dam wall collapsing. This terrible roar! Indiscriminate destruction! Everything engulfed and obliterated ... Then afterwards, this amazing calm – a gentle sun, a washed-denim sky.

Glenys rarely bore a grudge for long – except with you, Donovan.

I remember that Easter – three years after your final, huge row – when you drove up from Derby (you were on your sabbatical), bringing her that exquisite, miniature Japanese maple as a peace offering, and she snatched it out of your arms (it was a fair old weight in the pot!) and tossed it into the road. It lay there for hours. I saw the argument that followed (you didn't see me – I was sheltering behind our greenhouse). I watched you storm to your car, climb inside, slam the door and then sit there for a while. I longed to do something – to say something – but I didn't dare interfere (I wanted to. I really wanted to. More than you will ever, ever know).

I could tell how upset you were as you drove off – heard you accidentally sound the horn as you knocked the left indicator – and my heart literally broke for you.

It may cheer you to know (all these years later), that after you'd gone – a fair while after – I braved Glenys's rage, went out into the road and rescued it (the maple – just as dusk was starting to fall). I planted it in our front garden (next to the brick path, by the gate) where it still stands to this day – almost taller than I am, now – a fine, lasting testimony, I often think, to a son's gentle magnanimity (I only pray there might still be some small remnants of benevolence remaining in your heart, for Rhona and me, today).

Glenys never said a word about it (the tree, your visit. In fact she didn't speak – to anybody – for almost a week) but I'm sure she knew what I had done. In fact I'm certain of it. Every time she entered our gate from that day onwards, she had to walk straight by it.

I saw her standing on the path and staring at it, deep in thought, early one autumn afternoon about three years ago (the leaves had just turned a deep vermilion and it did look especially lovely). It was difficult to read her expression at the time (apprehension? Uncertainty? Regret? As you know yourself, it could be so hard to tell what she was thinking), but I resolved to grasp the nettle and say something to her when she finally came inside (to comfort her? Confront her? Make a direct appeal on your behalf? I'm not entirely sure), but then the milk boiled over in the pan on the stove and the moment was lost in the chaos that ensued.

I suppose I never really had the stomach to stand up to her (I hope I'm not a coward, Donovan – although you often accused me of it. But I don't think it's cowardice so much as resignation, an inherent stoicism. I taught myself – ever since the trials of my childhood – never to expect too much. I like to think, of all the virtues, patience is the one I come closest to possessing. Patience: 'A minor form of despair, disguised as a virtue', as I believe Ambrose Bierce once called it!).

I'm still not sure what good – if any – would have come from a needless confrontation. Your mother was never really open to persuasion (when I visualize her, even now, in my mind's eye, I see her in the guise of an old seaman's chest: heavy, well-travelled, somewhat battered, ribbed by a set of thick, iron supports, fastened by a giant lock. The key is lost).

Glenys was always uncompromising – in both her habits and her views. She could be shrewish, hard-nosed and intractable. By the end (the very end), Rhona and I (and the poor parrot, and the cat) were her only remaining friends. Even the postman refused to deliver to her door (he dropped her mail off with us). She was barred from both the pub and the local shop. She'd driven everybody else away. She'd scared them off. It had been an almost calculated act. As if to be alone – truly alone – towards the end was the fulfilment of a life's ambition.

Thinking that – believing that – how could I have ever knowingly jeopardized the relationship we had? It was so fragile, so necessary. Glenys needed us (although she was far too proud to admit it). She needed me, and, in a curious way I was grateful for her need (the kind of gratitude you feel when an abandoned fledgling bites your finger as you struggle to feed it).

For all the pain she caused you (and the frustration and the disappointment), the end result of your awful rift – the marvellous upshot – was that you were set free (without guilt) to pursue what was to become your glittering career in the Diplomatic Corps.

Glenys often said things that were cruel. She could be savage and mean. But her assessment of me back then was clear-eyed and entirely accurate. I was a liability. I was a wreck. My epilepsy was so severe …

Now I'm not suggesting that it was ever just a case of 'shooting the messenger' (how could it be, when the messenger was the only one among us bearing arms?!), but I am saying that while it was a hard truth to bear at the time (for both of us), perhaps Glenys's greatest crime (although not her only crime, by any means) was simply presenting things as they truly were – the bald facts – without the calming balm of artifice.

I would never have coped with the life you were destined for. I would have smothered your hope, your promise and your desire. If you had stuck with me (and my numerous maladies), you wouldn't have married your ex-wife, Patricia, and she couldn't have borne you your two handsome sons. You wouldn't have taken on the greatest role of your life: to be a father.

The very thought makes me shudder.

And then, of course, there was always Rhona. She'd sacrificed so much for me, and with such a huge sacrifice comes a strong sense of obligation. I was obliged to her, Donovan (I think I always will be). She gave up her vocation in the Church to take care of me after Mother passed. She abandoned her calling. It would have been an unforgivable crime to desert her just when her faith – her trust in God – was starting to falter.

But let's not dwell on these things! The past is the past. It is gone and forgotten. Although (to hark back, for just a brief second) it would be difficult for you to conceive how much comfort I took over the long years that followed – and still take, every day – in your manifold achievements as a UN negotiator in West Africa.

You have moved mountains, Donovan. You have altered borders. You have shifted the world's emotional geography. You have shaped lives. You have saved lives. You have had a hand in making history.

How could I – one weak and waffling female – have dared to stand in the way of all that?!

If Glenys's temper was a dam wall – threatening, at every second, to collapse or implode – your will to make peace, to intercede, to unify, was a force every bit as compelling and as powerful.

There's a lesson in that, surely? And a rich irony. You have become one of the world's most admired and respected Conflict Resolution specialists, because the most important conflict in your own life could never be resolved. It was unsolvable. Glenys's implacability was the cruel spur that drove you. It was both your inspiration and your goad.

She was (in Rhona's words) a silly old trout (and sometimes worse!). But oh, how I loved her, Donovan, for all her many faults! I loved Glenys. I don't even mind admitting it, now. I loved her because she was the opposite of you, I loved her because to love her – the mother, your opposite – was as close as I could get to loving the son. I made loving her my life's work (my trial, my test, my passion), and I feel such a gaping hole inside of me – a ludicrously huge void – now that she has gone.

Of course I don't suppose for a moment that she ever loved me back! Glenys tolerated me, at best. It's not that she was entirely cold. There were signs of warmth, on occasion (not heat, no – just the dull, red coals that glimmer in a cooling grate at the end of a long, inhospitable evening).

She could be funny – often unintentionally. I wouldn't call her 'unkind', not as such; there was kindness there (microscopic little drops of it). It just wasn't very well distributed. It was like those tiny scraps of burned newspaper that fly out of a bonfire – delicate tornadoes – on a gusty autumn afternoon.

She certainly cared for her animals. In their case you might almost say she cared too much. Her love could be ruinous (not to mention her over-feeding!). She killed three dalmatians 'with tenderness' over the past twelve years. When the last one died – Faith, a fine, good-natured, liver-coloured bitch, only five years old – it took three men to carry her out (rolled up in two blankets). They could barely squeeze her through the garden gate.

But enough of all this! I'm straying, once again, from the real purpose of my letter (I can hardly bear to engage with it, the subject is so painful – to both of us, I'm sure), so here goes … Deep breath …

Please try and forgive us, Donovan, for all the crimes you feel we have committed against you. If they were committed, then they were completely unintentional. You are one of our oldest and our dearest friends – a brother to us both. Let us start afresh. Let us put aside all the misunderstandings and the rancour and the pettiness (it can be done, it is possible, all it takes is a small act of will)! Let us try and return to the way things once were! The good old times!

If only you could be persuaded to believe me when I tell you that Rhona and I had no idea – not the slightest inkling – of the many arrangements that Glenys had set in place prior to her death. Glenys didn't tell us about her burial plans, I swear (not so much as a whisper)! When I wrote to you (on the sad day she died), I had no notion (absolutely none!) of the strange events that were soon to unfold.

She had never (never!) discussed the details of her will with us (we didn't even think there was a will. We had no earthly reason to expect that there might be. You were her natural heir, her only child).

After she died we did not – as you suggested in your last communication – 'ransack the cottage searching for valuables' or 'take up partial residence' there (it frightens me to think who could have fed you these untruths, because I know – I'm certain – that you couldn't possibly have come up with them all by yourself).

I've racked my brains and I still can't settle on any one individual in the village who might have anything positive to gain by stirring up such cruel rumours against us (although Rhona, alas, is not of my bent). In fact I've become profoundly depressed about it all. I'm currently on a course of sleeping medication and Rhona has lost over two stone in weight (although her doctor says this is no bad thing: every cloud has a silver lining, I suppose!).

After thirty years in Burley Cross I've started to find the atmosphere here stifling and claustrophobic. I'm constantly on edge, staring at all the kind people I've known for years with nagging feelings of suspicion and disquiet.

It's been horrible.

It pains me to have to go into all the details once again, but just so that there can be no further confusion on the issue, since Rhona discovered poor Glenys's body on that awful day, I can assure you – hand on my heart – that we have crossed the threshold into Camberwell Cottage on only two occasions, in total (even the estate agent went in alone).

The first was to select a suitable dress for Glenys to wear in her casket (when we found her, as I mentioned previously, she was in her nightdress), and to clean out the perishable contents of her fridge (none of which we kept – all of which we disposed of).

The second was to facilitate the delivery of a commode (the driver refused to take it back, although he did kindly agree to dispose of the old one). I can only guess that the 'disinterested party' your lawyer referred to when he called was a witness to this transaction and leapt to all the wrong conclusions.

For the record, the new commode (which was ordered – and paid for – by me) currently sits, still boxed up, in Glenys's hallway (even if Rhona or I had found it a desirable artefact, neither of us – thank God – have any need of it, as yet!).

In regard to 'prettying the place up for ourselves' (and it cuts me to the quick to even write down those words) I can tell you that we have continued to trim the grass and prune the roses. This was something we had always done for Glenys, and something we have continued to do – as an act of good will – for you.

And why? Because the house is yours, Donovan. It was always yours. I thought we made that plain when this thorny issue first arose. It never entered our minds that it should be otherwise. Your extraordinary theories about Glenys being 'under our spell', 'subject to our wiles', 'frightened, desperate and vulnerable' (and countless other bizarre notions which bear no relation to the truth), I can only imagine were uttered in the dark haze of grief.

What confuses me the most (and forgive me for this, because I know I can be a little slow on the uptake, sometimes), is your apparent determination to make the whole thing 'a matter of principle'. Which principle? I don't understand! There is no principle at stake here! The house is yours, Donovan, both by warrant and by right!

As you are well aware, Rhona and I had already consulted a lawyer (and at considerable expense) to begin the process of handing it over. That process is now in abeyance. If it were down to me, this would not be so, but it is not down to me. Rhona must also have her say in the matter.

To put it plainly, Donovan, Rhona's feelings have been hurt – her pride has been deeply injured – and when Rhona feels something strongly, experience has taught me that there is only so much that I can do to guide and counsel her. It may help you to understand the apparent severity of her reactions to your accusations when you discover that, far from 'sitting on a nice nest-egg', Glenys had been under increasing financial stress over the last few years.

In the autumn of 2005, for example, her boiler stopped functioning and Rhona cashed in a portion of her own pension to fund a replacement for her. We paid Glenys's phone bill on countless occasions. We had Glenys's roof insulated when our own was done. For the final five or so years of her life, we fed Glenys at least two of her daily meals.

Wherever Glenys needed to go, we drove her. We arranged incontinence care (which she rejected, for the most part). Whenever Glenys came over to visit us in Threadbare (which was most days), we had to wash/clean/disinfect the upholstery (although we always tried to 'guide' her into a particular chair).

These are small things, silly things, things that shouldn't need to be mentioned, but I am saying them here, Donovan, I am writing them down, in my silly green ink, even though I feel humiliated by it, belittled by it, because I want you to understand that the only crime we have ever knowingly committed against your mother was the crime of kindness.

Sometimes I sit and I wonder why it was that Glenys made the decision that she did. Was it out of gratitude? (She was never very big on saying thank you, but then nothing we ever did for her was predicated on that.) Or was it simply to cause mischief? To break your poor heart? To forge a rift between us? Was it a final, cruel way of making it plain that she had never truly forgiven me for the breach I had (unwittingly) caused, all those years ago, between you and her?

I don't know. I don't want to know (I'm just so sad, so worn, so exhausted by the whole affair). What I do know, though, is that all this procrastination over the will and its outcome is costing Rhona and me dearly (and not just emotionally). Camberwell Cottage is presently being sold. Rhona and I had no choice in the matter (we are currently liable to pay death duties and under threat of losing our own home).

I also think it only fair to warn you that two days ago Rhona told me that she was withdrawing £3,500 from Glenys's account (last May Glenys's depleted finances received a much needed injection of cash after an old insurance policy came into fruition. Up to that point she was over £5,000 in the red, a debt we were liable for. I'm not entirely sure of all the exact details, but I can find them out, soon enough, if you want).

I have no idea what the money is for. I presume that it is to cover legal fees and other debts incurring to us as a result of this impossible situation (Rhona had sworn that 'nothing on God's good earth' would impel her to touch a penny of the money. I can only guess that something important has changed her mind).

I am unhappy about the withdrawal, and I felt that it was only right to let you know about it. Can I assure you, though (for my own part, at least), that my determination not to access Glenys's account remains as strong now as it ever was.

So there you have it. I'm not sure there's anything left to add. If you still are resolved to pursue the case against us, then all I can do is wish you well. I think it only fair to tell you, though, that both our lawyer, and Mr Baquir, seem to think your hopes of achieving anything by this course are not good.

Please see sense, Donovan! Don't let foolish pride get in the way of a happy outcome. Stop this mess while it can still be stopped. We are your dear friends. We love you deeply. You are always in our thoughts and in our prayers,

Tilly

PS On a slightly lighter note: someone bought us a duck! He's a Muscovy and very fine! Rhona sank a bath for him in the back garden, but he still persists in following me up on to the moor for a swim in the ghyll each morning. He had befriended a lone swan up there who unfortunately died after swallowing a load of fishing twine. By rights we should clip his wings (we've had complaints about him – he's quite a beast!) but we've yet to catch the little devil!

Do take care.
XX

[letter 4]

1, The Old Cavalry Yard
The High Street
Burley Cross
Wharfedale
WD3 4NW

20/12/2006

Dear Mr Vesper Scott-Jones,

I am writing to you, care of your publishers, because I have contacted you via your website www.sky-turns-black.com on three separate occasions and have received no direct answer to my enquiries. Instead my questions (and my email) have ended up – in bastardized form – on a 'fans' forum' to be chewed over and debated by other 'fans', which isn't at all what I'd had in mind (and, to put it bluntly, their various contributions have, by and large, been nothing short of asinine).

If I had wanted to know what Joe Bloggs thought on a variety of issues relating to your 'oeuvre' I suppose I could always have strolled out on to the High Street, right here in Burley Cross (West Yorkshire), and conducted a small random poll myself (I don't doubt that it would have taken me considerably less time and been infinitely more illuminating!).

It might interest you to know – by the by – that you have an Australian fan who haunts your site called AUSSIEHARDASS (I'm guessing he's an Australian – of course this can't be definitively proven) whose provocative views and coarse language I find especially difficult to stomach, as do many other contributors (I believe he answers to the general description of what they like to call 'a troll' in the lingo). I would suggest that his presence on the site is counter-productive and that all traces of him should be expunged from it as a matter of some urgency.

Perhaps this letter may serve to draw your attention to some of the other problems with the website: it's slow to download, the graphics seem a little amateurish – far too much lime green for 'average tastes' – and there's an irritating, somewhat gratuitous home-page which you need to double-click – several times, in my case – to gain proper access to the contents (I am presuming that you have some flunkey from your publishers running the show, or – worse still – that you are actually paying some wet-behind-the-ears graduate a living wage out of your own pocket to take care of it. I don't know. But either way … etc.).

May I now just say – to start my letter, proper – that I enjoyed the four books in your 'Sky Turns Black' series a great deal, although I thought the last book, *Chute to Kill*, took some of the ideas and themes explored in the earlier novels a stage too far – into the realms of the surreal in some instances, e.g. the girl, Lola, who dressed and acted like a circus poodle (to try and exorcize her experiences of childhood abuse at the hands of her dog-breeder uncle) was stretching a point, I felt, but the boy who spoke only in garbled rhyme? Way too much! I realize that he served as a kind of modern-day Greek Oracle figure, but I found both his use of the vernacular and his ability to conveniently pop up (muttering a tired, little 'rap' – apparently to order) whenever a new corpse was unearthed from one of the various high-rise blocks' many rubbish chutes a tad unconvincing, to say the least.

The book just didn't hang together as well as it might have – and I'd guessed the final twist by chapter four (having said that, I *am* very quick on the uptake. It sometimes drives my wife Moira around the bend when I leap up, ten minutes into a film or television drama yelling, 'The transvestite did it! He killed his father to fund his breast surgery …' etc. etc. I just can't help it. It's simply a knack I have).

But all credit to you for trying something different. A lot of young(er) writers don't seem to have the gumption for that, nowadays – especially after a period of success (when a sense of complacency often tends to set in, and they end up churning out any old trash).

Of course like most people I came to your work through the TV series, which – to be frank – I thought was arty-farty and over-directed. I only watched it because my daughter, Elise, who was visiting us at the time, twisted her mother's arm into giving it a go.

That said, I did rate Kenneth Hursley's cartoonish portrayal of Tim Trinder, the failed private investigator turned estate manager, solving crimes on the job (while a group of idiotic coppers and social workers weighed in with their size twelves, making the already delicate racial and social relations on the estate in the swinging sixties/early seventies even more parlous than they already were!).

As a matter of interest, I saw Hursley in the new Kenneth Branagh vehicle recently and thought he looked strangely out of his depth rubbing shoulders with more 'established' actors (which was a shame for the poor lad. The conclusion I was forced to reach was that he was one of those actors who performs at his best when playing a role very close to his own personality – not that this is entirely a bad thing: it's always worked for Scotland's Sean Connery).

Now I hear they're toting his name about as the new Dr Who! Who'd have thought it?

I suppose we'll just have to wait and see what he comes up with for the role; although he'll have his work cut out to do a better job than Christopher Eccleston, who brought a much needed measure of northern grit to the part (he'd be hard pressed to do a worse one than the effeminate boy they've had in the role since!).

In truth, I've never really made much of a habit of watching the show, myself. My wife watches it, on occasion. The BBC love to over-hype it – but it's just for kids, really, isn't it?

The TV series of *Sky Turns Black* was filmed in Coventry,

whereas the location of the original books was Manchester's Hulme estate. Presumably this change was necessitated by the demolition of Hulme's (by then) notorious crescents in 1993. As a Coventry lad, born and bred, who later lived in Manchester for some years, I was naturally keen to see if this drastic southward shift would prove successful. In the end, sadly, I felt it wasn't.

I read in a question-and-answer slot (in the *Radio Times*, I think it was – or possibly in something more down-market which I paged through at the dentist) that you were on a Media Studies course at the Polytechnic College in Coventry for almost a year (I know they like to call them all 'Universities' nowadays, but they're not kidding anybody, are they?). I wondered if this formative experience might have been a factor in your choice of a new location?

Either way, it seems you didn't enjoy the academic life and headed down to London to work as a runner for a film company before later moving into advertising where you worked on campaigns for Dairylea Cheese Triangles, and, later, Dove moisturizing underarm deodorant (I can't distinctly recall the adverts for either of these products, although I do remember partaking of the odd cheese triangle when my children were young, and while they weren't anything spectacular they were certainly perfectly edible).

Not only did I grow up in Coventry, but (cue the drum roll!) my father was the caretaker on a housing estate near the city centre for several years! I have extraordinarily strong childhood memories of the post-war geography of the town, and was a first-hand witness to the radical changes that took place from the late 1950s onwards (although I was lucky enough to move further north in 1964).

I won't pretend that there is much of the Coventry I knew so well as a boy present in your TV series – or, indeed, of the Manchester I knew later on in your books. It's obvious where the gaps in your knowledge are, but I like to think that this isn't simply a lack of good, detailed research on your part, but rather an author's artistic prerogative to reinvent a location (or setting) to better explicate their character and their plot.

When it comes to the 'caretaking' aspect of the books, I also have (as mentioned above) a special insight into this particular area of endeavour, although of course my father, Ken, was nothing like Tim Trinder; he didn't suffer from childhood polio, for starters (his hand was not malformed, and he didn't walk with a limp), nor was he given to dramatic flights of fancy on the job. He was, as you might expect, a very sensible, responsible member of the Coventry community (a stalwart of the Rotary Club), a much liked local figure with a great talent for plumbing (something he later exploited by becoming a plumber, full-time).

It never ceases to amuse me how little practical information about the caretaking trade is present in your fiction. I suppose I must just accept that this aspect of the narrative is probably more interesting to me than to the average reader because I have so much technical know-how and a personal knowledge of 'the business', so to speak.

This is not to imply that I am a caretaker myself – heavens no! I was lucky enough to pursue my childhood dream of becoming a member of Her Majesty's Royal Navy where I trained as an electrical engineer. Since leaving the forces I have made an excellent living in the security industry (running a company that manufactures burglar alarms. My son, Nick, has continued this upward gradient and is currently working in astro-physics).

While I'm about it, I suppose I should make a glancing reference to your latest novel, *Fast Track*, where failed policewoman turned British Rail Station Manager Hilda Fisher is horrified to find a number of her regular passengers (or 'customers') dying in a series of lethal 'accidents' and is obliged to step in to stop clod-hopping local detectives (and BR big-wigs and PR gurus) from botching up the investigation.

I haven't read the book myself (it's way out of my 'comfort zone'), but my wife Moira did after it was selected by her local book group (I think their interest was piqued by the Harrogate setting).

The novel was systematically ripped to shreds, Moira said, because most of the group (all women) said the female lead 'thought and behaved just like a stupid man'. I wouldn't let this get you down, though. Moira said most of them didn't know what they were talking about, having cast the book aside, in disgust, after only the first chapter.

On a more personal note, I have long been fascinated by your unusual name. It's a strange combination of Vespers (evening prayer) and Vespa (the Italian scooter manufacturer). I looked it up recently in my *Encyclopedia of Names* (I'd been considering giving the name to the hero of my first novel, a reformed sex abuser who has been made sole custodian of a small Romanian boy – I won't bother you with the backstory, but it's all perfectly credible – and is then obliged to go on the run with him to keep him from the clutches of a Russian crime syndicate).

Your name wasn't actually listed in the encyclopedia (the closest it came to was Vesta – the Roman goddess of the hearth, used in the UK during the 1850s). When I looked in my dictionary, though, it said: Vesper n. [L.] 1. a) orig., evening b) {Poet.} [V-] same as EVENING STAR.

In the end I decided it was simpler just to call the character William (after my paternal grandfather).

The aforementioned novel, tentatively entitled *Ceaucescu's Child*, is still very much in its infancy, but I am hoping that you might do me the honour of casting your eye over a couple of pages from the opening chapter to see if you think I'm heading in the right direction (also whether the characters and language have the right kind of 'feel' to them).

I have provided you with a brief summary of the plot (above), but do bear in mind that I am planning an extremely shocking and dramatic denouement towards the end which I won't describe here on the off-chance that you end up using it in your own work (inadvertently, of course!).

As a 'famous' writer I fully understand that you must get pestered with requests like this all the time, and so will appreciate any input or advice you can offer me, however sparse (although the sooner you can manage to get back to me the better; it would be irritating to do too much new work on the rest of the book only to discover that you feel a certain amount of 'tweaking' is needed in the early stages. I'm hoping to get the whole thing done before Easter, when Moira and I are heading off to Madeira for a month).

Wishing you well over the festive season (if you are an adherent of the Christian faith),

All the Best,

Matthew Endive

an exclusive excerpt from

CEAUCESCU'S CHILD
BY MATT ENDIVE

'NO WAY, MAN! *FUCK YOU, WHITE BOY!!* I IS HAD E'NUFF!!' THE BLACK GUARD SCREAMED.

WILLIAM LAY ON THE FLOOR, SHIVERING, LOOKING UP INTO THE SEEMINGLY-INFINITE TUNNEL OF HIS TORMENTOR'S RAGE-DISTENDED NOSTRILS. HE WAS DOWN, YES, FOR THE MOMENT, BUT HE KNEW HE WOULD NOT BE BROKEN BY THIS VAINGLORIOUS JAMAICAN THUG – HE *COULD NOT* BE BROKEN. NOT HERE! NOT NOW! HE HAD COME TOO FAR! HE HAD SUFFERED TOO MUCH!

AND HE HAD *LEARNED* – OH YES! THE PRIMITIVE DISCI-PLINE AND RANDOM VIOLENCE OF THE CARIBBEAN PENAL SYSTEM HAD SEEN TO THAT! WHAT LITTLE DIGNITY HE'D ONCE POSSESSED WAS NOW VANQUISHED. THE ARROGANT CONFI-DENCE AND POLISH HE'D ONCE EXUDED – THOSE INDELIBLE MARKS OF THE BRITISH PUBLIC SCHOOL SYSTEM – HAD BEEN ALL-BUT SCRUBBED AWAY.

WHEN SOMETIMES HE CHANCED, IN AN IDLE MOMENT, TO PONDER THE ISSUE (LOOKING BACK, SADLY, ON HIS SCHOOL DAYS, AS IF ON A DISTANT DREAM), THE IRONY DIDN'T ESCAPE HIM THAT THE RIGORS OF PUBLIC SCHOOL HAD ESSENTIALLY TRAINED HIM FOR THE DEGRADATION THAT WAS TO FOLLOW. THEY HAD ACTIVELY HELPED – NAY *ACCLIMATIZED* – HIM, IN POINT OF FACT!

AFTER ALL, WAS THERE ANY CRUELLER OR MORE MORALLY-CORRUPTING PLACE ON EARTH THAN THE LOFTY INSTITUTION HIS OWN, DEAR PARENTS HAD SO TENDERLY BEQUEATHED HIM TO: ETON [*I SHALL 'MODIFY' THIS NAME IN THE FINAL TEXT, OBVIOUSLY – TO SOMETHING LIKE 'RENTON' OR REATON' TO FORESTALL ANY KIND OF LEGAL REPERCUSSIONS*]?

WASN'T IT HERE THAT HE HAD BEEN TAUGHT – ALONGSIDE ANCIENT GREEK AND CHORAL CHANTS – THAT IT WAS NOT ONLY GOOD, BUT NECESSARY TO FIND PLEASURE IN THE HUMILIATION OF WEAKER AND YOUNGER BOYS? HE'D SEEN THE MASTERS DO IT, OFTEN ENOUGH, AND THEN, ONCE LIGHTS WERE FINALLY OUT ON THE DORM EACH NIGHT ...
THE HORROR!

WILLIAM KNEW THAT HE HAD BEEN WEAK. JUST BECAUSE IT HAD HAPPENED TO HIM, THAT DIDN'T MAKE IT RIGHT FOR HIM TO VENT HIS RAGE ON OTHERS ... NO. HE SHOULD HAVE STOOD UP AGAINST IT, HE SHOULD HAVE TAKEN A STAND (PERHAPS EVEN SOLD HIS STORY TO THE PAPERS) BUT HE HADN'T. HE'D JUST 'GONE WITH THE FLOW,' AND SOON, WHAT HAD ONCE BEEN JUST AN IDLE AMUSEMENT HAD BECOME SECOND NATURE TO HIM, A DEEPLY-INGRAINED HABIT ... ALMOST – HE FLINCHED AT THE THOUGHT – *AN INSTINCT!*

WHEN WILLIAM CAST HIS MIND BACK OVER IT, HE REALIZED THAT ALL HE HAD EVER TRULY DESIRED – PERHAPS MORE THAN ANYTHING, EVEN A MOTHER'S LOVE – WAS JUST TO FIT IN. *TO FEEL AT HOME.* HE WAS AN EMOTIONAL COWARD, YES, BUT THEN HADN'T COUNTLESS GENERATIONS OF POLITICAL AND RELIGIOUS LEADERS THROUGHOUT BRITISH HISTORY BEEN EXACTLY WHERE HE HAD BEEN, DONE *EXACTLY* AS HE HAD DONE?

GLADSTONE? PEEL? DISRAELI? HAD ANYBODY EVER TOLD *THEM* THAT WHAT THEY WERE DOING WAS SICK AND WRONG? WILLIAM SMILED TO HIMSELF, WRYLY. NO. SOMEHOW, HE SERIOUSLY DOUBTED IT.

SURE, HE'D BEEN TO HELL AND BACK, BUT THE ONLY PART OF THE JOURNEY HE CARED ABOUT NOW WAS THE RETURN: HE HAD EMERGED FROM THIS HELL-PIT A NEWER AND A STRONGER MAN. YOU MIGHT ALMOST SAY HE'D BEEN STRIPPED CLEAN, PARED TO THE BONE, REDEEMED, NOT BY YEARS OF INDULGENT MOLLY-CODDLING AT THE HANDS OF SOCIAL WORKERS AND PSYCHIATRISTS, BUT DOWN ON THE SKIDS,

'INNA DA HOOD', AN UNWILLING GRADUATE OF THE SCHOOL OF HARD KNOCKS.

'HANG ON A SECOND ...!' WILLIAM BLINKED – *'THE GUARD!'* HE TRIED TO REFOCUS, STRUGGLING TO PULL HIMSELF OUT OF HIS SUDDEN REVERIE. 'I CAN'T PLAY INTO HIS HANDS,' HE THOUGHT, TURNING TO FACE THE WALL, 'HE *WANTS* TO MAKE ME LOSE MY COOL. HE WANTS TO GET THE OPPORTUNITY TO CANCEL MY PAROLE SO THAT I END UP ROTTING TO DEATH IN THIS MISERABLE SHIT-HOLE.'

HE THOUGHT BACK ON THE TREATMENT HE HAD RECEIVED AT THEIR BEHEST OVER THE SEVEN YEARS HE HAD BEEN IN-CARCERATED. THEY HAD TRIED TO DESTROY HIM WITH THEIR RACIST JIBES ('YOU STUPID, WHITE MAGGOT!' 'WHITE DONKEY!' 'YOU DAMN UGLY WHITE ASS!') AND HUMILIATING RITUALS: THE MOULD-ENCRUSTED DAILY PORTION OF 'RICE AN' BEANS', THE DEGRADATION OF THE SLOP BUCKET.

HOW THE HELL HAD HE SURVIVED IT? MORE TO THE POINT – HOW ON GOD'S EARTH HAD HE EVER ENDED UP IN THIS STINKING SEWER IN THE FIRST PLACE?!

OH YES ...' WILLIAM SMILED, CLOSING HIS EYES FOR A MOMENT, *'POLLY!'*

HE BRIEFLY REMEMBERED THE SWEET, BLACK-HAIRED GIRL HE HAD LOVED SO DEARLY AS A BOY. HER BROTHER WAS RUPERT, A 'SCHOOL FRIEND' (A NOTORIOUS REPROBATE AND SEXUAL PREDATOR WHO GAVE NEW MEANING TO THE PHRASE 'KEEP YOUR FRIENDS CLOSE AND YOUR ENEMIES CLOSER'). HE HAD INVITED WILLIAM TO SPEND A FEW WEEKS RECOV-ERING FROM HIS A'LEVELS AT 'DADDY'S PAD IN JAMAICA'.

WILLIAM HAD INITIALLY TURNED HIM DOWN FLAT [*I'M GOING TO GIVE REASONS FOR THIS HERE, POSSIBLY CON-NECTED TO THE BREAK UP OF HIS PARENTS' MARRIAGE*] BUT CHANGED HIS MIND AND AGREED TO GO, AFTER ALL, IN THE EXPECTATION THAT POLLY MIGHT ALSO BE THERE.

POLLY ... NOW FULLY GROWN, HER DARK HAIR CASCADING DOWN TO HER TRIM WAIST, THE ODD, STRAY STRAND OF IT

SLITHERING INTO THE MUSKY CREVICE BETWEEN HER FULL,
BROWN BREASTS WHICH WERE SPRINKLED IN PERSPIRATION,
DUSTED WITH SUMMER FRECKLES ... SHE WORE A YELLOW
BIKINI [*MORE DETAILS ABOUT HER BIKINI ETC TO FOLLOW*],
BUT SHE'D ONLY EVER REALLY HAD EYES FOR A LOCAL, BLOND
DRUG DEALER CALLED TRISTAN – AN OXFORD GRADUATE –
WITH HIS TAN, HIS MIRROR SHADES AND HIS READY ACCESS
TO 'PUFF AN' WEED'.

HOW FOOLISH THEY HAD ALL BEEN!
CRUSHED BY LONELINESS AND DISAPPOINTMENT, WILLIAM
HAD ALLOWED RUPERT TO LEAD HIM, BLINDLY, UNWITTINGLY,
SOMETIMES STAGGERING AS HE LOST HIS FOOTING, DOWN
DARK, TROPICAL PATHS HE HAD NO NATURAL INCLINATION TO
TRAVEL, AND THEN ...

WHAT?! WHO?! *HOW THE ...?!*
HE HAD ENDED UP HERE. IN THIS GOMORRAH. ON TRUMPED-
UP CHARGES. SOME THOUGHT HE HAD BEEN FRAMED (RUPERT
WAS THE TRUE VILLAIN OF THE PIECE, SURELY?) BUT HE
DARED NOT THINK ABOUT THAT – WHAT GOOD COULD IT
POSSIBLY DO HIM NOW?

SWEET POLLY HAD BEEN TO VISIT HIM BEFORE SHE FLED
THE ISLAND, HER CHEEKS STAINED WITH TEARS. 'THIS IS MY
BROTHER'S FAULT ...' SHE'D WHISPERED, 'IF ONLY YOU'D HAD
ACCESS TO A PROPER LAWYER ... IF ONLY I'D *SAID* SOME-
THING. IF ONLY I'D BEEN BRAVE ENOUGH TO STAND UP IN
COURT ... OH WILLIAM, WE COULD HAVE BEEN SO GOOD
TOGETHER!'

AND THEN, SEEING THE IMMEDIATE, AGONIZED RESPONSE
IN HIS BLOODSHOT, GREEN EYES, 'PLEASE! NO! *OH GOD!*
FORGIVE ME!'
'IF ONLY ...' WILLIAM THOUGHT, SMILING, AS THEY DRAGGED
HER, SOBBING, FROM HIS CELL, 'IF ONLY ... IF ONLY ...

(end)

[letter 5]

The Winter Barn
(off Old Woman's Lane)
Burley Cross
Wharfedale

21/12/06

Ivo,

I just sent you a text – in fact I just sent you an email (I sent you a text *about* the email) – because I'd just tried to phone you to make sure you downloaded it – *and printed it* – tonight (*all* of it, mind? There's about ten pages. I want them printed and then put into the Threadbare file, *pronto* – please, *please*, pretty-please).

When you didn't answer your phone I left a voice-mail (just ignore it – it was a gratuitous outpouring of hysterical waffle – although, knowing you, you'll ignore it anyway. You never seem to get around to listening to my messages. Why *is* that, exactly?).

Oh, God, *God*, I'm in such a crazy rush! I just want to be sure to catch the six o'clock post (does the post even *go* at six?). If I don't manage to catch it then the samples – there's only two of them, they're minuscule – won't reach you until the day after tomorrow and that would be a serious, *serious* pain in the arse (why am I telling you this? What good will it do? *Balls!* I'll *definitely* miss it at this rate! In fact … *Great.* I have missed it. I'm screwed. *You're* screwed. Carol-Ann's going to throw the most monumental strop. Brace yourself).

Hang on a minute … It's just this second dawned on me that it's Bengt's Birthday Bash tonight and you'll probably get pissed as a fart and throw a sickie tomorrow, anyway. I only …

No. No. NO! I don't *believe* this! I don't … My bottom's *soaked*! It's … *aaargh*! Remember how I told you about that tiny little hole in my bike seat which sucks up water into the foam padding when it rains so that the next time you sit on it ...

NOOOO!! I just ... I can't believe I've gone and done it again! Tilly, the woman in Threadbare Cottage, told me – she *warned* me on Friday – to put a plastic bag over it (the seat, Ivo, not my head – although I'm seriously starting to wish I had).

Damn! My beautiful *chair*'s all wet! It's that wonderful, padded, red-fabric office chair I got in the Conran Shop sale last year! You told me it was all wrong for The Winter Barn! You *told* me! You said, 'Jo-Jo, that thing's *completely* at odds with your country aesthetic.' But would I bloody listen? Would I hell! Well, you were right (*again*, you smug Teutonic swine)! It's looked stupid here from the very outset (I was too proud to admit it). And now there's this huge ...
Damn, damn, *damn*!

Okay. *Okay*. I need to calm down. I'm having a little panic attack. It's just all been so unbearably ... *urgh* ... stressful! I'm on HOLIDAY for Christ's sake! I just don't seem able to ... that small switch in my head you're constantly referring to ... I just don't ...
DEUTERONOMY!
NEHEMIAH!
ZEPHANIAH!
LAMENTATIONS!
EZEKIEL!!!
YES! YES! *YES*!
It's come to me, in a flash, like a divine revelation! The *name* of the new collection! Scratch the stuff I said in the email (it was all just a pile of crap)! This is *perfect*! This is *fabulous*!!!

'*LAMENTATIONS*: a modern exercise in old-fashioned restraint,' The lifestyle collection in colour, textile and print by designer Jo-Jo JOnes with a little help from Ivo-wots-his-name (Ha ha – serves you right, though).

———

'*LAMENTATIONS*: a tearful celebration of those good,
old-fashioned virtues of
thrift and temperance,'
[I've got goose bumps!]
The lifestyle collection in colour, textile and print by …

It's *brilliant*! I *love* it! So timely! So new! So atmospheric! And
so incredibly *appropriate* to the whole 'Threadbare story-board'
I've been working on all these long, hard months … *you* know –
all the bravery and the sadness and the heartbreak and the
making-do.

(Yes, yes. I *understand perfectly well* that 'Threadbare' was
always the best name for the collection – you've said it until
you're blue in the face! But it's just too blatant! Call me a
wimp, but I *do* happen to want to carry on living here, part-
time, in Burley Cross after the collection comes out. Their
cottage is literally around the corner! Thirty yards from my
front door! It'd be like, 'Hi, Tilly and Rhona. Yes. Yes. I totally
ripped off your *entire* life's work, but hey! Whatever …')

'LAMENTATIONS: a long, hard journey in
old-fashioned patterns and well-worn threads,'
[Oh,*God*, I *love* that! I'm *flying* now!]
from Jo-Jo JOnes, the designer who brought you …

Then, just *picture* it, Ivo: we'll use all the other books as paint
names, individual fabric names, wallpaper names etc. etc.
Effortless!
I mean, as I'm looking down the contents page, right now,
I'm seeing fifteen, eighteen, twenty really, really *meaty* titles!
LEVITICUS!
OBADIAH!
HABAKKUK!
(Habakkuk? *Hmmn.* Maybe not).
Have I lost you? Have I … ?! It's a *Bible*, stupid (you're

always harping on about your deep, Lutheran roots, aren't you?!)! I'm holding this incredibly, *incredibly* beautiful Bible in my hands (I'm going to photograph the cover this very second and send it direct to your BlackBerry! In fact, no, I'll photograph it and send it later, otherwise you'll just open the document and think I've gone loco. Actually, no, you won't. You'll understand perfectly. You always do).

I'm holding it in my hands (well, I'm not holding it in my hands – I couldn't *write* if I were – it's sitting on the table, directly in front of me, but I'm holding it in my hands, mentally, while rubbing a tremulous, slightly calloused thumb up and down its well-worn spine) and it's got this stunning (stunning, stunning, *stunning*) Arts and Crafts-style design on the front cover: a mix of these three, thick, bottle-green stripes (of irregular width) interspersed with these two very, *very* red-end burgundy stripes, intercut with four, thin, cream lines, then this absolutely perfect black and cream Coptic-style cross in the middle – the four quarters each with alternating A&C-style graphics going grapes/olives/grapes/olives.

Classic, generous, open font, in cream (I think it might be Baskerville, or something very like ... I *love* Baskerville. There's something so ... so *reliable*, so *trustworthy* about the spacing, somehow ...).

You've just *got* to see it! I borrowed it from Rhona (it's hers). She's the older of the two sisters. Always dresses in grey or black. Very tall with sloping shoulders. *Radiates* disapproval. Hair drawn back into an unforgiving bun. Should have been a nun. *Screams* nun. Never smiles. (Why are religious people always so unapologetically bloody miserable? You'd think being religious was a reason to be cheerful! What's the point of it all, otherwise?)

Well, it's hers. I asked if I could borrow it last week (just spontaneously). I *seriously* thought she was going to refuse, but then she handed it over, made some muttered excuse about 'digging over the raised leek bed', and left the room (I don't think she likes me. I don't think she likes anybody). By rights I should have returned it by now (but thank *God* I didn't! Thank *God* I hung on to it!).

Of course it was at *that* point – perfect timing, you know me – I discovered the wet bottom thing …

I was astonished! I was horrified! I was like – Oh, my God, my bottom's all wet! *WHAT THE FUCK IS GOING ON HERE?!?!*

Tilly – the younger sister (she's just so, so *gorgeous*, Ivo – you'd go perfectly wild for her if she was ten years younger. I'm *quite* in love with her myself, as a matter of fact. She's got this wild mass of black curls highlighted with tiny wisps of silver. She's thin as a pole with dark, *dark* blue eyes. Skin stretched over her cheekbones like strips of pale brown cow-hide. Dresses like some kind of crazed, pre-Maoist peasant refugee, or a young boy from a lost tribe of ancient Mongolian camel herdsmen; completely unintentional, mind – totally unpremeditated – clothes just *look* that way when she throws them on her. It's effortless! Doesn't have the first *clue* about how gorgeous she is. Product, make-up etc. an *absolute* anathema! Barely *glances* in a mirror … well, she told me … hang on … am I still …?) *Hello!* – well, she just gazes at my wet bottom, perfectly calmly (she's so unstintingly practical) and says, 'That'll be your bike seat. There's probably a small hole in it. It was raining earlier. Don't worry. It happens to me all the time. Just tie a plastic bag over it … the *bike* seat, not … No. It's fine. It's an old cushion anyway. In fact it's the special cushion we always used to try and give Glenys whenever she popped round, unannounced …'

At this point I leap into the air again, horrified (I've only just sat down) because Glenys was their revolting, senile old neighbour who died earlier this year. The fat, angry one – incontinent. Pelted Simpson with rotten apples from her garden when he barked at her cat that time. (The *cat*! Oh, my God! The cat – Chester, *her* old cat which they've adopted – is still

HUUUUGE! He's on a diet, but he's still massive. The sisters call him 'Puffen-bomf' [?!]. It's like this little joke they have going on between them – most odd – and when I asked if either of them spoke German they just exchanged amused glances and shook their heads.

He has this weird, fatty deposit near his back-end, to the right of his tail, but kind of tucked underneath it, so his bottom puffs out on one side. Apparently it's perfectly harmless, but once you've noticed it, it's impossible to stop staring at it. It's hypnotic! You would be *obsessed* by it, I swear! It's like this lopsided bustle. Most humiliating for a feline, I'd have thought. Although he doesn't seem to realize. I mean he's so fat it'd be a miracle if he could even *see* that far back.)

Anyhow, it transpires I've been cheerfully sitting on the cushion they always used to put out for their incontinent neighbour! I'm appalled (I'm wearing my favourite pair of beige cargo pants from Joseph)! But then Tilly notices my expression (hard to miss it, quite frankly) and says, 'Oh no! No! Please don't be offended! It was covered in plastic! We'd covered *all* the cushions in plastic by the end, because you could never predict … I mean we were always very careful to protect her feelings – we just pretended it was one of my little idiosyncrasies, because I make all the cushions myself, by hand … And I've washed it since, anyway. About a dozen times …'

So I sit back down again, nervously.

Then she starts going on about the duck – Eliot. She *loves* that duck. It follows her around the place, wherever she goes, getting into all manner of mischief. Do you remember the duck? Did I tell you about it at the time? I *must* have! He was like my little *in* on the whole Threadbare situation …

Well, I was cycling past the cottage – literally the first week after all the renovations on The Winter Barn had been completed – when Simpson suddenly disappeared from view and I realized – all too late – that the little shit had somehow managed to force his way into their garden (as it transpired, through a new badger hole running under their hedge. I *must've* told you?!).

So I bang on my brakes – stop – listen – hear barking – leap off the bike (*dry* bum) and charge into the property through the gate.

Simpson is nowhere to be seen (but is still producing an unholy racket). I run around the cottage into the back garden and there I see Rhona kicking Simpson away from her (*booting* him, savagely – *not* very Christian behaviour!) while holding a bloodied hen in the air above her head (a white hen. Drenched in blood. Like something from a voodoo ritual). Total, total nightmare!!

I charge into the fray, grab Simpson's collar and somehow manage to wrangle the little sod.

'I *hate* Highland Terriers!' Rhona announces (face like thunder, but still icy calm). 'They're such an awful, noisy, stupid, pointless, *aggressive* little breed.'
(Pointless?!)

Meanwhile – as Simpson barks on – she's trying to determine how a bad a state the poor hen is in (or was it a chicken? Are chickens and hens the same thing? I don't *know*! I'm just a foolish city girl! she wails). At this point Tilly emerges from the cottage, unfastened housecoat flying out behind her (Yes! She wears a housecoat! Isn't that adorable?!).

'Is it Gretel?' she pants. 'Oh please, *please* don't let it be ...' Rhona doesn't respond, just yanks at the hen's neck (cue: horrible clicking, cracking sound) and the poor creature is *kaput*. No discussion. No real ceremony, to speak of (and by the fierce look in her eyes I suspect she's more than ready to perform exactly the same 'mercy' on Simpson and myself).

Tilly bursts into tears. She *loves* Gretel (I'm glancing around, furtively, trying to locate a gingerbread henhouse. For the record: there isn't one).
Oh *balls*! I'm thinking. Another potential dinner invite goes up in smoke ...

And that was that, pretty much. I beat a hasty retreat.

But I felt so *bad* about it, Ivo! I mean that look on poor Tilly's face!

Anyway, to cut a long story short, I bought them a replacement hen (another white one. I thought it was the least I could do). I picked it up at a local farm and took it over to the cottage, two days later, in a small cardboard box (*sans* Simpson, this time).

Well, I knock on the door and Rhona answers it. '*Now* what?' she demands (Not 'hello' or 'so how are you?' She's absolutely terrifying. About seven foot tall. Face like a bucket). 'I've bought you a replacement hen,' I say.

She stares at the box, scowling. 'That really wasn't necessary,' she says, and makes a tiny gesture with her hands as if to encourage me to take it away again.

Thankfully, Tilly then appears at her shoulder, all smiles. 'A new hen?' she coos. 'But that's so incredibly *kind* of you! Come in! Come in!'

This is the moment (or soon to be the moment) when I see Threadbare, inside, for the first time (and that, I know for sure, is something I *have* told you about. In excruciating detail).

We go through to the kitchen and I place the box down on to the kitchen table, which is covered with the most amazing, lightly waxed 1940s-style tablecloth, decorated with all these tiny little ears of wheat (sample piece enclosed. I cut off a corner this afternoon when Tilly disappeared into the pantry to fetch me a dozen eggs).

Tilly opens the box and peeks inside. A short pause follows, and then, 'Oh my goodness!'

Rhona promptly elbows Tilly out of the way and peers inside the box herself. There's an audible intake of breath. She glares up at me as if I've committed the world's most heinous, criminal act (I hadn't even stolen one of their saucers yet! I can't wait to show it to you when I come back into town. It's darling! Pale yellow, decorated with jagged fronds of blossoming mimosa. I'm convinced we can manufacture something along similar lines, dead cheap, at that pottery in Croatia I told you about).

'Who sold you this?' she demands.

I stutter the name of the farm.

'He obviously saw *you* coming a mile off!' she snaps. And then (just in case I was in any remaining doubt), 'He keeps his livestock in the most appalling conditions. He's worse than a criminal. You were a fool to go there, an absolute *fool*!'

'Oh my goodness!' Tilly repeats.

'Is there something *wrong* with it?' I ask (peering over at the inoffensive little ball of fluff myself).

'No. I mean yes. I mean it's actually … well … a *duck*,' Tilly informs me, wincing, apologetically.

'A duck?' I echo, mystified.

'Quack quack,' Rhona smirks. 'You'll need to take it back, I'm afraid.'

She begins to close the lid on the box.

'But she *can't*!' Tilly squeaks, pulling the box towards her and opening it up again, 'She *can't* take it back! Look how *bedraggled* the poor thing is! He's half-starved!'

'A duck?' I repeat, horrified. 'Are you sure?'

(I mean how was *I* meant to know? I'm a *designer*, not a *vet*!)

'It's a Muscovy,' Rhona hisses. 'A Lavender Muscovy. The ugliest and most pugnacious of all the ducks …'

'This puts me in mind of "The Ugly Duckling",' Tilly interjects, trying to make light of it. 'The children's story,' she elucidates (having garnered no immediate response).

'Although, if I remember correctly,' Rhona interrupts her, 'that ugly duckling turned out to be a swan, whereas this "hen" *is* an ugly duckling. It's a *very* ugly duckling. And when it grows up, it will be a very ugly duck.'

Of course by this stage Tilly has the little scrap out of the box and is holding him in her hand and staring, devotedly, into his ducky face. She is in love.

'We could get Edo to build him his own, special duck-house,' she says, then, before Rhona can object, 'and we could sink that old bath – the one in the front garden I always plant up with hyacinths ...'

(I have shown you a photo of 'that old bath', Ivo, in full bloom. I actually took it when I was first up here, house hunting. Remember? You said it was the most beautiful thing you'd ever seen – four brass calf's hooves supporting a crazily elongated chamber pot. China. Not enamel. Never seen another one like it ... Well, they've sunk it in the ground now and turned it into a pond. Please, *please* stop crying. I've shed enough tears over it myself, already.)

It's at this point (I've been staring around the kitchen, my design-dar starting to sound loudly in my ear. I mean they have a *treasure*-trove of stuff in that room ...) that my eye alights on a series of exquisite, antique medicine bottles on the dresser, each one delicately hand-painted with scenes from Greek mythology.

'What are these?' I say, nudging one, awed.
'*Urgh*. Tilly does those,' Rhona grunts.
'It's just a silly hobby,' Tilly interjects. 'I find them in the garden and then I ...'
'Could I *buy* one off you by any chance?' I demand (heart a-pitter pat).
'Absolutely *not*. Don't be ridiculous! She couldn't *possibly* sell them,' Rhona exclaims, shocked. 'They're just therapy for her epilepsy. They're not worth tuppence!'
'No. *No*. I couldn't possibly,' Tilly echoes, mortified, her cheeks pinkening.

'Tilly's always been the most terrible pest with a paintbrush,' Rhona expands, taking the duck from Tilly's hands now, and staring into its duck-face, herself. 'If something stays still for long enough then she's bound to start dabbing away at it – literally anything she can get her hands on – the curtains, the crockery, the table, the walls ...'

The *wallpaper*, Ivo! A perfect bunch of wilting bluebells tied together with a piece of string! Hand-printed *and* painted (I ripped off a piece from behind the door last week after 'spilling' my cup of tea on the floor so that Tilly would rush off to fetch a mop. Enclosed).

'You painted everything in here *by hand*?' I all but gurgle. 'I've run out of space, so I'm concentrating on glass now,' she sighs, 'old marmalade jars, jam jars, little broken fragments which I unearth in the garden that I fancy the look of … Sometimes Rhona even lets me buy the odd piece from Oxfam or Save the Children if there's a special occasion coming up.'

'Her birthday or something,' Rhona generously concedes. I don't actually respond to this. I'm just devouring the room with my eyes. I'm just drinking it all in, almost nauseated, like a bee overdosing on nectar.

Oh, Ivo, *Ivo*! All that unbridled *creativity*! It's stupefying! It's sickening! It's deranged! She just exudes it, quite unconsciously. She perspires it. She exhales it. But not a shred of ambition! Not so much as an ounce of it! She just has this … this astonishing *eye*, this instinct. They both do! And it's not just the stuff she creates herself – the stuff she makes – but the stuff she *owns*, the stuff she *acquires*. It's whatever she thinks! It's whatever she touches! It's in each teaspoon, each tea-cloth, each pepper-pot, each ladle …

It's a gift! It's a knack! It's like every object, every artefact is just another small part of this infinitely complex and coherent Threadbare Cottage Design Universe – a wonderfully evocative stage setting for the gentle Theatre of Threadbare; a further sweet detail in 'The Threadbare Diorama'.

Yet every time I try and talk to her about it – talk *business* with her – she just closes down. She refuses to engage. She either goes completely blank, starts blushing, makes her excuses and flees the room, or abruptly changes the subject ('It's almost time to start chitting the potatoes!', 'I'm so looking forward to spring this year!', 'We really should replace that gate. Can you hear it creaking? Isn't it maddening?', 'The parrot has learned a new word! Barnabas! Barnabas! Say "soup"!').

I'm at my wits' end, Ivo! She's driving me insane! I mean what am I to do? Where am I to turn? How can I possibly hope to help someone who refuses to help herself? More to the point, how long can I be expected to just stand quietly by and let all this astonishing talent go to waste? It would be wrong to do so, surely? Obscene! Little short of criminal!

I walked into her kitchen the other week, and there she was (this quaintly eccentric English dear, this unquenchable font of British Design Talent) sitting at one end of the kitchen table, totally engrossed in decorating a broken ashtray she's found (using this old brush with one – *one* – bristle stuck on the end of it), and at the other end sits Burley Cross's token African inhabitant (Eddy – Eddo – Edo – Edouard – I'm not 100 per cent sure, but he's Congolese – at least I *think* he is – he speaks with quite a pronounced French accent).

You rarely see him around town (he has his own, quiet alcove at the pub where he likes to sit and get quietly inebriated). He's in his fifties, but very well-preserved. Handsome. Beautifully dressed. Has quite an attitude – bordering on the arrogant. How he and the Threadbare sisters built up an acquaintance is a mystery in itself (they're like chalk and cheese! And from what I can tell he – like them – keeps himself pretty much to himself).

I'm told he's married to a Belgian heiress – she's much older than he is and spends most of her time in Bruges. Although I think her oldest daughter – by a former marriage – has visited him recently, once or twice.

So he lives alone, for the most part, in what's reputedly the oldest house in town. It's called The Bleachers (after a northern bleach magnate who lived there in the early 1800s) and is absolutely gorgeous. I've never been inside the place, but it's lower storey falls *under* the level of the road – you walk down some little steps to get in through the front door, which is tiny, only four or five feet high.

The house is in an awful state of disrepair, although (from what I can tell) he's an amazingly talented carpenter. The town's various big-wigs are always moaning on about it (I think it drives them all nuts that this odd, haughty African owns one of the village's landmark properties but never so much as lifts a finger to maintain it). He seems to actively delight in antagonizing them all (*very* weird).

Where was I? Oh yes. So they're sitting at the table together, in this companionable silence. She's painting her ashtray, at one end, he's whittling away at the other, working on a sculpture – an African totem thingummy – female, about four inches high, astonishingly well-observed, with a tiny pair of withered breasts and a hugely protrusive vagina (I've seen other examples of his work. It's really terrifying. Figures with amputated arms, blindfolded men with pliers hanging from their penises, African devils in Nazi uniforms. In fact one of his pieces – an African Christ writhing on the cross – has caused the most *humungous* stink in town after it was hung in the front portal of the church by the 'old' vicar without the permission of the 'new' one, who went completely nuts when he found out about it!).

The point I'm struggling to make, here, Ivo, is that if a quaint village in the wilds of West Yorkshire can generate such stores of unbridled creativity, then why the *heck* aren't people producing stuff of this quality in Hoxton and Camberwell and Shoreditch? And if they aren't (which they aren't), then surely it's my job to *share it with them*?!

The way I see it, the bottom line re Threadbare is that I can't (I *can't*) just sit here and let this amazing opportunity pass me by. I *won't*. I must act! I *must*! And I don't think what I'm doing is wrong! Not remotely! I'm a *facilitator*, Ivo. *That's* my role! I'm a 'cultural midwife'. I'm like one of the Medicis. It's my moral duty to bring beauty to the world! How can I simply stand back and watch it bloom and die, unnoticed, unloved, unmourned?

Ow. I'm starting to develop cramp. And there goes my phone! Perfect timing! Is it you? Oh, do let it be! I'm absolutely *longing* for a proper chin-wag.

But *hasn't* this been fun? We should write letters more often! It feels so healthy, so *rustic*, so wholesome!

Simpson's scratching at the door. My bottom's quite dry again. I'm dashing straight over to pick up and answer just as soon as I can scribble –

Toodle-pip!

(And stuff this thing into an envelope ...)

XXX

JJ

17 THE BECK
THURSDAY, 3.15PM

RHONA BROOKS,

I HAVE SPOKEN TO YOU <u>TWICE</u> NOW ON THE SUBJECT OF THAT DUCK OF YOURN AND I WILL NOT SPEAK AGAIN ON THE MATTER I CAN ASSURE YOU. NEXT TIME I WILL COMMUNICATE WITH YOU THROUGH THE PERSON OF THE LOCAL CONSTABULARY.

THAT I SHOULD BE OBLIGED TO FORK OUT FOR A STAMP ON ACCOUNT OF NOT BEEN ABLE TO WALK TO YOUR DOOR AND KNOCK (OR POST THIS THROUGH YOUR LETTERBOX IF I DIDN'T FEEL AS I <u>WANTED</u> TO SPEAK IN PERSON) BECAUSE OF <u>FEAR OF ATTACK</u>, IS NOTHING SHORT OF CRIMINAL!

I HAVE STROLLED 'THE CALLS' MAN AND BOY, LITTLE THINKING THAT ONE DAY I WOULD BE HALTED IN MY PERAMBULATIONS BY SOME PESKY BIRD THAT OUGHT TO BE IN A PEN OR ON A DINNER PLATE, NOT CAREENING UP AND DOWN THE WAY LIKE A JUMBO JET.

SHAME ON YOU, RHONA BROOKS, AND SHAME ON THAT GIDDY SISTER OF YOURN. I THOUGHT BETTER OF YOU BOTH (ALTHOUGH WHY I DID SO I AM CURRENTLY AT ODDS TO REMEMBER).

I'VE A GOOD MIND TO HAVE A WORD WITH REVEREND HORWOOD ON THE MATTER – NOT THAT I'M MUCH GIVEN OVER TO SPEAKING WITH MEN OF THE CLOTH, BUT I KNOW HE STILL HOLDS SOME PALTRY SCRAPS OF INFLUENCE IN YOUR CORNER. PERHAPS HE MIGHT BE ABLE TO TALK SOME SENSE INTO YOU! BETTER STILL, PERHAPS

HE MIGHT FEEL INCLINED TO BASH YOUR TWO
SILLY HEADS TOGETHER! I CERTAINLY FEEL
INCLINED THAT WAY MYSELF!!

IF YOUR OWN DEAR MOTHER COULD SEE WHAT
A WILD COURSE YOU PAIR HAVE TAKEN OF LATE
SHE WOULD BE TURNING IN HER GRAVE! I'LL NOT
PRETEND HERE THAT ELIZABETH AND ME EVER
HAD SO MUCH AS A CIVIL WORD TO SAY TO EACH
OTHER, BUT THAT'S HARDLY THE ISSUE, IS IT?

THE ISSUE – POINT OF FACT – IS THAT INFERNAL
DUCK OF YOURN! I CALL IT A DUCK BUT IT'S THE
SIZE OF A GOOSE AND IT KNOWS IT AN' ALL! THAT
DUCK IS A WRONG 'UN. IT HAS THE EYES OF A
KILLER.

WALTER FRANCIS SAID THE THING ATTACKED
HIM WHILE HE WAS CHECKIN' OVER SOME EGGS
AT MRS RHODES'S STALL. HE SAID THE WRETCH
CAME DOWN ON HIM OUT OF THE SKY LIKE AN
EAGLE! HE SAID IT POOPED ALL OVER HIS JACKET.
HE DROPPED THE EGGS IN SHOCK AND BROKE
THREE OF 'EM. HE SAID HE DIDN'T FEEL INCLINED
TO PAY FOR 'EM AFTER THAT, GIVEN AS THEY WAS
BROKE, BUT THEN MRS RHODES CAME CHARGIN'
OUT OF HER HOUSE AN' GIVE HIM A PIECE OF HER
MIND FOR'T! HE SAID, 'I'M HARDLY GOIN' TO PAY
FOR THAT WHICH IS ALREADY BROKE, MADAM!'
SHE SAID, 'WELL THEY WASN'T BROKE BEFORE
YOU HAD 'EM IN YOUR THIEVIN' HANDS, THANK
YOU VERY MUCH, MR FRANCIS!'
THEN ALL HELL BROKE LOOSE OR SO I'M TOLD.

NEXT THING I HEAR THE DAMN THING HAS
BROUGHT DOWN THE GUTTERING ON BRIAN
BREWSTER'S EXTENSION. THEN HE GOT INTO MRS
LOOSE'S KITCHENETTE AND IS FOUND MAKIN'
HISSELF AT HOME IN HER WASHING UP BOWL! SHE

SAID IT GIVE HER THE HORRORS WHEN SHE SAW IT
SITTIN' THERE WITH ITS BIG RED FACE ALL
DISFIGURED LIKE IT WAS SCALDED. I SAID THAT'S
AS HOW THE BREED IS MEANT TO LOOK, MRS
LOOSE – UGLY AS SIN, AND FULL OF SIN AN' ALL.
IT MAKES YOU WONDER AT THE KIND OF HUMAN
MIND THAT COULD CONCEIVE SUCH A SIGHT WAS
WORTH THE LOOKIN' AT!
SHE SAID I DON'T EVEN CARE ABOUT THAT, KEN, I
CARE ABOUT THE POOP WHICH WAS ALL OVER MY
COUNTER. SOME OF IT HAD EVEN GOT INSIDE MY
SECOND-BEST TEAPOT!
IT'S GREEN POOP, SHE SAYS, AN' IT STINKS TO
HIGH HEAVEN!
    THIS VILLAGE IS IN COMPLETE UPROAR OVER
THAT DAMN BIRD. I'VE NEVER SEEN OWT LIKE IT
IN ALL MY NINETY-FOUR YEARS. IF YOU DON'T
TAKE A PAIR OF SHEARS TO ITS WINGS THEN I'LL
SURE AS DAMMIT DO IT M'SELF.
I'M AT THE END OF MY TETHER, OR
THEREABOUTS.
DON'T SAY AS I DIDN'T WARN YOU, LADIES!

YOURS SINCERELY,
KENNETH CRANSHAW (SR)

Find enclosed: letter 7 by Edo Wa Makuna (of Bleachers) in some weird Franco-African lingo (completely incomprehensible) followed by the translation I commissioned (7a), in some kind of deranged, haut-bourgeois English (equally incomprehensible).

The translation costs amounted to the princely sum of £897. Given that the translation is almost twice the length of the original, I am at least confident that we got our money's worth,

Loz

[letter 7]

Bleachers
The High Street
Burley Cross
Wharfedale

20/12/06

Oh my dear Brother!

Every year the same, old charade, eh? Every year our mother's first-born puts pen to paper – his hand growing shakier, his French getting clumsier – in the pathetic hope that his brother – the second-born – will receive his letter and hungrily devour it with his crazy, shit-coloured eyes and be born to him again.

We both know the truth, eh, Bro'? We both know the truth, too well. But every year ...

Where are you, my brother? I see you, as of old, sitting on the thick stump of that rotted acacia outside the Catholic Orphanage in Leopoldville! Your sunken cheeks! Your quick, angry laugh like the yap of a hyena! Your long legs sticking out like twigs from a pair of tattered shorts. Those brown knees pinkened with scars! Those brown arms chalked a ghostly white with streaks of sweat.

How loud you were! How you stank! A maniac! A fiend! Stolen mango pulp festooning the gaps between your gnashing teeth! You always were the greatest thief! A terrible liar! A vagabond!

How mad you made me – eh?! Blowing on that whistle that you kept hung on a piece of string around your neck. What became of that whistle, dear Brother? What became of you? Why did they take you from me? So suddenly? Where did you go to? Where did they carry you?

101

Ah, no – no. Too painful!
Let me just fill my glass and toast you, Brother-mine.
Let me fill ...
Your health, Brother! Long life, Brother! God save
you!

Eh? What's that you say? My hearing's not ...
Eh?!
How am I, you ask? Me? Edo? How's Edo? Edo's
fine! Edo's always fine, Bro'. I told you my story last
year, did I not? The year before ... Remember?

Nothing changes, see? Nothing ever changes here.
The sky is still grey. The grass is still green. My wife
is still gone. My heart is still sore (but not for her.
Ha! Don't make me laugh! You know me better than
that, dear Blood!).

I must confess that it pains me sometimes when I
think of the old times ... Does your heart ever pain
you? My memory is still bad. I try not to think about
things from the past. I try not to ...

Although sometimes I think about my journey to
The Gambia. Sometimes I think about my escape from
The Helmsman (the tight ship he steered! A ship now
sunk!), and all the wicked things he made me do.
Sometimes I think about those stinking beaches at
Banjul.

Oh ho! Good times, Bro'! Good times! Me, in my
tiny swimming trunks and my scuffed old panama hat.
With my lean, muscled body and my ready smile. Quite
the catch, I was!

And at night? Out on the town! In my pink, wide-
collared shirt, my flared brown pants ... I was
irresistible! They called me 'The Congolese'. Women
would ask for me by name! And why not?! I was all
the talk in the European hotels.

How happy I was back then! If only I had known it! I should have stayed. I should have taken a stake in that beach-side bar. I should have swallowed my pride and smoked fish for a livelihood - sold it on the market.

There was a special girl who worked there, Bro'. She covered her head with a polka-dot cloth. A modest girl. I broke her heart. But that was my profession, Brother dear, or, at least, that was one of them. There were others ...

These habits are hard to break, eh? Remember - always remember, Bro'; scratch it deep into the bark of your heart - one brief show of weakness and all is lost! No room for tenderness! No room for compassion! Pain is quicker, eh?! Easier to control. Start off small - a mouthful of ice, a slight adjustment to the balance of a chair (an inch off the front legs, Bro', that's all, nothing more!) - then gradually, over time, augment, expand, increase ...

Never flinch. Never waver. Be consistent. Be unyielding. Let them know, up front, to expect the worst. It's always kinder that way in the end, eh? Eh?!

Oh, Brother, sweet Brother-mine! Whoever would have guessed it? Whoever could have imagined that Edo - shy Edo, bookish Edo, the boy who always led the procession to mass - should have developed such a cruel and deadly skill as this? It's always the unlikely ones, they say - the cold ones, the quiet ones - who end up embracing a course most vehemently. But me? Me?! Edo? A child of God? I was always the gentle one! I was always the peacemaker!

What happened, Bro'? What happened to poor Edo? Did Edo get taken too, Bro'? Did Edo become you, Bro'?

No. No. No ...

In the end, it was only fate that drew me. And
insolence. I never took pleasure in hurting others, but
I needed to find out. I needed to know. And there was
a hunger in me, Bro', once you were gone. There was
an appetite that could not be satisfied. There was an
anger and a recklessness and a lethal arrogance.

The Guide saw it in me. He sensed it in me. He
could read people like that. It was my curse - his
genius.

But let's not get caught up in all these details, now.
It is done. It is over. It is long forgotten.

Other news, you say? What?! Stop kicking out your
feet! Why all this fidgeting? Do you tire of me
already?

Well ... okay ... (impatient boy! Impertinent boy!) I
have started carving again (I say 'again', although you
were always the better carver, were you not? Always
fighting! Always whistling! Always spitting! Always
whittling).

Well, now I am the carver, Bro'. It happened quite
suddenly. My dear friend, Tilly - my new Guide, my
sweet, English apothecary - has brought out this
hidden urge in me. There is something about her ... She
is different from the others. She is more transparent.
Cleaner. Like fresh rainwater caught in an old enamel
cup. She is wilder. She resembles the Blue Gum: skin
white like the trunk, eyes blue-grey like the leaves.

We work together, in silence. It is a great relief to
me. There is no need to talk.

She has a sister. The sister is fierce - powerful.
Strong as an ox. There was an old pastor, lately
retired, who the sister admired (a vengeful man, full of
bile, like Brother Francis - remember Brother Francis,

who beat us so? After you were taken and I joined the Force Publique I had him dispatched. The act of a moment. Strange, really, to think about it now ...).

Well, this pastor, a man called Horwood, came to the kitchen where I was carving last week - a figure on a cross, a nkondi. He asked me if he could look at it. He admired it for a while. It pleased him. I told him that I had yet to finish it - to pierce the chest with nails (because how else might the fetish work otherwise?).

'The chest?! Surely just the hands?' he said, winking. I merely laughed.

He asked if he could have it.

'Take it, Pastor,' I said, 'and pray for me.'

He nodded. He took it away with him. The next thing I know he's hung it up in the church. In the front portal - the fool! - for all the village to gawp at!

The new pastor - Reverend Paul - comes to pay me a visit in my home. He wants to confer with me about the nkondi.

'Would it offend you terribly,' he asks, 'if I took it down?'

'Mortally,' I say, with a ferocious scowl. Then I laugh. He laughs with me, nervously, the way the English do.

(What do I care, Bro'? Eh?)

'It's just that Reverend Horwood hung it up without consulting me,' he says. 'Members of the congregation have been complaining. It's not that they don't like it, as such. But the church is Anglican - there are certain, unspoken rules about decoration ... We tend to prefer the plain cross over the crucifix—'

'Crucifix?' I interrupt him, smiling. 'But it isn't a crucifix, Reverend Paul. It's a nkondi.'

He stares at me, blankly.

'A fetish,' I say. 'It's the figure of a man I tortured, a man I hung on a cross. He comes to me in my dreams and he haunts me, so I made the nkondi to frighten him away, that's all.'

'What happened to this man?' the priest demands. 'Was he killed? Did he die?'

'Oh no,' I shrug, 'he was cleverer than that. He confessed.'

Then I laugh again. After a long moment the pastor laughs with me. There are beads of sweat on his lip – on his brow.

'It's all right.' I grin, and slap him on the shoulder. 'Just a joke!' I say, then I offer him a drink. To my surprise he accepts one. A whisky.

As he sits and drinks it he ponders something for a while and then he says, 'Jesus was just a man, a mortal man, like you and me, hung and tortured on a cross ...'

Then he laughs. And I laugh.

'We all nailed him up there,' he says, 'every one of us.'

His eyes are suddenly full of tears.

'A touch of water?' I ask.

'What?' He blinks.

'The whisky? A touch of water?' I repeat.

'God bless you,' he says, passing me his glass.

Happy Christmas, Brother.

I miss you, my Blood.

May God keep you.

May God love you.

May God forgive you, and all of us.

Edo

[letter 7a]

121 Juniper Street
Pevensey Bay
Pevensey
East Sussex

28th January, 2007

Dear Sergeant Everill,

Further to our earlier telephone call (26/01/07), I have enclosed the commissioned copy, finally complete. I'm sorry that it took me longer than I had originally estimated to turn it around, and I hope you'll forgive the delay. As I said on the phone, I like to think that I provide SOMETHING ABOVE AND BEYOND over and above what might generally be considered 'a standard translation service'.

You are probably aware of the fact that I have translated some crucial items of evidence for the police on several previous occasions (I believe a translation of mine was critical in the arrest and deportation of a group of Congolese pygmies who were planning an environmental protest against the headquarters of a European multinational mining and logging company, in London, 1998. In 2004, my testimony was considered fundamental to the incarceration of a woman – a former sex-slave with the Hutu militia, no less – who was trying – and with some success! – to run an illegal cleaning company in Stoke).

Perhaps you may find it illuminating if I briefly let you in on a few 'tricks of the translator's trade', so to speak (if you *aren't* sold on the idea, then feel free to skip the next couple or so pages, recommencing the letter at 'But enough of my grandstanding …'. I won't mind in the least).

By and large, a good translator often finds that rather than translating a given manuscript 'piecemeal' – or word for word – it's far more important to try and recreate the general

---

107

'ambience' of the piece, to let the piece – a letter, in this case – 'chime within you, like a bell'.

A successful translation doesn't so much depend on the factual details (i.e. the pitch of the bell, the size of its ringer etc.) as on 'the rich beauty of the song itself' (this 'bell/song' image is not my own – alas! – but borrowed from my esteemed varsity linguistics tutor, the legendary Dr Rendl Gull PhD, author of the Translator's 'Bible': *The Vagrant Affirmation: Yes! Mais Oui! Da!*).

Bearing the above in mind, the proficient translator generally seeks – so far as they are able – to mimic the rhythm of the language, its subtle innuendos, its gentle cadences. They hope to recreate a profound and abiding sense of 'mood', of 'atmosphere'.

A translator's most important duty is to hear the person's 'voice', to absorb it and be true to it. We must be compassionate. We must be flexible. Above all, we must be empathetic.

It's undoubtedly an art, Detective, since 'communication' – in its deepest and most abiding sense – is often embedded in the smallest details: those light brush strokes, those 'minor notes' (to extend Dr Gull's bell/song simile). Translation is – to all intents and purposes – a kind of archaeology. Meaning is buried (preserved and entombed) in a person's 'little ticks', their stylistic 'nuances', their quirky mannerisms and idiosyncrasies.

Indeed, one generally finds that a translator's skill lies as much in making explicit what is *not* being said (and why) as what is being said (right there, on the page, in irreducible ink!).

An almost impossible task you may think, Detective (and you wouldn't be far wrong), but I still find myself happy – excited, even – to engage with the challenge of it: to pull on my translator's battle-suit and wrestle with the imponderables, to confront the vagaries of language, head-on, and to try (wherever necessary) to subdue them, to *wrangle* them – as best I can – into a new and more compliant form.

It can be an emotional journey – a *dangerous* journey, at times – full of treacherous by-roads and frustrating cul-de-sacs.

The implications, as I'm sure you can imagine, are often wide-ranging and profound.

The letter you kindly sent me (3/1/07) certainly proved no exception to this rule. I found myself perplexed and confounded – from the very start – by its 'playful' tone, its elusive character, its informality of style and heavy reliance upon 'the vernacular'.

I have naturally endeavoured – so far as is possible – to keep some of these elements in place during my translation, while, at the same time, struggling to dredge a more 'conventional' narrative out of the mire.

As always, there's that niggling disparity a translator always feels between the urge for something to 'make sense' (to the average reader), and one's own deep and abiding drive towards professional veracity (the scrupulous need for accuracy, in other words).

It's a delicate balance, Detective, and quite a hard one to sustain (I can't begin to count the number of times I've fallen prey to the nagging anxiety that something might have been 'missed along the way' – or Lost in Translation, as I believe the saying goes).

It's broadly for the above reasons that I have seen fit to 'interrupt' the letter's narrative at certain points (something I am generally loath to do, although I have done it before) with some pithy interjections of my own to illuminate some of the more obscure and intangible elements in the writing (the emergence of an 'unconscious backstory', for example, and some other things which, to the untrained eye, might seem utterly unremarkable, but which, to the translator, with their greater expertise in language and its Byzantine psychology, offer invaluable 'clues' to the overall meaning/thrust of the piece).

Of course it goes without saying that I am well aware that my role as translator begins – and ends – with the meaning of the printed words on the page (and that's exactly as it should be). It would be nothing short of a travesty, for example, if I allowed an over-weening inquisitiveness on my part to stand in the way of the voice of my subject (the integrity of 'the voice', as I've already stated, is always, *always* paramount).

But enough of my grandstanding! Let's get down to 'the brass tacks' now, shall we? 'Lokele's letter' (as I'm calling it, mentally, given that you have obscured his real name for reasons of confidentiality) is most certainly a linguistic hotchpotch, a puzzle, an intellectual minefield, written in what I like to call a kind of 'corroded French of the old, Colonial style'. Just to make my job especially difficult, there's the odd word of Lingala thrown in for good measure (Lingala became the national tongue of – as was then – Zaire – now the Democratic Republic of Congo – about thirty-odd years ago. It was introduced by President Mobutu, aka Joseph Désiré Mobutu, the Father of the Nation).

As you will read (in my occasional parentheses), I believe him to be an African man in his mid-fifties (I enclose these details in the unlikely circumstance that you have yet to identify/apprehend him). He was orphaned as a child and has a brother (to whom the letter is addressed). He is handsome (by his own admission!) and moderately well-educated (by African standards).

I'm sure it will come as no surprise to you that this complex translation – these few, humble pages which you now hold in your hand – is the result of many, many long days spent poring over mountainous piles of well-thumbed dictionaries, countless hours of intensive research on the internet, a smattering of emails to various obscure parts of the globe, and a desperate, last-minute trip to the Rare Books section of the British Library in London (the cost of travel, and the price of – as it turned out – *two* nights spent at a mid-range hotel, have naturally been included in my bill).

In between there have been interludes of deep soul-searching, numerous bungled attempts, a small period of writer's block, the acquisition of a new kitten, a thirtieth wedding anniversary party to plan and execute (a roaring success, but with the odd inevitable hiccup – the cake turned up a total of four weeks early!), countless re-thinks, revisions, re-writings etc.

A good translator rarely feels as though their work is 'complete' (I'd be 'tweaking' things forever given half a chance!), but now that my job here is, to all intents and purposes, 'done', I must confess that I feel a certain amount of pride in what I've achieved.

Of course along with the natural 'high' one experiences on completing any large and demanding project, there comes the unavoidable 'low', i.e. the overwhelming sense of dislocation, the crushing numbness, the physical and mental exhaustion, that is part and parcel of 'inhabiting' a character like Lokele's mind for so long – and intense – a duration (you may laugh at this, Detective, but in some small way I almost feel as if I had become temporarily 'possessed' by Lokele's spirit for a while, although I'm not suggesting that anything remotely 'paranormal' took place, nothing tangible, anyway. Or even, God forbid, that Lokele might have passed from his current, earthly incarnation to – as they say – 'a better place').

It's a difficult process to describe (still more difficult to understand, I don't doubt!), but the exercise of translating this letter feels loosely comparable to the act of thrashing my way into the heart of a tropical jungle and somehow – quite miraculously – conniving to fashion a small garden (fourteen feet by fourteen feet, approximately) in its dense and heaving midst.

I have brought order where once there was chaos. I have dug borders, grown a lawn – even plumbed in a small fountain (atop of which a charming stone cherub dribbles water from an upturned bowl). I have planted lavender and begonias where before there was only an inhospitable tangle of weed, thorns and wild grasses.

Welcome to my garden, Detective. Take your time, look around … relax. I do hope you enjoy your visit here …

Sincerely Yours,
Rosannah Strum-Tadcastle

*******,
*** **** ****,
****** ****,
*******.

20/12/06

Dearest *******,

[*I'm guessing this deleted word is 'brother' because it is seven letters long and the suspect 'Lokele' addresses his brother throughout the unfolding text – he also refers to him as the 'second-born', i.e. a younger brother, in other words.*]

My, how time flies! It's Christmas, once again, and I thought I should drop you a quick line (is it me, or doesn't it seem to come around that little bit sooner every year?!).
Do find it in your heart to forgive me my awful French …

[*From this we can deduce that 'Lokele' has been away from his place of birth for many years.*]

… and my terrible handwriting, there's a good chap.

[*Possibly 'Lokele' has 'the shakes' because he is a drug addict, or else an alcoholic – he refers to 'toasting' his brother on several occasions. Perhaps he is under some kind of unendurable pressure connected to the crime he is being investigated for – gold, diamond or uranium smuggling naturally spring to mind, since these are all activities that are virtually endemic in the place of his birth – the Democratic Republic of Congo.*
Other possibilities are that he has sustained a hand injury through carving wood – a so-called 'hobby' of his – or even as a result of some other, rather more 'nefarious' activities – who am I to judge?! Finally, of course, 'Lokele' might spend much of his time working – as we all do, nowadays – on a keyboard, so his handwriting skills may have deteriorated as a consequence.]

I was only thinking about you the other day – pondering those many, colourful, childhood experiences we shared together in Leopoldville at the Catholic Orphanage …

[*Ah! Leopoldville, now Kinshasa! The name was changed in the late 1960s. This small slip tells us that the writer of the letter – i.e. the suspect – is a man who was probably a boy in the late fifties, early sixties – a detail I made passing reference to in my notes, above.*]

What japes! What high jinks! Hard times but good times, eh? Not all of them a barrel of laughs, by any means, but when we had fun, *what* fun we had! The trees we climbed! The music lessons we enjoyed! The delicious fruit we devoured!

[*If this cunning monster's barrister harps on in court about his 'difficult childhood' to try and get the 'sympathy vote', nip it in the bud, Detective, pronto!*]

I recall how proficient you were as a student of the recorder – but how irritating it could sometimes be to hear you practise the same refrain over and over. I often wonder whether you made a career of it. You were certainly talented enough!

[*My younger daughter is a dab hand at the flute – she recently passed grade 5 – and I'm exceedingly proud of her achievements, but when I hear her tooting away at her scales some mornings the hair on the back of my neck stands on end! I can't help it! It's just instinctive! I sometimes wish she'd taken up the oboe, or something with more of a 'bass' sound.*]

If only we hadn't lost contact! It tears me up inside to think about it, it really does, but I suppose life has a cruel habit of sending us these little challenges, and, at the end of the day, it's not so much about the challenge itself, but how we chose to rise to it, eh?

[*This is so true, Detective – and a keystone philosophy of my own, as it happens.*]

Let us lift a metaphorical glass to our mutual good health, old boy!

[*I say metaphorical, but ….!*]

Well, I suppose it's about time I filled you in on some of what I've been up to over the past few months …

[*Hmmn. Very useful …*]

It's been a dreadfully wet year …

[*True. We can certainly trust the accuracy of 'Lokele's' grasp on the facts. He isn't a raving lunatic, or so far 'gone' on 'junk' that he is incapable of coherent thought. This may be an essential detail to share with the criminal psychologist if an assessment of his mental status is pending. It may also be something a judge might be interested in if sentencing is imminent.*]

We barely had any summer to speak of, and while it was – I must confess – rather maddening (to say the least!), on the upside, the lawns in ****** have never looked better.

[*The lawns … This is a complete shot in the dark, but I'm guessing 'Lokele' dwells in suburban anonymity, somewhere.*]

I'm experiencing a few health problems at the moment, I'm afraid. There's been a certain amount of chest pain, and my memory is certainly not what it once was … I'm unsure what the family history is in this regard. I'd love to find out (an incipient strain of dementia in the blood line, or a major history of heart issues would undoubtedly be of interest). Do you have any comparable health problems yourself?

It can be so difficult for us orphans to track down this kind

114

of information. I find it's one of the major downsides of being an orphan, in fact. But let's not harp on, endlessly, about my piddling health concerns – it's Christmas, after all, a time for joy! I mustn't be too much of a misery-guts – Bah, Humbug and all that!

[*I've opted to 'reconfigure' the structure of the letter at this stage, to bring all of 'Lokele's' health worries into a single paragraph. I think we could say I've 'condensed' them to a degree. He does have quite a tendency to witter on about this stuff.*

I don't imagine the information involved will be of much significance to his case, overall. I have the distinct feeling that he's probably a bit of a hypochondriac. That said, if you're planning a surprise arrest – e.g. smashing down his door in the middle of the night; plucking him, unannounced, from his bed – and he suddenly starts panting and clutching at his chest … Well … consider yourself forewarned!

While 'Lokele' is undoubtedly a bit of an old whinger, I must, nevertheless, commend him for his spirited attempt to try and turn things around towards the end of the last paragraph. Christmas is a time of joy. Absolutely.]

My wife finally died …

[*The word 'Lokele' actually uses is 'gone', – i.e. 'my wife has gone …' – so she could easily have done a runner with his 'stash', I suppose.*]

… I've been pretty broken-up about it, actually, although I won't pretend – least of all to you – that things were 'picture perfect' between us. I'm trying to focus on the positive. Her passing was definitely a 'blessed relief' for all parties by the end.

[*Good attitude. No use crying over spilt milk, as they say.*]

To try and cheer myself up, I headed off to The Gambia for a spot of winter sun …

[*There's a brief phase in the letter here where 'Lokele' starts reminiscing, incomprehensibly, about his 'escape' from the Congo many years ago on an illegal fishing trawler. He had to work his passage and the captain treated him rather shoddily, it would seem. The boat has since sunk, he says, but he's not crying any tears over it.*

This section is completely out of context and gets in the way of the main thrust of the narrative, so I've opted to delete it, although – of course – it's my professional duty to make a quick, passing reference to it.]

… I ended up in Banjul. It's a charming place but the beach isn't all it might be (too close to the big port and all those shipping lines for my tastes).

[*I've heard this complaint about Banjul before. I've also heard – on the BBC's World Service – that homosexuality has lately been outlawed in The Gambia. From this we can deduce that our suspect isn't 'that way inclined'. We are dealing with 'a man's man' in other words.*]

I tried to make the best of it, just the same, parading up and down the beach in my natty swimsuit and panama hat (I'm not in bad condition, physically, and like to think I cut quite a dash, even if I say so myself!).

[*He's either unusually well-preserved, ridiculously vain or utterly deluded – and in this respect bears a startling resemblance to every other middle-aged man I've ever met!*]

The night life was lively, although sometimes everything does feel a tad dated – like you're trapped inside some sordid television serial from the 1970s; all big-collared shirts and flared trousers!

[*Welcome to Africa, 'Lokele', welcome to Africa. The suspect is extremely arrogant and judgemental.*]

The staff at the hotel were very friendly. They quickly got to know all of my little habits – my regular evening tipple, the kind of fish I prefer at dinner … They referred to me as 'The Congolese' among themselves …

[*Oh-ho! A code name, perchance?*]

In the end I would've quite liked to stay on a while longer, but my flight was pre-booked so it simply wasn't possible …

[*Pre-booked? Or was there, perhaps, a vicious, square-jawed, gun-toting, Russian thug at the other end of your flight keenly awaiting an illicit 'delivery' of some kind, eh, 'Lokele'?!*]

… I'd barely had the opportunity to check out Banjul's legendary market, which is apparently second to none (full of an amazing array of coloured cloths, leather goods, seafood stalls etc.) …

[*As a matter of interest, there are some fabulous photographic images of Banjul's famous market on the internet. It does look wonderful. 'Lokele' obviously really missed out.*]

Shocking as this may sound, I met a girl on holiday. She was a lovely, little thing, quiet, very modest …

[*Muslim*]

… who I called The Girl with the Dotted Scarf …

[*Another code name! Has to be! This girl was plainly instrumental in 'the drop'. Although it's just conceivably possible that she was actually the girlfriend/wife of the local gangster 'Lokele' was dealing with – in which case: Ouch! You're playing with fire, there, 'Lokele'. Back off, my friend, if you know what's good for you!*]

I beat myself up a little, emotionally, about moving on so quickly (although nothing physical took place) …

[*I should hardly think it would! She's in purdah, you lunatic! And she's married to a hooligan from the Gambian Underworld!*]

It's always been my philosophy, Brother, that a man needs to keep a little something back in matters relating to the heart. Don't throw out the baby with the bath-water, in other words. Stay cool and collected. Show restraint. There's no point charging in with all guns blazing …

[*Not if you're hoping to get out of The Gambia alive, eh, 'Lokele'?!*]

Play things cool, but always try to be a gentleman. Pay special attention to her needs. Make her feel cherished. Ask if she wants extra ice in her drink, pull out her chair for her – perform all these basic acts of chivalry, but still guard your heart carefully. Don't give yourself over entirely – or you're asking to be hurt. Show a measure of restraint, but still try to be gallant …

[*I can't fault 'Lokele' on his dating techniques.*]

Consistency is often the key, I find. Don't make the error of giving away too much up front – or of making too many rash promises which you won't be able to keep. The 'hearts and roses' stuff never lasts that long. What you need to build are strong foundations.

Relationships aren't ever easy, Brother. They take a lot of hard work.

[*Yes. And I should certainly know, thirty years on …*]

I must confess to having been less than 'the perfect spouse', on occasions. It horrifies me when I consider the 'merry dance' I've led the many women in my life. And to think what a good, Catholic boy I once was (always the first to lead the procession into mass)! Well, that certainly didn't stop me from 'putting it about' a fair bit.

How I cringe when I think of how selfish and arrogant I was back then!

You were quite a 'ladies' man' yourself, as I recall. I suppose some of it might have rubbed off on me over the years. And let's not forget my highly developed sexual drive – that's also played its part.

Let's make no bones about it, Brother: I've been a horny devil in my time. But I regret it deeply now, more than you will ever realize …

I suppose what I'm trying to say, in my own, clumsy, roundabout way, is that it's important to know yourself – what you're capable of, emotionally – and to conduct yourself accordingly. Don't make too many rash promises. Don't give your partner false hopes. Be up front about your fallibilities. Communication is the key, and honesty …

[*Thanks, Dr Phil. Can we move on now?*]

Just try and be yourself …

[*Obviously not …*]

Hopefully she'll still manage to love you with all your faults …

[*'Lokele' gets distracted again at this point and starts talking about a bad Tour Guide he had on holiday who led him astray. It's pretty much just gobbledegook. I can't even decipher whether he means 'astray' in a geographical or a moral sense – although my instinct is to plumb with the latter. I don't imagine that this is anything that need concern either the moral or the actual police, Detective. Boys will be boys etc.*]

But enough of me wittering on about my holiday. I must be boring you stiff with it by now!

[*You don't say!*]

119

Something that might actually pique your interest, however …

[*I wouldn't bet on it!*]

… is that I have started carving again. I say 'again', although you were always the better carver, eh?

[*The texture of the language here precludes me from telling whether he actually means 'carving' as in 'woodwork' or 'carving' as in 'mercilessly butchering an unfortunate adversary – or any other innocent individual he might randomly happen across – with a lethally sharp weapon'. A switchblade instantly springs to mind, or one of those large, African knives sometimes referred to as a 'panga'.*
    'Lokele' the brutal assassin, eh? This is certainly a most disturbing thought.]

I have been greatly influenced in this 'life change' by a new friend, Tilly, an English doctor. She's very wild, very tough, with skin like bark …

[*I think the simile he's really grasping for here – bless him – is 'skin as thick as a rhino's hide', i.e. she's highly insensitive, in other words.*]

… She's certainly 'one of the boys'. We have a great rapport between us. She's very discreet, and can definitely be trusted …

[*Narcotics! Bingo! The penny finally drops! So this woman doctor is his new accomplice – they're dealing counterfeit drugs together – and 'Lokele' is obviously very keen for his degenerate brother to make her acquaintance. This 'Tilly' is part of a criminal gang which includes a woman who is known only as her 'sister'; in African parlance this isn't necessarily a blood relation, 'sister' is generally a colloquial phrase for 'pal' or 'mucker'. The sister happens to be friends with an old gang warlord called 'The Reverend', who 'Lokele' doesn't entirely trust … Possibly he's had*

120

problems with The Reverend before … But I'm getting ahead of myself, here …]

Tilly has a 'sister', a bodyguard of sorts, who is powerful as an ox. She's the 'moll' of a man they like to call 'The Reverend'. This man is a brute, very violent. He puts me in mind of Francis, that thug we knew when we were young upstarts in Kinshasa who used to beat us, mercilessly, at the drop of a hat.

After you did a runner and I joined the Congolese Police Force …

[*A corrupt insider! It gets worse!*]

… I helped to bring about his undoing …

[*I say 'undoing' but the word he uses is 'dispatch' – as in 'I dispatched him'. The language is very 'sticky' though, very 'opaque', and – in all good conscience – I don't feel entirely comfortable in pushing the point any further than I already have.*]

A few weeks ago, while I was carving in the kitchen …

[*Terrifying thought! Such macabre images spring to mind! Although I think he is actually just doing some woodwork on this occasion, Detective.*]

… 'Reverend' Horwood paid me a visit …

[*You'll already be very familiar with this notorious individual I should imagine.*]

… and expressed a great interest in my work …

[*Turf war! Not a shadow of a doubt. Horwood plainly already has a counterfeit narcotics ring operating in the area …*

I do think it only fair to warn you that from this point onwards the narrative becomes very 'psychedelic'. The language is far more

*esoteric and abstruse, with a slight whiff of 'the occult' about it. I
don't think this is just an accident, either. It's 'Lokele' truly 'coming
into himself'. All marks of civilization gradually drop away as he
begins 'talking jive' or 'the language of the "hood"'.*]

I happened to be putting the finishing touches to a figure on
a cross, a 'nkondi' …

[*I have left the word 'nkondi' untranslated because there is no real
English equivalent for it. A 'nkondi' is a kind of traditional
Congolese wooden sculpture which is held to have magical and
spiritual powers. They are usually about three feet high and can be
found planted in clearings in the Congolese jungle, usually clustered
into small groups.*

*There is absolutely no doubt in my mind at this point that
'Lokele' is carving these objects, hollowing them out, and then filling
the insides with illegal, narcotic substances – fashioning a kind of
African 'Trojan Drug Horse', in other words.*]

… Horwood was very impressed by the standard of my work.
He had a good look at it, smiled at me, somewhat intimidatingly,
then gestured towards it and asked if he could take it away with
him …

[*A line delivered at gunpoint, I'll be bound – although this fact isn't
made explicit.*]

There was little I could really do but oblige him. I warned him
that the sculpture wasn't finished yet. I even went so far as to
suggest that it had latent, supernatural powers. Horwood wasn't
buying any of it, though …

[*'Lokele' says some stuff about banging nails into the chest of the
figure he's carved. In this manner the 'nkondi' traditionally becomes
a kind of 'fetish' or voodoo doll. Try not to be too alarmed by this
idea, Detective. There's nothing remotely controversial about it.
Most Congolese sculpture is held to have such properties.*]

… he just grabbed the sculpture and carried it off to his 'church' where he displayed it in full public view.

['Church' or 'gang hideout', i.e. the natural extension of the 'Reverend' metaphor.]

I can't pretend I wasn't fairly ticked-off by this development …

[Horwood made 'Lokele' look 'a pussy', in other words – out on the streets, where these things really count. 'Lokele' is now in danger of losing the respect of the wider criminal fraternity. Respect – as you will know – is everything to people of this ilk.]

Luckily, a short while after, I was visited at home by a man called 'Paul' …

[An Englishman, whose name – strangely enough – also has the 'Reverend' precursor. I'm presuming he's a member of Horwood's gang, but has recently usurped him as leader.]

The meeting was rather tense. Paul said that Horwood had taken the 'nkondi' independently, without his permission (or that of his 'congregation'). It seems they were all highly irritated by his actions. He asked if I would mind if he dealt with Horwood accordingly …

[The exact phrase this 'Paul' uses – I hate to nit-pick, but it's important – was more along the lines of 'he asked if I would mind if he took Horwood down'. 'Lokele's very careful not to give too much away, here, though. This whole segment is drenched with distracting religious imagery and other types of hocus-pocus.]

I just laughed him off and confessed that I didn't really care …

['Attaboy! Always be sure to cover your back, eh?!]

Paul became very jumpy at this point. He broke out into a sweat. I offered him a drink and he accepted a whisky …

[*A grave error. Alcohol will only dehydrate him still further.*]

We chatted away aimlessly for a while about nothing in particular – 'religion' and the nature of mortal sin etc …

[*This Paul is obviously having something of a crisis of confidence – i.e. talks the talk but can he walk the walk? In my honest opinion, I don't think he's man enough to take the old Warhorse, Horwood, down. 'Lokele' is right to hedge his bets on this issue.*]

… then Paul made his excuses and left.

Anyway, Brother, I do hope you have a Happy Christmas this year, and that it brings you everything you could possibly wish for – and more.

Do spare me a brief thought as you enjoy your festivities …

[*Poignant. The life of an outlaw is certainly a lonely one.*]

God bless you,

[*And you, my dear friend, 'Lokele'. Enjoy these final, few hours of liberty, while you still may … See you in court! R.S-T.*]

★★★★★★

[letter 8]

A dispatch from the desk of:

Baxter Thorndyke, Cllr
The Old Hall
Burley Cross

21/12/2006

Trevor Ruddle, Ed
The Letters Page
Wharfedale Gazette

Trevor,

See if you can fit this into your letters page next week, will you? Somewhere prominent – first letter would obviously be ideal (there *is* a Christmas theme to it, after all).

As I'm sure you can imagine, I'm literally flat-out right now, bogged down with the usual, heinous combination of personal, charitable *and* professional obligations (not least hosting the BCRSC annual Christmas Fund-Raiser on Monday – we're roasting a whole suckling pig this year; should definitely be worth sending down a photographer – and putting the finishing touches to a groundbreaking paper I'm due to deliver to The Royal Society of Anaesthetists in Birmingham – early Feb. – on 'The Physiology of Hypothermia'), so the prospect of throwing away yet another precious hour of my valuable time in responding to the ludicrous opinions of that idiotic blow-hard Tunnicliffe (*WG*,19/12/06) was not one I especially relished, I can assure you.
Yet respond I *must*.

I know you're just a local rag – and he's an OBE – but why do you persist in publishing his inane drivel every week? The man's a clown – a scourge (or 'a pea in the shoe' as I believe

I heard Julian Moxham call him in open session at council on Friday).

How old is he, anyway? Eighty-seven? Eighty-nine? Isn't it about bloody time he retired from public life? Put his feet up? Gave the good people of Wharfedale a much needed break from his endless, sullen preachifying?

I saw him staggering around in Ilkley Tesco's car park on Wednesday afternoon clutching an organic cauliflower in one hand and a bottle of Ruddles Ale in the other. Seemed lost. Or half-cut (can't quite decide which). Is he still following that bizarre raw-food diet he keeps banging on about? If so, can alcohol really count as 'raw'? (Surely there's a measure of heat involved in the brewing process?)

The man's hardly an advert for it (raw food *or* brewing). He's just a withered husk. He looks like the hollowed remains – the vile, yellowed carapace – of something an insect has recently hatched out of (a small, white maggot springs to mind).

My wife, Tammy, blanched when she saw him (she was with me in the car at the time). 'I almost feel sorry for him,' she gasped. 'He looks revolting! So grimy! So *thin*! Like a mouldy old piece of horseradish!' (And Tamm – as you know – doesn't have a bad word to say about anybody, due to her deeply held religious beliefs.)

I've a strong suspicion he's entering his second childhood (he displays all the radicalism of youth and yet none of the sense – or temperance – of maturity!).

What on earth was the Queen *thinking* giving an honour of such magnitude to a wretch of his stamp? So what if he 'helped to design the wind turbine'(as I read in Who's Who Online, recently)? 'Helped' to design it?! How wonderfully non-specific! (What did he do, exactly? Man the tea trolley? Refill the office photocopier at a critical juncture?!)

'Helped to design the wind turbine?!' Well, it's hardly a cure for cancer, is it?!

The sooner that rancorous, bile-ridden old canary topples off his artfully recycled perch the better, as far as I'm concerned. I'm as green as the next man (greener!) but his holier-than-thou attitude gives environmental causes a bad name.

If you ask me, he's never been quite the same since he was forced to quit BC. Selling Rombald House and moving into sheltered accommodation in Ilkley was obviously a severe blow to his fragile self-esteem (he was always at the heart of what I liked to call 'The Old Guard' in BC – thought he ruled the roost when I first arrived there!).

People generally like to pass him off as 'eccentric' (because of the title, I suppose), but I was never under any illusions about the real nature of the man. He was always a nutter. Very, *very* controlling (the way these 'idealists' – these 'men of principle' – so often are).

And – to be fair – he's never much liked the cut of *my* jib, either (probably sensed, from the word go, that I wasn't especially eager to buy into his whole 'left-leaning, aristocratic schtick').

I remember him starting the most ridiculous quarrel with Tamm and I pretty much as soon as we first stepped foot in the village (July, 1998). I'd begun legal proceedings to try and alter the public right of way which – at that time – ran alongside The Old Hall (tourists were using it as a temporary latrine – and worse. It was horrendous. I'd wander out into the garden and find my hydrangea festooned with used condoms – male *and* female).

The way Tunnicliffe overreacted to the situation you'd think I'd actually suggested redirecting it through his own living room! So what if the new route 'trimmed' a few feet off the back end of his garden? After I'd inspected the original deeds it became glaringly obvious that he'd 'accidentally' extended the boundary of his property on to the adjacent moorland by a distance of some five and a half metres!

I wouldn't even mind, but his back garden was already

enormous *and* completely overgrown. He was forever banging on about 'promoting biodiversity', and was an early proponent of that whole 'grow your own wild-flower meadow' racket (I always saw this silly fad for what it really was, i.e. a feeble excuse for not bothering to maintain your lawn. 'Gardening for Squatters' is Tamm's hilarious take on it!). He was always a lazy old sod. His late wife, Melody, was apparently the green-fingered one.

Of course Tunnicliffe didn't have a leg to stand on, but he still fought the decision, tooth and nail. He cost me a small fortune in solicitor's fees.

Then, no sooner had the issue been resolved than he started doing everything humanly possible to put the brakes on Tamm and I cutting down this half-dead yew in our front garden (which completely blocked the view from our dining room window).

Started up quite a little campaign (even a petition)! What a ridiculous carry-on! The way they harped on about it you'd think the damn thing (which had been self-seeded from a tree in a neighbouring garden) had been planted by Great Queen Bess herself, then celebrated in a sonnet by William Shakespeare! It was an absolute *farce*.

The really ludicrous part of it was that I'd always been universally derided as a bit of a closet 'tree-hugger'. I was BC tree warden for three years (started the BC Befriend a Tree movement at the local primary school). At my strict behest, Tamm only ever buys household paper products from 'managed sources'. I've been a member of the Woodland Trust since 1986, for heaven's sake!

Of course it can't have been a coincidence that around about that time I was chairing a committee on the council (aimed at making the local moorland more 'walker-friendly') when a committee member (I forget who, off-hand) idly raised the idea of changing the name of Tunnicliffe Bridge into something slightly more 'directional'.

When LT found out about it (heaven only knows how) he absolutely flipped! I've never seen anything like it! He was apoplectic! I mean it's not as if it's even a proper bridge – just a couple of large stepping stones crossing a small beck! And given that the main, practical function of that 'bridge' was to take walkers (principally tourists – *not* local people, by and large) to the Cow and Calf stones, it only made common sense for the bridge to take on the name of the famous site it led to (and was *directly adjacent to*!).

I was still relatively new in Burley Cross at the time. Little did I realize that my perfectly innocent involvement with this entirely reasonable scheme would bring me up against an ego of such extraordinary magnitude! Well, I certainly found out soon enough! And I'm *still* finding out nine years on!

But enough of LT and his ridiculous hobby-horses …

Thinking forward into the New Year, there are several, fascinating 'live' issues I'm currently grappling with which I don't doubt will be of interest to your paper. The first relates to our ongoing problems with the public toilets at Burley Cross. Tom Augustine (a founder member of the BCPTW, whose wife volunteers at the Gawkley Wildlife Refuge) has lately come up with an 'animal safety' angle on the story which I think may well warrant a small article (especially in the approach to the warmer summer months). I can pass on his number to you if you don't already have it (send me an email. I should be back online within the next day or two).

It has also come to our attention (at the BCRSC) that Wincey Hawkes has begun accepting coach parties at The Old Oak again. She insists on doing this full in the knowledge that there is insufficient room for the coaches to turn in the designated space. The resulting damage to grass verges is appalling (I have seven or eight excellent photographs – all of publishable quality – which I can send to you via email early next week, if you're interested).

The verges are obviously only the tip of the iceberg. As

always, my main beef with Mrs Hawkes is the serious threat her irresponsible actions present to pedestrian and road-user safety alike (there's actually more to this story, which I'll be more than happy to go into at greater length, off the record).

Thirdly (and finally), I am working on something pretty startling at the moment relating to manhole cover theft in the UK by the Chinese. This is something that I think may well blow up in the Wharfedale area in a very big way in the New Year – in fact, I'll all but stake my reputation on it. I'm presently in close communication with the local constabulary and Liam Holroyd MP on the matter. If you can manage to keep the issue under your hat for a while I'll definitely have something 'solid' for you within the next three or four weeks …

I thoroughly enjoyed your piece in Friday's paper about the current problems with the big cairn on Farnhill Moor. You opted to take a 'lighter slant' on the story. I can fully understand why you felt the need to (the week before Christmas etc.), but I do think there are some pressing, underlying angles to this scenario – both criminal *and* environmental – which I may want to take up with you at a future date (didn't have the opportunity to write a letter on this occasion, although I may yet, if I can somehow find the time next week … In fact, on further consideration, I think I probably shall).

And while we're on the subject: 'POC-"AT*CHOO!*"'??! So let me get this straight: you elect to give a front-page, banner headline to the 'scoop' about a man who pulled a seven-pound carp out of the Kidwick Reservoir (where fishing is *illegal*, incidentally) because it coughs up a small, plastic Pokémon toy ('At-choo!' for your information, is the sound of a sneeze, *not* a cough), yet three whole weeks later, there still isn't so much as a mention of Barbara Simmonds's fascinating talk to the sixth-formers at St Hugh's on the wider implications of the excavation work at Hamblethorpe?

Why?

A Pokémon toy?!

An inappropriate pun?!

Whose brilliant idea was *that*?!

Most disappointing, Trevor, old man.

Baxter

PS Am reduced to using snail mail due to a pesky virus on the Mac.

[letter 9]

A dispatch from the desk of:

Baxter Thorndyke, Cllr
The Old Hall,
Burley Cross

20/12/2006

Sir,

In February (*WG*, 12/02/06) Lance Tunnicliffe OBE kindly provided readers with a step-by-step guide on 'How to be a Green Valentine'.

Included among his many, novel suggestions for Wharfedale's environmentally inclined lovers were 'making your own card', 'not going out for a meal but staying at home and eating by candlelight' (for the record: sober lighting would certainly be de rigueur if *I'm* the designated cook for the night), 'turning off the TV and passing the time by playing a few hands of rummy', 'just talking' (a perfect way to *ruin* a romantic evening I'd have thought, especially if – by a cruel twist of fate – there happens to be a match on), 'going for a moonlit stroll', (a little risky if you live in Moss Side or next to Beachy Head), 'sharing a bath', and even (a course that could well prove fatal for Inuits) 'turning down the heating' and 'snuggling up on the sofa together to keep warm'.

A few weeks later, in March (*WG*, 18/02/06), we found Mr Tunnicliffe OBE focusing his considerable mental apparatus on yet another social and cultural institution: Mother's Day, and the 'questionable tradition' (his words, not mine) of 'saying it with flowers'.

This tradition is 'questionable', it transpires, chiefly because of the 'tragic, even criminal conditions' endured by workers in the third world flower industry. To illustrate this point, Mr Tunnicliffe went on to describe (in almost excruciating detail) the thirty or so flower farms surrounding Lake Naivasha in Kenya (suppliers of the excellent – my word, not his – £2/dozen roses offer at ASDA), where not only were workers earning, on average, a 'pitiable' £45 a week ('and remember, many of these poor wretches will be women, most of them mothers'), but where a combination of 'polluted run-off' from pesticide use and 'water depletion' (from, well, watering) were lowering the levels of the lake 'to a dangerous extent', culminating in (brace yourselves) 'Hippos slowly frying to death in the punishing heat, simply in order that pathetic, Western cheapskates might have the opportunity to buy their beloved mothers a bunch of cheap roses out of season.'

In April (*WG*, 2/04/06) Mr Tunnicliffe OBE weighed in against Easter ('Did Jesus die on the cross and rise again to bring the world the gift of eternal life, or simply to provide greedy, clinically obese Christians and their spoilt progeny with the opportunity to gorge and binge on irresponsibly packaged chocolate eggs?').

It transpires (according to the researches of our fastidious correspondent) that your average chocolate Easter egg consists of approximately 45 per cent packaging.

You might be forgiven for thinking that this is *good* news for the 'gorgers and bingers' among us, i.e. fewer calories (you can't *eat* the packaging), but it isn't. It's actually bad news – *very* bad news – because (as Mr Tunnicliffe is only too keen to inform us) 'the buffoons at Wharfedale Council' haven't seen fit to provide adequate numbers of foil and card recycling bins in the borough.

In November (*WG*, 1/11/06) we find Mr Tunnicliffe OBE working up a sweat over the negative implications of Fireworks Night. These are (as you have doubtless already guessed) manifold, and include 'noise stress', 'the danger of smoke and gunpowder inhalation to asthmatics and people with chest problems', 'fires', 'serious accidents, even death' , 'the threat of copper and other metallic compounds entering the soil, crops

and water table', and last – but by no means least – the 'stress imposed on birds and other animals' (who, according to LT OBE, 'experience Fireworks Night as the start of a terrible – and potentially infinite – war').
I could easily go on, but I'll spare you.

And now, finally (*WG*, 19/12/06), it's Christmas, and – *surprise, surprise*! – Mr Lance Tunnicliffe OBE has decided that this is an opportune moment in which to deliver the taxpayers of Wharfedale (already a rather joyless and brow-beaten bunch after the constant hectoring they've received at LT OBE's behest all year) a withering lecture about the 'wastefulness of the Festive Season', focusing principally on Christmas lighting displays (in our homes, our villages and our town centres) which he calls (variously) 'a glittering tribute to the hollow excesses of Mammon', a 'crass obscenity' and (my personal favourite) 'the perpetually exploding flashbulbs of a consumer culture turned tabloid'. (?!)

Mr Tunnicliffe reserves his special ire for Wharfedale Council (why change the habits of a lifetime, eh?) which he accuses of being 'criminally irresponsible for leaving the festive lights on twenty-four hours a day' and 'failing to transfer to LED Low Impact bulbs'.

Of course nobody could dispute the fact that Mr Lance Tunnicliffe OBE has a valid and interesting contribution to make on public and private ethical debates alike (indeed, many of his more salient points I have raised in council on countless occasions myself).

He speaks an awful lot of common sense. And yet … well, am I *entirely* alone in wondering whether the only reason he seems so determined to put a damper on all our High Days and Holidays is because (perish the thought!) the poor soul has so little to actively celebrate in his own life?

Has Mr Lance Tunnicliffe OBE officially become 2006's greatest party-pooper because he has no party left of his own to poop?

This thought makes me sad – *very* sad. In fact it makes me so sad that I've resolved to take a little bit of time out of my frantic Christmas schedule to raise a small – but deeply environmental – toast to the dear old sourpuss (hopefully *before* he launches his inevitable assault on 'The Horrors of Hogmanay' next week).

I hereby extend a cordial invitation to you – the long-suffering readers of the *Wharfedale Gazette* – to join me … In fact – moderation be damned! There's no time like the present: Merry Christmas, Lance! Cheers! I do hope it's a good one.

Oh …
And turn the lights *on* as you leave, eh? There's a good chap.

Yours Sincerely,

Baxter Thorndyke

[letter 10]

1 Fa'weather Cottages
'Paradise'
Burley Cross

19th Dec

Dear Mr Braithwaite,

I've changed my mind again. I do think I would prefer it with the plain terracotta trim (as you originally suggested), with the main body of the piece in a subtle off-white or soft cream (it was extremely kind of your wife to agree to engrave it for me at <u>no added cost</u>. She's such a talented calligrapher. Her 'Paradise' has received nothing but compliments!).

Around the outside edge I want:

IN MEMORY OF BRADLEY

2004–2006

A MOST LOYAL, WISE AND

BELOVED COMPANION.

If there's any extra room, then just a small, rough sketch of some marigolds (English NOT French, please!).

It's taken me a while to come up with the actual poem. I've been through about three boxes of Kleenex in the process (man-size)!

Bearing in mind what you said (and how busy your dear wife is with her new sign-writing business), I have tried to keep the number of words down to a minimum. Here is what I've finally settled on:

Oh my beautiful, handsome, irreplaceable Bradley,

You were cruelly snatched from us, way too soon,

You were loved so much,

You are missed so desperately ...

No more shall I hear the tinkle of your bell as you fly in
    through the cat-flap, hungry for your 'dinny',

No more shall I feel your nudging head against my calf
    as I stand by the sink up to my elbows in suds ...

There is a space by the fire where once you sat, my
    beautiful, handsome Bradley-cat.

There is a hole in my heart where once you reigned.

I shall not see your like again.

Bradley, Beloved Bradley, hit by a speeding car.

Safe in Heaven now with the cherubim ...

Playing 'chase', away from danger, with dear Portia
    and Fletcher, and Molly, and Dwain and Mia and
    Ricky and Sunny and Tasha. And of course, Porter
    and Gypsy and Marco and Iver. And fearless Pete
    and gentle Cedric.

REST IN PEACE, MY PRECIOUS,
PRECIOUS BEAUTY.
XXXX

What do you think? If it's a fraction long then remove the two lines that start 'No more …' (although I'd hate to see them go, quite frankly; I feel the sombre mood of the piece would be greatly undermined by their absence).

I was thinking the size of a large dessert plate (or one size down, is it? Same as all the others, in any event).

Thank you, in advance, for your patience and your craftsmanship.

You have made a poor, heartbroken widow very, very happy.

Merry Christmas,

Bea 'Bunny' Seymour

PS Cheque enclosed. I have post-dated it to February 19th. I do hope that's all right.

PPS I just noticed my price-list is dated from 1998! It's almost antique! I do hope I'm not diddling myself!

PPPS P&P is included, I presume?

Bless You.
X

[letter 11]

A dispatch from the desk of:

Baxter Thorndyke, Cllr
The Old Hall
Burley Cross

20/12/2006

Dear Mr Liam Holroyd MP,

I have yet to receive any reply from you re my – marked
URGENT – email on the Chinese manhole covers issue
(10/12/06). Following a brief – but extremely edifying –
conversation with one of the people at your Constituency
Office (a volunteer. I think his name was Derek – or possibly
Don – Hoon … a Scot, rough, slightly over-familiar, nervy, bit
of a stammer) I have subsequently decided that the situation is
sufficiently grave for me to 'break the trail' myself (so to speak)
and to forge forward with several independent pieces of
preventative action off my own bat.

The first has been to contact the local constabulary directly,
and to forewarn them of the problem, although – in all candour
– I'm not holding out much hope of a positive response on their
part. PC Laurence Everill (or is he a sergeant now?) – at
Skipton – as good as laughed in my face when I approached
him a short while back on behalf of the BCPTW with
incriminating photographic evidence + car registration details
of all those individuals caught behaving 'suspiciously' at the
public conveniences in the village during the month of August
(his patent indifference to our 'special initiative' has left us with
no option but to display all the information we gleaned on our
new website to try and 'name and shame' those involved into
desisting from their abhorrent – not to say anti-social –
behaviours).

As for PC Roger Topping – at Ilkley – well … where do I

even start?! I mean of what *earthly use* is the man?! He's just a huge, forlorn elk, a tragic bison, lumbering about the place in that improbably gigantic pair of perpetually squeaking loafers of his like some heavily tranquillized mastodon.

Those shoes *can't* be Police Issue, surely? (I mean to hell with 'the element of surprise', eh? You can hear his approach from the neighbouring street! Tammy – my darling wife – says it sounds like he keeps a tribe of gerbils held captive within the insoles which he sacrifices as he walks!).

Have you ever *looked* at his feet? They're ludicrous – absurd!

And the way he constantly sniffles and snuffles into that voluminous red hankie like some chronically hyperactive bloodhound … Unbearable!

As a point of interest, what is this curious malady he always seems to be suffering from? So far as I can tell it changes every week! Gluten intolerance? Hay fever? Something viral? The clap? Heaven only knows (or cares, more to the point)!

Whenever he pays a visit to The Old Hall, I get Tamm to stand guard over the ceramics. He collects Staffordshire figures, I believe, and always heads straight for the big display cabinet in the corner of our 'formal' lounge, where he drools and gibbers, inarticulately, over our prized Majolica, his massive, clumsy white hands flailing through the air like a couple of poisoned doves in the final throes of agony.

And those mournful looks! Those strange, watery grey eyes – like a pair of suffocating squid trapped inside a greasy bowl full of slowly congealing albumen. Repulsive! In truth, I'd sooner have him shot and mounted than do business with the wretch (and I think it would be *kinder*. He's certainly beyond 'fixing').

At least Everill – for all his unbearable arrogance and his smugness – has a measure of vitality about him, even if he never bothers putting it to any kind of positive use (you've probably already heard the rumours about his *actual* behaviour during the 'Great Conflagration' at Tilton Mill? Apparently, according to my source – who's utterly reliable – rather than 'staying behind and risking his life' to save that fabled 'disabled woman' during the fire, he was trapped inside the storeroom with her, very much against his will.

In fact he reportedly tried to use the back of her chair to scramble up on to the ledge of a high window and make his escape, but the buckle on his belt became entangled in her hair …

They took her to hospital afterwards, not for 'smoke inhalation' – *WG*, 12/08/06 – but because she needed stitches in her scalp after he ripped out a sizable chunk of it in his urgent desire to 'do a runner'. Now I hear he's even to be awarded some kind of public *honour* for his troubles! What a joke!).

The second piece of preventative action I've taken (and this was on Don – Dan – Derek's – advice) was to compile a permanent photographic record – an 'unofficial archive', if you like – of all the manhole covers in Burley Cross (over ninety, in total! Ninety-three, to be exact).

I completed this task last week, and must say that the whole process has been a real 'eye-opener' for me. I honestly had no idea how incredibly ornate and beautiful some of these metal covers are! As I believe I said in my last email, it would be difficult to calculate how great a cultural loss the theft of these 'individual pieces' might be to the village. They are a vital and precious part of our increasingly fragile heritage.

To head off on a slight tangent for a moment: I was surfing the web the other night and came across an Art Website (I duplicate their capital letters with a distinct sense of irony) called 'Ruavista' (simply go to 'manhole cover theft' on Wikipedia and then follow the 'signposts') who have a whole collection of manhole covers on show in their 'virtual gallery'. They call them 'symbols of the Industrial Revolution', and say how they 'offer living testimony to the industrial artistry of the second half of the nineteenth century'.

Pretentious waffle, for the most part (of course), but I became so excited by the overall concept that I actually sent them an email enclosing a couple of my own photographs to display online (I have yet to see them up there), and this, in turn, spurred me on to thinking about creating my own website – to showcase the wonderful selection of covers in BC (with a brief history of the town included etc.) – so that people from other parts of Britain, and the world, might get to share in this wonderful, hidden bounty of ours.

I then became slightly paranoid about advertising these precious wares in public, lest I might inadvertently encourage some thuggish vandal from Shanghai or Beijing to fly over and swipe them! (It's a delicate balance, I suppose, between one's natural pride and showing the necessary restraint such circumstances demand.)

For the record, I've even considered approaching Taschen – who I know will publish any old rubbish – with the outline for a book on the subject (all proceeds to the BCPC. If only I could actually find the time to throw together a quick proposal for them …).

My third initiative has been to reach out some tentative 'feelers' to the local press. I've contacted Trevor Ruddle at the *WG* (on the downside, he's a blathering idiot – as I'm sure you're only too well aware. On the up, he's like an eager little puppy – pathetically easy to enthuse, chastise and direct).

I've said nothing concrete to him on the subject (as yet), but have endeavoured to tantalize him with a little taster. I also took the liberty of mentioning your name in relation to the issue (I hope you won't object).

I don't think there's any question that publicity is the key, here, but we'll obviously need to be extremely careful about both our approach *and* our timing. We can't risk generating an atmosphere of fear or panic – especially among the elderly and more vulnerable segments of the community.

Another factor worth bearing in mind is the serious risk – in the current, fraught political climate – of engendering 'emotional burn-out' among members of the public, who, in a place so full of precious heritage as Wharfedale, can sometimes tend to feel somewhat overwhelmed by the weight of responsibility its general upkeep entails.

On this basis, I think it's probably for the best if we just sit quietly on the issue over Christmas and then reconvene in the New Year – revitalized and refreshed, with any luck! – to forge a more coherent and detailed plan of action together.

I look forward to hearing from you shortly.

Wishing you all the best of the season, in the meantime.
Yours Sincerely,

Baxter Thorndyke

PS While I have your ear – and bearing in mind your extensive background in Town Planning – I wonder whether I might quickly seek some advice from you about the nefarious activities of one of your constituents, a woman by the name of Beatrix (née 'Bunny') Seymour?

She lives at 1 Fa'weather Cottages, on the outskirts of BC (to the due south of the village, if you're having trouble remembering it).

These cottages, you may well recall, were the main group of properties in BC to be affected by the building of the bypass seven years ago. There are three of them, in total, (although – for the record – I've always been a little sceptical about whether they're even entirely within the BC 'catchment area'. This is, I must confess, as much an emotional boundary as a geographical one on my part, since they're situated so far down the moor and aren't remotely 'in keeping' with the architectural atmosphere of the rest of the village).

It recently came to my attention, however (during the course of a small survey I was conducting on behalf of the BCPC), that Bea Seymour has actually undertaken some fairly major renovations to her property over the past eighteen months or so. The chief one of these was the demolition of an old outside toilet and brick wall to the rear of the cottage to make room for the addition of a modest conservatory on the back of the property (a move that I was unable to oppose in council because, by a cruel twist of fate, I was on an extended vacation to Tibet with my wife, Tammy, when permission was requested – and subsequently granted – for it).

Once the conservatory had been built, the former boundary of the brick wall was not then replaced – or even maintained (as you might imagine it should be) – but the entire area was subsequently cleared (denuded of bushes, borders etc.) and physically 'opened up'.

By dint of this cunning manoeuvre, Ms Seymour has, effectively, *turned the property around*, i.e. the cottage formerly fronted straight on to the bypass, but she has now planted the – as then was – poky front garden with a thick line of Leylandii (which are already at head height), and seems intent – so far as one can tell – on using the lower reaches of Piper's Ghyll Road as the *main source of access* to her home!

This access isn't direct – as yet. Ms Seymour is far too canny for that! She insists that she is now using the tiny back alley that runs to the rear of the three cottages – formerly used only by the refuse disposal services – as her chief means of ingress and egress. This small, dank lane she has named 'Paradise' (and has even hung up a sign to this effect!).

I was perfectly astonished when I ventured down there the other week by what an amazing coup our humble Ms Seymour had pulled off (I honestly didn't think she had it in her)! I promptly consulted a local estate agent (Rick Cullen, from Cullen and Speck) who told me that by suddenly, *effectively*, giving her home direct access to the lower reaches of Piper's Ghyll Road (one of the most prestigious addresses in BC) she has added a sum of at least £30,000 to the value of her property!

It now seems as though there are moves afoot for the residents of the other two cottages to follow her lead (they'd be foolish *not* to, I suppose!).

I must confess that I find the 'Paradise' sign especially infuriating. Not only is the name *utterly inappropriate* to the location of the property (and the property itself), but it's completely out of sync with other street names in BC. It simply isn't kosher (there's a silly, hippyish, deviant, almost heretical flavour to it). Worse still, it's a long-held tradition in BC – as you will doubtless already know – that none of the roads (least of all imaginary ones!) have signs on them. That simply isn't the way we do things here.

I have every reason to believe that Ms Seymour was compensated financially when the bypass was built, so find it doubly irritating that she has now connived to add *extra value* to the price of her ramshackle little abode by dint of completely disregarding local planning regulations etc.

I currently have two council lawyers working on the case. My main objective is to try and find out whether there might be any way to oblige her to return some of the original compensation she was paid, or possibly to force her – at the very least – to take down her silly sign and rebuild the old wall again (back at its original height of seven foot).

Of course you will know (possibly better than anybody) that if one person is seen to be 'cocking a snook' at planning regulations in a Conservation Area, then a very dangerous precedent is set, and all manner of breaches are liable to follow.

I mean whatever next, eh? A massage parlour on the High Street? Saxonby Manor turned into a temporary internment centre for asylum-seekers? The village church mysteriously transformed, overnight, into a functioning mosque?!
Is *nothing* to be held sacred any more?

I'm sure there must be something that we can do to set right this awful wrong …

Yours, etc.

Baxter

PPS Am reduced to using snail mail due to a pesky virus on the Mac.

[letter 12]

A dispatch from the desk of:

Baxter Thorndyke, Cllr
The Old Hall
Burley Cross

20/12/2006

For attn Sergeant Laurence Everill (Skipton) & PC Roger
Topping (Ilkley)

Re Manhole cover theft

Gentlemen,

I am writing to you today in my capacity as an elected
borough councillor *and* as a concerned – a *very* concerned –
member of the Great British Public, about the burgeoning
problem of manhole cover theft in the United Kingdom.

It is with a combination of astonishment and dismay that I
am obliged to inform you that these apparently insignificant –
you might think dreary, even inconsequential – items (a
constituent part of every road and high street in the civilized
world) have lately become the subject – the focus – of an
organized, international crime wave, sponsored by no less an
adversary than the Chinese.

If you are, as yet, unfamiliar with this startling phenomenon,
do not be dismayed. I am more than happy to fill you in on
everything you need to know …

The earliest, recorded cases of this heinous activity were
registered approximately three or four years ago in the Far
East. The thieves initiated this practice in China itself, then
gradually began extending their tentacles into India (I presume
certain cities and provinces in the Communist Republic started

---

146

predating, like parasites, upon each other, before turning their greedy, pitiless eyes on to greater riches lying slightly further afield).

You may (or may not) be aware that this particular segment of the globe has been industrializing – at an extraordinary rate – over recent years, which (by necessity) has generated a powerful need for basic raw materials (coal, oil, steel). This need is now so immense, so boundless, that certain corrupt individuals within the Chinese establishment are willing to go to any lengths – I repeat: *any* lengths – to acquire the precious resources they so desperately hanker after.

An insignificant hunk of steel – the humble, utterly commonplace and dependable British manhole cover – has now become an essential nutrient in the ravening appetite – and overweening political ambitions – of the Communist Republic.

As I said previously, the earliest known cases of manhole cover theft took place within 'the belly of the beast' itself. In 2004 at least eight deaths were reported as a consequence of such thefts in India and China.

Deaths?

Hang on a second …

You are probably drawing back, startled, as your eyes re-run over those two, stark words.

Eight *deaths*?!

'But … but *how* …?' you stutter.

I'll tell you how:

The manhole cover might appear to be a piddling, paltry, even meritless object, in principle, but *think* about it, Constables: when one is stolen, what's left behind is a whopping great hole for any innocent member of the public to tumble into (or drive over – generating horrendous damage to the wheels and bodywork of their vehicle – if the cover has been removed from the road itself).

This is a serious business. Still more serious when you consider how much these covers cost to replace. Steel yourselves, gentlemen (no pun intended): each individual cover costs *in excess* of £100.

Let me repeat that: in excess of *£100.*
And we aren't talking insignificant numbers here, either. This is a massive, professional operation, a major enterprise. In 2004, over 10,000 manhole covers were stolen from the Indian city of Calcutta in a period of only two months. Do the maths. That's around about 208 covers *per night.*

Baffled and infuriated by these thefts, the Indian authorities in that benighted slum replaced the steel covers with concrete ones, but were then appalled when these, too, were stolen – for the iron rods *within* the concrete!

Of course (I can hear you reasoning – and quite rightly) it is *illegal* for scrap dealers within the boundaries of the EU to purchase MHCs (Manhole covers).
Oh yes, it's illegal all right, but – trust me – it sure as hell still happens. And anyway, the Chinese are just as likely to ship the stolen covers back to China on a cargo vessel and melt them down secretly there.

An Important Question:
Why do I consider Wharfedale to be under special threat?

Here's the answer:
Most MHC theft started off in London (in Newham, east London, over 200 grates and covers were stolen during 2004 – 93 of these *in just one week*).

Since this time, MHCs have been taken, in considerable quantities, from places as far afield as Gloucester, Powys, Aberdeen and Fife (a batch of approximately 13 were stolen in Alness, but given that this was during a phase of snowy weather, the general consensus is that these may have been lifted by irresponsible locals to be employed as sledges).

The point I'm trying to make here is that Bradford, Leeds, and the outlying areas currently represent an immaculate – a pristine – hunting ground for these plucky, ruthless and tenacious Chinese thieves. Look at the map (enclosed): we lie *right in the middle* of their former targets. We are ripe for the plucking – a virgin patch!

So what the hell are we meant to do about all this?
I'll tell you what: keep our noses to the ground and our eyes peeled. That, and spread the word: get the general public on board. Get them involved. Warn them, prime them, prepare them for what lies ahead.

Let's *educate*, Constables, *together*. A campaign in schools and colleges (I'm more than happy to play my part, here), supported by the distribution of some well-designed posters and leaflets, followed by a media blitz, featuring some on-the-spot reports in local radio and television news programmes, articles and opinion pieccs in the local paper …

What people don't know – and what you yourselves may not yet realize – is that MHCs 'offer living testimony to the industrial artistry of the second half of the nineteenth century' (cf. Wikipedia under Manhole Cover Theft). These objects can be beautiful (see enclosed photographs – copyright BT), they aren't just 'hunks of metal' but precious little pieces of our social history, and, as such, are not just priceless, but utterly irreplaceable.

Those thieving Reds need to be stopped in their tracks!

One final question (and it's a tough one):
Do you two gentlemen have the *balls* for the job?
Well?

BT

PS Sergeant Everill. Further to our conversation in early Sept. re the BCPTW's 'August Initiative'. You didn't seem to take our endeavours terribly seriously when I initially approached you, but it may be of some interest to you to discover that our website is soon about to feature photographs of (and car

registration details belonging to) a notable member of the
Bingley Constabulary. Off duty, naturally …
Fancy a little chin-wag about it?

   You know where I am.

Bax

PPS Oh yes … And before you go to the unnecessary effort of
wheeling out that whole, rather tired 'working undercover'
dodge, there was nothing *remotely* 'undercover' about the kind
of activities that scoundrel was engaged in. Trust me.

B

[letter 13]

Highbank
2 Shortcroft Rd
Burley Cross

21 December, 2006

Dear Nadia,

This simply has to stop! I just can't bear it any more! I've had enough! And when I say stop, I mean stop – no more phone calls, no more letters, no more tantrums, no more tears, no more threats …

If you *do* come over on the ferry and turn up at the house, unannounced, then I shall hurt myself. I shall slash myself with a razor. I *mean* it, Nadia. I'm desperate. I have nothing left to lose. I carry it with me at all times, tucked into my bra, just in case. It's there right now – right this minute, pressing against my skin – wrapped up in a little piece of tissue paper.

Every time I hear a knock at the door I reach for it. Every time I answer the door – or Peter answers – I have it hidden in my hand. I will use it, Nadia. I swear on everything I hold sacred. I *will* use it.

It's over. It's *over*. Why don't you understand? How much more plainly can I state this? What more can I say? Why won't you just listen? (What's *wrong* with you? Are you deluded? *Insane?*) I want you out of my life! There! I'll say it again! I WANT YOU OUT OF MY LIFE!
Is that plain enough for you? Is that clear enough?

How did you track me down? How? *How?!* And *why?* Why did you persist when it was so obvious – so *obvious!* – that I didn't *want* to be found? I changed my name, my hair colour, my accent, my religion. I changed it all. I *lost* it all. I *wanted* to lose it, don't you see?

I'm a different person now. I'm someone else. I play bridge.

I do tapestry. I sing in the church choir. I raised £235 on the Walk for Life. I'm a good person, a stable person.

And I'm *not* your mother. I was *never* your mother. I never *wanted* you. I'm sorry to have to say that – to write that down in black and white – but it's the truth. I've given everything I had to give. I'm very sorry if it wasn't enough for you. I apologize. I truly apologize – but this is *who I am*, Nadia. This is *me*. I'm sorry if you find it disappointing. I'm sorry if you're angry. But have you ever bothered to think – even for a second – about what you're putting *me* through? You only seem to think about yourself – *your* feelings, *your* rights. But what about mine? If you honestly cared for me – as you insist that you do – then why can't you just show it by *LEAVING ME ALONE*?!

I didn't ask for this, Nadia. I didn't ask for any of this. It's making me ill. *You* are making me ill. I am very depressed and on edge. I can't sleep. I can't eat. I can't seem to concentrate my mind on anything. Peter has noticed. He's started asking me questions. I swear to God, if you turn up, unannounced, and ruin the life I've struggled so hard to build with him, I shall never forgive you. Never. *Never*. I shall hate you. I shall spit in your face and then slash my own throat.

I'm sobbing as I scribble all of these terrible things down, because I'm sorry. I am sorry. I'm sorry that it has had to come down to this. I'm not a maniac, but this situation is in danger of turning me into one. I have lost all sense of self-control. I keep bursting into tears. I am a different person. I can't seem to recognize myself.

This isn't normal for me. But I'm cornered, like a trapped animal. *You* have cornered me. *You* are in control of my destiny. You hold it in your hands. *My* destiny! *My* destiny! Not *your* destiny, but *my* destiny!
LET ME GO! LET ME GO! YOU HAVE *NO RIGHT* TO DO THIS TO ME!

I am afraid, Nadia. I am terrified. And I shall do anything – *anything* – it takes to survive this. I shall come out baring my teeth and my claws. I shall scratch and bite. You're giving me no other option. There is no other way.

And don't think for a moment that it's because I care for him *more*. Why do you keep on saying that? Why?! I don't understand the logic of your way of thinking! It's so stupid! It's so selfish! I don't care for him *more*. I care about the *work* I've invested! I care about the *years* of *work* I've invested. I won't have you just turning up and ruining it all for me. You ruined it all for me once before, thirty-six years ago. I won't let you do it again. I'd kill myself first. I won't go through it all again. I can't. I can't! Don't you understand? I can't! *It just isn't fair*!

Why all these questions about your father? What more do you feel you need to know about him? Why don't you just *let these things alone*?

It's almost like you *blame* me. You call yourself a victim, but *I* was the victim. Don't you understand? *I* was the victim. I am *still* the victim.

Of course I don't know what the medical implications are! Speak to your doctor! How am I meant to engage with all of this? It's monstrous! It's obscene! He was my uncle. I already *told* you he was a blood relation. My mother's brother. I already told that to the adoption people. I was *twelve years old*! A *child*! They swore to my mother – they swore to *me* – that they would maintain my anonymity.

I have rebuilt my life. I have paid the price. I was never able to conceive again. My womb was too small to go full term. The baby should have been aborted but my parents wouldn't hear of it. I nearly died in the delivery. I lost five pints of blood. I told you all of this on the phone. I never wanted to have the baby. It was a mistake, a terrible mistake.

I'm sorry the baby was you. But I never wanted you. I wanted another baby, my *own* baby, but that was never to be. I was denied a child of my own. *Peter* was denied a child of his own. I have been punished – by God, by him, by … I don't know … I have suffered enough. I have kept the secret all these years and I'm damned if you're going to spoil everything for me. I won't let you. I'll do anything, *anything* it takes. I am beyond fear. I am beyond care.

Please, *please*, let this finally be an end to it. Please.

Rita

[letter 14]

A dispatch from the desk of:

Baxter Thorndyke, Cllr
The Old Hall
Burley Cross

21/12/2006

Brian,

REMEMBER TO DESTROY THIS LETTER AS SOON
AS YOU HAVE READ AND MEMORIZED THE
CONTENTS!

DON'T BIN IT.
DON'T SHRED IT.
BURN IT!!

I thought it was probably advisable to pass on the details of
the Sex Hex by post, under the ingenious disguise of 'Boring
Council Business'. We don't want Petra accidentally happening
across it – in the form of a stray email – while idly going
through the online receipts for your annual tax return, do we,
now?

As I told you when we conversed on the issue in the bar after
council: I'm not prone to handing out information on the Hex
to just anyone, willy-nilly. Consider yourself lucky. Consider
yourself 'blessed'.

The Sex Hex works. It is *powerful magic*. Don't play around
with it. It is deadly, deadly serious. Use it at your own peril in
other words.

Got that? Good. So let's get down to business …

For a successful Hex, you will need:

1. A SHEET OF PLAIN, WHITE PAPER FROM A
PREVIOUSLY UNUSED BASILDON BOND NOTEPAD.
(Basildon Bond are a good quality paper manufacturer. The
original spell demands 'virgin parchment' – which could just as
easily be a stray page ripped from a scruffy student notepad.
But where's the fun in that? I find the spell is at its most potent,
its most powerful, when each individual ingredient you use is as
good and as 'pure' as it possibly can be.)

2. A MATCHING ENVELOPE (AS ABOVE).

3. A DOWNY FEATHER FROM THE BREAST OF A
TURTLE DOVE.
I have a casual acquaintance (the husband of Tammy's former
acupuncturist – greasy little chap, also an aficionado of the
Hex) who happens to breed grouse and doves. He has kindly
provided me with a ready supply of downy feathers. I have
taken the trouble to enclosed one for you, here.

4. A HAIR FROM THE HEAD OF THE OBJECT OF
YOUR DESIRE.
A good technique to acquire one, I often find, is to get into a lift
(or on to a bus – if you ever use public transport) with the Hex-
ee and stand directly behind them. You can then remove a
stray hair from the back of their dress/jacket with relative
impunity.

5. *ORCHIS MASCULA.*
This is the Early Purple Orchid (or 'Cuckoos' as it's often
called in the Midlands). It's fairly widespread all over the UK
and can be found in both woods and on meadowland. It
flowers from mid-April to mid-June, but the flower's of no
interest to us. What we need is the tuber (i.e. the root).

To complicate matters, the plant has two of them (both fleshy and egg-shaped). The difference between them is that one feeds the plant (then shrinks as the plant matures), the other receives all the excess nutrients that the plant accumulates throughout its growing season and so *expands* as the year progresses (thereby providing the energy the plant will need in order to germinate the following year). *This* is the tuber you want. The withered one is sometimes used in spells to 'check wronged passions' (the <u>last</u> thing you need). The fresh one is 'under the dominion of Venus' and will certainly serve our purpose.

6. *ORCHIS MASCULATA.*

It looks very like 'Cuckoos' (just to add to your misery) but flowers slightly later (July). You'll find it on heaths and commons. It's generally known as the Spotted Orchid (*Mascula* also has spotted leaves, so whoever you get your supply from certainly needs to know the difference between the two. Try looking on the internet if you get desperate).

The important distinction between the two species lies underground. *Masculata*'s tubers are divided into several 'finger-like' lobes (as a consequence, it is sometimes called 'Dead Men's Fingers' or 'Palma Christi' – I believe there's a reference to it in *Hamlet*. Ophelia is wreathed in them when she drowns).

This root is also referred to as 'the Female Satyrion'. The myth is that they were the special food of satyrs and excited them to terrible excesses. Once again, it is the plump tuber that you want (and to distinguish between the two types they must always be harvested in autumn).

Both kinds of tubers need to be prepared in the same way. First you'll need to immerse them in boiling water (briefly scald them, in other words – but be sure and keep the sets of tubers strictly separated throughout this process, or you'll forget which batch is which). The skins must then be rubbed off and the tubers placed into a pre-heated oven for around ten minutes (180 degrees Centigrade – 160 if your oven has a fan. Never, never microwave).

Once you've removed them from the oven, place them somewhere cool and airy for a few days (away from any damp). During this time they will change from looking 'milky' to transparent and 'horny'.

When fully dried they can be stored (indefinitely) in a glass jar or a plastic bag (remember, *do* label them correctly to forestall any future heartache).

For the Hex to work you will need a small slither of each, approximately the size and width of your littlest nail.

7. A SAMPLE OF THE SALIVA OF THE OBJECT OF YOUR DESIRE.

Sounds tricky, but this is easier to manage than you might initially imagine. Just invite the Object/Hex-ee out for a meal, or buy them a coffee, or – if needs be – just follow them around until you see them partaking of a random beverage and then acquire the can/glass/cup after they have gone and simply wipe a clean white tissue around its rim (a good quality tissue: white, pristine, with a high ply – none of that recycled rubbish). It is this tissue that you will employ in the Hex.

8. PAGE 85 OF THE *KAMA SUTRA*.

This is the Numerological part of the equation. The page number is acquired (a detail that had always deeply perplexed me before I finally worked it out during that especially long and boring debate about the future of the Ilkley Lido last spring) by adding together the numerical value of each individual letter in the words SEX HEX, i.e. nineteen for S, five for E etc. etc.

When I initially used the Hex I bought a new copy of the *Kama Sutra* for each fresh conquest. Now I just photocopy the page. It seems just as effective.

HOW THE HEX WORKS

Using a black pen, draw a large vagina on to the sheet of plain white paper – in as much detail as you like – and then print the name of your Hex-ee – in capital letters – around its perimeter (if you don't know their name, then their title will do just as well, so long as you keep a *clear vision* in your mind of them all the time as you are drawing, e.g. LOLLIPOP LADY).

Underneath it, draw a large, erect penis, pointing directly towards the vagina (try and give it the characteristics of your own penis), then print your name in clear, strong, capital letters along its immense, distended shaft.

Next, fold up the tissue, the page of the *Kama Sutra*, the hair, the feather, the two slithers of dried orchid tuber and place them all into the envelope alongside the drawing you have made. On the front of the envelope write SEX HEX. Underline it. Twice.

Take this envelope outside to a quiet corner (or if you have an open fireplace inside which is sufficiently private, use that) and set fire to it while repeating the phrase: - - - - - COME TO ME! - - - - COME TO ME! (- - - - is the name of your Hex-ee, obviously. If you don't know their name then – once again – use the appropriate phrase, e.g. SEXY BRUNETTE IN THE POST OFFICE COME TO ME! etc.).

Leave the burned remains where they lie. Do *not* touch them or move them.

Soon – *very* soon – The Object Of Your Desire will be beating a path to your door. Just sit back and wait. It *will* happen. On average, I find, it takes around forty-eight hours. When they finally do turn up (pulling off their clothes, gasping, *panting*), the sex will be astonishing. Explosive. Filthy. Unconstrained. Orgiastic.

The only negative effect is that there can often be an unpleasant smell in the room during the act of copulation. I have been told that this aroma is something to do with the

___

power of the Early Purple Orchid which – while generally odourless – can exude a foul smell as dusk falls. For this reason I always tend to burn sweet orange oil in the room (if I'm *in* a room and can plan ahead) for the duration of the coition.

Occasionally the smell clings to your skin for a while. It's not a terrible aroma – like burned butter. Quite acrid.

Another negative effect of the Sex Hex is that the Hex-ee will loathe you afterwards. They won't understand what it was that compelled them to initiate a random act of sex with you. They'll start off feeling dazed, then become slightly panicked and confused, then grow deeply resentful (but hey! Who cares? You've got what you wanted, so what the heck?!).

I have used the Hex twelve times now (and have yet another charming little Hex-ee lined up – unbeknownst to her – even as I type this!). It has worked like a dream each time – except once. I'd Hexed this sweet Danish nurse at work and she never showed up. It later transpired that she'd been knocked down by an ambulance while running across the road *directly adjacent to my office* (she broke both her legs, so was of no use to me then for several months. I don't think the power of the Hex lasts indefinitely – and I couldn't risk Hexing her again after that).

Do choose your 'conquests' carefully. I once made the mistake of using the Sex Hex on Sarah Jane's geography teacher (gorgeous red-head, straight out of college. A real goer!) Once the Hex had been fulfilled (two rampant hours locked inside the school sick-bay) and she turned all sour and vengeful, she opted (unfairly) to take out her rage on SJ. The poor child came bottom of her class that year (which was a shame – geography was her favourite subject). It really knocked SJ's confidence and finally put to rest all her ambitions of becoming Derby's answer to Sir Ranulph Fiennes (a pretty silly dream for a girl to have, anyway, I suppose).

I also used it on Pleasance Rutler (the wife of Ilkley's old Mayor – remember her? Blonde. Bossy. Great legs – ex-professional dancer. Thighs with the grip of a python).

She really, really bore a grudge. Nasty piece of work. Slashed the tyres on my car (well, it was Tamm's car, as it happens – I'd taken her little black VW Golf convertible to work that day – my Range Rover was being MOT'd).

My first Hex was on a young Nigerian traffic warden who gave me a ticket while I was parked on a double-yellow outside the hospital (a 'revenge fuck', so to speak. Although – of course – I was able to claim the money back on the grounds of it being 'a medical emergency').

I banged her inside a bus shelter, then several more times back at her home. She was the mother of twins. Lived in a crummy flat (on a still crummier estate). Kids screamed in their cot as we screwed next door. Her caesarean scars were still pink, which was slightly off-putting, but hey-ho …

In case you're interested, I was originally taught the Sex Hex by a heart surgeon I worked with in Derby. It was a teaching hospital. He'd been through half of the med. students there and I was desperate to know *how* … (can't have been much under seventy, the frisky old dog!). I'm not entirely sure where it was that *he* learned it from, originally …

So … yes. I think that's about the sum of it. Text me if you think I've left anything out. Good luck with it. Don't be scared to give it a whirl. And remember: it might seem fiddly to start off with, but it's foolproof, and a *hell* of a lot less trouble than the 'other' techniques we discussed.

Happy Christmas etc.

Bax

NOW BURN THIS, YOU HEAR?

[letter 15]

Saint's Kennels
Sharp Crag Farm
Nr Burley Cross

7 December, 2006

Hell's Bells, Prue –

It's been best part of a week – *longer* …
I scribbled the address on this damn thing *ten days* ago, and as
God is my witness, I've not had so much as a minute to call my
own since.

The fly strike's taken out three of the Romneys! Poor
Donal's at his wits' end. We never had it so late in the season
before – it's bitter out there ('Cold as the north side of a
gravestone in winter' as me mam always liked to say). A very
different story from Olonzac, eh?

Those filthy flies shouldn't be *alive*, let alone breeding …
Donal don't know if he's coming or going – me either (more to
the point!).

Then – as if that wasn't quite enough to be getting on with –
the Coombes kid (our newest recruit, tho' he's about as much
use on a farm as a chocolate teapot) has gone down with
sodding *measles* – caught it off our Lawrie (Ta very much,
Son!) who's been fretting about a constant headache for nigh
on a fortnight and won't eat a thing (apart from fruit smoothies
– home-made, <u>fresh</u> strawberry. Fussy little so-and-so … Oh,
and he *will* force a soft-boiled duck egg down his gullet, but
only if you ask him very nicely – *granary* soldiers, mind!
Whenever I trudge down to the local shop they've run out, so
then it's a pesky drive to Ilkley Tesco's to mollify the little sod).

Finally, to crown it all, Gayle's gone and had herself a huge
barney with Ryan (it would've been a year this Christmas; she
must've told me all of – oh – *three hundred times*) so she's

mooching about the place like a wet weekend, all heartbroke and love-lorn. 'The weddin's cancelled!' she announces at table on Friday (over a glamorous bowl of microwaved carrot soup). 'Weddin'?' Donal growls (he's been up best part of the night). 'Who said owt about a bloody weddin'?!'

Now she's hanging crape. Shooting him dark looks. Won't utter so much as a *word* in his general orbit (not that our man's noticed – he's that knackered!). 'Insensitive brute,' she mutters this morning after he turfs her out the bathroom (get *her*, eh? All *hoity*!). She'd been walled up in there over an hour – trimming her fringe (she's cut it way too short – silly mare – and has spent the best part of the day yanking and pulling at the damn thing in the hope of making it grow back again).

I'm still running the kennels single-handed. No sign of that extra help Donal promised after the Guy Fawkes Night hullabaloo (would've called it a 'debacle', but can't see my way to spelling it right … And we *still* haven't seen hide nor hair of that bloody Setter – tho' Arthur Wolf swore black is blue he saw the damn thing at Raven's Peak atop Kex Gill last week).

We're fully booked over New Year. Six months back I would've been made up about it – happy as Larry – but now? I dunno. I'm still not …

Sorry, Prue, love. Donal just hauled me down to the small paddock (Phew! Still short of breath, in fact!). Had to wrangle the ram as Donal teased about a million fly eggs out of the wool. The deeper he worked his way in, the worse things got. They'd hatched! An earlier infestation, Donal reckons. We finished up shearing the whole back end. It was far worse than we'd initially conceived of – they'd chewed through to the backbone, pretty much. Poor blighter was in agony! I just dashed back home to ring the veterinary (no mobile reception) …

Sorry, Prue – different pen – the veterinary turned up just as I was settling down. He said as how he thought we could save the poor blighter, but in the end it was too late (£94 too late!

Merry Christmas to you, too, Veterinary Crawford!). Donal shot him first thing (the ram – tho' if the veterinary'd hung around a minute longer than it'd took the ink to dry on his blasted cheque ...).

He's been ashen all morning (it was Pye, the first Romney ram he ever got. Donal doted on the tusty old codger).

Even Gayle clocked how riled her dad were (through that thick stew of heartbreak!) and took him his mug of tea out at ten – a timely *rapprochement*! (Looked up the spelling in the dictionary! Double-checked *debacle*! Nowt's too much trouble for you, Prue, love!)

I found mine (tea) nicely stewed on the kitchen table once I'd mucked out the stables – *her* job, coincidentally (Oh aye – and she was literally falling over herself to thank me, after ... uh ... *Not*).

You won't believe it: she's only back to worrying at her bloody fringe again! Looks like a Trappist monk! Ryan *still* isn't returning her texts (that was *some* row, eh?), but – like I keep telling her – he's on a walking holiday in Wales with the Scouts, so what's she expect? (I just thank God I'm not a teenager no more, Prue. All those new-fangled ways to feel rejected! 'He di'n't email, Mam! He di'n't phone, Mam! He di'n't text!' It's enough to send you do-bloody-lally!)

You'll doubtless be delighted to hear as Billy's in rare health. Still three bricks shy of a load, of course. Lawrie says he spent best part of an hour chasing his own tail in the yard yesterday, then collapsed – where he stood – and slept for three hours, solid. Wouldn't move a muscle – not even when Donal sounded the horn on the tractor!

I'm only glad you didn't risk taking him to Olonzac (what with the Gala virus running so rampant up in the hills there). He's having a whale of a time here! Loves charging about the place – tho' he's crouched over my boots, shivering (fit to bust!) as I write this (I had to hose him down after he rolled in a cowpat. He's *fine*. He's been sat by the kitchen range. The other Borders are all green with envy! Tarry and Rusty've had their noses pressed to the door throughout).

He just scoffed down all the cats' food while someone dropped off a Labrador – beautiful chocolate-brown bitch, five months old, name of Tess – and left their bowls in all four corners of the room.

How's your sister faring? Two broken arms, three kids, five months pregnant *and* a B&B to take care of? And there was me thinking as *I* was hard done by! You must be run ragged, poor sod! Bet you can't wait to get back home! Talking of which – I went down to The Old Cavalry Yard and dug out that recipe you was hankering after (Stewed Pork and Puy Lentils? Was that it?) *and* your rosary (enclosed). Then there's the seven cards I found on your doormat – and something you *won't* so much like the look of: a lengthy epistle about the Promise Auction from the reverend's good friend, Mr Sebastian St John (don't fret – I double-checked the deadlock on your door so as to be sure that BC's answer to David Dickinson couldn't wriggle his way in there and start pricing up the cutlery!).

Anyway, that's all my news for now – Oh, Lor! Apart from this month's Book Group! How'd *that* slip my mind?! *Life of Pi*! Total catastrophe! Hadn't had so much as a chance to look at the damn thing, but didn't dare confess it – being as it's my third book in a row I haven't read (folk'll start thinking I'm only in it for Sally Trident's legendary Cheese and Olive Scone Bake! Your lower digestive tract must be in uproar having missed out on it all these long weeks!).

As luck would have it, nobody else could make head or tail of the book (so I passed off my ignorance as confusion: 'But *why'd* they call the tiger Richard? Where's the sense in that?!'). Discussion was just getting started, when, next thing we know, Tom Augustine and Robin Goff start going at it hammer and tongs! (Don't have the first clue why the two of 'em turned up, quite frankly – I much prefer it when it's only us girls.) Clash of the Titans, it was! Tom Augustine jumps to his feet and sends a plate of bourbons flying. Robin's all up in his face, ranting and raving (poor Brenda didn't know where to put herself!).

I wouldn't mind, but the row wasn't even about the book! It was some pointless little dispute about 'the proper definition of a Farmers' Market'(!). Robin says as the produce has to come straight from the farm. Tom says summat to the contrary. The argument goes on for bloody hours, all manner of accusations flying hither and thither, the two of 'em crashing and butting like a pair of rutting stags!

Nobody else can get a word in (nor wants to, either!). Of course neither of 'em bothers asking me *my* thoughts on the matter (I'm just a farmer's *wife* after all …). Jill Harpington's down on the floor, meanwhile, gathering up the bourbons, trying to minimize the damage to her new cream Axminster (we're all in our stockinged feet – Tom, for the record, has a large hole in his sock) when her contact lens falls out. 'Don't move!' she's wailing. 'Don't move!'

Next thing we know, Tammy Thorndyke stands up, throws her book on't floor and commences mewling like a newborn! Sally Trident starts having a panic attack. 'Jesus wept!' she keeps panting (her glasses all steamy). 'Jesus wept!'

I'll tell you this for nowt, Prue: I don't know what the heck they've chose to read next month, but I've already booked my front-row seat! Wouldn't miss it for the world (am even thinking of taking young Lawrie along – you know how much he enjoys watching the WWF on the box)!

Donal nearly rolled off his chair laughing when I told him about it – first time he'd cracked a smile in weeks! I was only sorry you wasn't there yourself …

Come home soon, kid!

Merry Christmas,

God Bless,

XXX

Helen

PS. If what follows looks ominous, at least thank your lucky stars you don't have to tell Paula Coombes and her mob that the prefab in Lower Field's just been designated 'unfit for human habitation' by the local council. I saw Thorndyke sniffing around it – during one of his infernal 'rambles' – not a fortnight since (muttered something to me, in passing, about 'the strange angle of the chimney') and now this! I could happily swing for him!

We all know it's just tit-for-tat. The little creep's still filthy with Donal after he got behind Wincey at the public meeting in June.

Poor old Paula! With her luck, she'll end up sleeping in't stables (I know it's three days afore Christmas, but …).

Will fill you in on all the gory details over a large (<u>very</u> large) bucket of cheap plonk when you get back …

XX
H

[letter 16]

'Tiddlers'
The High Street
Burley Cross

19th December, 2006

Hi Prue, darling –

Seb here. You asked me to keep you up to speed on this year's
BC Auction of Promises, and I must confess – to my eternal
shame – that in spite of all my good intentions, I've been
actively *avoiding* getting in touch because I'm so deeply, deeply
mortified by the horrible way things have been panning out ...
(In fact this is how bad it's got, Prue: on Tuesday I spent the
entire afternoon sponging down my kitchen blinds – each,
individual wooden slat, front *and* back – with a warm water and
vinegar solution, having convinced myself that they were ever
so slightly 'claggy' to the touch. On Wednesday I lime-washed
a perfectly nice chest of drawers. On Thursday I spent hours
removing the lime-wash. On Friday I dragged my poor, dear,
long-suffering Chloe – who turned fifteen last week – over to
the Pet Parlour in Guiseley to get her teeth de-scaled, only to
be told by the receptionist – the moment we arrived, and in
tones of *some* astonishment – that she'd just recently had it
done, in late August, no less!)

In short, I'm basically at the end of my tether, Prue. I mean
call me naive, or stupid (or both, if the fancy takes you) but I
can honestly say that I had *no idea* when I agreed to take on this
precious 'baby' of yours that it would be quite so needy, or so
demanding – or so badly behaved, for that matter. (The late
nights! The early mornings! The ruined meals! And I've
virtually lost *count* of the number of times the little tyke's puked
down my shirt!)

All levity aside, Prue, it's been an absolute nightmare – a living hell. And I'm not sure if it's just because I'm relatively new in town, or whether you have some special kind of influence over people here (cue music for *The Stepford Wives* – original version. Bags *I'm* the gorgeous Katharine Ross …), but since you left for Olonzac the whole thing has quite literally 'gone to pot'.

It's no exaggeration (well, not much of one) when I say that BC, as it currently stands, is A Village At War. Threats have been made, Prue. Oaths have been forsworn. Dignities have been violated. Boundaries have been drawn, then flagrantly crossed, then painstakingly re-drawn (principally by muggins, here), then flagrantly crossed again.

I have been obliged (in my role as AOP 'caretaker') to transform myself, overnight, into BC's answer to Kofi Annan (and believe me, the traditional, garishly patterned African tribal tunic is so not my style!). I have put myself on the line, Prue – not just once, or twice, but *dozens* of times. Yet for all of that, none of the parties involved seems even remotely inclined to either relent or give quarter.

People are just being so selfish, so vile and pig-headed, that it actually almost beggars belief! I mean this is a *charitable endeavour*, Prue! I must've said it till I'm blue in the face! 'This is for charity, people! For all those skinny, shoeless little kiddies in the Sudan, *remember*?!' But nobody's listening! I feel like I'm basically just banging my head against a brick wall (or a beautifully reconstituted limestone one, in this particular instance).

What's become increasingly – agonizingly – clear to me over the past month or so, Prue, is that I totally lack your natural air of command; your authoritarian edge (I suppose this must be one of the pay-offs for all those years spent nestled deep in the bosom of HM's Prison Service … Well, that and the great pension allowance. And the dinky little baton. And the fabulous, *fabulous* uniform …).

Your name has a measure of *gravitas* in these parts, Prue –
you are respected, admired, even feared – while I, by
comparison, am just 'that skinny, camp antiques dealer who
likes to wear spats' (I overheard Jez Baverstock describing me
to Sally Trident with those *exact* words in the queue for the
post office last week! I literally didn't know where to put
myself! Although, on reflection, I suppose I *am* quite svelte …
and the spats *are* sort of my 'trademark' …).

To cut a long story short, Prue (or shorter, at any rate), I've
grown so frustrated (not to say disillusioned) with this whole,
torrid Promise Auction scenario that I took the liberty of getting
Reverend Paul involved (I do hope you won't be upset by this
decision; while I'm relatively new in town, it's still fairly
apparent to me how fiercely different local 'factions' like to
guard their own particular 'patch' – be it social, charitable or
ideological – although I like to believe the reverend, as a
representative of the Church, is above all that).

For the record, Paul's been amazing, a Godsend (an *absolute*
Godsend – an Angel of Mercy, in effect), and has doggedly
employed his – not inconsiderable – skills in trying to smooth
over some of the stickier disputes and get things back on track.

It's early days, though, Prue, early, early days, and, to quote
everybody's favourite poet, Robert Frost: 'I [still] have
promises to keep, and [many – *to help the thing scan*] miles to go
before I sleep …' (I'm sure a smart cookie like you will realize
that my real source of this poetic reference is actually the classic
seventies psychological thriller, *Telefon*, starring Charles
Bronson. I'm naturally type-casting Baxter Thorndyke in the
Donald Pleasence serial-killer role …).

On a more positive note (and I think there is a positive note
to be found here, although I'm not entirely sure what it sounds
like – probably a B flat), the auction itself went off fairly well.
As you strongly hinted before you left (and I must admit I
thought you were being perhaps a *tad* paranoid at the time), the
aforementioned Thorndyke *did* try to railroad the whole event

by taking to the stage (uninvited) and making a very odd, impromptu (at least I *think* it was impromptu) fifteen-minute speech about manhole cover theft, which had the overall effect of really shaking some of the more elderly bidders up (I saw at least two of them head for the door, panicked. One of them – that half-Chinese woman from Menston who works part-time at the local shop – almost in tears).

There really is no getting around the fact that this unplanned intervention of Cllr Thorndyke's somewhat soured the jolly mood. In the end, the only way we could bring a halt to his impassioned diatribe (the hall was booked till nine – The Burley Cross Players had it after that for early rehearsals of their *Passion*, which I must confess is going swimmingly. Meredith has finally found her Jesus! He's from Hebden Bridge, a professional, and *unbelievably* dishy!) was by turning all the lights off and pretending we'd had a power cut (this was Helen's idea; she said you'd been obliged to take this course of action before. It did seem quite an effective ruse – although the microphone still continuing to work was something of a giveaway, I suppose ...).

Anyhow, by the time *I* finally stood up to deliver *your* little introduction (thanks for that, it really did take the pressure off) the party atmosphere we'd all worked so hard to create – with the free rum punch, the Waitrose party finger-food and the balloons – had been somewhat undermined (although your joke about the BC Bell Ringers trying to get into the *Guinness Book of Records* went down a storm; you'll have to explain it to me properly when you get back).

That said, Helen was quite the star of the night when she paraded the second 'promise' into the hall on a leash. The turkey (a huge, repulsive-looking thing) trotted along beside her like a dog and was incredibly well-behaved (although no prizes for guessing who ended up spending the best part of an hour scrubbing turkey mess from the parquet ... Then, on top of that, there was the blasted cleaning bill for Baxter

Thorndyke's corduroy trousers – one of the biggest cheers of the night came when Helen inadvertently allowed the bird to evacuate what seemed like the entire contents of its bowels into his immaculately pressed turn-ups. Of course we offered to cover his dry cleaning costs. He sent me the bill last week: £38! This was almost as much as we raised on the bird itself! And he's *still* maintaining that they couldn't entirely get the stain out!).

Anyhow, to simplify things for you, I've gone to the trouble of breaking all the promises down, individually – in almost forensic detail – so you can get a general idea of where we currently stand (and trust me, it's no accident that I've chosen to employ the language of pathology here!).

I do hope you won't judge me too harshly on what you read below, Prue.

Hugs and Kisses,

Seb

PROMISE AUCTION
19th November, 2006

FOLLOW-UP REPORT

LOT 1

Promise made: Unity Gray of Finches, Lamb's Green, BC, promised a unique, handmade, patchwork quilt (size, colour etc., to be specified by the purchaser and agreed by mutual consent).

Purchased by: Catrin and Alan Crawford at Skylarks, Fitzwilliam Street, BC.

Amount paid: £109

Upshot: I'm sorry, Prue, but I would need to write a *novel* to explain the various ramifications of this fraught situation. It involves Catrin's psychotic second cousin, Lydia May Eardley, and an ill-advised trip she took with Unity (who I believe is teetotal) to The Old Oak on the night of the grand final of the Regional Darts Championships (with players from the local amateur Bingley and Otley darts teams in attendance – most of whom appear to've been either Hell's Angels or members of another, similarly unedifying, satanic, knife-wielding, long-haired, northern biker gang called The Otley Ridgebacks). This aforementioned 'ill-advised trip' culminated in the grand final being hijacked – after Lydia May Eardley stole the top Otley player's replacement flights and wouldn't give them back. The title was then awarded, by default, to the Bingley team. This shock result (Otley were long-time Champions, and by far the better side) led to the destruction of Wincey's prized nineteenth-century saloon bar, over £7,625 worth of damage to vehicles in the car park, and the renewal of a savage gang war between Otley and Bingley bikers which had apparently been in abeyance for the past twenty-five-odd years. As yet, no sure resolution has been reached re the quilt, either. Both parties are still feeling too 'raw' to meet up.

LOT 2

Promise made: Free-range Christmas turkey supplied by Helen and Donal Flint at Sharp Crag Farm.

Purchased by: Steve Briars at Chevin Cottage, 3 The Beck, BC.

Amount paid: £40

Upshot: Well, this is quite a bizarre one, Prue. The
particular turkey Mr Briars bought was later
stamped to death – in a brutal attack – by an
angry horse. The gentle turkey had apparently
been put into a field with the high-strung beast in
order to try and 'calm it down' (although I hear
this same animal had already killed a sheep by
the same technique!). Helen – Mrs Flint – made
the mistake of informing the purchaser of this
tragic fact (I rue the day she did this, Prue, but
then I suppose that's just our dear Helen all over,
eh? Utterly devoid of artifice, straightforward to
the point of bluntness, speaks as she finds, salt of
the earth, etc. etc.). Unfortunately, Mr Briars did
not take the news well. He is now insisting that
the replacement bird – which he's been up to the
farm to inspect – isn't of the quality of the
original one, and has kicked up a fair old stink
about it. He is also demanding that 'some kind of
punitive action' be taken against the horse.
(We're entering the realm of madness, here,
surely? I mean what does the man expect?! Fifty
lashes? No grooming for a week? A reduction in
its nose-bag?!) The horse in question (as you're
doubtless already aware) belongs to Helen Flint's
daughter, Gayle (who's *ballooned* in recent
months – must've put on three stone, at the very
least. Is it any wonder the poor nag's in such a
temper?!). So far as I can tell, the replacement
bird is an excellent creature, of comparable
quality, if slightly less tame (but that's hardly an

issue, is it? He's intending to *eat* the thing, not go on a date with it!). Having said that, I'm the first to admit that I'm hardly an expert on turkey flesh (Arts and Crafts furniture, yes, the literary works of A.A. Milne, yes, coins and medals from the Ancient Near East, yes, turkeys, no). On top of all this, we already have that cleaning bill of £38 to factor into the equation.

LOT 3

Promise made: Mhairi Callaghan of Feathercuts in Skipton promised a 'home re-style' to anybody – of *either* gender – who felt themselves in need of one.

Purchased by: Meredith Coles (your dear neighbour) from Flat 4b, The Old Cavalry Yard, The High Street, BC.

Amount paid: £20

Upshot: Meredith has actually already had her 're-style' and is pleased as punch with the results – although she went into the salon in Skipton to have it done, rather than getting Mhairi to come to her home (as she generally does) because the 'look' she had in mind required *both* a perm *and* a tint. I love Meredith to death, Prue (and don't let anyone dare suggest otherwise!), but I won't pretend that Mhairi wasn't somewhat put out that Meredith should demand *all* of her most time-consuming (and costly!) services while paying her £5 *less* than she usually does for a standard, basic trim! *Ouch!*

LOT 4

Promise made: Wincey Hawkes at The Old Oak, The High Street, BC, promised a convivial 'family lunch' in the pub's recently refurbished dining rooms.

Purchased by: Paula Coombes – c/o Sharp Crag Farm, nr BC.

Amount paid: £10

Upshot: As I'm sure you can imagine, once Paula put up her hand for this lot nobody else had the heart to bid against her. Wincey hasn't breathed a word about it herself (isn't that just Wincey, though? So wonderfully sensitive and discreet?), but I was talking to someone (they shall remain nameless – discretion *is* my watchword) who happened to be dining in the pub on the day Paula went to claim her promise (okay – you twisted my arm, Prue … God, you're so *good* at that! – it was Leonard Noble) and he told me – perfectly aghast – how her 'mob' ate poor Wincey out of house and home. He said it put him in mind of the time he was on safari in the Gobi Desert during the early 1970s and met up with a primitive clan of nomads who sacrificed a goat in his honour. Apparently they didn't waste an inch of the creature, but consumed the *entire* animal – brain, eyes, ears, hooves, tail … (Do goats even *have* tails?) He said the Coombes family behaved in a comparable manner, even going so far as to range around the dining rooms like a flock of locusts, devouring leftovers and scraps from other diners' abandoned plates. He said they licked the crockery clean, and one of them – the littlest – even ate the decorative sprigs of parsley which the fish dishes were served with (and pronounced them 'delicious'!). Oh yes, and they all talked – with their mouths full – throughout the meal, in unison, without interruption, and at a perfectly *deafening* volume. Leonard said the dining rooms were all but empty when they arrived and completely empty by the time they left. A uniform success, in other words.

LOT 5

Promise made: Nick Endive at 1, The Old Cavalry Yard, The High Street, BC, promised a rare tour of the 'Space Surveillance Centre' at RAF Fylingdales (where he is currently employed).

Purchased by: Nina Springhill, 7 Station Road, Ilkley (or c/o BC PO).

Amount paid: £45

Upshot: The tour took place a few weeks back and was accorded a 'triumph' by all parties (although I believe there was some difficulty with wheel-chair access for Ms Springhill's disabled beau).

LOT 6

Promise made: Tilly Brooks from Threadbare Cottage, The Calls, promised to decorate a piece of white porcelain – of the purchaser's choice – with one of her (I must say) *incredibly* beautiful flower paintings.

Purchased by: PC Roger Topping, 17 Dean Street,
Addingham (or c/o Ilkley Police Station).

Amount paid: £95 (much to Tilly's blatant
horror/embarrassment/astonishment!)

Upshot: I think this was a good result, overall, Prue. I
know it took a huge amount of persuasion (on
your part) to get Tilly to agree to auction some
of her work, but the demand for it really was
quite substantial! We even had a phone vote for
this one: Joanna Jones, who resides part-time in
BC at the Winter Barn, started the bidding off –
from her studio in London – at £50. The bids
then went up in £5 increments until, at £90,
the phone line suddenly went dead and PC
Topping (who turned up – out of breath –
halfway through) was able to secure Tilly's
services for himself! Strange man, the PC.
Grows on you, over time (rather like a mould,
I suppose). Collects Staffordshire figures, you
know. He once confided in me that his father –
a manic depressive who died by his own hand
when poor PC Topping was 'naught but a lad'
– had worked for a short but blissful interlude
as a painter in the Staffordshire Potteries. Some
of PC Topping's most prized pieces were
subsequently bequeathed to him in his father's
will. I must confess that he has a surprisingly
sophisticated eye for such a huge, apparently
gormless lunk of a man. Ms Jones – by the by –
is absolutely furious that she missed out. She
gave me quite an earful on the subject when
we met up, by chance, at Samson's Electricals
in Ilkley the other afternoon (somewhat

unnecessary, I felt … I mean am I now to be held responsible for the vagaries of technology on top of everything else?!).

LOT 7

Promise made: Norma Spoot of 13, The Beck, BC (or c/o Choice Cut's Butchers, The High Street, BC) promised one of her legendary sponges.

Purchased by: Jonty Weiss-Quinn at Saxonby Manor.

Amount paid: £12

Upshot: Mr Weiss-Quinn bought the cake as a surprise for his wife Rosabella's birthday (Rosabella wasn't actually in attendance at the auction), but when Mr Weiss-Quinn confirmed the details with Norma afterwards, he idly let slip that Rosabella was severely gluten intolerant. Poor Norma was utterly horrified! Her 'legendary' sponge comes from a recipe that has been in her family for generations. As you will know (probably better than I, Prue), it is soft and light and very, very wheaty (it's a *sponge*, for heaven's sake!). What Mr Weiss-Quinn wanted, in effect, was Norma's wonderful sponge cake but without its main, constituent ingredient. What he received was a delicious chocolate fridge cake made from dark chocolate, Kirsch, grated almonds and coconut (Norma apparently got the recipe from a gluten-free cake site after several thankless hours spent trawling around on the internet). The 'sponge' was delivered to the Manor on

Rosabella's birthday, with due ceremony. Rosabella professed herself 'delighted' with it, ate a large, sticky slice and promptly began to gasp (it transpires that Rosabella is also chronically allergic to nuts!). The emergency doctor was called. A buttock-full of anti-histamines/adrenalin was injected. Rosabella's eyes apparently swelled up 'like a toad's' (the change was almost imperceptible, then. Ho ho!). A weekend trip to London's Dorchester Hotel was cancelled, and the tickets they'd had booked for *Wicked* went to waste. (It was Rosabella's fortieth – I was astonished when I found out. She always looks so effortlessly 'well-preserved' I had her down for fifty, at the very least!) The following day a curt card was sent to Norma (via the butcher's), chastising her for not having informed them, in advance, that such a 'toxic allergen' had been 'thoughtlessly included' in the cake's list of ingredients. Norma was understandably furious. 'I mean what the heck did that pair of gormless idiots *think* the damn thing was made out of?'(she apparently said afterwards) 'Gypsy teeth? Fairy eggs? *Elf* breath?!' The Weiss-Quinns are now refusing to pay for the cake, 'out of principle', and Shayne Spoot, in turn, has unofficially 'banned' them from the shop.

LOT 8

Promise made: Jeremy Baverstock of The Retreat promised a 'no-holds-barred', private guided tour of the legendary dungeons at Saxonby Manor (parties of up to ten people accepted).

Purchased by: Emily and Duncan Tanner's son, Ned Tanner
                 (of 3, The Mead, Denby Lane, Fallow Hill)
                 who happened to be visiting his parents in BC
                 on the night of the auction (he's currently
                 resident in Bradford). It seems his daughter,
                 Cherry (aged seven), is 'obsessed by Vampires',
                 and Ned felt it might be useful to try and
                 redirect this (somewhat baroque) fascination of
                 hers in a more traditional, healthy, 'historical'
                 direction. Ned is a truly sensitive and wonderful
                 man. It never ceases to amaze me that he
                 managed to turn out so well with such a crazed,
                 hysterical blabber-mouth for a mother.

Amount paid: £27

Upshot: What the lovely Mr Jez Baverstock *didn't* get
                 around to telling us all was that he had
                 neglected to acquire *permission* from the Weiss-
                 Quinns for this wonderfully exciting tour of his.
                 Somewhat perplexingly, Mr Jonty Weiss-Quinn
                 was still in attendance at the auction when this
                 lot was being bid for and yet didn't see fit to
                 save us all from a world of heartache by
                 speaking up on the issue at the time. Instead he
                 phoned Mr Baverstock afterwards and
                 apparently gave him 'a piece of his mind' (it
                 would have to be a small piece, Prue, because
                 it's a tiny mind. Not by *any* stretch of the
                 imagination could we count Mr Jonty Weiss-
                 Quinn among the world's 'intellectual
                 mammoths' – although he is, on occasion, quite
                 a cunning little swine). Mr Baverstock
                 professed himself 'somewhat taken aback' by
                 Mr Weiss-Quinn's 'aggressive, not to say

uncharitable attitude'. He claimed that he had conducted 'numerous' tours of the dungeons during Lady Beatrix Morrison's long residency at the Manor (she was 'constantly pestering' him to do them, apparently, and, when he did, she invariably tagged along on the tour parties herself because she found Mr Baverstock's 'fresh, historical perspective so utterly riveting'!). In fact the Weiss-Quinns were so unnecessarily spiteful and hostile towards Mr Baverstock (and his charitable scheme) that his suspicions were aroused and he promptly decided to conduct a small investigation into the matter using 'a secret "contact" with ready access to the Manor' (Sally Trident, I'm assuming. Doesn't she polish their silver?). Using this 'secret contact', Mr Baverstock was soon able to discover that the Weiss-Quinns had actually converted the ancient dungeons into a luxury gym and pool room – *without acquiring the requisite planning permission*! Oh-*ho*!

So what does Mr Baverstock do? How does he choose to *respond* to this shocking piece of information? But how *else*, Prue?! *Blackmail*, of course! He promises to keep their flagrant act of architectural vandalism under wraps if they, in turn, offer him public support over some convoluted rights of access issue he is currently engaged in relating to his small cottage – The Retreat – which is located inside the Manor's extensive grounds.

And how am *I* privy to this information, Prue? Why, Mr Baverstock told me himself! *Bragged* about it, no less, when he phoned me up to tell

me that the tour was probably off, then airily
offered the Tanners a guided walk around the
church crypt instead (which – for the record –
he hasn't bothered asking Reverend Paul
permission for, either!).
Ned Tanner has yet to get back to me on the
matter.

LOT 9

Promise made: Rhona Brooks of Threadbare Cottage promised
to put her extensive horticultural skills to work
by offering a basic, Winter Garden Overhaul to
any resident of BC who felt their garden might
currently be in need of one.

Purchased by: The Jonty Weiss-Quinns at Saxonby Manor
(yes, they *did* have a busy night, Prue. Sorry?
What's that strange and powerful *aroma*, you
wonder? Could it be the pungent stench of
Noblesse Oblige, perhaps? Or did someone just
tread in a fresh cowpat?).

Amount paid: £25

Upshot: *God*. As soon as I even start to *think* about this
situation, Prue, my blood literally begins to boil.
I suppose this is because in the short time I
have been living in Burley Cross I have
developed a powerful admiration for the senior
Ms Brooks, who strikes me as a fair and
reasonable sort of female (not unlike yourself).
Admittedly there's always that gruff exterior to
contend with (she can be a fearful old battle-
axe), but underneath it – I'm convinced – beats

the kindest and most Christian of hearts. It is
this very Christian heart of hers, I fear, that has
allowed the superficially brusque and irascible
Ms Brooks to fall prey to a false sense of
'obligation' to the Weiss-Quinns (which I feel
sure is having a seriously deleterious effect on
her physical and psychological well-being).
When Ms Brooks promised a Winter Garden
Overhaul at the auction, she surely can't have
had any inkling that the garden she would soon
feel duty-bound to 'overhaul' would be one of
over seven and a half acres (possessing 230-odd
foot of yew hedges in desperate need of 'work').
And all this for the princely sum of £25! While
I don't doubt that Ms Brooks's constitution is
relatively robust, she is hardly in the first flush
of youth, and I have almost lost count of the
number of times that I have chanced to see her
in the Manor's grounds (on my daily
perambulations with darling Chloe), perched
precariously atop a ladder, brandishing some
shears, or trundling home through the village
after dark, plainly exhausted, pushing her
squeaking wheelbarrow full of tools. I have tried
to talk to her about it, but she simply brushes
me off. 'I like to think I'm as good as my word,
Mr St John,' is all she'll volunteer on the issue.
I've also had several '*tête-à-têtes*' with the Weiss-
Quinns, but they treat my interference with the
standard combination of fastidious hauteur and
lofty amusement. 'Oh, but Rhoda just *loves* to
potter around the grounds all day,' they say, or
– worse still – 'We're sure she'd be *dreadfully*
offended if we asked her to stop before she's
completed the job.'

For the record: their old, full-time gardener, George
Swinbourne, retired in June, after fifty years'
service, without a proper send-off. And they
still haven't forked up the £25 yet.

LOT 10

Promise made: Mrs Tirza Parry (widow) at Hursley End,
Lamb's Green, promised a piece of her
handmade jewellery to be 'created, to order'.

Purchased by: Mr Conan Hopkiss Jnr, 111 Wellington Drive,
Denver, Colorado.

Amount paid: £2,175

Upshot: Yes, Prue, I know. Utterly, utterly bizarre. But
then it gets still stranger!
All of the promises for the auction were listed
(by yourself) on the BC Village website for ten
or so days before the auction took place ('to
give people a general idea of the kinds of things
that were up for grabs').
Towards the end of this ten-day period (just
after you left), an email was received, from
America, offering £2,175 for Lot 10, sight
unseen! Well, initially I thought there must have
been some kind of a mistake (I swear I thought
she made those awful monstrosities out of Play-
Doh!), or that this was simply a cruel prank. So
I got back to Mr Hopkiss Jr myself (online) and
it transpired that he was a 'keen collector' of
Mrs Parry's work and extremely determined
that the new 'piece' should be his! I didn't
mention this extraordinary communication to

anyone, thinking it would be more exciting to announce the bid on the night in front of a live audience. This was a mistake on my part – a big mistake. I made the announcement – to audible gasps (and the odd snigger, naturally) – then was astonished when Mrs Parry stood up on hearing the bidder's name (and seeing his cheque, which he had already sent, sure in the knowledge that his bid wouldn't be bettered), declaring that Mr Hopkiss Jr was 'a pest', and that it was 'inconceivable' that she should make a piece of work for him. She then turned to the assembled mass and asked, 'Isn't anybody going to make me a better offer?' *Silence.* '*For a Tirza Parry original?*' she exclaimed (as though perfectly astonished by their reticence). I tried to move things along (as auctioneer) by suggesting to Mrs Parry that we might 'discuss the issue afterwards'. This we did. Mrs Parry remained adamant. It seems that Mr Conan Hopkiss Jnr has been collecting Mrs Parry's work for several years, and that his appetite for it is so great that he has effectively 'hoovered it all up' from the market – something Mrs Parry seemed to find deeply objectionable. In fact she repeated this phrase – 'hoovered it all up!' – with expansive gestures several times in her odd, Bulgarian accent, while stamping her white, cowboy-booted foot (I must confess that I find the woman absolutely terrifying). I asked her if she would just 'think about it' for a few days, and reminded her that the auction was 'for charity, after all'. Her immediate response was to tell me to 'drop dead' and then to storm out of the hall! She has refused to speak to me ever since. *Twice*, she has slammed her door in my face! After the auction I had taken the precaution of giving the cheque to Wincey (our lovely Treasurer) for safekeeping, but as my confidence in bringing Mrs Parry around began to falter I asked for it back (intent on returning it). Wincey then confessed that she had already *banked* the damn thing, naively believing that Mrs Parry would 'inevitably feel morally obliged to fulfil her promise'. I have consequently put Reverend Paul on the case (although I don't hold out much hope – I believe Mrs Parry is a passionate atheist). He has promised to visit Mrs Parry this very evening, so I just hope and pray some good will come out of his intervention.

LOT 11

Promise made: Tammy Thorndyke (at The Old Hall), promised a beginner's course of five private Kundalini Yoga lessons (a type of yoga at which she apparently excels).

Purchased by: Shoshana Baverstock (at The Retreat) was delighted to buy them.

Amount paid: £23

Upshot: I couldn't really see how this transaction might go awry, Prue (more fool me!). But after only two sessions I had Tammy Thorndyke banging on my door, in floods of tears, late at night (well, some time after nine, at any rate), begging me to think of some way – *any* way – to get her out of the promise (she even said she would refund Shoshana's money and contribute a further £23 to the charity herself to make up for the loss). And the *reason* for this sudden reticence on Tammy's part? Shoshana's eczema! Tammy had developed a sudden, extreme horror of it! Apparently Shoshana insisted on doing the sessions in just a bra top and g-string (she would've done them *nude* given half a chance) and Tammy had become increasingly obsessed by the idea that Shoshana was 'shedding skin' on her shagpile carpet ('I've tried vacuuming,' she said, 'but it just doesn't feel like it's nearly *enough* ...'). I explained to Tammy that eczema wasn't remotely contagious (and Shoshana's eczema's hardly that bad, anyhow. I've seen her almost naked myself on countless occasions – who hasn't? – and there's just the odd rough patch behind her knees and inside her elbows; hardly anything to write home about), but Tammy wouldn't be convinced. She said the thought of Shoshana's dead skin becoming 'embedded in my shagpile' was making her 'physically ill' (she *did* have quite a deathly pallor). 'But how on earth are we to get out of this promise without severely hurting Shoshana's feelings?' I asked. Tammy didn't have a clue. After some lengthy consideration, I decided that it might be a good idea if I approached Shoshana personally, telling her that I had heard 'really great things' about the health benefits of Kundalini Yoga on a recent repeat of an old episode of *Oprah*, and that I was 'desperate' to try it out for myself, so would she mind terribly if I offered a

contribution to the AOP Charity Fund and
joined the classes? Oh, and then if – on that
basis – we could *move the location* of the classes
from The Old Hall to Tiddlers? (I told
Shoshana that this was because I had bad
circulation and The Old Hall would be 'way
too draughty' for me to withstand in my
Lycra.) Shoshana promptly responded by
telling me that 'Kundalini Yoga is a huge waste
of time', and that Tammy 'doesn't have the
first idea how to teach it'. She said she was
desperate to get out of the sessions but hated
the idea of hurting Tammy's feelings. So there
I was, Prue, stuck between a rock and a hard
place. I therefore *persisted* with my scheme (in
the hope of sparing the feelings of both
parties), and the next session was duly held in
my cramped study at Tiddlers (Friday last):
me, resplendent in my yellow striped cycling
shorts and cap-sleeved tee struggling to grapple
with the many intricacies of the Downward
Dog as a small cassette recorder piped out the
tinny sounds of trickling water and harp (not
an easy union, Prue, believe me). Shoshana
made *yet another* trip to the bathroom and
Tammy finished a short lecture on The
Importance of The Perineum, relit the
strawberry incense, declared feelingly, 'Without
fresh air, even the finest fire dies,' or 'No one
can love you, unless *you* love you,' (I forget
which), lay down on her back and commenced
a frenzied interlude of Pelvic Bouncing (as I
gently averted my tormented eyes). One down,
Prue, two to go … May the Sweet Lord have
Mercy on my Soul.

LOT 12

Promise made: Arthur Wolf of Buck House, Old Woman's
Lane, promised to guide anyone 'fit, bold or
daft enough' on a hike up Raven's Peak on Kex
Gill (included in this 'package' was a short,
preparatory climbing lesson at Harehead Quarry).

Purchased by: Penelope McNeilly of Hawksleigh House, 5
Shortcroft Road, for her niece and nephew
(Astrid and Ethan Logan), who are currently
resident in BC while their parents are away in
London.

Amount paid: £45

Upshot: The hike took place a couple of weeks back and
was proceeding extremely well (by all accounts)
until Mr Wolf chanced to see a Red Setter
darting behind some scree at the base of the
peak and hared off in hot pursuit of it, leaving
the two young ones stranded for over an hour
(believe it or not). Arthur had determined that
this Setter was the same poor, mad creature that
had escaped from a car outside the public toilets
and had caused chaos at Saint's Kennels on
Guy Fawkes Night. He claimed that he would
'recognize the dog anywhere', since it came
from the same litter as his late, much beloved
Nell. During his extended absence (according to
Astrid – a lovely girl. Shy. Modest.
Extraordinarily *thin*) a sudden, moorland mist
came down, then the heavens opened up and
the two children were left without rainwear (or
refreshment) because Arthur was carrying the

rucksack. Ethan has a severe hearing disorder (as you probably know) and is not to get water in his ears *at any cost*. Both young people were getting drenched and so Astrid made an executive decision to guide her brother home under her own steam (although they later turned up in Hazlewood or Middleton or somewhere equally improbable!). By the time Arthur returned (*sans* dog) they were nowhere to be seen (obviously). The two of them finally made contact with the McNeillys over five hours later (having borrowed a stranger's phone to do so). A moorland search and rescue operation was already well under way. The whole thing was, all in all, an absolute bloody catastrophe. Arthur Wolf (for his part) swears that he didn't leave the kids unattended for more than five minutes, tops, and that during this interlude the weather remained dry – if cloudy. Of course he has *insisted* on paying the £45 to the charity out of his own pocket, in a pathetic attempt to redeem himself, but I think it's going to take a little more than *that* to rebuild the shattered tatters of his reputation, quite frankly.

LOT 13

Promise made: BC's own celebrity folk singer and storyteller: the legendary 'Little Wren with the Big Whistle' aka Frank K. Nebraska (as he now prefers to be called) of the beautiful Solstice (formerly Rombald House), Piper's Ghyll Road, promised an original song to be composed in honour of the purchaser, or an individual of the purchaser's choice.

Purchased by: Trevor Ruddle at the *Wharfedale Gazette*.

Amount paid: £475

Upshot: Oh-ho, I'm saving the best till last, here, Prue.
Trevor Ruddle bought the promise with the
intention of using it as the main prize in a raffle
at his newspaper, the *Wharfedale Gazette* (while
doing a large article on The Little Wren and his
recent move to the local area to generate reader
interest). He paid a generous amount for it and
we were obviously all absolutely delighted at the
BCAOPC for the extra publicity this generated
for us. The only spanner in the works, I
suppose, was that the promise was *actually*
made by Frank K.'s wife, Kizzy Nebraska, not
Frank K. himself (who was off on a
promotional tour of Japan at the time).
When Frank K. returned and found out about
Kizzy's promise, the famously modest and
'down-to-earth' star was apparently none too
pleased because he is (I quote), 'an artist, not a
performing f*****g monkey, in case you hadn't
noticed'. An added layer of complexity was
brought to bear on the whole scenario by dint
of the fact that the subsequent winner of the
raffle was a charming Sri Lankan gentleman
called Murali Arulpragasam, a successful
businessman (and huge Little Wren fan) who
lives just outside Draughton and imports/
exports special padded underwear for a living
(from his native land, which he sells all over
Europe, the US and Canada). The chief
function of these undergarments is purportedly
to help counter the problems of excessive

flatulence. The Little Wren, who was already somewhat put out by the thought of composing a song to order, was then 'dumbstruck' when he found out the name he was to be expected to grapple with (especially as he is currently hard at work on *both* a new album *and* his long-awaited autobiography, which – unlike most modern-day celebrities – he is actually writing himself!).

Mr Arulpragasam has been quite amenable about the whole situation and said that he is 'perfectly happy' to reach some kind of a compromise with The Little Wren if The Little Wren finds his name too much of a proposition to conjure with/scan in a song. He has suggested, as an alternative, that The Little Wren writes something 'loosely based on the issues of flatulence' which he can then use as a ringtone on his mobile phone and as background music on his website DraughtonFlatulence.com. The Little Wren has not, as yet, responded to this idea, but I know for a fact that Trevor Ruddle is champing at the bit to run an article in the *Gazette* on the whole farrago. I literally shudder at the thought of the kind of cheesy pun he might come up with as a headline for the blasted piece.

SUMMARY

After a brief confab with Wincey, it seems that the BCAOP has raised a grand total of £3,101, but is presently in receipt of just £2,838 of that, £2,175 of which we are liable to have to return. This means our *real* running total is £663, on the

---

understanding that The Little Wren can manage to come out of his artistic funk. If not, then it's £188, minus Baxter's cleaning bill of £38 and the cost of the party food, hire of the hall, balloons, etc.

On this (somewhat pessimistic) basis I'm reckoning it at approximately £107.00, all told.

Oh … And let's just pray that our dear Mr Conan Hopkiss Jr isn't of an overly vindictive or litigious bent, eh?

Happy Christmas, Prue.
Please come home soon and save me from this living hell …
Yours, resplendent in Lycra,
Seb

[letter 17]

The Rectory
St Peter's Church
Burley Cross

20th December, 2006

Dear Reverend Horwood,
(Further to our unfortunate little 'contretemps' on Sunday ...)

It's not that I didn't like the carving, as such – I think it's a
marvellous piece of craftsmanship, I honestly do – it's just that I
wished you'd consulted with me before hanging it up so
prominently in the church portal. It really did give me quite a
shock when I walked in, slightly behind time (you were right, I
was one or two minutes late), my mind running over the Order
of Service, making the odd minor mental adjustment to my
sermon (as one does), and then happened across it, totally
unprepared.

It blindsided me, Reverend (there's no point in pretending
otherwise). It gave me quite a turn. It threw me out of kilter.

The way I see it, the entrance to a place of worship plays an
important part in establishing the atmosphere of the entire
institution (it 'sets the scene', so to speak). As I think I said on
Sunday – although perhaps not as calmly (or as articulately!) as
I would have liked – St Peter's is an Anglican church, and
therefore it doesn't feel entirely appropriate to hang a crucifix
in such a prominent position, especially such a ... well, a
'powerful' and 'confronting' one as that!

When I accused you of hanging it up 'simply to provoke me',
what I really meant to say was that I am perfectly well aware
of the fact that you think my general theological stance borders
on the 'High Church' (and that this isn't something you
particularly welcome in my approach to the ministry), but
I certainly didn't mean to imply that you were trying to

undermine my work here at St Peter's in any way (not at *all*, Reverend – perish the very thought!).

I deeply regret it if your feelings were hurt by my speaking out so candidly on the matter, especially in front of Mr Simms, Miss Logan, Mrs Bramwell, Ms Brooks and Mrs Hawkes. Such an outburst is entirely uncharacteristic of me and I have felt profoundly troubled by it ever since.

It goes without saying that I have thought and prayed about this matter a great deal over the past week, and the only conclusion I can honestly reach is that the argument between us cast more light on *my* weaknesses and insecurities than on anything else. These are qualities in myself that I certainly need to work upon, and I shall (God willing – with His grace).

On a more positive note: in some ways I'm actually quite *relieved* that the sharp exchange of words we had on Sunday brought a few things out into the open that might reasonably be said to have been 'festering away between us' all these long months …

a) The Candles:

I am sorry that you don't like the candles. I can see why they might irritate you. I don't accept that they pose a fire risk, but I do concede that they alter the atmosphere of the church, overall. I don't think they are unduly 'Popish', Reverend – in fact I have had several very positive comments about them. Many parishioners seem to find a certain measure of comfort in lighting them and then using them as a direct means of focusing their thoughts and energies on a worrying problem, a sick friend, or a recently departed soul.

I have also been told that when worshippers enter the church to pray and find it unoccupied, the cheerful sight of the bank of flickering candles gives them a sense of community, a feeling that they are part of an ongoing series of conversations with the Almighty and a general, overall impression that their voice (and their predicament, more to the point) isn't a lone one.

Last – but by no mean least – the financial contribution the candles make (I pay just under 8p/candle and ask for a contribution of 20p/candle from the parishioners) *does* add significantly to St Peter's modest charitable armoury. Half of the money raised this year I am intending to donate to The Red Crescent, and to put the other half towards a mobile (i.e. with wheels), free-standing notice board, which I hope to use to promote local and international voluntary organizations and good causes.

b) My Cassocks:

As for my 'ridiculous robes', Reverend Horwood … Well, I suppose they *might* seem a touch theatrical to someone who prefers to think a sensible clergyman should always stick to the traditional black! Ultimately, I suppose, it is just a matter of personal taste. If I *do* look like a 'big, gallumphing fairy' in them then it's useful for me to be aware of it, and to alter my behaviour accordingly (perhaps I should sign up for Jill Harpington's tap and ballet classes at the village hall, and improve my deportment skills alongside the local six- and seven-year-olds! I might even try and galvanize some of the ballet mums into signing their little ones up for the new Sunday School while I'm at it!)!

c) The Flowers:

I do think the point you made about flowers in the church had a great deal of validity to it. I'm ashamed to confess that I hadn't seriously considered the possibility that some members of the parish might be allergic to them – the lilies especially. Gillian Reed is actually responsible for the majority of the displays. I think she has a real knack for arranging – a genius, even. She has spent a great deal of time and energy over recent months conducting a series of truly fascinating researches into the 'language of flowers', a medieval concept (the lily, for example, represents the Blessed Virgin!) and likes to

---

experiment with these wonderful ancient symbols and ideas in her arrangements.

Of course to someone like yourself, who doesn't welcome the sight of flowers indoors and finds them, at best, frivolous (even at funerals!) and, at worst, toxic, they might indeed make the church resemble 'the inside of some trendy, Chelsea fashion boutique and not a sober place of worship'.

I will certainly consult with Gill on the issue and see if we can integrate some more seasonal, less sumptuous flowers into the mix (more holly and ivy and dried flowers, perhaps). I'm sure she will be delighted to do this and that these restrictions will bring out a still greater creativity in her.

d) Music:

After what you said about my 'sidelining' Drew Cullen, I thought it best to go to him directly and have a private word with him on the matter. We spoke frankly and openly about many subjects relating to the church, the church organ, to music in general and its wider role (as I perceive it) in the liturgy.

Drew kindly confided in me that he had been finding it quite a strain to keep up with his commitments at St Peter's over the past year or so, and that he actually welcomed Shoshana's recent involvement, her fresh approach and her extended repertoire (not to mention her first-class fund-raising skills!).

The issue of music is probably one that you and I will never find true accord on, Reverend Horwood. While to you it is simply a bane (an awful, jarring cacophony!), to me it is an untrammelled joy (a true balm to the troubled soul!). When all is said and done, I suppose this is just something we're going to have to continue to agree to disagree about.

As a matter of idle interest, Reverend, just before I sat down to write this letter I chanced to look at my diary and saw that it was almost exactly ten months – to the very day – since I took my first faltering steps in this glorious parish of ours.

For a second I was perfectly astonished – the time seems to have passed so quickly! There's still so much I need to do! And then, with the benefit of some sober reflection, I realized how much had been achieved since I first arrived here.

It is also (and I hardly need tell *you* this!) almost ten months, to the day, since you formally retired. From my few snatched conversations with you (and my chats with your former parishioners – especially that redoubtable group of acolytes I like to call 'Reverend Horwood's Ladies'!) I knew that this was not a change in your life and circumstances that you felt entirely at ease with. I don't doubt that this transition (or 'evolution' as I prefer to think of it) has been rendered somewhat less precipitous (and hopefully less traumatic) by your unexpected decision to remain living in the diocese and to continue to engage with – and preach at – St Peter's whenever the opportunity arises.

I won't pretend that I wasn't initially rather taken aback by this decision of yours (which, in most parishes, would be considered a serious breach of Church etiquette!), but with the benefit of time and experience I have been able to realize how wrong (worse still, how arrogant) my misgivings (and my silly prejudices) were.

I have had plenty to learn about this small but dynamic new parish over the last ten months, and what better a person to teach me than someone who knows it like the back of his own hand?

Of course we approach things very differently, Reverend. We come from very different places – emotionally, theologically, socially, culturally – so it was almost inevitable that some feathers would be ruffled (on *both* sides) along the way.

I'm sure I thought – on the odd occasion – that you were far too uncompromising, old-fashioned and stuck in your ways. I'm sure you – in your turn – thought I was way too much of an 'eager beaver', too gung-ho, too touchy-feely, too liberal, too ingratiating, too intent on changing things for change's sake

(I believe 'Princess Pushy' was my nickname for the first six months or so!!). I don't for a moment doubt that there was some measure of validity to these harsh assessments of ours on *either* side.

But we live and we learn, Reverend (I thank God for that fact every day!). We sin, we err, we repent, and then we do our humble best to set things right.

We practise patience, fortitude and humility. We strive to 'enter through the narrow gate' as our dear, Sweet Lord prescribed, 'for wide is the gate and broad is the road that leads to destruction, and many enter through it' (sorry for quoting from the New International Version which I know you loathe, but I think you get my point!).

I hope it goes without saying that I have taken the time out to apologize, individually, to Mr Simms, Miss Logan, Mrs Bramwell, Ms Brooks and Mrs Hawkes for my terrible breach of last Sunday. Mrs Hawkes was exceptionally Christian about it (and this was all the more surprising since I hadn't so much as seen BC's charming publican anywhere near the church since I first arrived here; let's just hope her vision of the ministry hasn't been irreparably skewed by my appalling behaviour!).

Wincey was actually kind enough to help me to remove the bloodstains from my cassock (it was a new one! And it *had* to be the white one, didn't it?! Perhaps there *are* some virtues to the black ones after all!) with a hefty application of Cillit Bang (she's a dab hand in these matters, it seems, since she hand washes fourteen white tablecloths from the new dining rooms at The Old Oak each and every day of the week!).

Thankfully the nosebleeds have abated slightly as time has progressed. I went to the doctor (Dr Hardcastle, who was very good with me; I'm an awful patient – a shameful hypochondriac!) and he said he thought they were chiefly stress-related and really nothing to worry about (he gave me some tablets for my blood pressure and recommended yoga!

I should probably have a quick word with Tammy Thorndyke on the subject although … well, on second thoughts …!).

I was extremely grateful (not to say relieved) that my grovelling apologies were welcomed – and with demonstrations of great kindness, for the most part – from all those who were unwitting spectators to Sunday's awful *fracas*. In fact I could even go so far as to say that, in some instances, my horrible childish outburst has led to a slight (and completely unexpected!) 'thawing' in relations with certain parties (although I still don't have the foggiest idea why!).

One of your most loyal supporters, Rhona Brooks, has left three beautiful little packages on my doorstep this week: some wonderful leeks, some delicious duck eggs, and even an exquisitely painted milk jug (by the hand of her sister, Tilly, I presume) decorated with a perfect, tiny posy of hellebores (my favourite wild flower)!

So bolstered and enthused was I by these kind and benevolent gestures that I finally took my heart in my hands and went to see the enigmatic and taciturn 'Edo' at Bleachers, who (much to my great surprise) welcomed me into his home most cordially.

I explained to him that I thought his crucifix was extraordinary, but not, perhaps, entirely suitable for the front portal of the church. I then begged that I might be allowed to hang it in the vestry. He seemed touched and delighted by the idea and actually came along to the church on Thursday to take a quiet peek at it, *in situ*. We had a wonderful talk about a wide range of subjects. He's a complex and fascinating man – a tortured soul, a true artist – and I feel like I've learned so much from him already in just our two short meetings.

I don't know if he will become a regular member of the congregation (although I live in hope!), but I certainly think an important connection has been forged there, and I want you to know that none of this could possibly have happened without your involvement.

———

It only remains for me to thank you for your forbearance, and to wish you every blessing and happiness over the Christmas period.

Yours, united in God, and truly penitent,

Paul

PS Lily Beer approached me – out of the blue – and asked if I might baptize her grandson, Fergus, after all! Obviously I was absolutely delighted to accept her request. I'm presuming that you were forced to cancel for some reason and that you gently nudged her in my direction. If this *is* the case, then thank you, once again, Reverend. I have done so little to earn your support this week, but that you should have continued to offer it, and so graciously, honestly means the world to me.

[letter 18]

Buckden House
Piper's Ghyll Road
Burley Cross

21/12/2006

Dear Ms Squire,

Since I'm a chronic technophobe, I deputized my husband, Robin – who's the complete opposite – to send you an email with a link to our website on it, but given that I haven't heard from you since our conversation two weeks ago (and just happened across your address on a piece of paper by the phone), I thought I should send you one of our promotional leaflets in the mail, to keep in Mr Booth's files, just in case.

As I believe I said when we last spoke, Buckden House really is widely held to be one of the premium B&Bs in the Wharfedale area. We are situated at the prestigious 'top end' of this ancient and picturesque moorland village, on the legendary Piper's Ghyll, one of Burley Cross's most leafy and magnificent roads. All our rooms (or 'suites' – of which there are eight, in total) are quiet and nicely proportioned, with their own bathrooms (containing either a shower, or a deep, free-standing bath with shower fitments) and boast spectacular views of the surrounding moor.

I would envisage Mr Booth taking the Dragon Tree Suite (our equivalent of a 'penthouse'; it has a subtle, Mandarin theme, i.e. oriental silk bed wear and throws, shiny black skirting, gold fitments, Chinese wall hangings and screens) and possibly you in the Juneberry Suite (gentle lime-green walls, acres of crisp white calico, wooden floors, thick sheepskin rugs), just a short distance down the hall.

Obviously Mr Booth's needs are *very* specific, and you will know best what will suit him …

Although I didn't write down the date when we talked (and I'm kicking myself for it, now), I've had a nagging feeling that you said you were planning to come for your quick recce to Wharfedale today (the 21st). Given that I haven't seen you, I'm presuming that either you didn't make it to Burley Cross after all, or that you've happened across somewhere you think Mr Booth will prefer in Ilkley itself (although the noise will be a factor there, I can assure you, especially at the weekend. And if you're seduced by the apparent grandeur of The Railway Hotel – and it *does* look grand on paper – be assured that the central heating groans like a wounded heifer, every night, without fail, from 3 a.m. onwards).

Did I see a small advert in the latest edition of the *Wharfedale Gazette* saying Mr Booth would be 'appearing' upstairs at the Middleton Theatre on the nights of the 6th and 7th of January 2007? I think I possibly did. Well, I quickly checked our diary, and both Dragon Tree (which is at the top of the house – *very* private) and Juneberry are currently free for those nights (although Juneberry is booked for the 3rd, 4th and 5th by a regular couple who come every year, Mandarin on the 2nd and 3rd for some German honeymooners, then again on the 9th for local celebrity Frank K. Nebraska's mother-in-law – a lovely American lady, *extremely* cultured and affable, who always stays with us when she's in the UK visiting her daughter, Kizzy).

Obviously breakfast is usually served between the hours of 7 and 9 a.m., but in the case of Mr Booth (and yourself) I would be willing to extend that time-frame until 10 (you said he would be 'drained' by the performance, although I remember you didn't like to call it a 'performance'. I can't exactly recollect the word you preferred to use instead; it began with an e, I think. Was it 'evocation'? No. It was something else. Something slightly more abstruse …

That's it! I just asked Robin, who was wandering past in a terrible bate because a guest has cheekily purloined the crossword section from his *Sunday Times*: the *amanuensis*!

Starts with an a! Silly me! Kind of like a secretary taking down notes from dictation, Robin said.)

After seeing the advert in the *Gazette* (will they be doing an interview with Mr Booth? Photographs? If so, I'm very happy to free up my spacious back conservatory for the press. It's huge; Victorian; iron and glass, extremely beautiful and ornate, wonderfully 'atmospheric', full of fruit trees and a plethora of exotic palms) I idly mentioned my fascinating conversation with you to Wincey Hawkes at The Old Oak.

Robin and I had popped in there for a quick drink on Tuesday (bridge night, although the saloon bar where we usually prefer to sit is still presently closed after a small 'contretemps' with a local biker gang brought on by an abandoned darts tournament!), and she said you'd spoken to her, too (a couple of days after our conversation, I believe). Obviously we're all rather excited about the idea of having a famous psychic staying in the village (or 'a practitioner of the Esoteric Sciences', as I believe Mr Booth prefers to be known!).

Wincey runs a tight ship at The Old Oak, but I think it only fair to warn you that since the death of her late husband (Marmaduke Hawkes – or 'Duke' as we all knew him), she's been struggling somewhat to keep her head above water there.

Duke (I know, curious name for a Yorkshireman, but apparently it was common in these parts in the eighteenth century, and it'd been handed down through the male line of his family for years. Robin says – he's just wandered back past again, still searching! – it comes from Maelmaedoc or 'servant of St Maedoc' who was a famous Irish 'religious' at that time) had instituted a number of improvements to the pub (extending the car park, a new kitchen, a new 'dining room' – which isn't nearly so grand as it sounds!) and was then struck down by a throat cancer halfway through the process.

Duke was an enormous character, born and bred in Burley Cross. Fascinating life. Bit of an action adventure hero, really. He worked for years as a bare-knuckle fighter, then joined the

Foreign Legion, went AWOL, returned to the UK, became a nightclub bouncer, which is where he met Wincey, at a place in Newcastle, where she was employed as a hostess (all completely above board, mind! This *was* the 1970s!).

Duke was a big man, a real bruiser. Bald as a brush. Huge, red cheeks. Roaring voice. Curiously light on his feet. Did an amazing 'sand dance' once he'd had a few. Liked to play a portable harmonium, with his fists, sitting perched on the counter of the saloon bar (to see him hunched over that tiny instrument, pumping away like a maniac, sweat pouring down his face, was truly a sight to conjure with! And he didn't *sound* too bad, either, come to that!).

Becoming landlord of The Old Oak was apparently the fulfilment of a childhood dream for Duke whose parents both died young (and virtually destitute). He and Wincey (who's from Portmeirion, originally) were like a breath of fresh air when they first arrived here (oh, about ten or eleven years ago, now). They took Burley Cross by the scruff of the neck and really shook it up (not that it particularly *needed* shaking – but there you go!).

Wincey – true to type – has bravely battled on since Duke's death, but I'm not sure if her heart's still in it. And she's managed to become embroiled in a series of fairly rancorous disputes with a cross-section of local pressure groups (her decision to begin accepting coach parties at the pub – which used to be simply a cosy local – has caused a certain amount of ill feeling among some indigens). Not only that, but just at the point when she was starting to shake off her grief and move on – about eighteen months ago – the pub was burgled (completely turned upside down: obscene graffiti, paint trodden into all the new carpets, smashed up half the stock; they even defecated in the kitchen sinks!). I think this was the point at which her confidence took its most serious knock.

As I already said, though, Wincey runs a tight ship (a ghost ship, but a tight ship!), and I'm sure Mr Booth could do worse than to stay there.

I haven't spoken to Ruth Hitchens at Lumsden's (Burley Cross's other so-called 'quality' B&B). Ruth is rather a perplexing character. I think she could fairly be described as 'a bit of a shrew'. Her husband, Wyn, on the other hand, is perfectly wonderful. Very quiet. Fastidiously clean (which is always a bonus in a man!).

Unfortunately he and Ruth have been involved in a complicated legal dispute over Lumsden's for about four or five years now. They've divided the property in half and still run it in tandem, but they never speak. When they *do* communicate, it's only by hand signals and curt notes.

If you did speak to Ruth and she 'idly' happened to mention the animal crematorium at the bottom of our garden (trust me, this wouldn't be the first time!), let me assure you that she was only 'stirring the pot'. The crematorium is in fact just a small, ancient kiln which Robin – employing his entrepreneurial nous – put to use cremating pets when we first moved into Buckden House about twelve-odd years ago. The business never really took off, though, and we generally only use it now for 'special requests' on Thursday and Friday afternoons.

For the record, we've never run a cat sanctuary here, either. I kept Cornish Rex cats for many years, as did my sister, and my mother. When my sister moved to a flat in Plymouth and my mother passed away, I took on their animals. We had about seven at one point (and three on loan from the vets), but four of those have recently died, and the ones remaining are extremely sedate, far too old to manage the stairs, and chiefly inhabit the basement area.

Robin is actually an inventor, by trade. I don't doubt that he and Mr Booth would have plenty to talk about. Is Mr Booth into keep fit at all (Robin's a keen fell runner)? If he is, he will probably be intrigued by the prototype of a pair of shoes Robin has designed which he developed after hearing about a remote Native American tribe whose men run barefoot through mountains, apparently without sustaining any damage to their soles.

The secret to their apparent indomitability (and Robin can explain this so much better than me) is the tiny, almost mincing steps they take. It's a new way of running which completely eradicates a whole number of sports injuries!

Anyway, as a consequence of his researches into these fascinating peoples, Robin has invented a 'training shoe' which is effectively just a thin layer of transparent, blue-tinged jelly. The jelly is very durable. So powerful and innovative is his design that several of the large trainer companies have expressed an interest in it.

Robin was 'burned' once before at the hands of a large corporation, however, and is very suspicious about going into business with people of this ilk. The design has gained an almost 'mythical' status amongst the world's running elite (since it undermines the fundamental logic of all those 'air support' shoes), and this has led to a series of threats (by any other name!) being made by these huge corporations against Robin's reputation and his person.

When I say Robin was 'burned' once before, what I mean is that an earlier invention of his – 'The Key Maker' – engendered a huge commotion among international car manufacturers. The Key Maker is a small, portable device – a kind of laser, of sorts – which you (i.e. Joe/Josephine Bloggs) can use to gain access to any kind of lock. You simply point The Key Maker into the keyhole and it produces an instant 3D 'picture' of the missing key. You then take this 'picture' home, plug it into a small box (the size of a breadmaker) and it produces a replacement key, on demand (well, the entire process takes about half an hour, at best).

The car people (and the big insurance companies) were apparently so alarmed by this invention that they put pressure on the British government to gag the manufacture of this device. Not only did Robin have British intelligence on his tail, but members of a series of dangerous gangland fraternities, who were keen to get their hands on The Key Maker to fulfil their own questionable agendas.

Eventually Robin and I were forced into hiding (which meant I was obliged to abandon my promising career as a woman pilot). We destroyed all evidence of the prototype, and came up here, to Burley Cross, where we opened a bed and breakfast.

This move was entirely funded by the sale of another of Robin's inventions: 'The Cat Pill Remedy', which is a remarkable aid to the 'concerned' cat owner in feeding prescription medication to fussy felines (and we've had a few of these ourselves, over the years!). I won't bore you with all the details, but the device effectively transforms the prescription medication (whatever its original constitution) into a curious gel (gels really are Robin's speciality) which can be applied to any part of the cat's body (apart from the head, obviously!), and the cat will lick it off, immediately.

We have never understood why this invention has never gone into formal production. From what Robin can glean on the internet, the company went into liquidation shortly after it purchased the design but has still fiercely maintained its ownership of the copyright.

Given that Mr Booth is fascinated by 'the mind', I imagine that he might be interested in Robin's wonderful stress-busting device, aka 'The Heart Beat', which is a small, iPod-style object (tiny, hand-held screen, earphones etc., *very* portable) which completely alleviates panic attacks by reproducing a slow heartbeat (aurally, and as a palpable vibration), combined with a special visual graphic pattern which (and I won't go into all the science, but it's truly fascinating) automatically bypasses the conscious mind and instructs the unconscious mind to calm down. It can even put those who are especially susceptible into an involuntary trance!

It works within twenty seconds, without fail. The people at NASA have been on the phone twice this week, already. Google (a 'web engine') are apparently 'champing at the bit' to get hold of it. Apple want to integrate the device into their top-of-the-range mobile phones. It's all *very* exciting!

Was Wincey only waxing lyrical when she mentioned that you'd said Mr Booth was actually the by-product of a secret tryst between a prominent individual from the Salvation Army dynasty and one of the legendary Trebors (who I believe invented Extra Strong Mints)? What an utterly intriguing heritage that is!

Robin's great-great-grandfather actually invented nail polish (although my heritage is singularly unspectacular, I'm afraid)!

As I said on the phone, we would certainly consider reduced rates for Mr Booth (and yourself) on the basis of a small mention in the tour programme …

Do get back to me if you have any other thoughts or queries. Wishing you all the happiness of this wonderful season,

Yours Faithfully,

Brenda Goff

PS Please forgive the awful spelling mistake in the second paragraph of the brochure. That should be 'can't'.
PPS The photograph of the entrance hall needs to be updated. It was actually fully retiled in November.

[letter 19]

1, The Old Cavalry Yard

21/12/2006

Hello there, Nina,

I know this must seem a bit strange – me writing you a letter, when you're sitting at the post office counter not fifty yards down the road from here – it's just that I've been in about five times to try and speak to you, in person, but each time I've reached the front of the queue my nerve has gone (and I've ended up buying stamps, or airmail letters, or asking stupid questions about my television licence – for the record, I do actually know you don't need a special licence to watch TV programmes on a computer).

And then there's always the people waiting in line behind me; gossip spreads like wildfire in this place. Everybody always has their nose stuck into everybody else's business. I didn't want you to feel awkward, basically, or to put you on the spot by asking if I could meet up with you, privately, after work – just for a quick drink at The Old Oak or something – in front of … well, Emily Tanner on Monday (which was bad), Jill Harpington on Wednesday (which was pretty bad – she's thick as thieves with my mother), then Bunny Seymour on Thursday with – drum roll – Sebastian St John directly behind her (classic combination! I might as well have broadcast our imminent exchange from a public Tannoy system!).

The point – if I can actually *get* to it – is that I really didn't want anyone to misconstrue my intentions for something they patently aren't (although, to be perfectly honest with you, Nina, I'm not entirely sure what they *are*, as it currently stands).

I actually tried bumping into you as you were leaving work on Friday, but you always seem to have somebody with you. I even went so far as to follow your car (in my car – this was about a week ago), in the hope of attracting your attention on the road and getting you to pull over (I'm cringing as I type this – it all sounds so pathetic. It is pathetic! I don't really know what I was thinking … I guess I *wasn't* thinking – not coherently. In fact I probably shouldn't have told you. You'll definitely think I'm a freak, now – if you didn't think it already. You'll think I'm *stalking* you or something.

I'm not stalking you, I promise. I'm just … I'm just making a monumental arse out of myself – same as always, I suppose).

Lucky for me (or unlucky for me – I'm not sure which), just as I was pulling out of town (trailing you, in my car, like a psycho) I got hauled over by one of Baxter Thorndyke's Road Safety Committee monkeys (it was my dad, actually) who gave me a massive, public dressing-down for speeding (I'd barely changed into second gear, but he insisted that I had already reached 50mph. Showed me the reading on his special meter).

This completely freaked me out. I was already feeling a little weird about the whole thing. I mean it isn't normal to follow someone home in your car just because you're too socially inadequate to speak to them in public, is it?
(*Is* it?)

In my own defence (and I don't deserve defending; what I'm obviously crying out for is a massive, involuntary dose of horse tranquillizer, followed by a few sharp clips about the head), I was beginning to feel kind of desperate. But when they pulled me over (*Dad* pulled me over, dressed in that ludicrous yellow poncho thing – like some nightmarish, Day-Glo, neo-Nazi – a tragic, mid-life crisis in jack-boots) I suddenly started thinking that perhaps I was behaving irrationally and that I should just leave you the hell alone. (Let sleeping dogs lie. Butt out. Grow a backbone. Stop humiliating myself. Get a hobby: paragliding. Archery. White water rafting. Squash. Needlepoint. Karate. *Anything*)

I'm well aware of the fact that you have an awful lot on your plate with Glenn at the moment. Is he still very depressed?

(Bollocks. Scratch that. '*Is he still very depressed*?!' What am I *thinking*?! Of *course* he's bloody depressed! He had both feet blown off in a roadside bomb in Iraq for Christ's sake! Why wouldn't he be bloody depressed?!)

What I mean to say (and I'm typing this very quickly to try and push through my pain/embarrassment threshold) is that I fully appreciate the fact that you're under a huge amount of pressure right now, and I really don't want to add to it. I would never forgive myself if I upset you or made you feel uncomfortable – that's the last thing in the world I want. Although as you're reading this you're probably just wishing I would sod off. You probably think I'm a pest – a moron. In fact I probably won't post this thing anyway – it's just a pile of self-obsessed waffle, the sad and deluded ramblings of a maladjusted, twenty-something half-wit.

Nope. I definitely won't post this thing. My nerve will go at the last minute – like it did all those other times in that stupid queue …

Glenn was 100 per cent spot-on: I *am* just a big, myopic dweeb. A turd-brain. A dunderhead.

Oh yes – and while I'm on the subject – I'm really, really sorry about the arm-wrestling thing. I felt terrible about it afterwards. I honestly didn't think I had a cat's chance in hell of beating him. His arms are massive (huge! Ridiculous! Like a giant pair of steel hawsers!), and I'm such a puny little bastard by comparison.

But he seemed so determined to go ahead with it – got so, well, aggressive about it. I seriously expected him to thrash me, hands down. But then, when he didn't, when his wrist started to buckle, I half thought about reducing the pressure on my side, just subtly (to try and give him a break, help him get his breath back. I dunno). But there was this strange look in his eye, Nina – a furious look – kind of like: I might be in this chair, I might've lost my legs, I might've lost my job, but I still have my self-respect, my dignity (you patronizing little dip-shit). So

I didn't. I mean I tried not to. I just … well. You were there. You saw what happened.

I'm getting way off the subject – the actual point of this letter, the reason for writing to you – which is that I basically just wanted to say – to tell you – to try and … Oh *balls*. How to put this without …?

It's just … I just wish … Okay. *Okay*. Here it is: I just wish you hadn't said that thing you said to me on the walk back to your car after the tour of Fylingdales the other week. That's all (nothing earth-shattering). It's been playing on my mind ever since (what you said). I'm not sure why, but it's really knocked me for six.

And I didn't know how the hell I was meant to react at the time. I must've looked like such a gormless fool! Or perhaps I just looked blank. Completely blank. Unresponsive. I was blank. I was in shock! And Glenn was just behind us (talking to the sergeant). I was worried he might overhear what you were saying. Not that there was anything wrong in it – not remotely. I mean I knew you were just joking when you said it – you weren't taking it too seriously or anything – you were just referring to something in the past, making light of something you felt a long time ago – aeons ago – when we were both still at school.

I'm not saying it was *wrong* of you to hit me with something like that (sorry, I seem to be repeating myself), please don't think that – not even for a minute – because it really was one of the most wonderful things anyone has ever said to me (*ever*). I shall go to my grave happy knowing that you said it. Knowing that you felt it.

(*Wow*. That looks so dodgy written down – beyond dodgy. It looks *hideous* …)

I suppose what I'm struggling to say, Nina (in my own clumsy, feeble-minded way), is that I simply didn't know what I was expected to *do* about it at the time. I didn't know how I was meant to respond. I was just dumbstruck. I felt so inadequate – completely out of my comfort zone. I nearly burst into tears (I can't believe I just wrote that. Oh, God. Just take me out and shoot me).

Because I swear I always thought my feelings for you were completely one-sided. I *do* have feelings for you – of course I do! – I mean I did, at school. But then you were the girl everybody had a crush on. I don't think there was a single boy at St Bart's who wasn't head over heels in love with you. You're so beautiful – so ridiculously beautiful. And kind. And sweet. And funny. And modest. And you always smell so lovely, like … like … (keep on typing, Nick) … like, I dunno, like a newly strung bale of fresh hay. (Fresh *hay*?!)

I mean why the hell wouldn't everybody be just crazy about you?
(A bale of fresh *hay*?!)

I actually only started dating Linda Prichard (please don't tell Linda this, whatever you do) in Year Five because she was your second best friend (cruel, I know, but I was a fifteen-year-old boy, and a total dildo). I thought if I dated Linda then you might actually notice me. I just wanted to be around you. I just wanted to get to know you.
(Well, I suppose it's got to be better than *soiled* hay …)

What a dick I was! I don't even know how you tolerated me (let alone harboured fond feelings for me, on the sly). I was so smug! So bumptious! So ludicrously opinionated! And I was criminally bad at sports. With that acne! That ridiculous haircut! The *hat*! The Jamiroquai obsession! Those awful, low-slung, shit-brown hessian-style trousers and the turquoise, llama-wool jumper with all the heavy stitching and the hood! God. No wonder you were always ripping the piss out of the way I looked! What was that nickname you coined for me? 'The Funky Swot'?!

You were so much more clued into things than I was – even then – so much more grown up, so much more hardcore. You were mad about the Prodigy way before anyone else had the first clue who they were.

Remember how I won those four tickets in a quiz on a local radio show to go and see them, live, in Leeds? And you were desperate to come along, but then your mum said no at the last minute – just as you were heading through the door – because there was no one left at home to babysit your sister?

I didn't win them, Nina – I *bought* them. I just pretended I won them to try and come up with a legitimate-seeming excuse to meet up with you after school. Then, when you couldn't go, I had to take Linda and Peter Hannon (your ex) and his idiot friend Spanky. Spanky got out of his head on cough syrup and spent most of the night spewing up (ruined my best trainers, the idiot!). Worse still, I then had to sit through a bloody *Prodigy* gig! Surrounded by Prodigy fans! It was a nightmare! Like having my ears drilled!

I wouldn't even mind, but the next day (and I was still leaking blood from all my main orifices, coincidentally) you secretly confided that the Prodigy thing was only really a pose (to impress some older boy you fancied on the school bus). You were actually obsessed by Peter Andre! So I threw away my glo-sticks and started working on my six-pack (okay, I didn't get very far with that …).

I was absolutely besotted by you, Nina. I thought it was completely obvious! I mean I tried to mask it with sarcasm, sometimes, but I thought you'd have to be stupid not to realize (not that you *were* stupid – you're very intelligent. Extremely intelligent).

The only inkling I ever had that you might find me even vaguely interesting (romantically) was at Jason Flight's seventeenth birthday party when some pissed-up jerk chucked cider over your top – the black, silky one with the silver squiggles on it – and I lent you my jumper to wear (I treasured that jumper for years afterwards. I never washed it. I actually still have it. I even took it over to America with me).

We went and sat in the garden and had that really odd (but funny) conversation about how much you hated Chris Evans.

Then you said you were 'starving' and I bet you a fiver you couldn't eat a whole banana in one mouthful. And you very nearly did it! But the minute you'd crammed the whole thing in and started to chew, you got wildly over-excited (sensing victory, I presume), set off your gag reflex and regurgitated half-chewed banana all over the kitchen tiles (much to the obvious delight of Jason's Jack Russell, Olly, who devoured the whole lot in thirty seconds flat!).

Then Linda turned up. She'd just started working Saturdays at that posh salon in Leeds and the stylist had cut her hair (for a competition or something) into this weird, space-age bob. We were both laughing at it behind her back all night (every time I caught your eye you'd collapse into hysterical giggles).

You'd just started dating Michael Watson, I think. He'd gone away skiing that week with his parents. When I thought about it afterwards I convinced myself that you were only being friendly because you were bored. I didn't let myself believe it was anything more – I'd already won the American scholarship at that stage. I left for Houston about a fortnight later. And that was the end of that.

I remember how you signed my leaving card with a cartoon of a frog holding a heart. I spent hours analysing what that damn frog might represent (I never worked it out!).

It was ridiculous that you thought I was 'too clever' for you back then. When you said that the other day I was dumbstruck (too clever?! Are you insane?! *Seriously*?!).

You're one of the brightest girls I've ever met. I always thought you could've done so much better (academically) with the right kind of input from your parents (you invariably solved those difficult physics problems in around about half the amount of time I took! I'd glance up from the textbook and you'd be gazing out of the window, bored, or filing your nails, or scribbling something in a black marker pen on to your school bag). Because you came from such a large family I think you missed out on some of the opportunities (and encouragement –

the extra tutoring and stuff) that I simply took for granted.

But that's all water under the bridge now, anyway. You're with Glenn. I'm with Yasmin.

(And Yasmin's great. She's a truly lovely girl. Very natural. Very uncomplicated. Very genuine. Speaks four languages: English, Arabic, French, some German, a smattering of Italian. A talented biochemist. A wonderful cook. Way too good for me, really.)

Glenn's a great guy, too. I mean he's a hero, a bona fide hero! He carries himself with such confidence, such swagger. His stories are amazing (terrifying!). Is there any corner of the globe he *hasn't* received a medal in?!

He's had so much life experience. Squadron leader at twenty-two (wasn't he saying that the other day)? Twenty-two's so incredibly young to be given such a huge amount of responsibility. I'd imagine it's pretty much unheard of in the military (quite remarkable, come to think of it).

I honestly – sincerely – couldn't be any happier for you, Nina.

Although, having said that, I *did* think he was a little tough on you during the tour the other week. I know he's in constant pain, and that he's still only just coming to terms with his injuries (how long's it been now? Eighteen months? That's hardly any time at all, really, is it?), but even so, I thought he was a little tough on you (sorry, I'm repeating myself, again).

And I don't like to nit-pick (that's not my style, as you know – I'm a fairly easy-going kind of character), but if I'm going to be completely frank with you, Nina, I wasn't entirely happy with the way he kept calling you 'a blonde' all the time. And accusing you of being clumsy. And snapping at you. You're not remotely 'blonde' *or* clumsy (you're the polar opposite of that!).

You were so gentle with him, and so patient, I thought you were just amazing. I thought you were an angel. For the first time I could really see why you decided to take that nursing degree. You're such a natural! It's a real shame you felt you had to abandon it halfway through.

I mean don't get me wrong, he was obviously just joking

some of the time (or at least he tried to pass off some of the crueller put-downs as mere casual banter – that's soldiers for you), but I must confess that I didn't find what he was saying even remotely funny. I could see how much he was upsetting you. I saw your eyes fill with tears at least twice. And your hand was shaking when I gave you those headphones to put on.

I hated seeing how much he was getting to you, the way he was bullying you. It was so relentless, so unnecessary. It tore me up inside. And to see you backing down so readily – not standing up for yourself, not defending yourself at all – just letting him get away with it, time after time. *God!* It made my blood boil!

Just because I didn't say anything doesn't mean I hadn't noticed. I *had* noticed, but I didn't feel it was my place to intervene. I didn't think you'd thank me for it if I did. You seemed so diminished by it. You seemed so nervous around him, so flustered.

That's not the Nina Springhill I know! I kept thinking. That's not the funny, silly, mouthy, independent Nina I know.

I keep wondering where she's got to – the old Nina. What happened to her? Sometimes I still see a tiny glimpse of her; like that time we bumped into each other outside the bank in Ilkley (remember?) and you tore a strip out of me for wearing trainers with my suit. And at the Auction of Promises, when you secured the promise against Brian Brewster and then jumped into the air, whooping – in front of the entire hall – and did a funny little victory dance! (That completely cracked me up!)

And when we were walking to the car, of course, and we had the aforementioned 'chat' …
(But let's not get back into all of that.)

The bottom line (and I hate talking 'bottom lines' – it always sounds so unbelievably twatty) is that I'm simply not sure if you're getting enough support, Nina. I mean financially, emotionally, physically … I know Glenn will've had a certain amount of help himself (from the Royal Air Force), but how about you? Has anyone offered you counselling? Do you have someone you can talk to about things? Someone discreet you can confide in who might have a special insight into the peculiar kinds of pressures you're under?

I'm not volunteering myself for this job (of course not! That would be completely inappropriate of me!), I'm just very, very concerned that you shouldn't feel lonely or isolated. And if you did happen to need someone to chat to, confidentially (but very informally), without any pressure, then I'd be extremely happy to lend an ear. I'd be honoured, in fact.

We could just go for a walk on the moor together (blow off some cobwebs! Not talk about anything, in particular, just pass a bit of time together). Or we could go out for a bike ride. Or a swim! How about that? You used to love swimming! And nobody would need to know, Nina. I could be very discreet. I'm perfectly well aware of how delicate your situation is.

Perhaps – if you're nervous someone might see us together and gossip – we could meet up in Bradford and just go out for a coffee (do you still like custard Danishes? Can you still eat three in one sitting?). Or we could go and see a film. Any film. You could chose. We could pretend to bump into each other – randomly – at the cinema, like it was just a happy accident.

We could even …

Oh, God, Nina, who on earth do I think I'm kidding, here? This is impossible! It's absurd! I'm so crazy about you! I'm just mad about you! It's so painfully obvious (isn't it? *Isn't* it?!). I'd almost given up hope, and then – without any warning – the Promise Auction, the tour, the snatched conversation, that lingering look you gave me …

I'm just so confused now, so freaked out. I hardly know what to do with myself. And every day it gets worse. Just knowing that you're sitting at that stupid counter, not fifty yards away, but that you are, to all intents and purposes, completely unapproachable. I don't even dare text you, just in case …

I don't know … Just in case you wouldn't like it. Or just in case Glenn might find out. Or just …

Bollocks! I *hate* this! I can't *stand* it! I feel so helpless! So *stupid*!

Please put me out of my misery, Nina. Take it all back, if you must. Just set me straight, once and for all. Laugh in my face, if you want to – or tell me I've got completely the wrong end of the stick … Just do something to release me from all this horrible indecision (this pathetic mooning about the place)!

I'll do anything for you, Nina, you must know that. I'll do anything. Just say the word. Just give me some sign – some tiny show of encouragement …

I know it'll be messy. I'm not an idiot. But I don't care how messy it gets. I don't care. I love you. I think you're incredible. I just want to be with you. And don't worry about Yasmin. I lied about Yasmin – I mean not *about* Yasmin. There *is* a Yasmin. We are engaged. But America just seems so far away right now. America just seems like a whole different world, in fact.

Oh yes. And in case there's any remaining confusion about why I came back here (because Glenn's take on it was so weirdly off-kilter) I *did* mainly come back to Yorkshire to support my father (once his business started going under), and I'm living at home not because I *want* to, but just to try and help Mum and Dad out, financially, for a while.

Glenn was wrong to think that my transferring to RAF Fylingdales was some kind of a demotion. It was actually a promotion. The job came up and I put myself forward, hardly thinking I would get it (there's this whole, new, high-tech system of radars and tracking devices being installed at the base by the US over the next decade or so – an upgrade, in effect – and they've brought me on board to head the whole operation up).

Obviously I couldn't say anything about this on the tour – it's all totally hush-hush. And I was happy to let Glenn believe what he liked (I don't need his approval) but I didn't want you thinking I'd returned here with my tail between my legs, like some kind of pathetic 'Mummy's Boy', a failure, because that couldn't be further from the truth.

When I accepted the post at Fylingdales I knew the thing with Yasmin probably wouldn't be sustainable, long-term. She's got a teaching job in Houston which she really enjoys, and family there, and tons of friends. Over the past five or so months it's pretty much fizzled out between us. She was originally meant to visit this Christmas but in the end she decided not to (by mutual consent).

The truth is that she's never made me feel the way you do, Nina. Nobody can. Only you can. I'm crazy about you – I'm crazy in love with you (like Beyonce keeps on singing in that infernal song of hers).

I had to say it. I *had* to. I just had to put it out there – if only to stop myself from going slowly insane. I'm sorry if this has upset you. I'm sorry if I've behaved inappropriately in some way. I apologize if I somehow managed to misconstrue what you said the other day.

If you don't respond to this letter I promise I won't bother you again. I won't pester you. I'll just pretend this never happened. I'll move on. It'll be fine. *I'll* be fine. I don't want you to worry about me. Forget about me! You've got enough to worry about!

Whatever happens I just want you to be happy, Nina. You deserve to be happy. You deserve every good thing the world has to offer, and more, so much more …
I'm talking crap now. Yes. I should probably just quit while I'm ahead.

Have a lovely Christmas.

Forget I ever wrote this (if you want to).
I honestly won't hold it against you,

Nick

PS You were right about the A4 envelope. The book fitted into it just perfectly.

[tape transcript]

TRANSCRIPT OF DICTAPHONE TAPE RECORDING
(transcribed on 7/01/2007 by WPC Helen Graves – Front
Desk, Skipton)

*I don't know if it's relevant to the case at all, Sergeant Everill,
but the suspect appears to be located in a small, tiled room as he
dictates this message (I'm guessing it might possibly be a bathroom,
a cellar, or – at a stretch of the imagination – a cell of some kind).
There's an echo to his voice as he speaks, some audible 'straining'
(I've italicized these segments for you), the rustle of tissue paper,
and, at the very end, the sound of a low-flush cistern being pulled.*

*You may notice that I have taken the decision to blank out much
of the swearing in the text; this is actually because I named my only
daughter, Bronwen, after one of The Little Wren's most beautiful
songs – 'My White-Breasted Bronwen' (off his 1994 album Up on
the Downs). Bronwen is currently only twelve years old.*

*Prior to transcribing this tape, I had considered myself quite a fan
of Frank K. Nebraska (as he now insists on calling himself). I even
played his first hit, 'A Big Whistle (for a Little Wren)', as the first
dance at my wedding! Of course at that stage I didn't have the
slightest inkling that in real life he would turn out to be such a
stuck-up, arrogant, filthy-mouthed little b*****d.*

*Please feel free to get back to me if you have any queries about the
text, as it stands –*
WPC Graves

Troy – Frank here – and I'm so f***ing, *f***ing* ANGRY I
hardly know where to put myself …
Where *are* you? I need to *talk* to you for f**k's sake!
[*Sound of FKN grappling, clumsily, with a door handle*]
I'm still lying low in the wilds of West Yorkshire struggling to
get some s**t together for the new album … [*Sound of FKN
pushing a door open and entering a small, tiled room*] Of course

---

223

this is on the remotest off-chance that you actually even care where I am or what I'm doing with myself right now …

[*Sound of FKN petulantly slamming the door shut behind him*]

I tried your mobile, but I kept getting sent direct to your message-bank, so then I tried the office, and your haughty, jobsworth of a secretary tells me you've swanned off to the f***ing *Maldives* for three weeks, you jammy c**t!

Why the f**k aren't you picking up your messages? I mean who the hell gave *you* carte blanche to suddenly go all f***ing Garbo on me?

Huh?!

Because I'll tell you something for nothing, here, Troy: if you *had* picked up those messages you'd be shi**ing your f***ing Bermuda *shorts* right now. You'd be standing, weeping, in the full glare of the tropical sun, on a wide expanse of f***ing, steaming tarmac, desperately trying to hitch a ride back to the UK on the next available f***ing flight. Your *ears* would be bleeding, Troy, because I am f***ing *livid*. I am incandescent with f***ing *rage* here, Troy.

Oh, yeah, and I can't be f***ed writing all this down, so I'm recording it on my Dictaphone – as per – then couriering the tape direct to your hotel – or your t**tty stilted *chalet* – or wherever the hell else you're parking your slack, white, lazy, pock-marked arse right now.

Kizzy's sitting by the front door with her coat on, as we speak, primed and ready to make the drop.

[*FKN expectorates, noisily, into what sounds like a sink*]

The poor kid's been in f***ing *tears* all morning, Troy. She's inconsolable. She *hates* what this sh*t is doing to me! She thinks it's *criminal* that you've fucked off like that, without so much as a f***ing by-your-leave. She thinks it's completely, f***ing unprofessional, as it happens.

So f*ck you, Troy! You've made a beautiful, heavily pregnant young girl sob her gorgeous little heart out. You've broken her f***ing *heart*, Troy. You've broken my *unborn* *child's* heart, Troy. So I hope you're f***ing satisfied with that! I hope your three, tawdry weeks in the f***ing Maldives was *worth* all that, huh?!

Huh?!

I also hope, for the sake of our twenty-year-long relationship (I won't call it a 'friendship', that'd be rather stretching the point) – as well as your miserable little *career*, Troy – that you have a Dictaphone handy in your five-star f***ing paradise island retreat … [*FKN expectorates, noisily – for a second time – into what sounds like a sink*]

So you'd better have a nice big sip of your Jim Beam, Troy, pay off the syphilitic ladyboy, raise the blinds, turn the volume up to max, and listen very, *very* carefully, because I'm only planning to say this once, okay?

Okay?

Right. Good. Now cast back your booze-addled mind for a moment, if you will, and try to recall how directly before you thoughtlessly buggered off to the Maldives (casually leaving all your hardworking clients – especially *this* one – totally in the lurch) you kindly forwarded me the first draft copy of my so-called 'autobiography' (working title): *Frank K. Nebraska's: Blowing The Whistle* (a title which, for the record, I hate. It sounds like a coy pseudonym for the act of gay fellatio).

D'you remember that, Troy? Gradually coming back to you yet? *Yeah*? Great! Fantastic!

Well, what you might *not* realize, Troy, is that in your frenzied rush to catch your stinking flight, you also inadvertently enclosed the letter which the esteemed 'scribe' of said autobiography – Robert Pole – sent, for your private perusal, with the first draft of the book.

Yes, Troy, the letter. Remember the letter? Remember Robert Pole's 'entertaining' letter about the many 'hilarious' foibles of your loyal client and gullible paymaster, Frank K. Nebraska? Remember the letter, Troy? You do? Good. Excellent.

Well, you accidentally *enclosed* that disgusting letter *in* the book.

You sent the letter to *me*, Troy.

Like I say, it was a private letter, addressed to you, personally, so just as soon as I realized the mistake you'd made, I folded it up and sent it straight back.

[*Sound of a hand slapping repeatedly against a tiled wall*]

OF COURSE I BLOODY DIDN'T!

WHAT KIND OF A FEEBLE IDIOT DO YOU TAKE ME FOR?!

I READ IT, TROY!

I F***ING READ IT!

OF COURSE I F***ING DID!

[*Heavy panting*]

I *read* the letter, Troy … [*Slightly calmer, now*]

I read *every damn syllable* of it!

You forwarded the letter to me, Troy – is this actually sinking in yet? *Is it*?! – and I have *read the letter*, Troy.

[*Dramatic five-second pause*]

So thanks very much for that [*Insincere*]. No, I mean it. Thanks a f***ing *bunch* for that, old boy.

[*Sound of heavy, plastic lid being lifted*]

You've done me a great service there, my friend. I really mean it: a *great* service. It was just what I needed – *exactly* what I needed. It was a gift, Troy – a *gift* – to finally find out what that repulsive, cock-eyed, snivelling little secretary *you* hired (and generously paid over *10 per cent* of my piddling advance to) actually thinks of me.

That was great, Troy.

That was very, very special.

Merry Christmas to you, too, Troy.

That was just … just f***ing *wonderful*.

It really was.

[*Sound of zipper being unfastened*]

I call him a 'secretary', Troy, because that is exactly what he is. A secretary. A glorified f***ing secretary. Nothing more, nothing less. And – for the record – I don't give a flying f**k

how many other books he's co-written. He could've co-written *War and* f***ing *Peace* for all I care. He could've co-written Katie Price's f***ing *Pony* novels for all I care …
Bollocks to him!

He's just a *secretary*, a pointless, gibbering, insignificant little secretary. He took dictation. That's all the slimy, self-important little turd *did* in my case.

So maybe he indented the odd paragraph or two … Maybe he added the occasional comma and full stop … Maybe he did a smattering of *entirely gratuitous* editing … I mean where's all the fascinating stuff about the development of my political philosophy gone? That was gold dust, f***ing *gold* dust! Why'd he get rid of it all?

Huh?!

I mean I *told* you how I didn't want …
[*Straining*]
I *told* you, right from the start, how I didn't want anyone ghosting the autobiography for me. I was determined, from the very off, to write the damn thing myself.

And *why* was that, Troy? Eh? *Why* was that?
[*Expectant pause*]

Because I'm a famous *storyteller*, you bloody moron! It's what I *do*. I have a special *genius* for telling stories! I was kissed by the f***ing *Blarney* Stone! It's in my *blood*! And we both know that if I'd had even so much as a *minute* to f***ing spare I would've put pen to paper myself – or I'd've got Kizzy to put pen to paper *for* me – and I would've written one of the best autobiographies of ALL TIME, Troy. Absolutely no f***ing doubt about it.

But the turnaround was way too tight, Troy. You bungled the contract, and I ended up with only a paltry *three years* in which to *deliver* the stupid thing, and by the third year I was still gestating, Troy! I was still cultivating my ideas. I was still marinating my themes.

I just didn't have the f***ing *opportunity* to get this project

fully operational, Troy, because – unlike our wonderful Mr
Pole – I actually have a flourishing and viable *career* to manage.
I have a *profile* to maintain. I have a hungry – an *insatiable* –
f***ing *public* to entertain.
[*Straining*]

I mean this thing is a f***ing *outrage*, Troy!
It's a f***ing *outrage*!
[*The noisy flapping of what sounds like a piece of paper*]
The sheer cheek, the *gall* –, the downright *effrontery* – of the
man! It's an absolute bloody *scandal*!
[*FKN adopts pantomime, nasal, upper-crust accent*]
'There was obviously a certain amount of work involved in
trying to depict Mr Nebraska as a *sympathetic* character. I tried,
on more than one occasion, to explain to him that the average
reader – even the die-hard fan – needs to find something *likable*
about the book's protagonist, something to *empathize* with. The
odd – even slightly disingenuous – display of humility, modesty
or self-awareness goes a very long way in this respect, and a
gentle touch of humour often helps.

'Unfortunately, Mr Nebraska didn't appear to understand
this approach ("Why mollycoddle the f***ing idiots?" was all
he'd volunteer on the issue), so, for the sake of the book, I took
the necessary liberty of adding these small touches myself.'

D'you hear that, Troy? Pole *added them himself*! D'you *hear*
that?! The little shit 'took the liberty'. He acted *entirely* against
my wishes! He stuck his oar in and *made* me 'sympathetic'
without my permission, for the sake of the *book*! For the sake of
the f***ing *book*, Troy!

But I told him – till I was blue in the f***ing *face*, Troy – that
I didn't *want* to be 'sympathetic'. I don't *want* f***ing
sympathy, Troy! I'm an *artist*! All I want – all I desire – is to be
true to my muse! My *muse*, Troy! My *creative imagination*,
Troy! But how the hell is some grubby, slimy, inconsequential
little *hack* meant to understand a concept as pure and
unblemished and lofty as *that*? *Eh*?

F***ing *sympathetic?!*
What absolute, bloody *b*lls**t!*
[*FKN blows his nose, forcefully*]

   I mean is *Bob Dylan* sympathetic, Troy? Is *Jerry Lee Lewis* sympathetic? Is *Little Richard* sympathetic? Is *Neil Young* sympathetic? Is *Janis Joplin* sympathetic? Is *Frank Zappa* sympathetic? Is *Captain Beefheart* sympathetic?
Well?!
[*Suspenseful pause*]
*OF COURSE THEY F***ING AREN'T!*
*THEY'RE F***ING <u>ARTISTS</u> FOR CHRIST'S SAKE!!*
   GENIUS DOEN'T *DEMAND* SYMPATHY, TROY! IT DEMANDS RESPECT! *RESPECT!!*
UNDERSTAND?!
[*Interlude of quiet panting, enlivened by a small fart*]
   And this isn't even the *half* of it, Troy!
I've barely scraped the surface, yet!
Just listen to ...
[*Scuffling of piece of paper, throat clearing, re-adoption of nasal whine ...*]
'Of course he would then invariably go off on one of his typical, ten-minute rants about how Bob Dylan wasn't 'sympathetic' (because he was a poet and therefore didn't need to be) and I was then obliged to have to try and explain to him – in the kindest possible way – that a couple of novelty hits in the nineties, a catchy nickname, a scandalous private life and a green straw hat do not – I repeat, do *not* – a Bob Dylan make.

   'I mean, if the producers of Britain's most brilliant and long-running comedy sit-com hadn't used one of Nebraska's songs for its theme tune five years ago (and purely out of a sense of irony, to boot!), then that huge American Emo band hadn't done the dreadful cover version of it which was then promptly snapped up by those tone-deaf film people – he'd be pretty much on his uppers right now and there wouldn't be a musical career, or an autobiography for that matter!'

Good *GOD*, Troy! D'you *hear* that?! The unbridled *cheek* of
the little c★★t! 'Green straw hat?!' I haven't even *worn* the hat
since 1999! I ditched it for the Millennium. I burned it, live,
onstage, at that pub in Bedford! The Little Wren died that
night – he was *immolated* that night, Troy, and Frank K.
Nebraska arose, phoenix-like, from the ashes (you were there,
Troy, as I recall. You had to pay off the fire department).

A *legendary* moment in my career, Troy! A *critical* moment
in my career! A turning point! The cuddly and lovable Little
Wren – Great Britain's favourite tabloid cheeky-chappie –
commits public *seppuku* so that the Nietzschean Superman, the
sleek, intellectual monolith that is Frank K. Nebraska, can
finally come bursting into life!

Yet how many pages does this astonishing turn of events
warrant in the book, Troy? How many?! *Three*! Three piddling
pages! Pole gives *at least* as many pages to that insignificant
episode at The Royal Variety Performance where I was arrested
and sectioned for trying to hand the Queen a secret message
about f★★★ing radishes! It was a message about *radishes*, Troy!
Utterly insignificant! Ludicrously over-mediated at the time!
Has no bearing at *all* on my creative output! In fact I actively
avoided mentioning the stupid interlude in our discussions
because I didn't want it featuring too prominently in the book.

And for the record – the hat wasn't f★★★ing straw, it was felt! It
was f★★★ing *felt*! A *felt* hat! My infamous green *felt* hat, for f★★k's
sake! And the arrogant slime-ball calls himself a 'professional'?!
Huh?!

[*Yet more nasal whine*] 'I also told him that there needed to be
a sense that the subject of the book had been on a "journey" of
some kind (a cliché, I know, but the arc of the narrative usually
demands it), and that his "experiences" had taught him
something valuable – about both himself and the world he
inhabits. Unfortunately, in the case of Mr Nebraska, they
hadn't, so once again I was obliged to …'

A *journey*, Troy! The little pri★k wants a *journey*? I'll give him

a f***ing *journey* all right! I'll give him a swift kick up the arse
all the way down to his local Accident and Emergency! *That's*
what I'll give him! I'll give his winking anus a journey it'll never
forget into deepest recesses of his strangulated throat!

[*FKN readopts nasal voice*]

'One of the major problems with our sessions was that Mr
Nebraska cancelled most of them, and refused to reschedule,
preferring to tape his "recollections" on that infernal
malfunctioning Dictaphone of his, which seems to record his
voice at *twice* the normal speed and makes any benighted soul
lumbered with the task of deciphering it feel like they're
listening to the hyperactive rantings of a foul-mouthed, deeply
demonic Pinky or Perky …'

[*This is absolutely true, Sergeant Everill – H.G.*]

What *guff*, Troy! What arrant, f***ing *bull***t*! Is the fool on
acid or something?! Is he hallucinating?! Something *wrong* with
my Dictaphone?

*Boll**ks*!

He was just *smarting*, because by deftly employing my handy
Dictaphone I cunningly redirected the course of the narrative! I
excluded him from the creative process! His fragile ego simply
couldn't handle it!

[*FKN commences reading again*]

'A major downside of Mr Nebraska's refusal to see me in
person – and answer my many questions about his life – was
the fact that it allowed him to avoid interrogating his past (his
"history") with anything amounting to a critical – or
dispassionate – eye. This rendered him wholly incapable of
seeing any of the situations in his car crash of a personal life
from any other perspective apart from his own. To "bulk out"
the details of these segments of his life (the "missing years"
between 1989 and 1996 being a case in point) I was often
obliged to mine other sources.

'Mr Nebraska has that rare and wonderful ability to be
completely self-involved and yet not remotely self-aware (quite

incredible, really, when you consider how many idle hours he's frittered away in rehab over the years) …'

[*Long pause*]

So *that's* how he came up with the section about my mother's early vaudeville career, Troy! *And* the whole chapter about the cottage in Aylesbury I shared with Luella! I *wondered* how he managed to get all that detail about the blue Dalton crockery she kept arranged on her old dresser … I thought he'd just made it up and struck lucky!

God! The little sneak actually *spoke* to Luella? Well, *no wonder* I'm so nice about the thieving cow in the book! Now it all makes sense!

How many other of my exes did he buddy-up to?

[*Shocked pause*]

Holy f**k! He contacted *Mel*! He visited the asylum! *That's* how he knew it was a *teapot* I threw at her when she told me she was up the f***ing duff again in '89, and not a slice of parkin!

Christ! And all the pointless filler he put in there about my sister's kleptomania, and how her relentless shoplifting as a kid got us all put into care … And Anthony's breech birth in the back of my Reliant Robin … And how I originally got the 'Wren' moniker from a barman in Llandudno …

He f***ing *researched* all this rubbish behind my back?! Without even *telling* me?! The sneaky, conniving, two-faced, little c**t! I *knew* it! I *knew* he couldn't be trusted, Troy! My instincts were right all along! My instincts were spot-on!

I mean I *told* you how I didn't want some jumped-up little nobody, some *hack*, putting his mark all over my life …

[*More straining*]

Well, there's absolutely no question about it, Troy, the whole teapot section will have to go. And anything favourable I say about Luella. We've got to delete it. And we'll need to re-insert all my ideas about astrology and political philosophy. And the stuff he didn't include about how that thieving b**tard Robbie Williams ripped off my entire act.

I need to wrest this book back from his filthy clutches, Troy. I need to wrest my f***ing *life* back – because what remains is all *me*, it's *mine*, by *right*. It's the stuff I recited, verbatim, into the Dictaphone. It's 100 per cent Frank K. *110 per cent Frank K …*

Point of fact: I don't know why we even *hired* the little turd, Troy. I mean I effectively wrote the damn thing myself, didn't I? I *am* The Little Wren, after all, and The Little Wren *is* a storyteller … ergo … well, that's what he *does*, Troy. That is his gift. That's what he's celebrated for, what he's *loved* for: he tells stories. He *weaves* stories …

[*More straining*]

And the bottom line is …

[*More straining – followed by a small plop – followed by a grunt*]

… that I effectively wrote this alone, Troy. The magic is all mine, eh? The content is all mine. The *life* is mine. Robert Pole just conducted a couple of crummy interviews, sent me a list of fatuous questions to answer and then typed my answers up in some semblance of order. *I* did all the donkey work on this thing, Troy. *Me …*

[*Straining*]

Now I've finally seen it all written down, I realize how much of the overall content is just pure, undiluted Nebraska – it's Frank K., through and through …

[*More straining – followed by two further small plops*]

Writer's f***ing credit, my arse!

I mean who the f**k does this little worm think he is? *Huh?* He expects a *credit* now? For what?! For taking a little dictation and moving a few sentences around? For sorting out the odd place name and date? For confirming the odd bit of sequential detail? For meeting my mother a few times and finding out the colour of the kitchen lino, or how slow I was to be potty-trained? Is seven *really* that late, Troy? *Seriously*?! I mean do we honestly need to make such a f***ing *issue* out of that?

[*More straining, another plop*]

I mean the f***ing *gall* of the little twit!

Who the *hell* does he think he is, Troy?! *Huh?*

To call *me* 'High Maintenance'!

There it is … [*Rustle of paper*] … in black and white!

To call Frank K. Nebraska 'High Maintenance'!

It's downright bloody *vindictive*, Troy. It's creepy! And to sneak around interviewing people behind my back? He's like a stalker! I think he's probably deranged! I think he's fixated! He's jealous, Troy! That's it! He's literally *eaten up* with jealousy – *consumed* by it! It's pitiable, Troy, *pitiable*! If I didn't hate him so much I'd almost feel *sorry* for him …

But lucky for you I *do* hate him, Troy, so that means you can fire him, with total impunity. We need to get rid of him, Troy. And let's do this properly. Let's take out a restraining order on him, and use a couple of contacts to blacken his name in the press. Say he was unstable. Say he was incompetent. And withhold the last payment, obviously. I don't want the little pr**k getting *paid* for this drivel! He doesn't need a f***ing *reward* for what he's done here – he needs to be chastised, Troy! He needs to be brought up short. He needs to learn a harsh lesson, here, Troy – the harshest lesson …

No mercy, Troy. *None.* Because it's probably *kinder* to treat him this way in the long run. I mean, who knows, in the end he might even end up *thanking* me for it.

Yeah.

Right.

Good …

And we need to do all this *now*, Troy. Okay? We need to do this immediately – like, *yesterday*. You need to contact the accountants and stop his cheque.

[*Straining*] This is *urgent*, Troy. It's critical. Time is of the essence …

[*More straining*]

I mean where the f**k *are* you, Troy? What the hell are you *playing* at?

[*Yet more straining*] I mean who else's agent f***s off to the Maldives for three weeks over f***ing Christmas?

Do you see *me* flitting off to the Malidives for f***ing Christmas, Troy? *Do* you? *No*! No! I'm at f***ing *home*, Troy, with my gormless, weeping, pregnant mare of a girlfriend. I'm saving my autobiography. I'm starting a new f***ing *album*. I'm just back from a promotional 'tour' of f***ing Japan – I turned up at the store in Kyoto and they didn't have a single copy of my last album! Not a single copy! What kind of a shonky, two-bit operation is this?! I flew to *Japan*, you t**t! And there wasn't a *single* copy of the last album in Kyoto for me to sign! That's *your* responsibility, Troy. That's *your* fault. I'm holding you *personally* accountable for that, Troy! Hear me?!

[*Sound of tissue being pulled from a rattling holder. Dabbing. Grunting*]

OI! KIZZY! *KIZZY*! THIS STUFF IS LIKE F***ING *SAND*PAPER! WHAT'VE YOU DONE WITH THE *GOOD* STUFF? *EH*? WHERE'S THE F***ING *WET* WIPES? *KIZZY*!!
WET WIPES!
WET WIPES!
KIZZY!
WET WIPES!!
NOW!!!

[*Silence*]

Bollocks!

[*Disgruntled noises. More scuffling with paper. Sound of toilet being flushed*]

Well, I guess that's me pretty much done for the moment, Troy. I'm just gonna …

[*Sound of distant female voice shouting something*]

Huh? Oh. Yeah. Kizzy says enjoy the rest of your honeymoon …

[*Sound of yet more distant female voice shouting*]

She says she can't get a courier to come to the house so she's banging this tape straight into the post.

[*Pause*]

KIZZY? *KIZZY*?! WHAT HAPPENED TO THE *WET* WIPES?

[*Silence*]

THE *WET* WIPES, KIZZY!

KIZZY …?

[*Tape is turned off. Tape is turned on again*]

Troy. It's me. It's Frank. On second thoughts, leave in all the stuff about Luella. Leave in the good stuff about Luella. Let's keep her sweet and then try and reduce the f***ing alimony payments early next year at some point.

Good.

And *you* can sort out all the other stuff, yeah? The other stuff? Just tell Pole to return the tapes and then get some office dogsbody to type them up and gradually filter the bits I mentioned back into the text.

Now I come to think of it, I actually remember saying something really insightful – really profound – about Nostradamus at one point. Definitely put that in. Or – better still – get Pole to do it before you sack the little s**t.

Yeah …

Thanks, Troy.

Just get the f**k back here, now, okay?

Pronto.

Okay?!

[*Tape is turned off again. Tape is turned on again*]

Three weeks in the f***ing *Maldives*?!

Are you *serious*?

Is your secretary just taking the f***ing *p*ss*, or what?

I mean how much am I f***ing *paying* you for Christ's …?

[*Tape runs out*]

[letter 20]

Finches
Lamb's Green
Burley Cross

21st December, 2006

Dear Mr Jennings (or 'Claw'),

May I just start off by saying that I am so sorry (so very, *very* sorry – words just can't express) for my unwitting role in the dreadful events of the fateful night of December 12th.

Given your persistent refusal to accept all my visits and phone calls since that momentous date, I can only imagine that you're still absolutely furious with me – and heaven knows, you're certainly in good company!

The Crawfords remain utterly implacable, I'm afraid, even to the extent that Veterinary Crawford claimed he was 'far too busy' to come out and see my ailing love-bird, Tyrone, on Tuesday last, obliging me to depend on the services of his genial assistant, Mr McGraw (who is the first to admit that he has no special expertise in avian health issues!).

Then I saw Wincey – who nobody could deny has a heart forged from pure twenty-four-carat gold – dart and hide behind a parked car to avoid bumping into me outside the PO. To add insult to injury, I was actually being gently ticked off by Sebastian St John – this year's AOP Events Manager (more of which, anon) – at the time!

Wharfedale's dog warden, Trevor Horsmith (his beautiful, silver Clio was destroyed in the riot – I believe it was the one you purportedly 'torched'), can barely find it in himself to exchange so much as a civil 'hello' ...

And they're just the tip of a rather large iceberg, Mr Jennings! In all candour, I'm starting to feel a little like a pariah in my own home (although please don't think – not even for a minute – that I'm looking for sympathy here. Good heavens, no! Not a bit of it! I wouldn't *dare* to! Because I'm perfectly well aware that by comparison to you I've got off very lightly – or at least relatively unscathed …).

I suppose all I'm really trying to say (if I can somehow manage to get my teeth in straight!) is that I do hope you don't think that you're suffering this awful trial of yours entirely alone. I am here for you (every inch of the way), as is the Gentle Nazarene ('He is never far from us and is always close at hand. If he cannot remain within he goes no further than the door …' Meister Eckhart).

Always remember, as St Paul says, 'Virtue is perfected in weakness' (2 Cor. 12: 9), and that all things finally must work to the good – 'Yes, even sins!' (St Augustine).

That said, Mr Jennings, I must confess that my poor heart sinks (it dives – it quite literally plummets!) every time I think of you, stuck in some tiny, overcrowded cell, on remand, in Leeds, knowing that I must bear at least *some* partial responsibility for the tragic turn of events that prompted you to end up there.

Oh, it must be such an unbearably grim and lonely time of year to be incarcerated (not that there's ever a *good* time, I'm sure!). I do hope you're managing to keep your chin up.

At least know that you are never far from my thoughts. I've been into our local church – St Peter's – and have lit a candle for you every day since I first learned of your awful plight. I suppose you might almost say that I've been mounting a small vigil there on your behalf.

And if it isn't too self-indulgent of me to mention it, I have also been reciting a special prayer – morning and night – which I found in an ancient little book of *Meditations and Prayers for Particular Occasions* which my grandmother (who was a devout, Catholic lady) gave me as a child. The prayer in question is 'A Prayer Before Going on A Journey' (because this is how I have chosen to perceive your cruel incarceration, Mr Jennings, as a journey, of sorts).

If you can stand it, I would like to take the opportunity to copy it down here for you, in the feeble hope that it might give you some kind of sustenance in your hour of need (you will see that I have taken the liberty of inserting your name into its fabric – to give it a more personal and authentic feel. I do hope you won't consider this too much of an impertinence).

O Almighty God, who fillest all things with thy presence, and art a God afar off as well as near at hand, Thou didst send thy angel to bless Jacob in his journey, and didst lead the children of Israel through the Red Sea, making it a wall on the right hand and on the left; be pleased to let thy angel go out before Mr Jennings and guide him in his journey, preserving him from dangers of robbers, from violence of enemies, and sudden and sad accidents, from falls and errors. And prosper his journey to thy glory, and to all innocent purposes; and preserve him from all sin, that he may return in peace and holiness, with thy favour and thy blessing and may serve Thee in thankfulness and obedience all the days of his pilgrimage; and at last bring him to thy country, to the celestial Jerusalem, there to dwell in thy house, and to sing praises to thee forever. Amen.
(Jeremy Taylor)

You may – or may not – be aware of the fact that I spoke (at some length) to your barrister, Mr Tracey, yesterday. It was he who actually suggested that I write to you, not only to assuage my guilt, beg your forgiveness and wish you well for your court appearance on January 3rd, but principally to explain, in the plainest possible detail, why it was that I behaved as I did on that horrible night of December 12th. He hoped that by dint of this enterprise, I might finally provide you with the best chance of understanding how it was that the Cruel Fates connived to bring this sorry situation into being.

To start at the very beginning, Mr Jennings, I should tell you that I am a seventy-two-year-old widow, a practising Christian and a grandmother of three beautiful girls (Sophie, Zoe and Victoria, who live in Ontario with my only son, Patrick, and his wife, Renee).

I have chronic arthritis in both of my knees (which tends to flare up more severely in winter, and means I am sometimes obliged to walk with the aid of a stick).

As a consequence of this (the arthritis, which can be quite disabling, although I'm not complaining here, Claw, since God has blessed me – and quite copiously – in countless other ways: I have excellent eyesight, for example, which I thank him daily for), I have developed a keen interest in tapestry and sewing, and am fairly well known in Burley Cross for my handmade patchwork quilts (sorry to rabbit on about myself like this, but these boring details *are* pertinent to the story and aren't simply the senile witterings of a lonely old crone, I can assure you!).

Over the past couple of years I have been very happy to participate in the Burley Cross Auction of Promises, an annual event where citizens of the town auction off their humble services in the hope of raising money for charity (this year I believe it was to support a wonderful school for deaf children in the Sudan).

For the past three years (like I say) I have auctioned the promise of one of my patchwork quilts. The quilts come in all shapes and sizes and can take anything from a month to six months to produce. This year the proposed quilt was purchased by Catrin and Alan Crawford (Burley Cross's resident vet and his wife) for the princely sum of £109!

Obviously every quilt I make is unique. The overall look and feel of the thing depends on a whole variety of factors, the colour, shape and texture of the individual patches being but three (square or honeycomb, plain or patterned, cotton or satin, the choices run on and on, virtually *ad infinitum*!).

When (as in this instance) the quilt has been specially

commissioned, I generally like to have a good chat with the person (or persons) I am making the quilt for, well in advance of commencing work, so that their preferences are clearly established (some people are perfectly allergic to bright colours, for example!). I suppose you could call this highly informal process 'a consultation', of sorts.

During this 'consultation', I often take along a few photographs of some of the quilts I have produced in the past (I have a whole scrapbook of the things, believe it or not!), then go though some colour swatches with them, and even (if it is deemed in any sense helpful) have a quick peek at the room/the bed/the chair for which the quilt is finally destined.

In the case of Catrin and Alan, this 'consultation' had been rather difficult to arrange because they both have quite demanding jobs (Catrin is the local school secretary, and she is also doing a part-time course in Reflexology, while Alan is obviously a vet, so his hours can be long and somewhat erratic).

Two initial attempts to meet up both went awry and on each occasion the fault was entirely mine (on the first, the gas boiler in my cottage suddenly started making an extraordinary screeching sound, and I felt compelled to call in a twenty-four-hour plumber. On the second, I made the unwelcome discovery of a wasps' nest inside the trunk of an old hibiscus – a mere three yards from my front door. I was pruning the hibiscus when this happened, and inadvertently pushed my elbow right into the heart of it! I was stung at least thirty-seven times).

A third meeting was eventually scheduled for six o'clock on the evening of the 12th, and I knew that under no circumstances would it be acceptable to register yet another no-show.

As luck would have it, Mr Jennings, it had been a particularly long and stressful day, after I was awoken, at an ungodly hour, by the refuse disposal men, who were kind enough to inform me that a fox had somehow managed to upend my new green plastic composting bin (which had recently been delivered –

free! – by the local council) and had spread the contents (kitchen scraps, in the main) all over my front lawn.

I then spent the following forty or so minutes painstakingly gathering up tiny fragments of egg shell, torn tea bags and little pieces of grated carrot by torchlight (an eccentric piece of behaviour, I'm the first to admit, but I was anxious that it might rain and the mess become permanently embedded in the grass).

This laborious process – and the cold weather – duly set off the arthritis in my knees and compelled me to take double my usual dosage of painkillers.

I was late to start my breakfast (always a mistake if you're on heavy medication!) and was just bolting down a quick Shredded Wheat when Baxter Thorndyke appeared at my window, irate, because he'd driven his Range Rover over five bags of poo (dog poo) which had been placed (inexplicably), at regular intervals, along the edge of the grass verge in front of my cottage.

Without delving too deeply into the sordid ins and outs of the affair, Mr Jennings, the bags of poo had burst under the pressure of his vehicle's wheels, festooning the under-carriage of his car with a stinking layer of excrement (why he'd felt the need to drive his huge 4x4 up on to my small grass verge in the first place still remains something of a mystery!).

I explained to Mr Thorndyke that the poo wasn't my responsibility (I don't own a dog – or even cat – only a lone, ailing love-bird), and that it had obviously been placed there, out of pure mischief, by some deeply troubled and unstable individual (but let's not get in to all that right now, eh?).

It quickly transpired that Mr Thorndyke was on Lamb's Green to photograph the local manhole covers (I have an especially beautiful one – apparently – in front of my property!). Even though I was in no way responsible for the filthy discharge, I did feel obliged to lend a hand in cleaning it from Mr Thorndyke's car with the aid of my trusty pressure-hose.

I'd just returned inside (to towel myself off) when Janine Loose – my neighbour – phoned me, in a complete panic, because a Muscovy duck (which belongs to two sisters who live on The Calls – the road backing directly on to ours) had somehow connived to force its way into her kitchen. The duck (a large, rogue male) was perched, quite contentedly, in her kitchen sink, and was in no particular hurry to leave!

I rushed around there and tried to encourage the cheeky devil out. This took quite some doing since it had inadvertently pushed its foot through a scone cutter, which had, in turn, become tangled up with a fork.

I don't mind telling you, Mr Jennings, that by the time I finally made it over to the Crawfords (having filled the previous three hours overseeing the hanging of a tapestry exhibition in the village hall – quite a trying process, physically *and* emotionally) I was an absolutely spent force.

When I arrived at Skylarks (Fitzwilliam St) on the stroke of six, I was not a little surprised to discover no one home. I knew that Catrin had been planning a quick dash into Bradford after school to collect a dress for an engagement party at a boutique there, so presumed that she had simply been held up.

After a long fifteen minutes, Veterinary Crawford screeched to a halt in his battered, old Land-Rover, full of apologies. Catrin had phoned him on his mobile to say she was stuck in traffic. We went inside and waited for about ten or so minutes, then Veterinary Crawford offered me a sherry. I told him that I didn't generally indulge in alcohol (except at Communion!), but that I certainly wouldn't object to a nice, warming cup of tea!

Veterinary Crawford disappeared off into the kitchen, from whence an impressive volley of crashes and curses then emerged, before the – somewhat harassed – veterinary reappeared again, his cheeks all flushed, claiming that not only had he been unable to locate any tea bags, but that they also appeared to be completely out of milk!

After a few pointed enquiries (on my part) it soon became evident that the poor dear soul had never actually produced a cup of tea in his own kitchen before! Sensing his embarrassment, I quickly swallowed down my misgivings (I *am* generally teetotal) and suggested that we share a small glass of sherry together, after all. This we did, Mr Jennings, and very convivial it was, too.

Another twenty or so minutes passed in idle chit-chat, during which time Veterinary Crawford received an urgent call on his mobile saying how a cow had been hit a glancing blow by a car on the A65 (just past Ilkley, the same incident that was holding up Catrin, it later transpired!).

The veterinary tried to get his assistant (McGraw) on to it, but McGraw was engaged in his own little drama in Leathley (where a poor terrier had a large hide chew stuck in its throat). I naturally insisted that Veterinary Crawford should attend the call (who knows what that poor creature was suffering?), and, after much resistance, he relented, begging me to hold on a short while longer for Catrin, who had assured him that she wouldn't be any time at all.

Well, I sat down and I waited, Mr Jennings, and after a few minutes I must've nodded off. I'm not sure how long I was asleep for (probably just a couple of seconds), but I was suddenly awoken from my light doze by a sharp knock at the door. I hurried to answer it, adjusting my hair (all right – my dentures! The bottom plate had briefly slipped forward!), somewhat startled and confused.

Imagine my surprise, then, when on opening the door I was greeted with the spectacle of two large (by large I mean tall – imposing – muscular) gentlemen, in uniform (the details of which I can't entirely recall) standing either side of a small, pale-faced brunette with a pair of large, one almost might say 'burning', brown eyes. I remember wondering at the extraordinary length of her scarf. It was long, very long, green and white, and wound around her neck countless times (like a

woollen boa constrictor). It hung down in front of her, almost
to the floor.

'Mrs Crawford?' the men asked. 'Mrs Catrin Crawford?'
'Well, yes …' I answered, meaning, of course, that it was Mrs
Crawford's *house*. 'But I'm not—'
(I was intending to say, 'I'm not she. I am not Mrs Crawford. I
am simply waiting for Mrs Crawford in her delightful home.'
But I didn't get the chance, obviously.)
'This is just a formality,' the girl interjected, irritably (and with
great authority, if I say so myself), waving her hand around,
airily, 'just a formality. Come on, dear, *quick, quick* …'
She grabbed hold of the pen (which one of the two men was
proffering me) and pushed it into my hand.
'Crawford,' she said. 'Sign.'

The second man passed me a clipboard with an official-
looking document attached to it and she pointed to the space at
the bottom of the page, next to the word SIGNATURE.
'Crawford,' she repeated, prodding at it, forcefully, with her
forefinger, 'Catrin Crawford.'

Now obviously, with the benefit of hindsight, Mr Jennings, I
realize that it was a mistake – a terrible mistake – for me to take
that clipboard and to sign Catrin Crawford's name on it. In
truth, I can't actually even *remember* signing it. I was still half
asleep at the time. I'd had the sherry, remember, on top of a
rather large quantity of painkillers. I was physically and
mentally exhausted after an exceedingly long and trying day.

And I *know* it probably sounds rather like I'm just making
excuses for myself, here, Mr Jennings (and I probably *am*, truth
be told), but the girl who stood before me, Miss Lydia May
Eardley (as it later transpired), had an extraordinary *presence*
about her (one might almost call it a *surfeit* of character!). She
exuded this strange atmosphere of … of calm implacability, as
if she must – by necessity, by pure force of will – control any
situation she might get herself in to.

I signed the name, Mr Jennings. Indeed I did. I knowingly

and calculatedly committed perjury (the legal consequences of which have yet to be fully thrashed out). Although may I just say, in my own humble defence, Claw, that my motives, I believe, were entirely good and honourable (I have a tacit agreement with *both* of my immediate neighbours on Lamb's Green, for example, to automatically sign for deliveries on their behalf. It can so often be the case with modern delivery companies that if they fail to make a drop on their initial visit to your home, it can take literally *weeks* for them to arrange to come back).

As soon as the document was signed (I *know* it was wrong, Mr Jennings, but I sincerely believed I was helping Catrin out) Lydia May pushed past me (somewhat rudely) and disappeared into the house. The two men thanked me, cordially, then turned on their heels and left. I closed the door and limped back to the living room (I had forgotten my stick in the rush), fully intent on seeking an explanation of some kind from Lydia May about the unusual circumstances of her arrival.

When I re-entered the room, however, I was somewhat astonished to discover the girl – large tumbler of sherry in hand – going through the Crawfords' compact disc collection, looking for something to put on. Yet instead of simply reading the names of the discs as they sat in the rack, or removing each disc, individually, and inspecting it more closely, she was pulling them out, in fistfuls, and then hurling them down on to the carpet around her!

I immediately tried to encourage her to desist from this somewhat disruptive (one could even say violent!) behaviour, but she was talking all the while (ten to the dozen!) and asking a series of these infernal questions that one couldn't really find an answer to, saying things like, 'This is such a *taupe* house, don't you think? Catrin's so very *taupe*. Don't you just *loathe* taupe, Laura?'

(She called me 'Laura' throughout the time we spent together.

It later transpired that Laura was the name of Veterinary Crawford's dead mother.)

At last (at long last!) she happened across a compact disc that she didn't mind the look of and shoved it into the CD player – Rável's *Boléro*, I think (yes. The *Boléro*. I'm *sure* of it, now), but it was almost impossible to tell *what* it was when it actually began to play because Lydia May had turned it up to such a deafening volume.

The rattle of the drum (is that how the thing starts?) during the opening refrain sounded not unlike a volley of gunshots. In fact I was so startled by this explosion of sudden harsh sound that I lurched to my feet, in alarm (I was crouched on the floor, trying to gather the wretched CDs together, some of which had slipped out of their plastic containers), and inadvertently knocked Lydia May's sherry glass from her hand!

The sherry went everywhere, Mr Jennings: my cardigan, the CDs, the carpet (which isn't taupe, for the record, but what I'd call a very modern and attractive 'pale mushroom' colour).

'Oh, you clumsy old *fool*!' Lydia May exclaimed (once I'd finished grappling with the volume controls; I remember her words exactly, for some reason). '*Now* look what you've gone and done!'

Well, I tried to keep my wits about me, Mr Jennings (even in the face of this abusive onslaught!), and hobbled into the kitchen to look for a cloth to clean up the mess with. I'd just located one (under the sink) when I thought I could hear a phone ringing in the other room. By the time I'd returned, however (cloth in hand), Lydia May had already finished her brief conversation and was hanging up the receiver.

'Was that Catrin?' I asked, slightly breathless.
'Uh … yes,' Lydia May answered, turning and inspecting an abstract watercolour on the wall behind her with a sudden – very intense – level of interest. 'Yes. I do believe it was.'

'Did she mention whether she would be home any time soon?' I followed up.

Lydia May didn't respond to my question at once. Instead, she continued to inspect the painting, very closely, until, 'What the hell is this?' she demanded, pointing to it.

'An abstract,' I answered promptly (and why not? The question seemed perfectly uncontentious). 'A bowl of fruit, I believe.'

'A bowl of fruit?!' Lydia May echoed, plainly astonished. 'A bowl of *fruit*?! *Seriously*?!'

She drew in still closer to the painting, until her nose was almost pressed up against the glass.

'Is there a problem?' I asked (somewhat querulous, now).

'*Fruit*, you say? Fruit? But what about …?' She stepped back again, scratching her head, obviously deeply puzzled. 'I mean how can you *possibly* ignore …?'

'Ignore what?'

I stared at her, nervously.

'*Those!*'

She pointed.

I gazed at the painting, blankly.

'*Those! Those!*' She continued to point. 'The two, huge *iguanas*, stupid!' she exclaimed (although she pronounced it ig-hu-anas). 'The two of them, right there, just … just …'

She threw up her hands, horrified.

'Iguanas?' I murmured, hoping that if I gazed at the painting for long enough, the iguanas might just magically materialize (but I could see *no physical evidence* of the iguanas, Mr Jennings! All I saw was an apple, an orange, some grapes and possibly a pear).

'Urgh!' Lydia May grimaced, turning to face me, again, appalled. 'Don't you just find that perfectly *disgusting*?!'

I didn't answer her immediately. Instead I pretended to busy myself (to win a little time) with the sherry stain on the carpet.

'I mean in a *public* space like this? A *lounge-cum-diner*? To hang a picture – a painting – on your wall, of two, huge, taupe reptiles sodomizing each other? Doesn't that *revolt* you, Laura? Doesn't that just make you *sick to your very stomach*?!'

I stopped dabbing at the carpet for a moment and gazed up at her, dumbly.

'I mean here we supposedly are, in this safe, taupe world,' she continued blithely, 'this safe, *respectable*, taupe world. Everything in its place ... Everything "just so" ... And then hanging there, in the *middle* of it, *right* in the middle of it, at the very *heart* of it, these vile and brazen reptiles, these two, huge, *deviant* reptiles, engaged in a *blatant* act of filthy, lusty, uninhibited—'

'But are you sure?' I quickly interrupted her (terrified she might actually use that awful word for a second time).

'Sure?' she echoed, surprised.

'Yes. I mean ...' I grabbed hold of a sherry-soaked CD and quickly began drying it off. 'I mean are you absolutely *certain*?'

'*Certain*?' she repeated, her chin lifting, her two hands settling, combatively, on her hips. 'How d'you mean?'

'It's just ...' I stuttered (struggling to hold my nerve in the face of her sullen glare), 'it's just that I'm not entirely sure if they *are* iguanas, exactly.'

'Really?'

She turned to look at the painting again. 'What? You think they might be monitor lizards?'

'No. *No.* I mean ...'

'Geckos?'

'No. *No.* I mean I don't think that they're ...' I swallowed, hard. 'I don't think that they're reptiles *at all* ...'

She gave this controversial statement a moment's consideration.

'Ah. I see,' she finally mused, 'so you think they're *amphibians*? Is that it? You think that iguanas are actually amphibious?'

'No. *No.* Good gracious, no!' I exclaimed (I do like to think I'm quite knowledgeable in the field of Zoology, Mr Jennings!). 'Iguanas aren't amphibious. Amphibious creatures are born in water, and I certainly I don't think iguanas—'

'But *of course* they're born in water!' Lydia May snorted, waving a dismissive hand at me.

'No. No. I think they're actually hatched from—'

'Frogspawn!' she interjected.

'Eh? What?' I paused, confused. 'Oh. Like a *frog*, you mean?'

'Yes. Exactly! Like a frog.'

(Lydia May seemed very pleased with this notion.)

'Well, to be perfectly honest with you,' I still persisted, 'what I was actually going to suggest was an egg. I think iguanas might possibly be hatched from—'

'*WHO CARES HOW THEY'RE HATCHED*?!' Lydia May suddenly yelled. '*God*! Why get so *uptight* about it?! Why get lost in all the *details*, for heaven's sake?! The fact is that they are *here*! In this lounge! On this wall! In awful taupe! *FORNICATING*!!'

A short silence followed.

'Yes. Well. *Good* ...' I murmured, softly. 'I suppose I'll just have to take your word on that, eh, dear?'

I tried to look calm and obliging (perceiving this statement as a kind of tacit retreat).

'My word?' Lydia May parroted (obviously not seeing it in quite this way herself). 'What's *that* supposed to mean? "My word"?'

I opened my mouth to respond—

'I'll *tell* you what it means,' Lydia May promptly interrupted me, 'I'll tell you *exactly* what it means! It's just a weak and mealy-mouthed way of saying you don't *believe* me! Isn't it? *Isn't* it?'

Lydia May stuck out her chin again, defiantly.

'No! No!' I insisted. 'Not at all!'

'Are you standing there and calling me a *liar*, Laura?!'

Lydia May's wan cheeks had reddened, perceptibly.

'No! No!' I exclaimed, shocked.

'Or deluded? Are you calling me *deluded*?' Lydia May clenched her fists and took a couple of threatening steps towards me. 'Is *that* it?!'

'No! Absolutely not! Not at *all*. I'm just … I'm simply …'

I began to flounder. My throat contracted. The CD I was holding accidentally slipped from my grasp and clattered to the floor. Then, before I knew it, Mr Jennings, Lydia May was advancing on me, at speed! In just a matter of seconds she was almost upon me (her fists still clenched, her arm swinging out), and as I uttered a strangled cry and flung myself, flinching, against the shelves (preparing for the very worst!), she snaked down, grabbed hold of the CD, straightened up again and proffered it to me, gently, with an ingratiating smile (it was a movement of such extraordinary grace and beauty, Mr Jennings! A movement of such marvellous fluidity! And the instinct apparently a benign one! But the *smile*, Mr Jennings? The *smile*? Extremely cold! Immensely cruel! Horribly intimidating!).

She was standing very close to me, now, her warm breath on my ear.

'Do I make you uncomfortable, Laura?' she whispered, in insinuating tones, and then, before I could answer, 'Does the *truth* make you uncomfortable, perhaps?'
Her voice hardened. 'I mean some people *are* uncomfortable with the truth. It doesn't sit well with them, eh? They seem to much prefer it if we all just gaily *pretend*.'

'Did … did Catrin happen to mention if she would be home any time soon?' I all but squeaked, turning and enthusiastically dusting a couple of imaginary drops of sherry from the front of the storage unit (to try and mask this sudden – and clumsy! – change of subject).

'Catrin?' Lydia May frowned.
'Yes. *Yes*. Catrin. On the phone …'
'The phone?'
'Yes. A little earlier, remember? When she rang …'

'Oh. *Oh* …' Lydia May took a sudden, quick step back again, her tone now studiedly cool and off-hand. 'Yes. Of course. When *Catrin* rang …'
'Did she leave any kind of … of *message* at all?' I persisted.

'A message?' Lydia May paused for a moment, thoughtfully. '*Hmmn*. A message … Well, yes, yes, I suppose she *did*, as it happens …'

She gazed at me, enigmatically.

'And … and what was it, exactly?' I eventually prompted (since no explanation was forthcoming).

'The message?'

'Yes.'

'Catrin's message?'

'Yes.'

'You actually want me to *tell* you?'

'Yes.'

'Oh.'

Lydia May thought deeply for a moment.

'Well, the message – *Catrin's* message – was that she wanted us all to … to …' Lydia May paused again, frowning, then her face suddenly lit up with a luminous smile, 'to go for a drink! *All* of us – you, me, her – down at the local pub!'

'Sorry?'

(This wasn't remotely the kind of message I'd been anticipating, Mr Jennings.)

'Yes. Yes! In fact Catrin was very strict about it, Laura. She wanted us to leave straight away – immediately! – she virtually *insisted*.' Lydia May was gradually picking up speed. 'She'll probably be waiting for us by now, all in a rage! What time is it?'

I peered down at my watch: 'A quarter after seven.'

'Oh dear!' she tutted. 'How dreadful! We're a whole ten minutes late, already!'

'Really? Ten minutes … ?' I gazed at my watch again. 'The pub? The Old Oak, you say?'

'Yes. The Old Oak. I'm afraid so,' Lydia May sighed, unwinding her scarf with a look of studied indifference, then carefully rewinding it again.

I adjusted my cardigan (which had fallen from one shoulder in all the previous excitement), then dabbed away at it, ineffectually, with the cloth (to try and win myself a bit of breathing space).

'But are you sure that's an especially good idea?' I eventually queried, glancing up again, nervously.

'No!' Lydia May exclaimed (her tone extremely heartfelt). 'No! I'm *not* sure it's an especially good idea! I personally think it's an *awful* idea, a *terrible* idea, but it's what Catrin *wants*, I'm afraid. She as good as *demanded* it. She's set her dear little *heart* on it. And anyway – if I can be perfectly honest with you, Laura – the thought of hanging around here, for so much as even a *second* longer, with that … that thing, that *monstrosity …*'

She pointed, grimacing, at the painting of the iguanas (I mean the fruit), emitted a strange, haunting 'bleat', then bolted for the door. What else could I really do under the circumstances, Mr Jennings, but quickly retrieve my stick (and my bag, and my book of samples) and clumsily stagger after her?

So there you have it, Claw: an exhaustive account of exactly how it was that we ended up in the local hostelry that night (and the <u>real</u> reason why I purportedly 'reeked' of sherry when we initially arrived there!).

Of course I had no idea at the time – not an inkling – that the earlier phone call hadn't been from Catrin at all, but from the secure institution where Lydia May Eardley is usually resident, apologizing for delivering her to the Crawfords' home a week early (she'd been given special dispensation to attend an engagement party – the one Catrin was collecting that designer dress for) and instructing her – in no uncertain terms, I'm told – to stay put.

I had no idea *at all* about any of these things, Mr Jennings. If I had, I would have behaved quite differently, I can assure you, but as it was, I felt compelled to follow Catrin's strict 'instructions' and to accompany Lydia May Eardley to The Old Oak.

I can see no real point in detailing the series of disturbing events that transpired during our short walk to the pub together, Mr J. Suffice to say that in that brief, 200-yard journey Lydia May climbed a tree, urinated against a wall (standing up! Extraordinary! I could barely believe my own eyes!) and tried to steal a scooter (although she only actually succeeded in knocking the thing over. On to my foot. You will probably have noticed my exaggerated limp when we initially encountered each other).

I also think it's important to state, at this pertinent juncture, that I didn't (as I believe has been suggested by local gossip-mongers), 'ply Lydia May with alcohol' when we first arrived at The Old Oak. Quite the contrary, in fact! I didn't order *any* drinks at all (intent, as I surely was, on staying there for as short a time as possible!).

What actually happened when we arrived at the pub was that I instinctively guided Lydia May to the new dining rooms (which were empty that night – as they are most evenings – although the fare there is generally excellent, if a little steep for local budgets), having noted that some kind of function – i.e. your darts comp. – was under way in the saloon bar. I sat her down at a table, gave her a menu to peruse (as a form of distraction) then went off, on my own, to try and locate the elusive Catrin.

Of course it was naive of me (in the extreme!) to imagine that Lydia May would stay put for any lengthy period of time once I'd abandoned her to her own devices, but I could hardly have conceived of the fact that she would head off to the bar *the very instant my back was turned* and order four pints of 'snake-bite' from the barman there.

It later transpired, Mr J, that 'snake-bite' is not generally sold in The Old Oak. This lethal combination of cider, lager and a dash of blackcurrant cordial (so beloved of 'ravers' and 'Goths' in the 1980s, I've since been told) is considered 'too dangerous' to be served in most responsible hostelries. As luck would have it, though, Wincey had a temporary barman working that night who was unfamiliar with the rules of the house, and consequently had no reason to think that it would be a problem to serve this toxic brew.

I had barely popped my head into the snug, Mr Jennings (then turned around to quickly scan the window seats adjacent to the front entrance), when I espied Lydia May at the bar with four pints of revolting, purplish-brown liquid set out in front of her. I immediately dashed over there (well, as immediately as it was possible for me to dash given the slight injury I had sustained after the accident with the scooter; it later turned out that I had cracked two small bones in my foot!) and tried to intervene, but it was too late. The barman was already engaged in a heated argument with Lydia May about payment for the beverages (Lydia May wasn't carrying any money with her! He was threatening to throw her out!).

The barman was absolutely irate (I'm not sure what Lydia May had said to him, just prior to my arrival, but I later heard her snidely referring to him as 'bunny boy'. You may recall the gentleman in question had unusually protrusive ears). He was so angry, in fact, that I instantly felt compelled to take the edge off the argument by simply settling the bill myself (£10.80, no less!). I told Lydia May to go and sit down, quietly, while I fished around in my bag for my purse.

Lydia May did as she was asked (a rare occurrence, indeed, Mr Jennings – although she plainly balked at my use of the word 'quietly'!), grabbing all four glasses in one go (I don't know if you noticed during your brief encounter with her what an extraordinarily long reach she has – I'm sure she'd be quite a wonder on the keyboard!) and heading for a corner table.

It was at this moment, I fear, that the die was truly cast for the horrors that were soon to unfold, because on her way to that table, Lydia May bumped into one of your party (on a quick visit to the Gentlemen's toilets) and her drinks were almost upended during the collision.

255

The individual responsible (if he was, indeed, responsible: I believe it was your dear friend – and comrade in arms – 'Mutley') apologized politely, but having duly noted that no drink had actually been spilt, reasoned (and quite rightly!), that no real damage had been done.

I think it would only be fair to say that Lydia May was *not* of this opinion, Mr Jennings! By the time I came to join her at the table (and she was already halfway through her first pint at this point – and wearing a small foam moustache, into the bargain!) the poor girl had worked herself up into a rare old bate about the incident. This was, after all, the *second* near-mishap relating to alcohol of the evening (I say 'near-mishap', although the first was an *actual* mishap, and my fault entirely).

It wasn't just the little incident with Mutley that set her off, however. A secondary factor was the thudding of the darts against the wall directly adjacent to which we sat. It seems (I have since been informed) that Lydia May has extremely sensitive ears. Loud and sudden noises (except for the ones she makes herself – and she *does* make such noises, Mr Jennings, and at very regular intervals!) are apparently extremely distressing to her.

The regular thud of the darts was accompanied by spontaneous cheers of support (from the teams and a small, but enthusiastic, cadre of fans), and the loud and often colourful tally of the caller.

None of these appeared to improve Lydia May's irritable mood. To counter her frustrations she 'took refuge' in her glass (as so many are wont to do, Mr J!), and I don't think it was much more than three minutes flat before the first one had been completely drained – to the very last drop!

I should probably mention that I had taken the precaution (on sitting down at the table) of moving two of the glasses to my side (determined, as I was, to maintain the – frankly, quite laughable – pretence that these had been ordered by Lydia May for my own enjoyment). Every so often I would appear to take a sip from one (although I was only really just touching the revolting concoction to my lips). Even so, Mr Jennings, I quickly began to feel the 'snake bite's' lethal impact (remember, I had already partaken of the earlier sherry, and am completely unused to alcohol in <u>any</u> form).

Lydia May, meanwhile, was determinedly attacking her second full pint, and loudly holding forth about how green was her 'favourite colour in the whole world!' (I don't know if you noticed or not, but the corner benches in that part of the bar are upholstered in a fine, green velvet plush).

'Green! Green! Oh, I *love* green!' she kept saying. 'Isn't green the best? Isn't it just fantastic? Don't you think green must be God's favourite colour? I mean if God didn't love green then why would he have made the grass green? *Huh*? And plants! And trees! And leaves! Leaves are always green – *always*! – aren't they, Laura?'

'Absolutely,' I concurred (fool that I am!). 'Except in the autumn, of course, when our Dear Lord gently transforms them into a magnificent kaleidoscope of red and orange and yellow and burned ochre …' (I now hold that my curious urge to wax lyrical about the change of the seasons was at least partially engendered by a perilous combination of nervousness and alcohol.)

These words had barely left my lips, before Lydia May began to glower at me, ominously. 'Don't talk about autumn, you *fool*!' she hissed, glancing nervously over her shoulder (although there was only the wall behind her). 'Autumn's strictly prohibited! It's on my miss list!'

'Sorry?' I stuttered, lifting a tentative hand to wipe a fleck of her spit from my chin. 'Your …?'
'My *miss* list,' she reiterated. '*Miss*! *Mis*-take! *Mis*-chance! *Mis*-conduct! *Mis*-demeanour! My *miss* list! You *mustn't* say it, Laura! It's one of the bad words. It's one of the words that makes me *very* angry. In fact I *am* angry, right now, simply because you've said it – simply because you brought it up! And

having to *explain* it to you like this – and saying it myself, *rehearsing* it, again and again: Autumn! Autumn! *Autumn*! – makes me angrier still! It makes me *seethe*! It makes me *boil*!'

She paused for a moment (to draw breath), peering down, somewhat forlornly, at the fabric on the bench. 'Not like green,' she sighed, inspecting it, fondly, 'green is on my hit list, but *autumn*? Urgh!'

She jabbed at the bench, savagely, with her knuckles.

'Then let's talk about green!' I rapidly interjected. 'Please! Let's do that! Let's just talk about how truly wonderful green is!'

'Really?'

She instantly perked up.

'Yes! Of course!' I enthused. 'Because green is wonderful! It's marvellous! I mean when I think of all the green things in the world and how amazing they all are, like … like apples! And pears! And … and …'

Lydia May winced, dramatically, as another dart hit the wall behind her.

'And … and certain types of grape! Wonderful grapes! Seedless grapes, from the Cape! And kiwi-fruits, which are brownish on the outside but bright green on the inside with hundreds and thousands of tiny, crunchy, little black pips …'

'Yeah, I guess,' Lydia May conceded (not quite so enthusiastically as I had hoped, perhaps). 'But can't we think of any *other* kinds of green stuff, Laura? More *interesting* kinds of green stuff, maybe?'

(She winced, once again, as yet another dart hit the wall.)

'*Other* kinds of green stuff?' I echoed, astonished. 'But … but why, when there's so much more exciting *fruit* to consider, like … like limes, for example?'

'But I'm *tired* of fruit, already!' Lydia May grumbled. 'It's so safe, so dull, so … so *pedestrian*!'

'Well, how about lettuce, then?!' I exclaimed. 'And cucumber! And courgettes! And marrows! All wonderful, healthy, green vegetables! How about some of those?!'

Lydia May shuddered as another dart hit the wall, and a roar of approval – followed by a ringing, 'One hundred and eighty!' – all but drowned out my words.

'Then there's always cabbage,' I doggedly continued, 'and broccoli, and sprouts—'

'What I suppose I'm *really* trying to get at, here,' Lydia May promptly interjected, 'is the stuff that isn't just vegetable in origin. More *interesting* stuff … like … I dunno … '

'Like the green baize on a snooker table!' I smiled, confident of engaging her enthusiasm again. 'Or … or your beautiful *scarf*, for example.'

'But they're man-made, Laura,' she sighed, 'and I want to talk about things that are really green, things that are *truly* green …'

'Oh …'

I was momentarily floored, Mr Jennings, and my mind began desperately groping around for yet more green things with which to tantalize her. Then suddenly, out of the blue, the word 'frog' sprang into my head (if you'll pardon the pun!), but I hesitated to pronounce it, out loud, for some reason (I can't begin to explain *why*, Mr J – perhaps there was something in her strangely pale and languid expression that gave me temporary pause … I don't know … a kind of smouldering expectation, an evil torpor, a dangerous quiescence, like she was just *toying* with me, at some level, like I was merely a tiny, insignificant little fly unwittingly tangled up in her voluminous web).

It dawned on me, in that same instant (and forgive me for contradicting myself here, Claw, because this is an explanation, of sorts) that perhaps 'frog' might lead us back, ineluctably, to 'iguana' (also green! Could that actually be just a coincidence? Or was it – God forbid! – a trap?!), and I definitely didn't want to risk returning to *that* thorny old ground again!

In order to avoid this terrible eventuality I tried to think creatively – tangentially, you might almost say …

'Well, here's an idea,' I suggested, with a blazing smile. 'How about we focus our minds for a while on all the wonderful *words* for green that there are in the world, like … like *emerald* green, for example?'

Lydia May was instantly engaged.

'Emerald green,' she echoed, impressed. 'Yes! I *like* that! I like it *very* much! Let's think of another one, quick!'

She gazed at me, expectantly.

'Olive green!' I promptly followed up.

'Yes! Good! Another one!' she squealed, clapping her hands together, delighted.

My mind briefly went blank again, Mr Jennings (although, in retrospect, I should have just gone with 'lime green' or 'pear green' or 'apple green' – they're all the most obvious ones, I suppose – but I fear a part of me was worried that Lydia May might consider these some kind of a 'cop-out').

Truth to tell, Mr J, I actually looked up 'greenness' in my Thesaurus when I finally got home that night, and was honestly shocked by how few green words there really are out there. *Real* green words. I mean if you consider purple, for example, there are loads of them: I can think of lilac, violet, lavender, plum and amethyst just off the top of my head. Sage green isn't a bad one (it just this second came to me!), and bottle green, of course …

'Well, how about *you* think of one?' I eventually suggested.

'Why?' Her eyes narrowed. 'What's in it for me?'

'Pardon?'

I was shocked by her baldly acquisitive attitude.

'I mean what do I *get* if I think of one?' she demanded.

'Get?! You get a wonderful sense of satisfaction, of course!' I exclaimed.

'Oh.'

She drained her second glass and then eyed my spare pint covetously.

'A marvellous sense of … of *achievement*,' I expanded.

Lydia May just gazed at me, darkly, as yet more darts thudded into the wall.

It was at this precise point, Mr Jennings, that a small 'need'
(which had been nagging away at me for quite some time now),
suddenly transformed itself into a powerful 'urge'.
(Fastidiousness prevents me from discussing this issue in too
much further detail, but suffice to say that by some strange
process of osmosis, a quarter of my pint had miraculously
chanced to 'evaporate' and I was consequently experiencing
nature's call.)

'Very well,' I eventually compromised, 'I'm willing to strike
you a deal. I'm going to dash off to the lavatory for a couple of
minutes, and while I'm gone I'd like you to sit here, on your
own, and try your best to come up with another word for
green. If, when I return, you've come up with something
especially good, I'll give you a very, *very* beautiful gift – a prize,
of sorts – which I currently have hidden away in my bag.'
(A lovely bookmark, Mr Jennings – plastic-coated – which I
acquired on a wonderful trip to Wordsworth's house in June. It
had an abridged version of '*I Wandered Lonely As a Cloud*'
printed in pretty gold lettering on to a calming, daffodil-yellow
background.)

'Okay,' Lydia May instantly obliged me. She then gazed up
at the ceiling, frowning, as if deep in thought.

I clambered (heavily!) to my feet, grabbed my stick, and set
off for the Ladies' lavatories. And yes, *yes* – I know *exactly* what
you're thinking, Mr Jennings: that it was utterly foolhardy, even
downright irresponsible, to leave Lydia May entirely to her own
devices again at that sensitive juncture! And you're right, of
course (100 per cent!), but a call of nature is a call of nature, is
it not?

Aside from that, I was determined to locate Catrin now,
come hell or high water. I had a fairly good idea that she wasn't
in the pub (I had a partial view of the car park and the front
entrance from where I was sitting). My only sensible course of
action, I felt, would be to try and persuade some charitable
individual to let me use their mobile (I don't own one myself,

more's the pity) in order to phone her from the pub and find out what the delay was all about (better still, to try and locate Wincey, and convince her to perform this small service for me).

I visited the lavatories, Mr Jennings (really beautifully done out, they are, in subtle shades of grey and ivory), then returned to the bar in the hope of locating an obliging local whose phone I might use, but even as I did so, I became aware of some kind of a 'commotion' in the saloon bar (the regular 'thud' of the darts had been temporarily interrupted, and the caller was instructing the crowd to 'please remain calm').

I have subsequently been informed of the extraordinary sequence of events that apparently played out during my short *sojourn* in the lavatories (all – or most – of which you yourself were a direct witness of, Claw).

Can I just say that when I saw that Lydia May was gone from our corner table (and that every remaining scrap of alcohol had been consumed – totalling one and three-quarter pints!) I turned and literally *sprinted* to the saloon bar to try and protect my young charge from any of the potentially hazardous scenarios that instantly crowded into my overheated mind (*none* of which, may I add, were anywhere near as bad as what later transpired!).

I use the phrase 'my young charge' advisedly, Mr Jennings, because I'm sure it's clear by now that I considered Lydia May to be my sole responsibility (in so far as one *can* be 'responsible' for such a wild and wilful creature!). It was in this spirit that I entered the saloon, full in the knowledge – in other words – that I was 'standing in' for Catrin (Lydia May's temporary – but official – carer).

Imagine my horror then, Mr J, when my old eyes (and forgive me for playing the age card again at this point; as I believe I said before, I have perfect vision, so this is cheeky of me, to say the least!) were greeted by the unwelcome sight of my young ward, Lydia May (I say 'young', but I fear this is an emotional description rather than an actual one; I've since been

---

262

informed that she is actually thirty-eight years of age!), in the midst of a bellowing throng, having her breasts manhandled (her breasts!) by an imposing, bearded, somewhat ferocious-seeming, silver-haired fellow in full biker apparel (this 'imposing fellow', it later transpired, was no less an individual than you yourself, Mr Jennings!).

I didn't know (indeed, how *could* I have known?) that this incident wasn't simply a cruel and random attack, but the culmination of a series of immensely provocative (nay, wrong-headed) acts on the part of Lydia May herself (i.e. acts that might almost be said to have *demanded* the kind of response they ultimately garnered – not that manhandling a young woman's breasts is *ever* justifiable, Mr J! Perish the thought!).

These aforementioned 'acts', e.g. staggering on to the 'oche' and parading around, annoyingly, in front of the dartboard (thereby interrupting play at a critical juncture), 'mooning' the caller (when he politely asked her to desist), pushing over Mutley's table (festooning his wife and your oldest daughter with drinks/bar snacks), and, finally, stealing your highly prized, reserve flights (as I understand the feathers on the dart are called) from the top pocket of your leather jacket (where you usually have them displayed during crucial matches as a kind of lucky 'talisman', I've been told) cannot and should not be supported under <u>any</u> circumstances.

Although – in Lydia May's defence – they were *green* flights, Mr Jennings! Fluorescent green! That's why Lydia May persisted in yelling, 'Fluorescent green! Fluorescent green!' throughout the subsequent brawl; the foolish girl was *still* hoping to win her prize, I imagine (and as a matter of fact I posted the bookmark to her, a couple of days later. I do, of course, realize that 'fluorescent' isn't really a type of green, as such, but I had to give her top marks for tenacity, Claw, if nothing else, and a deal *is* a deal, after all).

Like I say, Mr J, I knew *none* of these pertinent details at the time. If I'd had even so much as an inkling that your precious flights had been cunningly shoved inside her bra (for safekeeping), how different things might have been! (It seems that Lydia May *always* stores precious objects inside her bra. When we were strip-searched at the police station an hour or so later, they found not only your flights, but a £50 note, a crumpled picture of Gordon Brown, a small plastic model of Father Abraham from The Smurfs and half a 'bumper' packet of Maynard's Fruit Gums all stuffed in there.)

Had I been better informed (and feeling a tad more like 'myself') then I may well have resisted the rash, not to say ill-advised course of action I consequently took (in fact I'm *sure* I would have thought better of it!).

What I did was obviously wrong, Mr Jennings, but it was not premeditated in *any* way! And yes, I *am* seventy-two years old (pretty much 'over the hill' in most people's estimations!), but I still can't ignore the fact that I was a reserve for the 1960 British Women's Olympic Hockey Team (my usual position was right back, formally a defensive role. I have a hefty 'thwack', in other words – no matter *what* manner of stick I happen to be employing!).

But enough of me, now, Claw! I can find no earthy justification in 'mithering' on any further about these issues (to do so, at this late stage, would surely be pure self-indulgence!). Although I think it only fair to tell you that once I'd hit you with my stick (and had dragged Lydia May, kicking and screaming, from the saloon bar), I seriously believed that the worst of the affair was over – 'done and dusted', so to speak!

Little did I realize that the worst was yet to come! Because Lydia May still had those precious flights hidden about her person (your late father's flights) and you consequently felt unable (once you eventually came around, that is) to play on. The match was then awarded to the opposing team – a cruel decision, I feel, under the circumstances: you were suffering from quite a serious case of concussion, after all, an important detail which, I have been assured, your solicitor will be *very* keen indeed to put forward in your defence in court come January – and your thwarted hopes, profound sense of bafflement, deep feelings of frustration and disappointment simply combined to overwhelm you …

What more is there left to say, Mr Jennings, but simply to repeat that I am sorry, truly sorry, for my pivotal role in this dark and dire farrago, and that I hope you will some day find it in your heart to forgive me?

If I may beg your indulgence for just a few brief seconds longer, I would like to finish this letter with the first four stanzas of one of my favourite hymns: adapted from Rev. 3: 20, which always gives me solace, I find, even in my bleakest hours:

REV. 3: 20

Behold a stranger at the door!
He gently knocks – has knocked before;
Has waited long, is waiting still,
You use no other friend so ill.

But will he prove a friend indeed?
He will – the very friend you need:
The man of Nazareth – 'tis he,
With garments dyed at Calvary.

O lovely attitude – he stands
With melting heart and open hands;
O matchless kindness – and he shows
This matchless kindness to his foes.

Rise, touched with gratitude divine!
Turn out his enemy and thine;
Turn out that hateful monster – sin,
And let the heavenly stranger in.

Thank you for reading this letter, Mr Jennings. I do hope it's cleared up a few of the outstanding questions that may still have been niggling away at you during those long and wearisome nights in your cell.

If there is anything else you need to know, then please do not hesitate to contact me at the above address.

It goes without saying (but I'll say it, nonetheless) that you are constantly in my thoughts and prayers …
God Bless You,
Yours Faithfully,
Unity (Gray)

PS I have yet to hear back from Lydia May re the bookmark – although something tells me that she isn't one of life's natural correspondents!

PPS I have been utterly bemused by the extensive coverage of the 'Old Oak Riot' in the local press. It took my dear nephew Timothy upwards of ten minutes to explain the *Wharfedale Gazette* banner headline 'Flight Night!' to me – and I'm still not sure if I've grasped it entirely!

[letter 21]

Hawksleigh House
5 Shortcroft Road
Burley Cross

21st December

Darlingest, Darlingest-est-est Mummy,

Ethan says I must tell you, <u>straight away</u> (because he's far too lazy to write himself, but he loves you VERY VERY VERY MUCH!!!!), that Mrs Jeyes awarded him a gold star for being Best in Class on Friday. He was so happy about it that he wore it all weekend – mainly on the tip of his nose (Yik!). It kept falling off (even though I glued it back on there, twice) so we all had to search for it.

One time I found it floating in the toilet bowl AND HE STILL STUCK IT ON AGAIN, SOAKING WET!!!

Oh, my God! He's just *totally* DISGUSTING, Mum! (And I honestly don't know why he can't simply pick up a pen and tell you all this himself! HE ISN'T A BABY ANY MORE!!!)

NOOOO! HE JUST HIT ME WITH UNCLE A'S BADMINTON RAQUET AND MADE ME GET BLACK MARKER PEN ON MY FAVOURITE, YELLOW SKIRT! I HATE HIM SO MUCH! HE'S SUCH A PEST!

Ha! Aunty P's confiscated his PlayStation and is making him peel all the vegetables for dinner! 'But what's wrong with frozen peas?' he keeps whimpering.

I just made a special request for *extra* parsnips!
Yes!
The pile's even bigger than he is!
SERVES YOU RIGHT, YOU EVIL LITTLE MUTANT!!
(I do love him, really, though – honest I do, honest, honest, honest …)

Mum, if Dad is reading this to you as you lie in bed, *please*

---

tell him not to use that silly voice he always uses when he reads things out loud! I'll be FURIOUS if I find out he did!

Oh, Mummy, I miss you so much and I wish you were here with us. Aunty Penelope and Uncle Angus have been really kind and lovely and everything but we miss you LIKE CRAZY!!! Yesterday we had Steak and Kidney Pudding for dinner (with dumplings – Granny Jane's recipe) and Ethan COVERED his in brown sauce because it reminded him so much of yours that it made him want to cry.

I ate all of mine! Every last scrap! Even the dumplings and I had THREE! Aunty P was really, really pleased with me, although she <u>still</u> won't give me my phone back!

Aaargh!!

So UNFAIR!!

But I won't go on about it. I know you've got much more important things to think about: LIKE GETTING BETTER! TRY REALLY HARD, OKAY??

OKAY?!

Remember how I said I was going to send you something very special I was making at school for Christmas? Well, I'm not sending it, now. DON'T BE CROSS! LET ME EXPLAIN! I'm sending you something MUCH BETTER instead. Aunty P and I are making a HUGE batch of chocolate truffles on Saturday (with edible Christmas decorations etc. It was ALL my idea! We bought these really, really cute holly leaves made out of icing sugar from this AMAZING site on the internet) and we're giving them to everyone we know in these pretty little boxes (which we got at the same place. You have to build them yourself, but it's easy).

Well, anyway, we are making you a special batch ALL OF YOUR OWN with 70 per cent cocoa chocolate. REALLY bitter, like you love! (And there might be something else, too, but it's a surprise. DON'T LET DAD BLAB!!!!!!)

Aunty P has just said she's planning to send an extra few boxes down – one for the consultant, and a couple for those two nice nurses (but they <u>won't</u> be as gorgeous as yours, I promise!).

The thing I was working on at school (the other secret) was a piece of calligraphy (sp?). I was going to copy you out your favourite page from Jonathan Livingston Seagull, but then this girl I know gave me an even better idea (Kayla Dove – remember her? SHE'S BRILLIANT! *SOOO* FUNNY! I JUST <u>LOVE</u> HER NAME, DON'T YOU??!! She's from New South Wales and has a belly-button piercing with a pink crystal on the one end and a silver dolphin on the other – it's *soooo*, like, Britney-2004-tacky! AND she knows it, but she doesn't care! She's *soooo* FIERCE, I swear!!!).

Kayla had found this beautiful poem on the internet for her grandad called 'The Road Less Travelled'. When I read it I was just, like, wow! and immediately wanted to copy it out myself and give it to Mr Wolf.

It took me two whole hours! IT'S REALLY LONG!! Then I made this stupid, little mistake in the third last line and thought I was going to have to start all over again from scratch! I was like, *NO! NO! NO!* THIS CAN'T BE HAPPENING TO ME!! But then Mrs Turnbull came up with the idea of just covering the bottom half of the page with another piece of paper. She said because I was laminating it you wouldn't really be able to tell, and she was right. It looked almost perfect!

I took it over to Mr Wolf this morning and he was just, like: This is the nicest thing anyone has ever done for me!

I mean I *know* everyone's still really cross with him for deserting us on the hike and stuff, but I wanted to show them all that I still like him and trust him, even after what he did. He just made a mistake, Mummy, and, like I said to Aunty P (who didn't want me to give it to him, but I stuck to my guns, because I just *knew* it was the right thing to do): We all make mistakes in life. I've done some things in the past that I really, *really* regret (you know this better than anybody, Mum, but you carried on loving me just the same) and people have forgiven me – mainly because I'm a kid. Well, I want to forgive him, and that's that. Even Ethan thought it was a good idea (and his ear infection was nowhere near as bad in the end as everyone thought it would be).

I wish you could have seen his face, Mummy! He said he knew the poem already and it was one of his favourites. He had tears in his eyes. He thought my calligraphy was amazing. He just kept saying, 'I can't believe you did this all by yourself! That's incredible!'
He just couldn't stop staring at it!

Anyway, I hope you won't mind about Jonathan Livingston. If I get time over the holidays I might do it for you anyway.

Aunty P is taking me and Evaline (the girl from school I told you about with all the amazing, red hair – her mum and Aunty P are friends from bridge) into Leeds early next week to look for some boots and the black skinny jeans I want. Evaline has a pair *exactly* like the ones I'm after. She got them at H&M in August. I just really hope they still have them in stock. She says you can only get the ones I want at the bigger branches – so fingers crossed.

I was telling Aunty P that Evaline gets the Otley bus to school in the morning and says it's really well supervised. She said we could meet up every day and I could catch it with her, then Uncle Angus wouldn't need to drive me, although – don't get me wrong – I do enjoy getting a lift in the morning, especially in wet weather!

Uncle A and I always listen to the news together and then have heated discussions about the big issues of the day. It's fun! I would definitely miss that if he gave up driving me. But then I know how far out of his way he has to go to take me, and he works such a long day! It makes me feel guilty sometimes.

Did Dad tell you about the speech I made in school assembly for Macmillan Cancer Relief? I raised £33! Some kids even gave all their lunch money. People said I was really brave, but I said I wasn't brave at all, I said *you* were the brave one. I said you were so brave that it made us all want to try harder to be the best people we could be. I said you were an inspiration (AND I DIDN'T CRY! NOT EVEN A SNIFF!), because it's true. I said that I loved you SO MUCH and that you are the cleverest and the funniest and the kindest, sweetest, most generous person in the whole universe (Okay. Maybe I *did* cry, just a little bit).

Afterwards Mr Benson said that it wasn't only about the money (he gave £5!) but about spreading information and creating awareness. Anyway, I just wondered if Dad had told you?

Oh, I wish I could speak to you more, Mum! I know it's hard for you to hold the phone, and that you're very weak, but if I could just text you sometimes and tell you what I was doing – silly little things about my day etc. I would love that so much! I wouldn't even need any texts back from you! I'd just like you to know that I am thinking about you ALL THE TIME!!

It would be great to have my phone back so I could do that, although Jake Spencer says the electromagnetic fields caused by mobiles mean that sparrows can't reproduce properly. He said it's, like, *destroying* the sparrow population!

Weird, huh?
So maybe it's good I'm not using my phone after all!
See?! I'm trying to look on the bright side of things!!!

Okay. I've got to go now, Mum. Aunty P wants to set the table for dinner.
I love you SOOOOO much!
Please, please, please, please, please, please, please, please, please, please, please, please GET BETTER SOON!!!
LOVE YOU, LOVE YOU, LOVE YOU!

Astrid
XXXXXXXXXXXXXXXXXXXX
(+XXXXXXXXXXXXXX from Ethan, too)

PS. He's just finished the vegetables. What a mess! Bits of peeling all over the table and the floor. And the veg are so small, they look like Dolly Mixtures! Aunty P's getting the peas out after all!

AAAAARGH! *BOYS*!!!!

XXXXXXXXXXXXXXXXXXXXXXXXXXXXXXXXXXXXXXX
XXXXXXXXXXXXXXXXXXXXXXXXXXXXXXXXXXXXXXX
XXXXXXXXXXXXXX

[letter 22]

Hawksleigh House
5 Shortcroft Rd
Burley Cross

21 Dec '06

Dear Gabriel,

This'll have 2 be quick because Aunt P is watching me like a hawk. I CAN'T blow it this time. That fat old cow notices my every move. I am 6st.2oz. I have gained 2oz since I spoke 2 U on the phone from Hazlewood. It might just be water, though. I hid the plastic cup in the cistern like U said and it works a treat! You're a genius! I have at least three glasses every time I'm in there! She ALWAYS knows if I'm drinking from the tap. The pipes in this hellhole start screaming whenever you turn them on. It's sick.

I HATE THIS PLACE, GAB! I AM GOING INSANE! U'VE *GOT* 2 COME AND GET ME!!!

We don't have much time, now – I'm sure Ethan's starting 2 buckle. There's a new teacher at his school who's making a real effort with him – there's only so much longer I can get the stupid, little troll 2 keep his fat mouth shut about the hike etc.

I can't wait 2 tell U about the move I pulled with Mr Wolf! OMG! It was a masterstroke! What an idiot! I almost felt SORRY 4 him! They're all so easy 2 play, it's, like, *totally* ridiculous! I've been being everybody's perfect little miss! I have Uncle A eating out of my hand, now. I even made a speech at school to raise money 4 charity! I'm being the perfect, little ZOMBIE CHILD just like they all want me 2 be!! They're all so stupid and pathetic! They make me SICK!!! I can't wait 2 make them pay for what they've done 2 me!!

None of them understands me like U do, Gab. None of them speaks 2 my soul like U do, my sweet, dark blade, my blood,

---

273

my black, black Prince, my beautiful, brave and broken, skinny, Skinny Lad.

I am working on a scheme 2 get my phone back, but it might end up taking too long. They watch my EVERY move – esp. Penelope. That ugly, fat cow HATES me. She's so jealous of me, it's pathetic! She keeps telling me lies about you, just like Mum did. WHY DO THEY NEED TO DO THAT?! DON'T THEY KNOW IT JUST MAKES US STRONGER?!

WE R INVINCIBLE!!!!!

I'm pretending to write 2 mum right now (in hosp.) so that I can write 2 U instead. They won't even allow me 2 keep my pencil case when I get home from school! First the internet, then the phone, now this! I even have to *ask permission* to write my diary! I know they are reading it behind my back! How stupid do they think I am?!

Is there NOTHING they won't take from me? Is there NO DEPTH these zombies won't stoop to?

The plan is that we meet up on Christmas Day, behind the church (St Peter's) at 3pm EXACTLY. I'm planning 2 feed them a cock&bull story about going 2 light my mother a special candle in church. Nobody will suspect. I won't be able 2 ring U again or contact U 2 confirm.

REMEMBER! Our Song! 'STICKWITU'!!!!

UR my life!

UR are my blood – my smooth, smooth knife – my Guardian Angel – my soul!

Until the 25th, then – and eternity.

Sing our song if U feel low:

And now,
Ain't nothin' else I could need …
I'm crying cause you're so, so into me,
I got you,
We'll be making love endlessly,
I'm with you,
Baby, you're with me …

Nobody gonna love me better,
I'MMA GONNA STICKWITU FOREVER,
Nobody gonna take me higher,
I'MMA STICKWITU.

A X

PS PLEASE, PLEASE DON'T FORGET ABOUT ME, GAB!
I AM DESPERATE! I AM ALL ALONE! I AM
DEPENDING ON U!!

[letter 23]

Tollhouse Cottage
Fitzwilliam Street
Burley Cross

20/12/2006

Dear Teddy,

Festive Greetings from Burley Cross, England!
I have enclosed the set of Christmas stamps, as requested.
Once again, secular designs. They're perfectly passable, I
suppose. Two each for First Class and Second Class. I
especially like the £1.19 Christmas Tree and Presents. Can't
help thinking the Father Christmas on his Chimney and the
Snowman are somewhat workmanlike, however ...

They're by Tatsuro Kiuchi. He's a very reputable Japanese
digital illustrator. Perhaps I'm getting a little picky in my old
age, but I can't help feeling like there's something a fraction
'hollow' about the set, in general.

Is it just the preponderance of blue? I've never been a great
fan of blue tones at Christmas. I much prefer the warmer,
interior tones of red and green. Of course I fully accept that
those perennial Christmas themes of snow and ice demand a
blue/white palette, but I loathe the fashion for blue trees and
blue lights at the moment. People hang them all over their
houses nowadays – outside, too! I fear we've become terribly
American since you were last in the UK. You'd probably hardly
recognize the old place!

Call me an old grump if you like, but when I see blue lights I
immediately think 'emergency': Police! Fire! Ambulance! I
certainly don't think 'festive' or 'relaxation'.

It surely must have some bearing on the issue (the stamp
issue – no pun intended!) that they don't celebrate Christmas
in Japan. It isn't even a proper holiday over there.

On a somewhat more positive front, my Tristan da Cunha collection is almost 'definitive', now. The 1995 Queen Mother's Birthday arrived on Friday via Stanley Gibbons. I'm very pleased with it and am currently only hankering after the 1977 Naval Ships/Crests and the 1973 Anne and Mark's Wedding (neither very expensive – I'll probably order them for my birthday in late Feb).

Thanks so much for your letter. It was funny and informative, as always. I was delighted to hear that the long-anticipated talk by the man from the Organic Soil Assoc. went down so well on the island. I can't pretend I'm not eaten up with jealousy that he got government support to fund his trip over there.

From your brief précis I didn't get the impression that he had much of great interest to offer on the subject of soil erosion. This was definitely a missed opportunity. There's so much to be said (and done) on the matter – and not just in Tristan da Cunha, but worldwide (Africa! Asia! India! Even here, in the UK!). Imagine the differences we could make, environmentally, if we just put an end to tilling, if we finally resolved to stop using crop residue for other purposes (like fencing, animal feed etc.) and opted to proceed the *natural* way.

I know seed-drilling technology can appear prohibitively expensive at the outset, but just consider the money to be saved, in the long term, on diesel and fertilizer! Our topsoils are so vulnerable, so fragile. It's taken literally millions of years for them to evolve on this planet, and yet what people seem signally incapable of comprehending is that once they're gone, they're gone for good (unless you have a spare million or so years to wait around for them to gradually reconstitute, that is!).

World populations are growing at an alarming rate, millions go hungry every year, more and more pressure is being placed on the remaining soil stocks we have left, but *still* we persist in using farming methods whose long-term (even short-term) prognosis leads to erosion and sterility. This isn't just carelessness or stupidity, it's nothing short of criminal.

As I always like to say: people – the general public – really need to stop thinking of soil as just 'muck' or 'dirt' (denigrating it, in other words) and to start realizing that it's the foundation, the very lifeblood, of this beautiful earth we inhabit.

Part of the problem has always been that we (and by 'we' I mean governments, the big corporations etc.) are addicted to short-termism. That, and the fact that we invariably have a *vested interest* in shoring up an unsatisfactory situation (and thereby cheerfully maintaining the status quo). What exactly am I getting at here? Well, that real money – *serious* money – is always made from supplying treatments, not from inventing cures. Where's the logic in solving a problem if it means that the numerous institutions/industries that have been carefully developed over the generations to support it (pretending to counter it, but actually only sustaining it) will be rendered obsolete?

I was listening to a programme on the radio the other week about the huge increase in cases of Type 1 Diabetes, worldwide, and the various ways politicians and scientists have set about responding to this crisis (for the record, your average diabetic requires approx. £1 million in healthcare spending during the course of their lifetime). It became increasingly obvious (as the report progressed) that scientists were only really getting substantial, private and public funding to try and improve the kinds of treatments already in existence, not to grapple with the fundamental problem outright. Because where's the profit to be had in finding a cure for something?

Let's think about it this way: if your local street 'dealer' suddenly found himself in possession of a pill to cure heroin addiction (in one fell swoop), would he opt to sell it to his regular clients, even if they were willing to pay ten times as much money for it as for their regular hit? Not likely! Even your lowliest street punk understands the rudiments of capitalist economics! Supply and demand! These same principles apply across the board, not least to farming and to soil.

Sorry, Teddy – here I go again, banging on, relentlessly,

about my favourite topic! You must be heartily sick of my
incessant rantings by now! In fact you've probably accumulated
about as much 'core' knowledge on this subject as *I* have after
all these years (merely by acting as my sounding-board!). On
that basis, there's no 'earthly' reason (Oops! A little inadvertent
geological joke!) why you shouldn't host a public meeting
yourself to discuss this vital issue in an island context (I can
certainly supply you with a good set of crib notes!) instead of
patiently waiting for me to turn up and host one.

If only Joanna's sister hadn't moved to Stuttgart … She
insists on seeing her twice a year, and our already frugal holiday
funds are rapidly depleted on flights and hotels (Pam, her
sister, lives in a one-bedroom flat). As things stand (and much
as this grieves me), I can't see me fulfilling my childhood
dream of setting foot on 'The Loneliest Island in the World'
any time in the foreseeable future.

Curious to think that it's been all of forty-four years since we
last saw each other, face to face. I remember waving a cheery
farewell to you from the docks in Southampton like it was only
yesterday (the memory of that moment remains crystal clear!);
a blithe twelve-year-old, so full of hope and heat and heart and
confidence … Where'd it all go, eh?!

I suppose I shouldn't let myself get too down in the mouth
about it. These things are generally always best left in the hands
of the Gods ('Insh'allah' as the Muslims are wont to murmur).
If it hadn't been for a series of entirely unpredictable and earth-
shattering events, after all (an erupting volcano, no less!), we
would never have met up – or have become such firm friends –
in the first place. So who am I to pronounce with such certainty
(or such resignation) on what the future may hold?

'The Loneliest Island in the World' …
I couldn't help but smile wryly to myself as I wrote that down
just now. Because I don't mind admitting – at least not to you,
Teddy – that sometimes I feel rather like a lonely island myself
(even the loneliest island, on the odd occasion!).

I shouldn't complain. I have so much to be grateful for: good health, a loyal wife, a charming home. Burley Cross is such a beautiful place (a 'chocolate-box' village, to all intents and purposes), and I've grown to truly love West Yorkshire over the seven years since Joanna and I first moved here, but I must confess that I sometimes struggle to find people I can really talk to, people I can exchange ideas with or truly 'open up' to.

I sometimes feel starved of intellectual stimulation, of decent conversation. I used to enjoy the odd chat with Lance Tunnicliffe (OBE), but it's been difficult to maintain the relationship since he moved into sheltered accommodation in Ilkley. I'm not entirely sure why … Perhaps I serve as too much of a painful reminder of his old life (now over)? Hopefully this feeling may alter, in the fulness of time.

Then there was Robin Goff (the inventor – or 'The Prof' as he's known about the place). He's an odd man, somewhat scatty, slightly sensitive and irascible, very intense, a keen fell runner, but extremely interesting for all of that. Unfortunately our blossoming friendship has recently been soured (I won't go into all the sordid details) and I'm not sure if it will be possible to get it back on track.

The point I'm struggling to make here, Teddy, is that I still feel I have so much more to give … I just long to do something useful, something substantial, something of consequence, to break free from my shackles (self-imposed as they undeniably are) and purge this gnawing maggot of frustration that constantly and relentlessly seems to worry away at me.

I suppose this is all just part and parcel of the aftermath of Robbie's death. A child's death is never easy, but the death of a chronically disabled child takes its toll in so many quiet and insidious ways. It's much less straightforward than you might imagine (on an emotional level), so much more difficult to 'unpick'.

Joanna has coped with things by throwing herself, wholeheartedly (the only way Jo knows how!) into her many charitable pursuits – chiefly her animals. She's become absolutely indispensable at Gawkley. I was speaking to one of the other volunteers in Ilkley the other week who said they were thinking of naming her their 'Patron Saint'!

But it's always been that much harder for me, Teddy, not least because I found the situation with Robbie so much more demanding – so much more challenging – than Jo ever did (Jo's faithful as a Fox Terrier – loyal to the bone). I was always that little bit less 'easy' with it, less 'natural' with it, right from the start. I resented more. I gave less (or less willingly).

After he passed away I honestly believed life would just miraculously 'start up' again, that I would somehow (almost effortlessly) pick up where I had left off. But it seems like time has got away from me. Things have changed. They've moved on. And it's a cultural shift as much as anything. I keep reading articles (in *Nature*, the *New Scientist*) about how geology is 'the coming science', but I still have this nagging feeling that I'm 'old hat', that I've jumped off the carousel, that I've missed the bandwagon to some extent.

Seventeen years ago, I felt like a lone voice crying out in the wilderness on soil erosion issues, but today there are many voices, all clamouring together, in unison. How to make oneself heard among them, I wonder? How best to stand out and yet still to fit in?

Of course, on a rational level, I know that this upsurge in interest can only really be to the power of good (politically, environmentally) and yet still I find myself almost *resenting* it at some level (absolutely ludicrous, I know!).

I was watching a nature documentary on television the other week about the life-cycle of the earwig. It transpires that earwigs actually have a set of wings on their back – perfectly functional wings – which they never bother to use! I found this fact both strange and extraordinary. Where's the sense in lugging around a spare pair of wings all day, I thought, and yet never going to the trouble of unfurling the damn things? I mean why not just throw caution to the wind and cut loose, for once? Take to the air? If only as a novelty – for the sheer thrill of it? As an experiment! Because you can!

Then it suddenly struck me (with a sense of almost thudding dismay) that here I was – in all my hubris and my insolence – expecting the humble earwig (a mere *insect*) to step up to the plate and take exactly the kinds of life-altering decisions that I have always been signally incapable of making myself! Because sometimes *I* feel as though I had a pair of wings on my back – folded up but never opened, never tried, never extended, never truly and fully stretched out …

Have you ever felt that way yourself, Teddy?

On a more cheerful note (and much as it galls me to admit it), Baxter Thorndyke has definitely been of some positive use in this regard. He's helped to snap me out of my funk (to pull me – kicking and screaming – out of my rut). As you know, I've always had my misgivings about the man. I'm not sure if we really see eye to eye on an emotional or intellectual level – and certainly not politically! It's principally a 'social' connection, a 'local' connection, engendered, in the main, by my deep admiration for his prodigious energy – his enviable vitality.

There's certainly no denying his magnetism. He's deeply – even dangerously – charismatic (although cut more along the lines of 'a pocket Stalin' than a young Guevara, to be frank!).

I'm still somewhat at odds to understand what it is, at root, that drives him. I remain to be convinced that his motivation is entirely altruistic. But then who am I of all people (the personification of somnolence and ennui!) to stand in judgement on such matters?!

You may well remember that our 'partnership' (such as it is) began during his campaign to preserve the village's grass verges. Joanna and I happened to have just such a verge outside our cottage, and were often frustrated to find people (generally tourists) parking their vehicles hard up against it before setting off on a ramble or a hike on the moor. The verge would invariably be either crushed or irreparably dented, and a considerable amount of work was involved in setting it right.

By and large the campaign (which consisted of a series of rehearsed, public 'interventions', a small flurry of newspaper articles, a firmly worded 'Statement of Intent' placed in a prominent position on the notice board outside the PO, and some tastefully produced, portable, plastic signs – on supporting spikes – to be pushed into the more vulnerable verges as a warning during wet weekends and Bank Holidays etc.) has been very successful, although there have, inevitably, been some notable casualties.

Wincey Hawkes (the landlady of our local pub, The Old Oak), came in for a bit of stick in this regard. She's been encouraging coach parties to stop in the village (over recent months) and several prominent, central verges have suffered quite badly as a consequence. Don't quote me on this, but I get the general impression that her trade has been rather poor of late (especially after that unholy bust-up following the darts competition on Dec 12th: a succession of tabloid-style 'pub from hell' headlines in the local rag are hardly conducive to an increase in your overall customer base, I'd have thought!).

Poor Wincey. From what I've heard on the grapevine, she's still struggling to pay off the loans they took out for the extensive 'improvements' to the pub instituted by her late husband, Duke, who – just by the by – cultivated the most bitter and rancorous feud with Baxter while he was still alive. The two men quite literally loathed each other!

From what I can recall, Baxter was accused of using his influence on council to block the expansion of the pub car park. Duke was furious about it. His response was to spontaneously compose and perform a series of the most filthy songs about Mr Thorndyke – to general acclaim – while perched at his harmonium on the saloon bar!

He truly was a most extraordinary sight! While playing this wheezing instrument (and due to his enormous girth, he wasn't entirely immune to emitting the odd wheeze himself) he looked not unlike an over-extended walrus, gently tinkering with a walnut!

A remarkable man, and greatly missed (but I do seem to be getting slightly drawn off the subject here) …

Baxter's other notable campaign – against speeding in the village – has likewise had a pretty positive impact. Not so much in preventing the aforementioned traffic from taking this slightly shorter route (BC is favoured by 'boy racers' – and more sober folk who really should know better – as a short cut), but in giving people a sense of empowerment, a feeling that they are taking action themselves rather than just sitting back and letting standards slip.

My most significant involvement with Baxter, to date, has, of course, been with the BCPTW – his campaign to 'clean up' the local public toilets (which are located just at the end of Fitzwilliam St).

Given that these facilities are the only public lavatories for many miles around, they are naturally considered a vital resource for tourists, ramblers and local tradesmen alike, but they have also become the backdrop for what I shall simply call 'more nefarious' pursuits.

I must confess that I hadn't even really registered this unsavoury underground activity until Baxter first drew it to my attention (during a National RSPB-sponsored Big Garden Birdwatch Campaign at the end of January; we were part of an elite team of volunteers tabulating the number of wild birds in a small area of common ground directly behind the toilets at the time), but since he did, I have become increasingly preoccupied by the amount of undesirable 'traffic' these toilets seem to attract.

Sometimes I drive my car up there (it's only a distance of thirty or so yards from our cottage, in actual fact) and park it in the designated zone to try and get a proper sense of how bad the problem really is. I have started taking notes – writing down the car registration details of the men who enter the facilities and then seem to be taking a suspiciously long time to reappear.

I showed this information to Baxter and he was very pleased and impressed by my levels of diligence, and promptly set up a BCPTW website on the back of it (another example of that boundless energy I keep harping on about!)! He even went so far as to appoint me 'chair' of the committee (a kind gesture, but an empty one, given that there are currently only three members, all told!).

As a part of our overall strategy, Baxter then suggested that we might start taking surreptitious photographs of the worst of the offenders in order to establish some kind of a formal, visual record of the main participants in these degenerate activities. I was initially a little slow to warm to the idea, but after he invested some committee funds in a digital camera, and acquainted me with the fundamentals of how to use it in the most effective way, I must confess that I've become quite the 'secret snapper' (taking some pretty impressive shots – even if I say so myself!)!

Of course the police refuse, point-blank, to consider amateur photographic evidence as a sufficient incentive to take these vermin to court. It's deeply frustrating, but Baxter still feels it may serve a purpose (could be a useful resource to use as a 'bargaining counter', for example, and to show the police – and the perpetrators – that we are deadly serious in our concerns about the matter).

My experiences at the toilets have certainly proved to be quite an eye-opener. I've been astonished by how many local men are frequenting these facilities on a regular basis. Many of them bring their dogs along – as a kind of 'cover'. I'm presuming that a good proportion of these gentlemen are married and pretending to their ignorant spouses that they are out on the moor, exercising their benighted (and patently neglected) animals, while what they are actually doing is driving them over to the toilets, 'parking up' and then leaving the poor, confused creatures mouldering away inside the car for hours!

I made the mistake of mentioning this gruesome scenario to

Joanna (who had hitherto remained determinedly disinterested in the matter, being very much of the 'well, if they're not hurting anybody …' frame of mind) and she quite literally went ballistic (proving – if proof were needed – that while people are perfectly welcome to do pretty much what they like to each other in Jo's book – however sick or perverse it might be – once a dumb animal gets tangled up in the equation … Well, you'd better watch out!).

I suppose it was partly as a consequence of Jo's avowed militancy on the issue that I felt compelled (almost against my better instincts) to take some direct action in this regard during an especially bad instance of what I perceived as 'serious neglect' a few weeks ago.

I had observed a man – youthful, brown-haired, quite fit and handsome, dressed for hiking – entering the toilets at approximately 14.00 hrs on a quiet Tuesday afternoon. He was driving a dark, metallic-green hatchback (some kind of Hyundai, I think). When he initially pulled up I noticed that he had a very beautiful, large and finely bred Red Setter accompanying him.

I ducked down in my seat upon his arrival (so as not to be observed) and took a couple of preliminary shots (he definitely looked familiar to me – I presumed I'd probably seen him loitering in the vicinity before), then kept my eyes firmly trained on the toilets for the next fifteen or so minutes, patiently waiting for him to re-emerge.

After he had been gone for five minutes (tops), I noticed that his dog was growing increasingly distressed (I was busily scribbling down his registration number at the time; I have a very handy 'single binocular' – a 'mono-ocular', I suppose you'd call it – a tiny black telescope which I bought at Millets for specifically this purpose). The dog was shifting around, frantically, in the back of the car and pawing at the window. Eventually it began barking, mutedly (but emphatically) through the glass.

As the minutes gradually ticked by, the dog became more and more hysterical, leaving slicks of foam on the window, even hurling itself against the car's interior bodywork (principally the wire mesh that separated the poor deranged beast from the rest of the car's interior).

Enough was enough! Disturbed and infuriated, I climbed out of my car and walked over to the Hyundai to try and calm the Setter down. It clawed at the window, still more frantically, upon my arrival. I tried to talk to it through the glass, but it simply ignored me (far too agitated). I cursed under my breath, impotently, and was about to turn towards the toilets (intent on heading in there and confronting the owner directly), when I noticed – with some astonishment – that the car was actually unlocked!

At this point (and don't ask me why – I can't really *say* why) I found myself applying some slight pressure to the back handle, twisting at it, gingerly, and feeling the mechanism of the lock unlatching itself with a smooth, satisfying *clunk*.

I suppose (in retrospect) that my instinctive aim was to open up the door by a couple of inches simply to try and give the dog a bit of fresh air, or perhaps to talk to it, soothingly, through the gap, and – if it didn't seem unduly snappy or aggressive – to pat it or stroke it to try and ease its distress.

No sooner had the mechanism sounded, however, than the dog (a large animal – larger, even, than you might imagine) had thrown its entire body-weight against the door and had violently burst its way out – sending me flying (I landed flat on my back)!

Before I could so much as draw breath – let alone clamber to my feet again – it had bolted off, at speed, into the undergrowth (following a route I presume it knew all too well, down a nearby moorland path and then up on to the moor itself). I remained seated on the ground for a few seconds, somewhat dazed and confused, then quickly scrambled to my feet, breathless and slightly flustered.

What now? I glanced around me, nervously. How to proceed from here with the absolute minimum of fuss and embarrassment? Did I quickly shut the boot (carefully wiping my fingerprints off the handle with my shirt sleeve) or just leave it gaping open (as if the dog had – by some miraculous fluke – managed to release the mechanism by itself)? Did I pursue the dog on foot and attempt to retrieve it (but what chance was there of that when I didn't have a lead to attach to its collar, or even know the name to call out?)? Did I try and alert the owner, or simply (the cowardly option, perhaps) head back to my car and lie low (or nonchalantly drive home, as if none of this had ever happened)?

I scanned the horizon for any witnesses. The coast seemed clear. I then quickly wiped the door handle with my handkerchief (better safe than sorry!), drew a long, deep breath, smoothed down my hair (or what remains of it!) and headed back to my car, fully intent on beating a hasty retreat. I'd barely taken five steps towards the car, however, before I was tormented by sudden, violent pangs of conscience. How could I possibly just walk away from this? Wouldn't that simply be wrong of me? Even criminal (delinquent, immoral?)?!

I stopped dead in my tracks and then turned, with a grimace, to face the toilet block. What would Joanna do, I wondered? How would 'St' Joanna behave under such trying circumstances?

Need I even ask?! I gazed over at the block for several seconds, vacillating wildly, then swallowed down my qualms and set off, determinedly, towards it.

It's difficult to describe at this point – with any real clarity or lucidity – the extraordinary series of events (one might almost call them 'phantasmagorical' or 'hallucinogenic', even 'chimerical') that now commenced to unfold around me (everything still remains such a strange, unconsolidated mess – a blur – in my mind, so please do your best to bear with me, Teddy). Suffice to say that I coughed, sharply, several times, before first entering the men's lavatories. I may even have stamped the mud off my boots (although I wasn't actually wearing boots) and whistled, nonchalantly, to telegraph the fact that my intentions were entirely legitimate, above-board and non-predatory. The door, as I recollect, felt extremely heavy against my shoulder as I pushed up against it, and opened with a loud, heartfelt – almost ecstatic – groan.

On entering the block, 'proper', I rapidly glanced around me, fully tensed, expecting to see the dog's owner lounging against the latrine, or standing by the sink, but there was no immediate sign of him. I suppose I could have just called out something (in retrospect, I think that would've been the most sensible plan of action). I could have called out something like 'Hello? Is anybody there? I've just come from the car park where there's been a most unfortunate mishap involving a dog ...' (I've rehearsed this scenario since, a thousand times, in my mind.) But I didn't. I didn't speak. I just glanced around me, slightly spooked. Then I walked over to the latrine (it seemed the obvious thing to do – I was nervous, my bladder was full and I desperately needed to relieve myself).

As I made use of the latrine, my ears were pricked and my eyes were peeled for any unusual visual or aural stimuli. There *were* noises – very slight noises, but noises, nonetheless. They seemed to be coming from the furthest cubicle (there are three cubicles, all told). Once I'd finished passing water, I automatically turned and walked towards them (the noises), tensed, anxious, my stomach churning, almost holding my breath.

I was preparing myself to say something – something like ... like ... I don't know ... like: 'Hello? Is anybody there? Would you happen to be the owner of a Red Setter by any chance? Because if you are, then I'm sorry to have to inform you ...' but before I could utter so much as a word, I noticed something glinting on the floor – a coin – a silver coin – a ten pence piece ...

Of course I automatically bent over to pick it up – to retrieve it. I leaned down, I leaned forward (to take hold of it, this coin, this dropped coin), and as I leaned over, as I bent down (to retrieve this coin) I glanced up (as you do when you lean down, sometimes), and unwittingly found myself staring straight into the furthest cubicle – the end cubicle – where the door, it now transpired, had been left propped slightly ajar …

It's important to underline how *utterly unintentional* this was, Teddy. I mean if it hadn't been for the coin (which turned out not to be a coin at all, just a small metal disc of some description, embedded in the tile), then I wouldn't have bent down, I wouldn't have leaned forward (not at all! Wouldn't have dreamed of it!), and, in this idealized scenario (this fantasy scenario) I would have consequently avoided … would never have seen or borne witness to … to this extraordinary scene – this bizarre tableau – this strangely inchoate and confusing spectacle of … of …

It took a few seconds to make any sense of it, a few seconds to render intelligible the complex arrangement of their bodies, the curious positioning of their limbs … It took a few seconds to assimilate. And then that natural pause – that shocked hiatus – as the brain tries to process what it's witnessing (on a social level, a moral level), as the brain tries to fully fathom the sight it's beholding …

Thirty seconds, at best, until my brain could make any real sense of it. Forty seconds, at most. And remember, I was still thinking about the coin – distracted by the coin, the metal disc – embedded in the tile, which I'd thought was a ten pence piece (just processing the confusion of that whole silly incident) and steadying myself, physically, as I straightened up after bending down.

And the most ridiculous thing of all (you'll laugh at this, I know you will) is that in my confusion – in my natural confusion – having been initially alerted by those perplexing sounds while standing, innocently, by the latrine (or 'nervously' by the latrine – I forget which it was, now), in the inevitable confusion that followed (and I wish you could have been there to see how swiftly time passed – so swiftly! – and to judge the distances involved – it was so close – it's so very cramped in there, barely any distance at all!), in those few vital seconds that followed, I had somehow not quite managed to ... I had yet to ... to finish off my ... to tuck away my ... to put away my ...

It was still idly propped in my hand! Suspended in my hand! But utterly unconsciously! Like a girl holding an old rag doll! Like a child holding an empty pop bottle! I was just caught off my guard, that's all! Still dazed from the fall (remember?). Still confused from the incident with the dog by the car, the sudden pang of guilt, the change of heart, the whistle, the cough, the stamp of my foot ...

Yes.

And there I was, all agog, struggling to make any sense of that strange tangle: that mess of limbs and heads and lips and hands ... Just this extraordinary abstract. This sensual *Guernica*. The one figure sitting down, his back slightly arched, his eyes closed. The other kneeling – on his knees – kneeling (did I already just say that?) towards his lap ...

And the moment of horror – of shock – of recognition – when the seated gentleman (I call him a gentleman) chanced to open his eyes for a second, with a groan of ecstasy, to invite me in, almost, to include me as a player – an unwitting player – in their little drama ... In that moment – in that brief moment – we looked – we saw – we recognized ...

Robin?

The *Prof*?!

Robin *Goff*?!

Oh *God*!

No!

And I had completely forgotten about the dog (in my confusion). I was all ... I was just ... I should have *mentioned* the dog before – or even then, right that second, perhaps. If I had mentioned the dog – or the coin – then it might not have

seemed quite so … so … But I didn't mention the dog. No. I
didn't mention the coin. I just stared. I just stood there,
helplessly, holding my … I just … How long? I'm not sure.
How long did I stand there, in shock? In horror? In awe?

I'm not … I don't …

Of course you mustn't breathe a word of this, Teddy! Please!
Make no mention of it in your next letter. Or if you do, then
encode it. Refer to it as … as The Wreck of HMS Julia
(*Shipwrecks; first series; 1985*). I'll pretend that I've lost it (the
stamp). You can say something casual like, 'Have you found
The Wreck of HMS Julia yet?' or, 'You were a damn fool to
lose The Wreck of HMS Julia,' or even, 'I feel so sorry that you
lost the … so *dreadful* for you … I've been there myself, many
times, and I understand completely …'

Yes. Something comforting like that. Because Joanna likes to
read our correspondence, on occasion, and we couldn't – I
mean if you accidentally let something slip, that would just be
so … so *horrendous*. Unthinkable! I couldn't possibly … Let's
keep this our little secret, shall we? A private exchange, between
the two of us?
(I just needed someone to confide it, Teddy. Someone I can
trust.)

They still haven't found it, I'm afraid. They haven't found
HMS Julia (the dog). It's been all the talk in the village. There's
a Lost Dog photograph on the notice board outside the shop.
There's been a small article run in the *Wharfedale Gazette*. And
the best part of it? The crowning glory? The identity of the
heartbroken owner? PC Peter Richardson!

A police officer!
What a fool I've been! What a fool *he's* been (because there
were photographs – already downloaded on to the computer
from the camera; I *had* seen him parked up there before – and
Baxter suddenly came across them, randomly, a couple of
weeks ago, while going through the files … So I think he knows,
now! I think he suspects!).

The circumstances of the dog's loss are being called 'suspicious', but that's currently about as far as it goes … Although it's been sighted, at least twice, over the past six weeks: once, on Guy Fawkes', up near Saint's Kennels (the day after it first went missing), purportedly worrying a sheep. Another time, a couple of weeks later, by a local man out hiking near Piper's Crag – or Herber's Ghyll – I forget which …

Nothing since.

I keep thinking about that poor animal, Teddy; out there, all alone on the moor in the cold. It's been six weeks! Sometimes I lie awake at night – as Joanna sleeps beside me – and I think about it ranging around up there: hungry, unbidden, almost feral. I can't get it out of my mind! It haunts me! And when I do finally fall asleep, it fills my dreams: this handsome, burgundy animal, tormented by ravening appetites. This powerful, proud, red beast: untrussed, unfettered; uncowed; truly wild and utterly unconstrained.

But how will we ever bring it back into the fold, now, Teddy? That's the thought that torments me the most! How can we possibly hope to civilize it again after such a sweet and tantalizing taste of liberty?

How?

Oh, God! That's the door! Joanna's home. I must finish up. I promised to pre-heat the oven for the lasagne. I swore I'd fill the coal scuttle … So much still to say, old friend. But enough for now, eh?

Enough.

Thank you for bearing with me. It means the world. Please, *please* don't judge me too harshly …

Tom

PS Hope the asthma has improved. A Very Merry Christmas to Merrill and the kids. Do enjoy the stamps.

[letter 24]

12 Rivock House
Jaytail Crescent
Ilkley

20th December, 2006

Dear Dr Bonner,

It's good news, I'm afraid (or bad news, I'm happy to say. *You* know what I mean …).

I'm pregnant, in other words.

Pregnant.

Me, Nina Springhill, up the duff.

A bun in the oven.

It's official.

I finally plucked up the courage to tell Glenn last week and he just stared at me for about a minute (no expression) and then said, 'Is it mine?'

I wish to high heaven it wasn't, Dr B! Not that I mean I wish it wasn't *his*. I just wish *it* wasn't. I just wish *I* wasn't.

A baby is pretty much the last thing on earth this situation needs right now – and I think even Glenn's starting to gradually appreciate that fact (no matter how hard he worked at bullying me into it in the first place). Not that he's actually *said* anything (Mr Monosyllabic? *Say* anything? Actually talk about his feelings? Are you kidding me?!), but he made me one of those flowers out of tissue paper (like the ones you learn to make at school) and left it on my pillow the other day. It was sweet.

I don't know what I'm going to do. An abortion's out of the question (obviously). I'm just going to have to make the best of things, I guess; quietly reconcile myself to my fate. Make a virtue out of necessity, as my mum always says. And why not? It's the legendary 'Springhill Way', after all … That's one of the only positive benefits of coming from a family of unholy

---

294

screw-ups: you always know how best to react when the shit really starts hitting the fan …

Hang tough, Nina!

Bite the bullet!

Take it on the chin!

Or, in my particular case: like it or lump it! (Like it *and* lump it … Ha ha.)

This isn't your problem, anyway (not that you needed me to tell you that!). And I'm fine, actually. I'm doing okay. A cloud of quiet resignation is settling all around me.

From the middle of this cloud (and it's quite dreary in here, quite damp!) I just really wanted to write and say how sorry I am that I was so rude and off-hand with you when we met up the other month. Everything you said was true. Everything! It just took a while for it to sink in properly, that's all.

I suppose I was still trapped in the stupid mindset that it was only Glenn who needed to talk his problems through, not me (I was just great! I was completely brilliant! Rock solid! Everything was just hunky-dory! Still is, in actual fact!). I honestly didn't realize how caught up in the situation I'd become. And you were right when you suggested that our relationship was doomed from the start (I'm sorry I bawled you out when you said it. I was just shocked. You were telling me all these things that I already knew were true in my heart, but I just didn't have the balls to face up to them at the time).

I've been so naive! Such a bloody idiot! I was just playing at being Florence Nightingale (like you said). It was all just a silly fantasy. I was just being … I don't know … A stupid dick-head! Arrogant. Self-important. Holier than thou. I was so busy making this huge, grand gesture – this dramatic 'statement' – that I never bothered to sit down and think through what it all *meant*, what it would ultimately add up to, what the actual consequences would be … ('Oh yes, I know he's just lost his legs, I know he's already married, I know things will be difficult, but he loves me, and I love him, and nothing else matters …')

I was living in cloud-cuckoo land! I was caught up in all the drama. And I've paid a high price for it, Dr B. I threw everything away that I'd worked so hard (so *bloody* hard) for: my little flat, my friends, my new nursing career (which I loved) and all for what? For some childish schoolgirl crush? A crazy, half-formed gesture of self-sacrifice? (That's a Catholic upbringing for you. I suppose it had to reveal itself, somehow, somewhere along the line!)

I honestly thought I was being so brave – so noble – when in fact all I was being was a big, immature kid. So *unprofessional*! Trying to worm myself right into the heart of this awful tragedy (Glenn's awful tragedy – which had nothing remotely to do with me). Making myself the centre of it.

Unbelievable, really, when I actually come to think about it. I was like Erin sodding Brockovich (in the film. Although *she* actually achieves something worthwhile by the end, and all I've done is create a horrible mess – a terrible mess – and make everyone feel even worse about themselves. Well done, Nina! *Great* work, lass!).

It just kills me when I think back on it, now.

I mean I knew Glenn was married, and that the travel arrangements were difficult for his wife (especially with two young kids to look after and no proper family support to speak of), but I didn't give a damn about it. *Seriously*. I was so ready to judge her. I was so busy being the perfect little nurse, bustling around the place in my neat starched blue uniform. So happy playing the part, in other words.

She didn't stand a chance – not a chance. And Glenn's … well, he's just Glenn. He's just … just the man he is – a bit of a bully, a bit controlling, a bit of a blow-hard, a bit of a 'glass-half-full' type of person (with legs *or* without them). He was vulnerable. He was flailing around. I was just an escape route. Something new. Something that *hadn't* actually been destroyed by that land mine. Something positive (or so he thought) to emerge from the whole mess.

I'm not proud of what I did, Dr Bonner. I suppose my head was just turned. I was like some awful Angel of Mercy – a Love Vampire (here we go: that wonderful knack for self-dramatizing you talked so eloquently about!). But it wasn't even love, was it? Just grandstanding.

And everybody told me it was a mistake (everybody – even Mum!), but would I listen? Would I hell! I've always been a pig-headed little cow.

Well, my chickens have certainly come home to roost, now…

You asked me about Divine Retribution, remember? I said I didn't believe in it – and I honestly don't think I do – but if I did, then, yes, Nick arriving home (dropping out of the clouds like that – completely without warning) was definitely a strong indicator!

I was so freaked out when I tried to say his name during our session and then found that I just *couldn't* – began stuttering like a crazy-woman and then burst into floods of tears! I was mortified! It just stuck in my throat! It was like I could barely get it out of my mouth! Like I was choking on it! I had no idea (till that moment) that I was so cut up about the whole thing, that my feelings were still so strong for him.

After we talked, I really thought about what you said: about how it was crueller to keep Glenn hanging on if I still had such powerful, unresolved feelings for somebody else – no matter how much Glenn said he loved me, or what he was threatening to do to himself if I left (no matter how much of a bastard he was being; the fault was still mine, to some extent. The *power* was still mine, more to the point). Not that it's even relevant any more – what with a baby on the way. Nick wouldn't be interested now. How could he be?

Anyhow, it turns out that he has this amazing American girlfriend! She's a biochemist or something. She speaks four languages. She's a really great cook. He's constantly coming into the post office to get stamps and envelopes for packages he's sending her. It's pure torture! He's so devoted – so dedicated! It's like he never stops writing to the bloody woman!

Even if I did think I had a hope in hell with Nick (which I obviously don't), I could never, *never* jeopardize his current relationship (not after what I did to Glenn and Laura).

I did follow your advice and try to tell him how I felt, though (before I really knew how serious he was about Yasmin). I set up this tour for me and Glenn at RAF Fylingdales (the base where Nick works). I partly did it for him and Glenn to get to know each other better (Glenn's been so paranoid about him since he saw us having that joke together outside the bank in Ilkley – when I took the piss out of Nick for wearing trainers with his suit. Afterwards he kept making all these loaded comments like, 'Well, at least he has feet to wear trainers *on*. Do you *like* a nice pair of feet in a man, Nina?' Stuff like that.

It's just so exhausting, sometimes – second-guessing everything I say around Glenn. Although perhaps it *was* insensitive of me to kid around with Nick in front of him. I just didn't really think about it at the time. I was caught up in the moment. Nick seems to have that effect on me).

I also set up the tour in the hope that it might give Glenn the incentive to consider going back to work again. Nick actually told me that he would hire Glenn if Glenn was at all keen on the idea. He insisted that it wouldn't be as a favour to me, but because Glenn would've earned it in his own right (there's plenty of appropriate work there for someone in a wheelchair. The base is basically just full of nerds sitting around logging space junk all day; it's pretty static work, but apparently the jobs are really sought after).

It didn't quite pan out in the end. Glenn was really aggressive with Nick – really hostile. I think it's probably still too early for him to seek full-time employment. He's still too raw. And anyway, I get the feeling that a clean break with the military might be necessary (being around other soldiers just seems to be a constant reminder of what he's lost. I think you may've hinted at that possibility during our chat).

One good outcome of the tour was that it finally got him off his arse (out of his comfort zone) and made him think about his long-term goals. He's considering applying to a college (down south) to do that sound engineering course he's always fancied. It's made him think about the future in a more positive light.

Anyway, at the end of the tour I plucked up the courage to tell Nick (on the walk back to the car) about how I'd always had this huge crush on him at school. And guess how he reacted?!

He didn't!!

It was a disaster!! He just kind of stared at me, blankly. He seemed really confused – even embarrassed. So then I got all embarrassed myself and made a big joke out of it (same as I always do). He then turned on me and started lecturing me about how I'd 'really changed' since school. That upset me quite a bit. It was like I'd let myself down or something – like I was this massive disappointment to him now.

He's always really nice whenever we meet up, though, very attentive, always makes me laugh (which is something I really love about him – and something I've really missed, too). But I think it's more out of pity than anything.

When he finds out I'm pregnant he's just going to flip! He'll think I'm such a fool – that I've made such a mess of things! And he'll be completely right! Just the idea of seeing his face when he finds out actually makes me feel physically sick. That's partly why I've decided to do as Glenn wants and move down to Taunton with him. It'll mean he's closer to his wife and kids. He has way more friends down there – lots of them pre-army, which is good.

I just think he deserves a fresh start, with my full support. I'm dreading making the move, but it's a sacrifice I feel I should probably make. And it's a real sacrifice, for once – a true sacrifice.

On a more positive note, it'll be a huge relief to get away from this place (Burley Cross – Ilkley – the post office). It's just too painful seeing Nick around all the time and imagining what could have been if I hadn't been such a bloody fool. I'm so much in love with him, Dr B – crazy in love with him. Every time that song comes on to the radio (by Jay Z and Beyonce) I just break down in tears.

Pathetic!

I blame it on the hormones.

Anyhow, that's me about done and dusted. I just wanted you to catch up with all my news, and to tell you how much I've appreciated your kindness and your honesty. It really was such a great relief to speak to someone who wasn't directly involved in the situation. I'd been feeling so lonely and I didn't even know it!

We're planning the move for early/mid Feb, so I can work out my notice at the PO. Hopefully I won't be showing too much by then – I'm keen to keep my pregnancy under wraps until we go (with any luck).

Before I finish up, remember how you asked me towards the end of our session if I would think of my favourite memory – my most beautiful memory – and tell you about it? But I couldn't actually think of one?

Well, you'll be relieved to know that I've thought of plenty of them since (loads of them!), but the one my mind keeps coming back to is of when I was seventeen and I was at this party (it was just some boring party in Ilkley, a birthday party for this boy I knew from school) and everybody was completely drunk (I was sober for some reason – can't remember why, exactly). Then Nick turns up, out of the blue. He'd just won this scholarship to America (I was totally devastated that he was leaving, so much so that I'd started dating this guy I met on the school bus – who I didn't really fancy at all – simply to try and put a brave face on the whole situation).

Anyway, Nick turns up just as some idiot is accidentally tipping cider down my top. I was soaked! (I don't remember what I was wearing, but it was definitely something new.)

Nick was horrified. He got me to take it off, hand washed it in the kitchen sink and stuck it in the tumble dryer. He gave me his jumper to wear as it dried. Then we went outside and sat in the garden together. He was ranting on about how much he hated Chris Evans, and making me roar with laughter.

We were sitting on the bottom step at the far end of the patio. This kid's house was halfway up the hill (the moor) and had an amazing view into the valley below. All the lights were twinkling. There was this powerful smell of lavender (two huge plants stood on either side of us, and we kept nudging them with our elbows as we talked, releasing this wonderful, heady scent into the atmosphere).

It was so beautiful! And I would have kissed him, right there and then, but he was dating my best friend at the time, so I just gazed up at him – really, kind of, melting inside. I honestly thought he was the most wonderful boy I had ever met.

I still think that. And while I know nothing can come of it now, just having seen him again, after all this time (taking into account all the pain it's caused me and everything), a part of me is still incredibly glad – that non-disillusioned part, that non-resigned part – because I can hold the memory of him in my heart forever, and cherish it, and finally believe in something – something honest, something unchanging, something constant. Real love. True love.
(Okay, I'm done! Stop retching! You can put away the sick-bag!)

Well, I think that's probably quite enough of me rambling on about myself for a while … I doubt I'll see you again before the move etc., so thanks (so much) for everything you've done for me. You've really made a big difference.

Hope you have a great 2007!
All the best,
Nina (Springhill)

PS Here's something a little strange that just happened (I thought you might appreciate it, being a shrink and everything). While I was working in the PO this afternoon, one of our customers (a man called Baxter Thorndyke) accidentally left his wallet behind on the counter. During my tea break I volunteered to take it around to his house. Oonagh (the postmistress) said she was happy to do it after work, but I was like, no, no, I really need to get some air (which was kind of weird, really, in retrospect).

Anyway, I walked over to his house (it's this big place called The Old Hall), and when I got there (it's about half past three in the afternoon – freezing cold), the front door is wide open! I knocked a few times (no answer) and considered just leaving the wallet on the hallway table, but then became convinced that a passing stranger might come in and steal it (unlikely, really, and I could've just closed the door after me, anyway).

As I stood there (unable to make up my mind – classic case of Pregnancy Brain!) I could hear music in a distant room – up a small flight of stairs (awful, South American pan-pipey stuff), so I headed towards it, barely noticing my surroundings, almost like I was in a dream or something.

Eventually I found myself walking into this large room, this huge bedroom (thick, shag-pile carpets, four-poster bed, embossed velvet counterpane, oriental wall-hangings etc.), and there, in the middle of this room, at the heart of it, was a massive, free-standing bath (you know the kind of thing: gold taps, lion's claw feet …).

The bath was steaming hot and full of bubbles. The room reeked (it stank!) of this really strong, really awful scent (orange blossom, I think, which made me want to vomit). But best of all, sitting in the bath, completely starkers, wearing this crown made out of ivy leaves (like something you might see at a really tacky toga party) and holding a glass of what looked like champagne, was Mr Thorndyke!

I just stood there for a second, my mouth hanging open, barely knowing what to say. Then he smiled and said (in this really creepy voice), 'Ah, Pretty Post Office Girl, COME TO ME!' and toasted me with his glass!

He held out his other hand. I gazed at it for a few seconds, totally astonished, before realizing that he probably just wanted me to give him his wallet back!

I said, 'Your wallet. Of course ...' (all, kind of, mechanically) and passed it to him. Then I curtseyed (I curtseyed! I've never curtseyed in my life!), turned on my heel and sprinted off!

I've felt all tingly and light-headed and woozy ever since ... So there you go! More crazy adventures from the weird and wacky world of Burley Cross!
Make of it what you will!

XN

[letter 25]

Fewston Grange
Hardisty Hill
Blubberhouses

21/12/06

Mr Brogan,

Yet more incidents to report. I went down there yesterday morning early (must've been around 8 a.m. – sun'd hardly rose) and found that confounded bloody woman (Tilly Brooks) accompanied by that confounded bloody duck (repulsive thing it is – face like a piece of broiled tongue), swimming around – trespassing – in my Private Fishing Lake again.

I've given her fair warning, Mr Brogan (a fact you yourself can testify to), and I've had a gut-ful of her sass an' all. There are others (as you well know), but this one's the worst. This one's what I call 'the ringleader'. It's an arrogance she has – although I wouldn't say as it was an arrogance, as such … Can't think of the right word just off the top of my head (it's not my job to be thinking up words all day! It's my job to run this Private Fishing Lake in the most efficient and cost-effective way possible!).

Fact of the matter is: she's old enough (and ugly enough) to know better.

I put up the extra signs (like you suggested – at considerable cost!). Hasn't made so much as a scrap of difference! The gate is locked. The fence is secure. But she still persists in …

Heedless!
That's the one!

She's heedless! Worse than heedless! She's cocky! Indifferent! Like I'm just some pesky little fly as she can't be bothered going to the trouble of swatting off her shoulder! Does the woman think I'm down here all the hours policing this

Private Fishing Lake because I *want* to be? Eh? Does she think I'm doing this simply for the benefits of my bloody <u>health?!</u> *Jesus wept*!

Like I says to her the other week (during that incident I reported to you involving Miss Sissy Logan), 'I'm not petty enough to want to hinder a couple of harebrained, local women from swimming in this Private Fishing Lake just for the sheer hell of it! The implications are wider – *much* wider! The implications start when tourists and local youth observe you at it and then get to thinking it's fine and dandy to do the same thing theyselves! The net result is chaos. *Chaos*!'

It's a Private Fishing Lake, now, Mr Brogan, not a public swimming baths, and their heedless behaviour is completely unacceptable. It's out of line! Intolerable! I don't care as how long they've been swimming in it or what their nutty reverend instructed them to do! There's a new reverend now, anyways – I can't see the likes of *him* encouraging a troop of saggy, middle-aged females to set about 'purging' theyselves (or whatever it is they think they're about) in a freezing, bloody Private Fishing Lake at all hours!

Like I says to Sissy Logan: 'What happens if one of you idiotic women has an accident? Eh?! What happens if one of yous gets into trouble and drowns? Am I expected to take the rap for that?'

'But I've read all the signs, Mr Tooth,' she answers (quick as a flash), 'so I'm perfectly capable of taking responsibility for myself!'

At which point Ms Brooks interrupts our discourse: 'Signs?' she says, peering around her, all vague like. 'Are there signs …?'

'Of course there are signs!' I yells (she was standing directly in front of one!). 'Of course there are bloody signs! What the hell do you think *that* is? Eh?'

I points to the sign.

'Oh,' she says, turning to look at the thing, blinking with surprise, 'That's a sign, is it?'

That's a sign, is it?!?

I don't know as which is worse, Mr Brogan: her stupidity, her lawlessness, or her sarcasm (the lowest form of wit, they say – and quite rightly so)!

Of course she thinks she's a cut above – she thinks she's a damn sight better than all the rest of us lot put together, that one! *Heedless*, she is. Uppity. Quiet-spoken, but a real smart mouth on her (if you actually stop and listen to the drivel what's coming out of it). Always very polite, though.

Is it any wonder she's been stuck a spinster all these long years? Living in that tiny cottage with that giant, galumphing sister of hers?

Never bothers making anything of herself. Have you noticed? Dresses like a refugee – like one of them Vietnamese Boat People! Hair like a bird's nest. Not so much as a scrap of make-up on her! People say as it's 'bohemian' or 'artistic' (or some similar kind of clap-trap). I say as it's peculiar! It's unnatural! I've never come across a woman so unattractive! *Never*! You might as well make love to a boy as to that! Can't abide the thing! Can't abide her!

And I know people think as she wouldn't say boo to a goose (Oh yes – that's how she likes to put it about the place), but I've seen her dark side, Mr Brogan. I've seen her pushy side. Because not only is she persisting in trespassing on my lake – a Private Fishing Lake – but she then has the barefaced gall to tell me as how I ought to be running the damn thing!

I sees her yesterday and she's floundering around in the middle of the water, pulling something along behind her on a rope! I'm squinting over the lake for upwards of <u>half an hour</u>, trying to see what the hell she's up to now. I'm standing there, absolutely fuming – mad as a bull – waiting for her to come back to shore again so's I can give her a piece of my mind! Freezing my blooming b****cks off (if you don't mind my saying so)! God only knows how she didn't get struck down with hypothermia – and if she did it'd be my fault, I shouldn't wonder!

(Would it be my fault? Will you get back to me on that?)

By the time the ignorant creature is pulling her scraggy personage out of the water (although I won't deny as she has a fine pair of legs on her – a very fine pair), I'm at my wits' end, Mr Brogan!

I've gone and rammed the tip of my rifle into the soil so deep (with pure frustration!) that I've clogged the damn thing up! Compacted, it is! It took a full ten minutes to dig it all out with a corkscrew when I finally got back to the workshop (an' it's still not back to as how it should be, neither!).

'Look as what you've made me do to my rifle, you ignorant besom!' I says, furious, pointing the rifle at her (just to show the woman what I've done, mind).

'Oh dear,' she pants (still short of breath from all her exertions). 'You'll need to be more careful next time, won't you?'

Need to be more careful!!
I says, 'I wouldn't *need* to be anything at all if you wasn't trespassing on my Private Fishing Lake, Miss Brooks!'

She directs me one of them vague looks of hers. 'But you should always try to be careful with expensive pieces of equipment, Mr Tooth,' she says.
'I wouldn't need to be careful if you wasn't trespassing on my Private Fishing Lake, Miss Brooks!' I repeats.

'Oh, but I think you would,' she chides me, pulling off her swimming cap. 'A sensible person should always do their best to try and preserve the useful life of functional objects, Mr Tooth.'

I was stunned by this, Mr Brogan – dumbstruck! Was the impudent chit of a woman calling me unsensible, now?!

'Are you calling me unsensible, Miss Brooks?' I yells.
'Good heavens, no!' she says, shocked. 'I wouldn't dream of it, Mr Tooth!'

'Because if you don't mind my saying so, Miss Brooks,' says I, 'the only unsensible person as *I* can see around here right now is the one who's splashing around, for upwards of half an hour – not a week afore Christmas – in the middle of my Private Fishing Lake!'

(Ho! Had her bang to rights, there, Mr Brogan!)

'Yes, I did stay in the water for a little longer than I might ideally have liked,' she acknowledges, then begins unwinding this length of rope from around her waist.

'Where'd you get that rope?' I demand.

'Why?' she asks, struggling with the knot (on account of her fingers being half-froze, I suppose). 'Are you in need of some, Mr Tooth?'

Am I in need of some?!

'I think as I already *had* some exactly like it,' says I, 'which was stole off my rowing boat on Friday last!'

(I already sent you a letter about this incident, Mr Brogan – dated 12/12/06. My rowing boat had its rope stole and was left floating in the middle of the lake, remember? Took me all of three days to retrieve the damn thing.)

'How utterly maddening for you!' she says, then adds, 'Would you mind awfully just giving me a moment's privacy so that I can fetch my towel and dry myself off properly?'

Give her a moment's privacy?!

'I'll grant you exactly as much privacy,' says I, 'as you have accorded my Private Fishing Lake, Miss Brooks!'

(Ha! *None*, in other words, Mr Brogan!)

She stands there for a second or two, frowning slightly, as if calculating something: 'That would be approximately twenty-three and a half hours per day,' she says, 'which will do me very nicely, thank you, Mr Tooth.'

Eh?!

She then stares at me, all expectant like.

'Confound your cock-eyed logic, woman!' I explodes, at which point that pesky duck of hers comes waddling its way out of the water (a giant wretch, it is – size of a swan, ugly as the back end of a chimp) and commences acting in such a manner as I'd call 'intimidatory' (hissing, flapping its wings and suchlike).

In an act of pure self-defence, I points the gun at the little blighter.

'Calm down, Eliot!' Miss Brooks snaps.

'Don't you be telling the likes of me to calm down!' I yells (incensed). 'Try having a word with your demented fowl!'

'I *am* speaking to the duck,' she says, then repeats her instruction for a second time:

'Eliot! Calm down!'

On this occasion, the duck responds to her order (promptly desisting from its hissing and a-flapping), but it still continues glaring at me, sullenly, through its evil eye.

'I suppose as you thought it was a real *hoot* to name that ugly broiler of yourn after a man of my complexion,' says I, severely affronted (my high colour has oft been remarked upon by men of a medical stamp – although I think as they make too much of it, myself).

'After you, Mr Tooth?' says she, batting her lashes, like butter wouldn't melt.

'Don't come the innocent with me!' I yell.

'The thought had honestly never crossed my mind!' she insists. 'If you must know, we actually named him after T.S.'

'T.S.?'

'T.S. Eliot – the famous poet.'

I stares at her, blankly.

'Macavity: the Mystery Cat!' she cajoles me.

I stares at her blankly.

'*Macavity's a Mystery Cat*,' she declaims, '*he's called the Hidden Paw –*

For he's the master criminal who can defy the law!'

I stares at her, blankly.

She stares back at me, brows raised a-way, as if she can't quite believe any person of passing intelligence might not be instantly familiar with this so-called 'poet' of hers. Then she quickly qualifies, 'Although if *I* were you, Mr Tooth, and the duck was named in *my* honour, then I think I should probably take it as an enormous compliment. Eliot is very highly bred, after all. You can see it in the pride of his bearing, in his magnificent plumage, and in the wonderfully refined, pale blue of his eye.'

She gazes at the duck for a moment, full of admiration. 'A marvellous, forget-me-not blue,' she sighs, before adding, 'I believe you have eyes of exactly that fine shade yourself, Mr Tooth ...' Her intense gaze turns to me, now. 'What a startling coincidence!' she exclaims, with a small laugh.

'You have yet to explain to me,' says I (determined not to let the woman sweet-talk me off the subject), 'what kind of questionable enterprise you was just lately engaged in – employing a ten-yard piece of rope, of uncertain origin – in the middle of my Private Fishing Lake, Miss Brooks.'

'Oh, that ...' She shrugs. 'It was nothing. I was just submerging a dead badger.'

'Sorry?' says I.

'I was just submerging a dead badger,' she repeats, 'the one I told you about the other day, in fact ...'

'Do I hear you a'right?' says I. 'You was submerging a dead badger in the middle of my Private Fishing Lake?!'

'Indeed, Mr Tooth,' she says, cool as a cucumber.

'Well then,' says I (mad as a bull again), 'might I suggest as you go and retrieve the blasted thing, Miss Brooks?!'

'Retrieve it?!' says she, appalled. 'But I couldn't possibly do that!'

'Why not?' says I (stamping my foot).

'Because I'm not permitted to swim in the lake, Mr Tooth!' she trots out.

Not permitted to swim in the lake!

Not permitted ...!

'Perhaps you might like to inform me,' says I, removing a notebook from my pocket (white with rage, now, Mr Brogan), 'as to *why* you felt the need to submerge a dead badger in that particular hard-to-reach – not to say out-of-bounds – location, Miss Brooks?'

'Why?' she repeats, plainly astonished by this question (and intimidated by the notebook, too, I shouldn't wonder).

'Yes, *why*, Miss Brooks,' I enunciates sharply, priming my pencil with a small dab on my tongue.
'Well, because after poor Gracie died from swallowing all that carelessly abandoned fishing twine …'

'Gracie?' says I.
'The dear swan,' says she, with a baleful look, 'and you neglected to remove the corpse in time.'
'Neglected?' says I (insulted).

'Absolutely,' she confirms, then seeing as how I am pausing a'fore writing down this detail, she kindly spells out the word for me: 'n-e-g-l-e-c-t-e-d,' she says.
'*I KNOWS AS HOW TO SPELL NEGLECTED, MISS BROOKS!*' I yells.

'Oh … Good,' she says. 'Well, anyway,' she promptly continues, 'this young badger happened across dear Gracie at some point, decided to have a little nibble on her, and then before you could say "Bob's Your Uncle", he'd dropped dead, too! I looked for any evidence of twine lodged in his throat, but couldn't find any. It was at this point that I asked if you might consider disposing of the poor soul, because I wasn't sure of the cause of death, and felt his continuing presence on the shore line wasn't entirely conducive to—'

'You asked me to dispose of it,' I quickly interrupts (having turned to the relevant page in my notes), 'because you said as how several local dogs was "worrying away" at the corpse.'
'Exactly!' she says, beaming. 'Spot-on, Mr Tooth!'

'And if I remember a'right, Miss Brooks,' I calmly venture, 'I then responded by telling you that so far as I was aware, all the "local" canines involved in this unfortunate scenario was in the company of your confounded "swimming ladies" who, for the record, was *TRESPASSING ON MY BLOOMING LAND*!'

She completely ignores this, Mr Brogan, and instead says, 'Obviously the ideal thing to do would've been to bury the corpse, and I initially pursued that approach, Mr Tooth, but the ground around here was much too cold and hard for me to hack out a hole of any real depth. The dogs and foxes simply dug it straight back up again. It was then I decided that it might be an idea to submerge the corpse in the lake itself.'

'Submerge a corpse?!' I scoffs. 'And how does a person go about submerging a corpse, Miss Brooks, when the very nature of a corpse is to *float*?'

'Well, there you have my dilemma in one, Mr Tooth,' she says. 'At first I thought I might just weigh the feet down with rocks, but then logic told me that it would be impossible to transport the badger out there, manually, with the rocks – and obviously I don't have access to a boat ...'

As she speaks, she rubs away at her arms with her hands (so as to try and generate herself a bit of heat, I suppose).

'Then my sister, Rhona, came up with the wonderfully innovative idea of attaching deflated, biodegradable plastic bags to each of the four paws, swimming to the middle of the lake and then inflating the bags and allowing the weight of the water itself to sink the animal.'

'Deflated, biodegradable plastic bags?' I echo, gaping at the notion.

'It's apparently the technique they use when sinking wind turbines in the ocean,' she explains. 'They pin them to the ocean bed by filling these huge, empty containers with the surrounding water – it's actually extremely clever when you come to think about it.'

'Sweet Lord have mercy!' says I.

'I reasoned that the bags would soon biodegrade,' she continues, 'and that while this process was under way, the bigger fish in the lake might feed on the badger and thereby gradually dispose of it.'

'Which is ideal for me, Miss Brooks,' says I, smiling (almost beatific), 'to have a large, potentially toxic, dead badger in the middle of my Private Fishing Lake for all the fish to gorge theyselves upon.'

'Precisely!'

She beams.

'I'M BEING *SARCASTIC*, MISS BROOKS!' I bellows – at which point the duck commences its big old performance again (the hissing and the posturing and the wings all a-flap).

I points the rifle at it, Mr Brogan. 'Call the damn thing off!' I cry. The duck takes not the blindest bit of notice of the firearm (sensing as it was temporarily jammed up with mud, perhaps). It approaches (at high speed) and delivers my shin a savage nip. I turn the rifle around and try to beat it away with the butt.

'Call the damn thing off!' I cries again. 'Or so help me, God, I'll shoot the wretch!'

I glance over towards Miss Brooks and see as how she is swaying, gently, on her feet. She's looking very queer, Mr Brogan! Her eyes is all a-flutter, her arms and shoulders commence to convulse, and then she topples over, backwards, into a dead faint.

(I say a dead faint, but t'was more of a fit than a faint, in point of fact.)

'Damn you, Miss Brooks!' yells I. 'Get thee up, now, woman, get thee up!'

(She shows no sign of obliging me, Mr Brogan.)

Of course the duck now thinks I am to be blamed for its mistress's sudden collapse and continues its attacks on me with a redoubled ferocity. When I approach the body and kneel over it (to tend to it in some manner), the damn thing delivers me a violent nip on my right thigh, then another, hard upon it, on my right buttock!

It is at this precise moment (midst all the fray) as I discover something most untoward, Mr Brogan: the strap of Miss Brooks's swimming costume (a copious, dark blue garment of questionable age and construction) has worked its way loose

---

from one shoulder (fine shoulders she has, Mr Brogan – I won't bother denying it!) and has fallen down, almost to her waist, revealing a single, pristine breast (this is not yet the untoward part), and lying on that breast (the breast is small as a poached egg, purple from the cold, but a breast, nonetheless), giving suck on the tender, pale flesh thereof, is a leech – fat, black and not less than two and a half inches long, one inch across (around six centimetres by two in the metric – but don't quote me on that).

Hell's bells! I shy back for a second, horror-struck (being no great fan of leeches), and then, struggling to keep my wits about me (and my gorge from rising), I reach forward a tentative hand to try to pluck the leech from its delicate mount. It takes several attempts (the thing is stuck on quite firm).

With the fourth try I have some success – detaching the tail section (if such it were), then gradually peeling the rest of the body away (careful not to leave any mark or tear on the pale flesh beneath). Once the vile parasite has been removed, I toss it over my shoulder (grunting, in disgust), and blow me if I don't see my puce-faced assassin taking a quick break from his savage campaign to dart off and gobble the damn thing up!

By this stage the worst of Miss Brooks's fit seems over with. Eager to preserve what remains of her modesty, I commence to start readjusting her costume. As I do so, however, two unrelated events takes place in what I can only call a 'startling conjunction'.

The first is that the duck delivers me a hefty nip on the other buttock (the left). The second is that I am addressed by a voice from directly behind me which says, 'Hello? Mr Tooth? Can I possibly be of any assistance here?'

I am naturally jolted by both eventualities (the nip *and* the voice, Mr Brogan), so much so, that I lurch forward, unexpectedly, and (being obliged to reach out my hand for support) am forced to rest my weight for a second on Miss Brooks's still naked and rapidly purpling orb!

As soon as it is done, it is undone (you can be sure of that!), and then I turn, in shock, to apprehend no less a person than PC Roger Topping (out on call after receiving a tip-off about a missing dog – which turns out to have been naught but a patch of rust-coloured bracken).

'Ah, Constable Topping,' says I, 'how timely! Miss Brooks seems to have been subject to some kind of an attack – I mean a fit …' I quickly corrects myself, and then moves back a-way to let him fully apprehend her where she lies.

Well, the look on PC Topping's face was quite something to behold, Mr Brogan! Not the kind of look – I can assure you – that is generally to be seen on the face of a professional officer of Her Majesty's Constabulary! (If I didn't know better, I might as almost think the giant nit-wit had a distinct *preference* for the shabby little baggage!) In two seconds flat he's down on his knees beside Miss Brooks, cupping her wan face in his two giant mitts.

'Tilly!' he cries. 'Tilly! Are you all right?'
'She was standing there, right as rain, one minute,' says I, 'and the next she's gone for a Burton!'

Constable Topping now observes (with an expression of blatant disquiet – nay consternation) that one half of Miss Brooks's bosom is currently on display, and that there is a large, suspicious-looking hand-print spanning its neat circumference.

'Have you been administering CPR, Mr Tooth?' he asks, darting me an accusing look (before promptly rearranging the garment). 'Don't you know she's epileptic?'
'T'weren't CPR,' says I, 'I wouldn't know as where to start with all that … She had a leech stuck on her brisket, as it happens – a giant one, Constable Topping, two inches at least – and I felt as I was obliged to pull the damn thing off.'

'A leech? he echoes, checking her airwaves for any impediments. 'A freshwater leech? And of such improbably huge proportions? Where did it get to, then? What happened to it?'

'I tossed it aside,' says I, 'then that dratted duck went an' hoovered it up.'

'She's freezing cold,' he murmurs, barely acknowledging my testimony (nor congratulating me for my prompt action, neither). 'Fetch me her towel, Mr Tooth.'
He begins taking off his jacket so as to wrap her up in it.

'I hope as you don't think there was anything untoward,' says I.
'She's freezing cold!' he yells. 'I said fetch me her towel, you bloody idiot!'
(I was not over-impressed by the 'bloody idiot' part, Mr Brogan, but I nevertheless obliged the gormless clod and went off to retrieve the thing.)

'I'm glad as you're here, Constable Topping,' says I, on my return, 'because Miss Brooks has been caught trespassing in my Private Fishing Lake – worse still, she has been apprehended in the act of submerging a dead badger in it!'

'Damn you and your Private Fishing Lake, Mr Tooth!' says Constable Topping, snatching the towel from me, then scooping up Miss Brooks in his arms (like she's naught but a piece of thistledown) and promptly carrying her off with him.

I watch his swift departure with a sense of some astonishment, Mr Brogan.
Damn you and your Private Fishing Lake?!

The duck tarries behind a few moments longer, holding me, once again, in its fierce, blue-eyed gaze (blow me if that duck isn't a double for my old grandmother – Flora Tooth! A legendary local Tartar, she were!).

'Don't know as what *you're* staring at,' says I, kicking out at the beast with my boot. It side-steps my assault, delivers me a final, hoarse hiss, then waddles off in hot pursuit.

I'll tell you this for nothing, Mr Brogan: there is something *seriously amiss* with that piece of poultry, and make no mistake about it! It's a reprobate, Mr Brogan, a scoundrel! A villain!

I've since been told that Muscovies are the only breed of

duck not to be furnished with a quack, and I thank the Lord for it! If it quacked even half as bad as it looked, I can't as begin to conceive of the foul disturbance it might produce!

Damn that bird, Mr Brogan! And damn Miss Brooks, an' all! And damn the moronic constable, into the bargain!

I've since wrote the man a stiff letter about the submerging of the badger. I said as I'd be contacting my lawyer over the issue (and here I am – a man of my word – doing exactly that). Do you think there is a legal case to be answered here at all?

If not, then perhaps we should seek ourselves a more subtle form of retribution (in the form of another 'supportive' letter to our dear gullible 'friend' Mr Donovan Lefferts)?

Revenge is a dish best served cold, eh, Mr Brogan? The way turkey (or duck) is oft best enjoyed on Boxing Day, alongside a good, rich dollop of fruity pickle …

Yours etc.,

Eliot Tooth

[letter 26]

Coombes Cottage
Lower Field
Sharp Crag Farm
Nr Burley Cross

December, 2006

Dear ___COUSIN SALLY ___,

Welcome – be you friend, relative, old neighbour, ex-workmate, former sexual partner or all of the above! – to this year's bonzer Coombes Family Christmas Round-up!!!!!

Surely it can't be a whole twelve months since I sat down to write the last one, out of my mind on prescription painkillers (after an agonizing kidney infection), utterly broke and freezing cold, huddled up in front of a malfunctioning bar-fire, from our tiny bedsit in Hull?!

Of course we were all still struggling to come to terms with Ramsay's sudden death at that point (when you marry a partner so much older than you are, you're naturally resigned to the prospect of losing them prematurely, but under such awful circumstances? I still – to this day – can't pick up a steam iron without shuddering …).

Then there was the loss of Thornton Manor (our beautiful, ancient, family home), poor Hayden and Dylan were taken into temporary care (although the problem *wasn't* scurvy, after all!), Jared was facing those trumped-up shoplifting charges, Madeline was still coming to terms with her recent diagnosis and little Poppy was screaming the rafters down because I'd run out of teething drops!

Definitely *not* the best of circumstances in which to be composing a Christmas message – so please forgive me if my spelling was dodgy (or even more dodgy than it normally is!) and my tone was slightly hyper!

There's been a hell of a lot more water under the bridge since then (many miles on the – currently broken – speedometer of our old camper van, countless Happy Meals devoured, numerous games of Ker-plunk lost and won, endless idle – and not so idle – threats issued from irate debtors, hundreds of GREAT, *GREAT* ADVENTURES in other words) and I really can't wait to tell you all about it!

We miss Hull like crazy: those long, bracing walks collecting scraps of firewood on the muddy Humber beach in the pouring rain; 'illegal' chocolate fondues held on the roof of my flat (so as not to wake the baby!) dressed in gloves and balaclavas with my kind 'comrades' from the slaughterhouse; that mouth-watering aroma of curry and chips from the rowdy Balti Hut downstairs; the Coombes Family Band, Exoskeleton, performing outside M&S (me on accordion, Madeline on fiddle, Hayden on bongos, Poppy on tambourine, Dylan passing the hat around); my brief but intensely erotic relationship with Mr Nolan, our bailiff, which, while it ended quite badly (he was just manipulating my feelings to gain full access to our home, and when he managed it he took virtually everything, including the kids' instruments) taught me the very, very valuable lesson that one day – *yes, one day* – I might finally be ready to open my heart and find 'true love' again …

What life-affirming times they were! And things have only got better, since …

You will have seen (from the new address) that we've moved back to West Yorkshire. It seemed the only sensible thing to do (once the boys were released from care) since Jared was on remand in Leeds and the journey from Hull wasn't the easiest to manage with limited resources and a large family in tow.

We initially stayed for a few weeks at a B&B in Haworth – Brontë Country! (until it was closed down by Health and Safety) – then, after a chance meeting with an incredibly charming and 'centred' individual called Brother Julius (a shaman with the Church of the Broken Lyre – they're amazing!

Really screwy – really kinky! Look them up on the internet!) and his gorgeous wife, Iona (named after the windswept Scottish island), who were running a stall at a New Age Fayre selling dream catchers (exquisite ones, which Iona makes herself out of local hides and crystals), we ended up moving into a fabulous teepee, just outside Timble near the Washburn Valley.

We stayed there, rent-free (brilliant!!!), for several months and the entire family got involved in the manufacture of wire cranial massagers (a spider-like metal implement which you push on to the top of the head and it stimulates various, crucial pressure points), but unfortunately the locals weren't too keen on the encampment (there was a problem with our sewage pit – which was located just behind their tea shop).

That, coupled with unpredictable weather (May was very wet, so much so that two of the children developed trench foot), and a terrible flash-flood (which took literally all of our remaining possessions – bar Ramsay's mother's favourite blue glass decanter, which I never really liked in the first place!) meant that we were obliged to move into more 'traditional' quarters for a spell.

After a month in an abandoned warehouse (amazing parties! – incredible acoustics!) we actually ended up getting our own little council house after Jared's case-worker, a beautiful, passionate man called Vito (the Spanish for 'vital' – read into that what you will!) pulled a few strings on our behalf.

Unfortunately, much of the equipment for the manufacture of the cranial massagers had been lost in the flood (soldering irons and the like) so we initially struggled to make ends meet. Then Iona moved in with us, temporarily (along with her two daughters Pearl and Lunar – Vito had gone back to his wife by this stage), and taught me the ancient method of hair removal – 'threading' – which originated in India but is widespread all over the Middle East.

It's a rather fiddly and complicated process which is strictly

non-invasive and simply involves holding a piece of (clean –
well, cleanish!) cotton between your two hands and your teeth,
forming a tiny loop, trapping a single hair (or a line of hairs) in
it, then extracting it/them with a sharp, rapid movement.

I like to think that I could have become very proficient in this
amazing beauty treatment (and might easily have made an
excellent living at it) if it weren't for my two false front teeth
(one or other of them kept flying out at critical moments,
causing a certain amount of confusion and distress amongst my
clients).

It was at around about this time that Jared's case finally came
to court (Yay!!!). We were all very apprehensive about it, but
given that he's only eighteen, and it was only his seventh
offence, the judge went easy on him (double yay!!!). His closing
summary was a little severe, however. He referred to Jared as 'a
persistent thief'.

Of course Iona – who was with me, offering moral support,
and is very forthright by nature – said she couldn't just sit by
and allow him to say such awful things about a young man of
such obviously great potential. She leapt to her feet in the
public gallery: 'Persistence is a wonderful quality in a young
man,' she shouted, 'in an age of pikers and quitters, persistence
is a virtue that we should be actively encouraging in our youth,
not using it as a stick to beat them with!'

I couldn't have put it better myself! Unfortunately Iona's
outburst ended up in us both being evicted from the building.
Jared's lawyer even went so far as to say that the sentence was
made considerably harsher as a consequence (although I think
he was probably just caught up in the drama of the moment –
much the same as we were!).

Jared was eventually saddled with over 200 hours of
community service (poor soul, and that's on top of his lengthy
period in remand!). Yet, strange to say, this cruel-seeming
punishment (given that he only 'borrowed' the collection box in
order to study the design and use it as a starting point to make

me a jewellery box for my birthday) was to turn out to be the making of us!

Some problems had developed with the council house. Brother Julius had (understandably) become very bitter about my 'setting up home' with his former wife and daughters (although he wasn't officially married to Iona, and the two girls weren't actually related to him by blood). He expressed his bitterness by spreading a series of malicious rumours against me and the children: that I had formerly lived in a castle (ludicrous! It was just a stately home with a couple of turrets!) and had acquired the council house not through right but by cunning; that I was a wife-stealer and notorious lesbian (Iona and I were actually 'together' for a brief span, but it didn't really work out in the end, since neither of us is remotely bisexual); that Jared was a persistent thief etc. etc.; and this, coupled with a number of small fires (*very* small fires – Poppy was merely going through that whole 'fascinated by flames' phase) and some ill-thought-out DIY (Iona knocked down a supporting wall on the ground floor to try and make the place feel a little more 'open plan', then one of the upstairs bedroom floors collapsed!) meant that we were evicted from the house and obliged to move on again (Iona had already left at this point, to pursue her dream of attending Clown School in Orpington, near London).

As luck would have it, Jared was working out his community service in the beautiful, picturesque village of Burley Cross where he was employed collecting litter from moorland paths. During this time he was operating under the guidance of local councilman Baxter Thorndyke, who gradually began using him to do small jobs about the place, e.g. washing his 4x4, raking his path, gathering leaves in his garden etc. I turned a blind eye to it, initially (thinking that Jared might even benefit from a positive, male role model and mentor), but after he came home one day, deeply traumatized and covered – almost from head to foot – in filth (the councillor had made him clean out his septic tank!), I decided that enough was enough and made an official complaint.

Thorndyke then responded by making counter-complaints (I won't go into them here, but given that the bathroom was on the second floor and Jared is uncircumcised, his wife really didn't have a leg to stand on).

During his time spent in the village, Jared had made the acquaintance of a lovely boy called Lawrie, the son of a local farmer, who, when he heard of Jared's predicament, stepped in on his behalf (there was apparently already a feud between this Thorndyke character and the farmer, based on the farmer's support of a local publican in a minor planning dispute). He offered Jared a job on his farm (which satisfied the probation people), and then, later on, when he discovered that Jared and his family (that's us!) were currently living out of their trusty VW, took pity on them and gave Jared free accommodation in an old prefab.

Coombes Cottage (Madeline renamed it!) is where I currently sit – and write to you from – today. It's a tiny, scruffy old place, but it's home and we all LOVE IT!!!!

Since coming here we have been blessed in so many ways! The people of Burley Cross have been enormously kind and generous to us! Last week we had a slap-up meal in the local pub (all of us, for only £10!). It was a truly wonderful occasion and honestly made me feel as though we were turning a corner and entering a new phase in our fascinating journey together (the only thing that soured it was that Hayden – who's very technical by nature – got a little too 'involved' in the interior workings of a large grandfather clock that sits in the snug and managed to destroy the working mechanism. The bill to fix it will be over £100!).

In an attempt to scratch some money together (Wincey, the landlady, has been very good about it, but the clock was a twentieth anniversary present from her late husband, Duke, and I felt I really should try and contribute something towards the repairs) I decided to take Ramsay's mother's blue glass decanter to a local antique shop to see if I could raise any funds on it.

That very morning, Poppy had come down with the measles (a particularly vicious strain, caught from Hayden, who'd caught it from Dylan, who'd caught it from Jared, who'd caught it from Lawrie) and had vomited all over me (I was in my customary pair of frayed denim hotpants, teamed with some stripy woollen tights – the only clothes I currently own!!). The prefab is unheated, and it would've taken hours for them to dry properly, so I threw on a skirt (generously donated by Helen, the farmer's wife, although the last time I wore a skirt was circa 1989!!!) and jumped into the van.

Well, I hadn't been driving for much more than ten minutes, tops, when, completely out of the blue, a bee flew in through my window (which was propped open to stop the windscreen from getting too steamy) and flew straight up my skirt!!! *Nooooooo*!

I didn't even realize bees were still around so late in the season (Global Warming Alert!!!). In fact I was so shocked that I took my hands off the steering wheel for a second (to protect my Lady Garden – I wasn't wearing any knickers), the van swerved, and I crashed straight into an oncoming car.

Luckily nobody was very badly hurt, but the van was pretty bashed up (and the car was quite a mess, too).

This is the incredible part, though: I'd only managed to involve myself in a serious collision with an expert from the BBC TV series the *Antiques Roadshow* (on his way to do a reading in Ilkley from his latest book!)!! And, better still: he was their glass expert!

WHAT AN *AMAZING* COINCIDENCE!

I naturally showed him the decanter (after we'd exchanged insurance details – *his* insurance details, since I'm not actually insured: I just made a few up) and he was able to tell me that the decanter was actually very, very rare!!!! It was Norwegian and dated from around 1890. He said it could be worth in the region of £1,700!!!!!

He picked it up to inspect the hallmark properly (all excited!), and then the thing just *FELL TO A MILLION TINY PIECES IN HIS HANDS*!!!!

'Oh well,' I said, 'I never much liked the damn thing anyway!' and we both absolutely howled with laughter (he was great fun, really up for the craic – even with a torn shirt and blood dripping from his ear)!!

There's so much more I'd love to tell you all (about Poppy's first word, Dylan's round-worm infection, Hayden's incredible, new talent at online gaming and the like), but there simply isn't the time or the space to do so here …

All there's actually the time and the space to do is to wish you all A WONDERFUL, *WONDERFUL* CHRISTMAS, AND A VERY HAPPY AND PROSPEROUS NEW YEAR!!!

With HUGE love and hugs from us all:
Paula, Jared, Hayden, Dylan, Madeline and Poppy

PS Madeline just won the talent contest at her local school, armpit-farting God Save the Queen while standing on one foot! Perhaps it wasn't such a bad thing that Mr Nolan stole her beloved fiddle after all!

PPS Aunty Jinny is still diligently researching our family tree (on Mother's side). Turns out that I'm distantly related to William Huskisson, who was a famous British politician in the 1820s! He was apparently in charge of the expansion of the railways (perhaps that's where I get my itchy feet from!), although it seems his career was cut short after he was unlucky enough to topple under a slow-moving locomotive …

PPPS I've just got off the phone to Ramsay's old accountant, Denton Wade, who has recently uncovered some 'hidden' investments which he thinks might be worth a 'serious' sum of money!!!!! He told me not to get my hopes up too high, and that (because of various legal wrangles to do with the Estate, Death Duties etc.) it might be necessary to leave cashing them in until later on next year, but we're all wildly over-excited in the meantime (so please, *please* keep all your fingers crossed that in 2007 there will be bumper dividends at Kwik-Save and Leeds United FC!)!!

I honestly think this is going to be our <u>BEST FAMILY CHRISTMAS, EVER!!</u>
Up the Whites!!!!!
Lots and lots and lots of love (and cuddles, and good karma etc.)
XXXXXXXXXX
P

(*Via internal mail*)

For attn Inspector Laurence Everill, Skipton

CONFIDENTIAL

Dear Laurence,

A most heartfelt congratulations on the Bravery Award (and on the surprise promotion, come to that)! I sent you a fulsome text (*two* fulsome texts – one on both counts), but I imagine they must've got lost in the deluge ...

Either way, you really did the boys proud back in December. I watched the Awards broadcast, alone, in my flat, with a nice bottle of cheap merlot and an above-average, ready-made Tesco's Finest Boeuf Stroganoff. Quite a little celebration it was! 'That's Laurence Everill,' I kept saying to the cat. 'We went to school together, you know!'

I couldn't help but notice (during a couple of audience 'reaction shots') that Sandy (who was sitting with the chief superintendent and his wife, I believe) had a lovely new hairdo – and a host of pretty blonde highlights in her fringe. Quite a departure! She looked lovely – truly lovely. Dark green is definitely her colour. Do tell her how impressed I was (not that she'll much care, I'm sure!).

Several people have stopped me in the street (or flagged down the car when I'm out on patrol) to discuss the matter. One old dear (who I generally pop in on during my rounds – just to check she's all right, and have an amiable chat) said, 'It honestly helps me to sleep better at night, knowing we have men of Sergeant Everill's calibre working on the force.'

I couldn't have put it better myself.

———

Like you, Inspector (quite rolls off the tongue, eh?!), I am somewhat at odds to understand why it was that the BCPBT Case (as I prefer to call it) was transferred from your most capable hands in Skipton to my considerably less competent – if slightly more capacious – ones in Ilkley …

(Although which of us 'mere mortals' may hope to grasp the complex array of motivating principles guiding that subterranean army of shadowy forces – that 'silent, faceless vanguard' – who seem to inveigle their way into every corner of our working lives, overseeing our every, basic move – our every shallow breath, even – like ominous, lowering, ever-watchful phantasms?)

'Ours is not to reason why,' as I said, only this morning, to my part-time factotum-cum-administrative-assistant, Mrs Hope (who also sends you her heartfelt congratulations, by the way), 'ours is but to complete the paperwork – in duplicate!'

Please accept my deepest gratitude for sending me your additional thoughts on the case. They were immensely useful. It's an education (of sorts) for a rank-and-file copper like myself (a mere picayune, a booby, a hick, a poor shot, a galoot) to be given ready access to the elevated workings of a renowned (and superior) detective intellect.

I am forced to agree with you that PC – soon-to-be sergeant – Hill's spelling leaves something to be desired ('suspisious' is another one), but I still thought his energy and his commitment were thoroughly commendable – a shining example to all us cynical 'old stagers', in other words!

If (when he eventually returns from his extended sick-leave), you're ever stuck on a boring stake-out together (although I fear you may've become far too important for that grubby kind of caper, now!) and have nothing of any remote significance left to talk about, then perhaps you might tell him that I think I may've found my (clumsy) way towards solving the BCPBT mystery (audible gasps of astonishment!), and that his early leg-work in December contributed in no small part to this breakthrough.

My approach to the thing has, as always, been characteristically 'back-to-basics' (to borrow a much derided phrase from the John Major era); a man of your rank and experience might almost call it 'entry-level policing' (although I'm rather fond of 'bread and butter policing' myself – for obvious reasons!).

Either way, I slowly worked out (during an especially dull lecture about the benefits of cardio-vascular exercise at WeightWatchers on Tuesday) that there could only ever really be three good reasons for a person to feel inclined to break into a postbox at any given moment in time:

1 The hope of acquiring some kind of financial benefit
2 The desire to accrue private information
3 The desire to stop a letter from being sent (an incriminating one, perhaps, posted on the spur of the moment and now held to be a serious liability by either the letter writer him/herself, or by someone who knows the letter writer – and possibly the contents of the letter – and wishes to protect themselves/the future recipient from the potential fallout from the information enclosed).

It was based on these three, very simple notions that I proceeded with my enquiries.

As to reason (1), it soon became evident that this was not a viable option since the three cheques (sent by Wincey Hawkes) were left behind in the cache. So far as I am aware, nothing else of value was reported missing.

As to reason (2), I was able to discover (on inspecting the seals of the envelopes) that very few of them – if any – had actually been opened by the original thief. The majority had been opened by Mhairi Callaghan (the loquacious proprietress of Feathercuts, Skipton), prior to her ringing the police to notify them of her 'sudden discovery' of this mysterious yet tantalizing haul which had been randomly dumped in the back alley of her Skipton salon (I deduced this by dint of the tiny residue of red hair dye – Mhairi specializes in tints, something Sandy herself will attest to – on the top left-hand corner of the vast majority of the torn envelope seals).

I verified this suspicion during a subsequent visit to the salon, by passing Mhairi a letter, marked 'urgent', which I said I'd found on the doormat. This envelope was instantly torn open, using exactly the same technique as all the others in our body of evidence (the style of opening is highly idiosyncratic; a 'signature', of sorts).

Luckily, Mhairi didn't see her way to reading all of the letters in the cache (perhaps conscience overwhelmed her at some point). Baxter Thorndyke's Sex Hex letter remained intact (although it was in a fairly worn and dilapidated state by the time it reached my desk!), as did several of the other more 'sensitive' pieces (Tom Augustine's, which he still insists he didn't write, Nick Endive's and Nina Springhill's, to name but three).

Unfortunately Mhairi *did* see Rita Bramwell's poignant letter to her alienated daughter, Nadia, something that I feel may well have been a contributing factor to Rita's unsuccessful suicide attempt in early February (if only she'd been brave enough to tell Peter herself, what a world of pain and heartache she might have saved them both in the long run!).

Naturally, with the realization that Mhairi had opened several of the letters came the suspicion that she may also have been directly involved in the original crime (although her motivation for such an act would have been difficult to pin-point). I promptly abandoned this theory, however, on discovering that she had a rock-solid alibi for the evening of the 21st, having spent the entire night with Helen Graves – Skipton Constabulary's charming WPC – watching you and Sandy (whose hair she'd just tinted to such spectacular effect), during a 'special showing' of the Bravery Awards in Skipton's Royal Arms.

So with Mhairi now out of the picture, and with the thief (or thieves) patently having had no financial incentive for the crime, the only available option still remaining on the table (along with two cans of Red Bull, a large pork pie and a cream eclair – 'brain food', I like to call it!) was number (3), i.e. that the postbox had been broken into by a local; someone who'd posted a letter and then had thought better of it, or someone with good reason (in their own mind) to want to stop a letter from being sent.

Nick Endive now shot straight to the top of my list of suspects; his passionate but illicit declaration of love to Nina Springhill was, I reasoned, exactly the kind of confession a man might seriously live to regret …

Let me also just say, at this pertinent juncture, that I am not now (and never was) willing to follow the Thorndyke route and blame either Trevor Woods – BC's long-suffering postman – or his employers at the Royal Mail for this illegal act (had they been truly determined to replace the postbox with a more modern version, I'm certain there would have been countless far less complicated ways for them to have facilitated this process). In fact, so far as I can tell, the only illegal act the directors of *that* particular organization can fairly be accused of is asset-stripping a perfectly good, ancient and honourable British institution, then blithely running it – with due government approval, nay, assistance, even – into the ground! (As you already know, Inspector, this is something of a pet subject of mine – and one that I'm always only too happy to get exercised about …)

Re option (3): if the thief/thieves hadn't actually opened any of the remaining letters in the cache, I think we must, by necessity, deduce that the letter they wanted to get their greedy mitts on was – more than likely – subsequently identified, separated from the rest and rapidly disposed of (to behave otherwise would be illogical: why commit a crime and then cheerfully leave the reason for it behind you in the guise of a glaring piece of evidence?!)

Love-lorn as Nick Endive obviously was, surely even he wouldn't have been silly enough to dump a letter containing his innermost feelings in a bin bag behind the salon of one of Skipton's most famous blabbermouths!).

Bearing all of the above in mind, the BCPBT investigation was now effectively stuck in neutral – facing a metaphorical 'brick wall' – because without fingerprints (which PC Hill was unable to acquire, due to the rain, and the necessary distraction of his delicious-sounding fish dinner) or a witness (of which there were none), we were left without any palpable clue as to the thief's identity (and scant hope of acquiring any, either).

On this basis I decided (as you yourself had done before me) to make a study of the remaining letters in the cache to try and build up a picture of Burley Cross (as a crime scene/community, on the week/night of the robbery), in the pathetic hope that there might be some subtle clues to this mystery inadvertently sewn into the everyday fabric – the insignificant weft and weave, so to speak – of other people's lives.

I don't doubt that we all found out rather more about this small, attractive, relatively well-to-do moor-side village than we had hoped (or, indeed, expected) by this subsequent course of action, Inspector, not least that Astrid Logan was planning to instigate yet another of her surreptitious 'moonlight flits' with that troublesome, and evasive, internet pal of hers.

Part of me regrets the fact that the force was unable to take any kind of decisive action in this regard (perhaps we might have posted the letter on, in the hope of setting up a trap and catching the filthy bugger, red-handed … But the timing – as you comment in your 'further notes' – was, of course, way too tight).

It later transpired that the contact address, alone, proved very useful. I've since been told (in subsequent conversations with the Portsmouth Constabulary) that Marc Pym's home was raided (for a third time) in January and his computer confiscated, although little incriminating evidence was found on it (aside from a lengthy correspondence – mainly focusing on the subject of diet – and the contact addresses of forty-three underage girls, all of whom he had met on eating disorder websites as 'Gabriel', or in the form of his avatar, 'Skinny Lad', a nineteen-year-old boy suffering from chronic bulimia).

As we currently stand, the gentleman in question still remains 'at large'.

A further codicil to this story: after you contacted Penelope and Angus McNeilly with the news about Astrid (and told them that they were at liberty to do with it what they would), I have been reliably informed that they immediately made contact with Mr Wolf (he being the one person whose reputation might, quite reasonably, have been perceived as being the most damaged by Astrid's deception) and duly apologized to him on Astrid's behalf. He subsequently insisted – being ever the gentleman – that the matter should remain strictly under wraps. He was much less concerned about his own social standing, it seems, than for Astrid's long-term mental and physical well-being, especially in the light of her mother's tragic death from cervical cancer at the start of the New Year.

(I don't know why, but I have a nagging feeling that this won't – by any stretch of the imagination – be the last we hear of this particular story, more's the pity ...)

But let's get back to the real gist of the matter, now, shall we? Like I said before, there were many things I learned from my perusal of those twenty-six letters, Inspector (many things – enough to fill several notebooks, in fact), yet the piece of correspondence that drew me the most (the one that my eye kept on returning to, come what may), was the letter to Miss Squire (Miss Courtney Squire, 'personal assistant' to Mr Gerald Booth), from Mrs Brenda Goff (of Buckden House).

I have known Mrs Goff for many years, and she has never particularly struck me as the most forthcoming of women (it's sometimes as much as I can do to elicit a grudging 'Good morning' out of her!), and yet here she was, the busy proprietress of an extremely successful bed and breakfast, committing the time and the effort to writing a letter (ten pages in length!) to someone she'd actually never met – someone with whom she'd previously enjoyed only the most rudimentary of telephone conversations.

This Miss Squire certainly must have a very successful and dynamic cold-calling technique, I mused, since not only had she clearly impressed Mrs Goff during this short, introductory chat of hers (to the extent that Mrs Goff was willing to offer her reduced rates on two rooms at hardly any notice), but she'd had what sounded like a similar kind of impact on Wincey at The Old Oak – and who can guess how many others in the local vicinity?

During her letter, Mrs Goff mentions, in passing, that Wincey had been told that Mr Booth ('a practitioner of the Esoteric Sciences') was 'the by-product of a secret tryst between a prominent individual from the Salvation Army dynasty and one of the legendary Trebors ...'

Well, I don't think it takes too much of a stretch of the imagination to work out *which* prominent individual from the Sally Army we are automatically meant to think of here: there surely can't be many individuals more prominent than the Salvation Army's founder: Sir William Booth, himself (the clue is in the name, I suppose). Although the connection's never made completely explicit (how could it have been? As an illegitimate son, Mr Booth's theoretical ancestor would have had no right to claim membership of the family).

But how about the Trebors? A little harder to pin down. I did some research on the internet and found myself unable to find out anything about this 'legendary' clan – to the extent that I have now begun to have serious doubts as to whether they even really exist (might Trebor not just be the name of the sweet company itself? Also, quite coincidentally, the name Robert, back to front?).

———

334

What I do know is that the company was formed in 1907, that the famous Trebor Extra Strong Mint was launched in 1935, that shortly afterwards they merged with Bassett's (the Liquorice Allsorts people, formed by George Bassett in 1842) and then still later on with Cadbury's Schweppes.

I must confess that the more I thought about this supposed heritage of Mr Booth's, the more it began to strike me that this combination of two such prominent English brands was both an extremely clever and an intrinsically seductive one.

Here we have all the decency, staunch faith and charitable inclinations of the Booth side, coupled with the fierce, clean, sweet, traditional mintyness of the Trebor contingent. And the magical adhesive that glues them both together? A slight whiff of the transgressive, an element of the clandestine, something deeply romantic which is kept strictly 'under wraps'.

Of course the famously lofty, sensitive and spiritually inclined Mr Booth couldn't possibly stoop to discussing such private/intimate matters with 'the general public' himself, could he? (I mean where's the margin to be gained in doing that?!) He has a grovelling 'assistant' to do this for him, an eager skivvy, a loyal run-around, someone highly attuned to his complex array of needs and requirements, his fastidious tastes and his subtle preferences, someone to sort out the wheat from the chaff, in other words (note: 'Obviously Mr Booth's needs are very specific, and you will know best what will suit him ...').

Enter our Miss Squire, stage left!

Miss Squire has a functional nomenclature (a squire being a knight's attendant, his escort, and a landed gentleman in his/her own right), a name that somehow resonates a sense of fairness, a sense of squareness (is effectively – when you actually come to think about it – simply a loose conjunction of these two words combined).

Her role is a simple one: to ring ahead on behalf of Mr Booth and to sort out all his 'arrangements' (careful to generate the necessary atmosphere of reverence and awe in the process!).

Her manner is always reassuringly calm and authoritative, with the slightest touch of primness, the gentlest hint of candour (just enough to sweeten and then 'draw out' her gullible interlocutor).

A *technique*, Inspector, a clever technique! One that's as old as the hills, and used by con-artists of all complexions in all corners of the world!

But let's not get carried away here – let's think about this logically: if our Mr Booth is a psychic by profession, a talented clairvoyant (by all accounts), then his meat and his drink must be the insignificant detail of other people's lives. And on this understanding, the one – almost the only – thing a man of his stamp requires (the delicate axis on which all his mumbo-jumbo hinges)?

Information!

Gullible victims!

Opportunities!

So how does he set about acquiring these three basic necessities? (Better still: how does he quietly build himself up whilst effortlessly ingratiating himself at the same time?) By dint of the young Miss Squire and her genial enquiries in local B&Bs, of course!

A measure of flattery is involved ('Mr Booth has heard that yours is the best B&B in the area ...'), an element of doubt ('although Mr Booth's requirements are *very* specific, I'm afraid ...'), a further element of competition ('... and I've heard *incredibly* positive things about The Old Oak ...'), an element of disclosure ('Mr Booth's privacy is of the utmost importance – he has a fascinating heritage, but it's all terribly hush-hush ...') in order to encourage an automatic – even unwitting – desire on the part of the victim to *divulge something intimate about themselves*!

And our poor Mrs Goff? She falls straight into their trap! Ten pages deep! She gives away ludicrous amounts of personal detail, not only about herself, but about her local competitors, spurred on – in all probability – by wounded pride (didn't Miss Squire promise to pay her a cordial visit on the 21st, then cruelly stand her up?).

But hang on a minute … The 21st?! Isn't that *the very day* the Burley Cross postbox was broken into?!

Stimulated by this outrageous idea (and also because it happens to be located directly adjacent to my favourite bakery), I strolled over to the Middleton Theatre and had a word with the girl at the box office there about Mr Booth's appearance (Jan. 6th &7th). She said (much as I had suspected) that the show had been cancelled due to 'unforeseen circumstances'.

Hmmn, interesting, I thought, and toddled back to the station where I promptly instigated an official police search on our Mr Booth, only to be told that you had conducted one yourself – and I was already in receipt of it (it had been caught up in your further correspondence with Rosannah Strum-Tadcastle about what you, quite rightly, perceived as an excessively high translation bill. For the record: I actually showed the translation of his letter to Edouard himself; we bumped into each other at The Old Oak, and I just happened to have it to hand. He professed himself 'astonished' by its unerring accuracy, said it was 'a work of pure genius', and confided that he felt 'almost as if Mrs Strum-Tadcastle has forged a magical wormhole into the deepest, darkest recesses of my very soul …'

Can me an old sceptic, Inspector, but on the evidence of that, I'd definitely think twice about paying the London hotel bill).

After quietly perusing the police search on Mr Booth (aka Raymond Whittaker) I could find nothing of any consequence to detain me – aside from an excessive number of unpaid parking tickets – and was just about to abandon my inspection of this (quite frankly) unexceptional document, when I happened to observe (in the footnotes) that his local constabulary had planned to pay his neighbour (a suspected illegal alien) a 'surprise visit' on December 22nd 2006, but had inadvertently chanced to launch an assault on Mr Booth's property instead (kicking the door down and ransacking his flat – something they were highly apologetic about afterwards, and rightly so!).

Mr Booth wasn't home at the time of the raid, but naturally they promised to reimburse him – during a later visit – for a new door and any damage done.

These incidents took place the day *after* the BCPB theft (the very day on which the cache was uncovered in that Skipton back alley). Curious coincidence, I thought. My eye then returned to the parking tickets themselves, which hailed from all parts of the country, and had been acquired, I presumed, while Mr Booth was out 'on tour'.

I took the last three tickets as my guide (Shrewsbury, Mold, Bangor) and began to undertake some very basic enquiries. My aim? To discover whether there might be a measure of synchronicity between Mr Booth's visit to a town and a marked increase in the amount of postal crime in the area.

It didn't take much time to find out (so I'll spare you all the unnecessary build-up): in every instance I came up trumps! No postbox thefts, but in each place a significant theft of post had been reported exactly *three weeks* prior to Mr Booth's posited arrival!

In the cases of Bangor and Shrewsbury, postal vans had been broken into (although access had not been forced – in both cases two postal bags had been removed while the postman was busy emptying out a nearby box); in the case of Mold, a postman claimed that his bag was snatched 'by a large gang of kids' while he struggled to gain access to a block of flats.

All well and good, I told myself, but if Booth and Squires *were* involved in the BCPB theft (and countless others, by extension) how then to go about explaining why the Burley Cross cache was found dumped in Skipton – letters still untampered with – on the afternoon of the 22nd?

It didn't take long to come up with a solution (two crunchy sticks of Twix long, followed by a swift half-Snickers, in celebration!).

Here follows a brief outline of how I envisaged the whole scenario panning out:

21/12/2006, approx. 21.00 hrs. Burley Cross High Street. The Postbox. Mr Booth's assistant, Miss Squire, pulls up in her car. She is late. She had planned to arrive earlier in the day to host an inspection of the local B&Bs (which she has already contacted by phone) in order to drum up interest in Mr Booth's Ilkley show (also, perhaps, to 'case' these properties for any objects of exceptional value while accumulating a useful store of information, which she can then follow up on the internet, through detailed searches of local papers, obituaries, MySpace pages, websites etc.).

Unfortunately, Miss Squire has been delayed because of a problem with her tyre (a blowout on the A65). When she arrives in Burley Cross it is late – too late – but she pulls up in her car (or Ka) next to the postbox to check the collection times (which she suspects – and correctly – may have been temporarily altered in the week leading up to Christmas).

As Miss Squire inspects the postbox, it occurs to her that it is in an extremely poor state of repair. She kicks it, gently, with a peremptory toe. The door groans its protest. She kicks it again, still harder. The door caves in a little. Her face breaks into a broad smile. Incredible! Perhaps her luck is turning at last!

She goes over to her car and grabs the first sharp object she can find – a plastic knife and fork (which she'd earlier used to devour a takeaway M&S red onion and feta salad – this is pure speculation, she may've just used a stray screwdriver or a handy Swiss army knife, or the salad may actually have been tuna-based) – then returns to the ailing postbox and vigorously attacks the door again.

With hardly any wrangling, the door falls off its hinges, revealing a healthy bounty of Christmas post inside! She pulls out the contents and bundles them into her capacious handbag, then leaps back into her car and drives off.

Fifteen minutes later (21.22 hrs), Miss Squire arrives in Skipton where she is booked into a local B&B. This B&B is located directly across the road from Mhairi Callaghan's Feathercuts. Miss Squire informs the proprietress of the B&B (Margaret Bridge) that she is late because of a blow-out on the motorway, then heads straight up to her room to retire for the night.

The following day, at around lunchtime (having occupied her morning I know not how) she walks into Mhairi Callaghan's Feathercuts for a trim. Here she has a long and fascinating conversation with the proprietress about a broad range of issues – Mr Booth included.

In a subsequent interview (14/03/07) Mhairi describes Miss Squire as 'an absolute gem. Friendly. Very chatty. Beautiful hair, barely needed touching, really. *Very* loyal to Mr Booth …' who it turns out is 'the bastard son of some filthy high-up in the Methodist Church and a famous wine gum heiress – Maynards, was it?' (Yes. So Mhairi's memory on this score isn't quite all it might have been …).

Miss Squire then goes on to tell Mhairi how she and Mr Booth met 'after he relayed a message to her during a live performance about where her late mother had hidden a valuable diamond ring. It was tucked snugly inside a hollowed-out copy of Frank McCourt's *Angela's Ashes*, would you believe!'

Uh, no. I wouldn't.

'Which she'd been just on the brink of throwing out! Of course Miss Squire was so impressed by him that she booked a further, private consultation to try and make contact with her late mother again. He sat her down and said, "You're bored with your job," (she was an air hostess) "you have a strong psychic gift, but it needs bringing out. You want to become my personal assistant, but you don't have the first clue how to go about it." Incredible! The man's a genius!'

(And the rest, as they say, is history).

Oh yes … One small detail Mhairi *didn't* forget: while she was finishing up Miss Squire's haircut, Miss Squire received a phone call (at 13.15 hrs, approx., from Mr Booth) and apparently became 'quite agitated'. Mhairi is uncertain as to the finer details of this exchange because she was rushed off her feet at the time, juggling Miss Squire's cut with a difficult tinting job, but Miss Squires left the salon shortly afterwards (too flustered to remember to leave a tip!).

During a later conversation with Maggie Bridge (14/03/07), I was able to discover that Miss Squire cancelled her booking for the following night and left 'in quite a hurry'. When I asked her if she could remember anything else remotely unusual about Miss Squire's visit she said no, but as I was leaving she said, 'In actual fact, yes. I remember it struck me as being quite strange, when I came to make up her room, that Miss Squire had taken pretty much everything that wasn't glued down – the toilet roll, tissues, soap, napkins, even the bag from inside the wastepaper basket.' I asked her what kind of a bag it was. 'It was a standard black refuse bag,' she said, 'because I'd run out of the smaller, white ones that I normally use.'

Well, I don't suppose it takes much of a genius to put two and two together here, Inspector. I'm guessing that Mr Booth – presumably spooked on coming home and finding that his flat had been ransacked by the police – phoned Miss Squires (at the hairdresser's, where she was intent on sniffing out local gossip to use in his act) and told her that the police were on to them and that she should bail on her mission (who knows what other kinds of mischief Miss Squire was involved in: at this stage we can but conjecture …).

Miss Squire immediately remembered the incriminating bundle of letters in the boot of her car (where, presumably, she had stored them), and, in a state of high paranoia, ran back to the B&B, took the bin bag from the wastepaper basket, tipped the letters inside it, and dumped them, unopened, in a nearby back alley.

In her panic, Miss Squire neglected to seal the bag quite as tightly as she should have. There were high winds that day, and by the time Mhairi came outside to dump some rubbish of her own, a selection of letters were flying around in her small concrete yard. The rest of the cache she later discovered in the communal back alley … etc. etc.

So what do you think, Inspector?

Of course at this stage there is little I can do to bring about an official case against Mr Booth and his pretty cohort (my theories are just 'informed speculation', after all); certainly nothing that might have any hope of standing up in a court of law.

I find this deeply frustrating, not least because – further to my suspicions – I had a sudden fancy that it might be interesting to conduct a second search on Mr Booth (né Whittaker), but this time instead of Raymond I inserted Robert (Trebor?) into the mix. And you'll never guess what … Seven counts of theft by deceit, four of minor fraud, nine of theft … a veritable Aladdin's cave of lawbreaking and intrigue!

I am now hard on Mr Booth's tail. Through his web-page I have acquired extensive amounts of information about future appearances in the UK, and have contacted all the local forces in the areas involved with the details of this case. His Ilkley performance has been re-booked for late September. I await his return to these parts – and that of Miss Squire – with abiding interest.

Re fishing on Saturday. I'm afraid I'll have to give it a rain check, since I currently have a prior engagement to drive the Brooks sisters (Tilly and Rhona) to the L.S. Lowry museum in Salford.

I went to the trouble of hiring a Vauxhall Zafira for the
occasion, and was persuaded to invite Reverend Paul and
Tilly's friend Edo along as well (further to the hanging of Edo's
crucifix in the church, it seems the reverend and he have forged
a great spiritual and intellectual bond. Edo is now acting as
temporary church warden – since Steve Briars was taken ill
with suspected bird flu).

I have yet another surprise in store for them. Further to my
unfortunate meeting by the lake with Mr Eliot Tooth – and an
extended correspondence on the matter (during which, I'm
afraid, some rather harsh truths were exchanged: there really
was no palpable, visual evidence of a large, freshwater leech in
the general vicinity), I have taken the liberty of contacting
Donovan Lefferts and setting him straight on a couple of
issues.

Mr Lefferts has undertaken to drive up to Salford from his
home in Buxton and finally 'make peace' with the two sisters.
I'm hopeful that some kind of permanent accord may soon be
reached between them. Tilly's happiness (and Rhona's, of
course) is an issue of paramount importance to me. I am
absolutely determined to do everything within my power to
bring it about …

Could we try and reschedule for early May?
That would be lovely.

Yours, whistling at the wheel,
PC Roger Topping

PS I picked up a rare, Staffordshire monkey on the market in
Saltaire last Saturday for the princely sum of £4! Victorian.
Tiny chip to the tail, but pristine beyond that!

PPS Yes, I know that t'ai chi instructor of PC Hill's quite well.
Odd he should say he was Bulgarian – he's actually Austrian.
And he has a lisp, not a stutter.

Back problems can be very troublesome. I remember suffering from them myself, roundabout the time I first got together with Sandy (you'll know – only too well – how demanding she can be in the boudoir; her needs bordering on the athletic, even the gymnastic, on occasion!).

Now I come to think about it, weren't you wearing a corset yourself for a while back there (during the late 1990s – around about the time Sandy and I initially filed for our divorce?). Yes. I'm certain that you were. In fact I remember it troubling you, no end. The chafing was the worst part. Most aggravating for you, as I recollect.

PPPS County Wicklow? Really? Is my memory finally deserting me? I could've sworn Sandy's father was buried in the family grave just outside Bolton.

PPPPS I hear the tear in Janna Lee's scalp has almost entirely healed up, now – there are even promising signs of new growth!

R

Ilkley,
17/03/07
15.30 hrs

(Via internal mail)

For attn Chief Inspector Iain Richardson

CONFIDENTIAL

Dear Chief Inspector Richardson,

The evidence has now been unofficially 'buried' (just as you requested). Further to a short, private conversation with Mr Augustine, I have ensured that all remaining photographic proof of PC Peter Richardson's 'moment of madness' (there were three such 'moments', in total) has been destroyed.

You will be relieved to know that Mr Augustine was just as keen as yourself to keep the matter under wraps. The original copy of his letter has been burned (although I returned the stamps, which I actually thought were quite attractive: modern, but still reassuringly seasonal). I have obviously not opted to keep a copy of the original on file.

Mr Thorndyke won't be a problem. I believe Inspector Everill and Sergeant Hill have already seen to that – at a price, naturally (although I'm sure the force will be all the better for it).

How right you were to deduce that my desk in Ilkley was the perfect place to direct a 'tricky, little problem' so that it might (I quote), 'quietly breathe its last – in an atmosphere of shuddering obscurity – and then die'.

You were also correct to realize that I was one of the few people left on the force 'stupid enough to care about the difference between right and wrong, but still sufficiently respectful to take direction from above – without even the remotest expectation of personal gain …'.

———

345

I am, of course, thoroughly overwhelmed at receiving such a huge accolade from a police officer of your great stature.

Please extend my very best wishes to your son.

(Still no word on that blasted dog, I'm afraid ...)

Happy Easter.

Yours, as ever,

PC Roger Topping

PS Am thinking of giving up all remaining shreds of my professional credibility for Lent. How about you, Chief Inspector? Just chocolate again, this year?

Dear Mrs Hawkes,

Back on the old fags again, eh? And after you swore blind
that you'd given the damn things up! Of course it's really none
of my business (I'm perfectly aware of that), but I won't
pretend I'm not a little disappointed, Wincey. It's a filthy habit.

I quit because of Duke – we both did: you, me, five or six
others (Meredith Coles, Duncan Tanner, Mhairi Callaghan,
Joan Dunkley) on New Year's Day 2004 – ten months before
Duke finally passed.

I remember how pleased he was – how proud he was (of
you, me, all of us). He was a shadow of his former self by then.
So thin, pale, reduced … That terrible, hacking cough.

Quitting wasn't easy, but whenever I've felt the urge to
chuck in the towel and start up again, I've thought of Duke.
I've called to mind that autumn evening (that damp, early
autumn evening in 2003) when he clambered on to the saloon
bar with his trusty harmonium, sat down, cleared his throat,
began pumping away at it with his feet (and banging away on it
with his hands – doubtless intent on performing some
wonderfully libellous composition about certain, stand-out
members of the local community), opened his mouth to sing,
and then … then *nothing*. Nothing came out! Not a single note!
That awful look of confusion on his face – quickly surpassed by
one of haunting fear …

I'll never forget it.
I'll never forget Duke. He was an extraordinary man; the spirit
of Burley Cross (the old spirit, the true spirit), and greatly
missed by all of us.

Perhaps we don't get around to telling you that quite as often
as we should …

So how did I find out, you're wondering? About the smoking? Well, I've been suspicious for a while. The clues have been there: a slight whiff of smoke on your clothing, your eagerness to dash 'out back' every twenty minutes or so in order to 'check on the barrel', followed by a swift re-application of lipstick on your return. On one occasion – quite recently – I could've sworn I saw a trace of ash on the toe of your court shoe.

Oh, and then there's Mhairi, of course. She's back on the snout herself. Don't worry, she didn't tell me (didn't break the faith between you), this was just a little theory I came up with, all by myself. I was actually in Feathercuts on Tuesday, following up on a case I've just recently inherited from the Skipton Constabulary (the Burley Cross Postbox Theft Case – as one of the official victims of the crime, you'll probably have received formal notification to this effect from Skipton by now).

You're probably also aware of the fact that it was Mhairi who discovered the stolen cache (out in the back alley, behind her salon), and that – contrary to popular belief – the letters weren't found pilfered – violated, even – by the thief. They were pristine. Untouched. It was Mhairi herself who tore some of them open (and perused the contents), before finally doing what she should have done in the first place: ringing the police.

Did she tell you about Rita Bramwell's secret daughter? (You'd been pretty worried about Rita for a while, hadn't you? Hadn't everyone? I mean it wasn't just idle gossip on Mhairi's part so much as an act of charity – a gesture of honest concern.)

But when Mhairi told you *how* she'd acquired the information? From a letter in the stolen cache? Weren't you horrified? Truly horrified? And then, when Rita got wind of it and attempted suicide? How did you feel then? *Eh?* Bad? Conflicted? *Culpable?* As if you'd pushed that cruel, sharp blade on to her delicate wrists with your own hand?

Mhairi told you – she insisted, she *promised* – that the letter she had found was already torn open, but you knew that it wasn't, didn't you? Because when you stole those letters you didn't think of opening them. Not even for a second (you're far too scrupulous, too honourable for that!).

Although you *were* angry, weren't you? Underneath your studied veneer of cheery professionalism? Angry about a lot of things (not that anybody would have guessed it – with your open smile, your easy hospitality, your ready line in casual chit-chat …).

You were angry that Duke was gone, that he'd been taken from you, so cruelly. You were angry that he'd left you in a state of such crippling debt (from all those expensive renovations, instigated, in the main, because of that ridiculous feud of his – that pointless rivalry – with Baxter Thorndyke). You were angry after the burglary (and with good reason, too. The mess those vandals made of the newly refurbished bar! So cruel! So pointless! So unnecessary!). You were angry when your insurance premiums sky-rocketed. Angry that Timmy Dickson pretty much got away with it (after turning in crucial evidence on another, unrelated – but apparently more 'serious' case – and plea-bargaining with the judge).

You were angry about how long it took you to get back on to any kind of an even financial keel after the police confiscated a series of cheques and other critical pieces of documentation as 'evidence' (because Sergeant Everill had developed a – completely stupid and erroneous – theory that the whole thing might actually be 'an inside job').

And then, when it felt like you might finally be getting back on track again, that stupid riot after the darts tournament! The ruinous headlines in the papers! Your insurance premiums virtually doubling overnight! Harsh words from the brewery! All those bills! All that stress! Baxter Thorndyke sticking his boot in at every available opportunity …

It wasn't just important, now, but imperative that trade should improve in the run-up to Christmas. You were already living hand to mouth – so desperate, indeed, to make ends meet that you had actively started encouraging coach parties (even though a large proportion of the village was dead set against it). That huge stink over the damage to grass verges! Ridiculous! Exhausting!

And then last, but by no means least (the icing on the cake): that hyperactive Coombes kid tampering with the mechanism of Duke's prized grandfather clock! (Duke's beloved clock! Its steady, regular tick, representing for you – for all of us – the life and breath of The Old Oak.)

You wanted to throw in the towel that night, didn't you? That night of the Coombes family Auction of Promises dinner? Standing there, all alone, in the snug, tears running down your cheeks, the carpet around you scattered with a terrifying array of nuts and bolts and springs and gears and wheels …

But you couldn't throw it in, no matter how much you wanted to. You couldn't give up on Duke's dream. You couldn't let Thorndyke get the better of you both. *You simply couldn't let that bastard win*!

But cash was so short, wasn't it? So short, in fact, that you found yourself doing something you thought you could never, ever stoop to. You found yourself borrowing from the charity box (just briefly, just temporarily, just a harmless, spur-of-the-moment thing). You'd been placed in charge of the Auction of Promises budget after Prue dashed off on her mercy mission to France. And then there was the bridge night – the money raised for that donkey sanctuary in Cairo …

Good old Wincey, trusty old Wincey, so ashamed of having temporarily pocketed the charity cash that she ducks behind a car on seeing Sebastian St John and Unity Gray idly chatting outside the post office together. Not because you're angry with Unity (for the darts comp. catastrophe). No! Not at all! But because you're crippled with embarrassment. You can't bear the thought that they're going to ask (for the third time, the fourth time) if you've managed to bank that infernal charity money, yet.

You *can't* bank it – it's impossible – because there's not a penny of it left (and not so much as a bean remaining in your account to cover the debt!). But then that awful look of humiliation on Unity's old face! You hadn't managed to duck quite soon enough (she saw! She'd noticed!). So you quickly pretend you've dropped something (*what*? A coin? A bangle? A stamp?), that it's rolled down into the road and you're simply trying to retrieve it. You scrabble around in the gutter for a while, then you turn and you make a rapid bee-line for … Where? *Anywhere*! The church!

You dash inside, mortified. You lean against a back wall, peering around you in the half-gloom, catching your breath. Your eyes alight on a bank of candles, flickering, comfortingly, in a far corner. You smell the scent of flowers. It feels different in the church. Warmer. You've not been inside the place since Duke's funeral – which Reverend Horwood hijacked with some horribly inappropriate hell and damnation diatribe (about the social ills caused by alcohol). You swore you'd never enter its dark portals again after that.

But here you are, just the same. You're staring at the bank of candles and feeling strangely – unwittingly – drawn towards them, so you go and sit down on a pew. You're desperately sad – desperately alone. You inspect the exquisitely embroidered knee-rest for a while. You close your eyes. You rest your forehead, lightly, on the back of the pew in front. You find yourself whispering a little prayer. Your tensed muscles gradually begin to relax. You feel a sense of lightness, of peace, a brief moment of comfort, even …

But then your reverie – your brief, blissful idyll – is cruelly destroyed as a loud commotion breaks out directly behind you. Suddenly the church is full of people – full of argument and rancour. Reverend Paul is there, and Reverend Horwood, and several of Reverend Horwood's 'ladies', and Reverend Paul (usually so quiet and unassuming) is shouting at Reverend Horwood for displaying a crucifix in the church foyer without first seeking his prior permission.

You're appalled by this scene – jolted by it – disorientated – and you quickly rise to your feet and flee the building. You're in such a hurry to get out of there that you leave your gloves and your scarf behind you. Yet the gloves and the scarf aren't the only things you miss in your rush. You miss something else – something you couldn't really be expected to notice, but something significant, even momentous …

Rhona Brooks (one of Reverend Horwood's 'ladies', his most loyal acolyte) is also in attendance. You and Rhona have never been close. Rhona doesn't drink. She's very morose, very dowdy, very devout. She doesn't socialize much. You have nothing in common with her. But when that argument takes place between the new reverend and the old, and she sees you suddenly quit the church, Rhona notices your distress (your gloves and your scarf left behind on the pew), and something gives way inside her. A tiny shift takes place. A little knot of doubt enters her staunch, puritanical heart. She starts to question herself. She starts to wonder …

She plays the scene over – again and again – in her mind: the sight of you, Wincey Hawkes, the old publican's wife, cowering in the corner, hoping to find comfort in front of that flickering bank of candles (that frivolous bank of candles which Reverend Horwood disapproves of so much). She sees (not just sees, but *feels*, each time she replays the scene in her head), that palpable sense of hurt felt by the new reverend (the sense of betrayal), the atmosphere of contempt – of rage, even – emanating from the old (but … but it was only a little joke, wasn't it, after all? The carving? Edo's carving? Nothing more than that? Nothing serious? Nothing critical? Just a quick, mischievous yank on the tiger's tail?).

Let's push Rhona to the back of our minds for a moment, though, shall we? (But don't forget her – heaven forbid! – because she still has a small yet critical role to play in this story.) Let's think about Wincey again. Let's think about you, *eh*?

What happens next? You go home to the pub. You do
several hours' work behind the bar. You're re-stocking the
crisps in the snug – polishing the optics, perhaps – when you
chance to overhear a conversation between Kenneth Cranshaw
(Sr) and Walter Francis …

Seems that Mr Cranshaw (Sr) has just returned from a
council meeting where the old prefab on Sharp Crag Farm has
been designated 'unfit for human habitation' (at Baxter
Thorndyke's instigation!). Poor Donal Flint is *furious* about it –
it doesn't rain, it pours, they're saying; didn't he just lose three
sheep to the fly strike this week?

Your mind turns to the bill for the repair of Duke's
grandfather clock – how you pretended it was just a hundred
when it was actually over four … And poor Paula Coombes's
face when you told her – £100! An unimaginably huge amount
to her (an unimaginably huge amount to *you*, right now).

So the next day, when she pops in (still plainly ignorant of the
developments on council), you tell her to forget about the repair
bill. 'I'm sure the insurance will cough up, eventually,' you say.
But Paula already has a bee in her bonnet about taking her late
husband's mother's favourite vase – or decanter – to a local
antique shop to see what she can raise on it. And though your
every good instinct rails against this scheme (she's a widow
without so much as a change of clothes to her name, the older
boy's a reprobate, all the kids currently have measles), you find
yourself giving in to her. You're so broke! She's so eager to make
it up to you! And the actual bill is four hundred – you kept that
fact back from her, didn't you? To try and spare her feelings?

Poor Paula! So keen to make amends, so full of sincerity and
optimism, that you don't have the heart … you don't have the
luxury … Which is it, exactly? Does it really even matter?

The next afternoon, at lunchtime, you receive a piece of
most unwelcome news. Paula's been in a car crash – on her way
to Ilkley, or to Bradley, or to Kildwick – with the blue glass
decanter. The van is a write-off. The decanter is smashed. And

she doesn't even know yet that she's to be made homeless, at Christmas! Five kiddies in tow! You sit in the empty dining rooms, your head in your hands.

It's then that you receive a visit from Rhona Brooks. She has your scarf and your gloves with her (which you'd left at the church). And she looks so out of place in here, so ill at ease, with her stooping gait, her long, grey, almost nunnish dress, the prominent cross at her neck, those huge, calloused hands. But even so. 'You seem upset,' she murmurs, and she pulls out a chair.

So you tell her about Paula Coombes. You tell her about the clock. You tell her about the vase, the bill, the crash. And then, before you know quite what you're doing, everything else just starts tumbling out. About the insurance, and the numbers, and the articles in the paper, and how broke you are, and last – but no means least – about the charity cash.

'It's all such a mess,' you say, 'such a terrible mess!'

And you think Rhona will hate you, that she'll judge you (the way Reverend Horwood judged Duke); a part of you actually wants her to, a part of you actually needs her to. But she doesn't. She just sits there, quietly, and she listens, her giant hands knitted together, gently, upon her lap. And when she's done listening, she stands up, and she leans forward, and she squeezes your shoulder, and she nods, then she leaves, muttering something about needing to 'finish off a hedge, over at the Manor'.

When she's gone, you wonder if you only dreamed it. And the day draws, inexorably, onwards. Deliveries. A broken oven in the kitchens. The chef threatening to hand in his notice if he doesn't get a kitchen assistant to help with the chores. Then the cleaner's a no-show. And the phone keeps on ringing: salesmen, creditors. A coach party arrives, but nobody requires hot meals. One of the toilets gets blocked ...

You begin to rail against the world again. How could you not? And it's the evening already and the barman's cut his finger on a broken bottle – they're bandaging it up in the kitchen, so you're back behind the bar. And Sebastian (just on his way over to post a letter to Prue), pops in for a quick chat about the Auction of Promises. Mrs Goff is there, too, propping up the bar, her face full of sympathy. 'Numbers not up yet, Wincey?' she asks, scanning the half-empty saloon.

You're finding it difficult to talk. Your throat keeps contracting. Your eyes keep filling with tears. You're so tired – so exhausted. Then Sebastian mentions the money again. The fifth time, is this? The sixth time? And you don't know what to say, what to do … So you go and grab your cheque book and you write out three cheques – one, two, three of them, signing with a flourish (entirely for Brenda Goff's benefit): one for the Auction of Promises, a second for the clock repairs, a third for the donkey sanctuary. You address the three envelopes, leaning on the bar. You apply three stamps.

'Pop these in the post for me, Seb,' you say, 'there's a good lad.'

An hour later, though, and your stomach is in knots. You know there's no cash to cover the cheques in your account – you've already fallen behind on the mortgage.

What to do? What to do?

So you throw on your coat and head out. It's almost nine. You have a small can of lighter fluid in your hand – or a bottle of red wine vinegar. You must destroy those cheques – at *any* cost – or everything will be lost.

But when you reach the postbox you can't bring yourself to do it, can you? You just stand there, staring at the damn thing, grinding your teeth with frustration, with rage, with grief, with disappointment. And in a moment of pure, unadulterated pique, you kick out your foot. You land a blow on the box. One, small blow. Then the door pops off.

Good heavens! You take a quick, halting step back. What an unexpected stroke of luck! Then, before you know quite what you're doing, you've fallen to your knees on that icy pavement and you're feeling around inside, reaching inside, frantically

---

355

scrabbling your way through the letters (simply intent on removing yours), but then you hear the creak and clank of Susan Trott's gate. *Damn*! Now what?! You rapidly tip the entire contents of the box into your coat – or a plastic bag you've brought with you (the bottle of lighter fluid, the vinegar, hidden inside it), and you run.

Oh, God! Back in the pub again, upstairs, in your bedroom, turning the lock on the door, you finally return to your senses and wonder what the hell it is that you've just done. Am I crazy? you think. Is this just some terrible nightmare? Or could Wincey Hawkes – the respectable pub landlady, an upright member of the community, a gracious doyenne of local charity events, a rock, a brick, a shoulder for all the world to cry upon – have just casually (and with malice aforethought), *robbed the local postbox*?! A mere five days before Christmas?!

You struggle to draw breath for a while (Am I a thief now? A vandal?), but then your mind turns back to Timmy Dickson, to Baxter Thorndyke, to that stupid argument in the church, and your heart hardens, your resolve deepens. This needn't be so bad as it seems, you think. You make a plan. A good plan. You think it's virtually foolproof.

The next day you carry it out. You have an appointment with Mhairi at Feathercuts in Skipton (to get your roots touched up – your red roots). Mhairi's salon (what a happy coincidence!) just happens to back on to the same, quiet, scruffy back alley as Timothy Dickson's house.

Just prior to the appointment you park your car, make sure the coast is clear, then carry a black refuse-bag with the letters hidden inside it into the back alley. You remove three letters from the bunch and scatter them around inside Mhairi's small, neat yard. Then you go and get your hair done.

Halfway through (as is now customary), you sneak into the back kitchen for a quick fag, opening the back door (to air the room – as you generally always do). You place a further letter (which you'd hidden inside your pocket), on to the back step (to draw her on), then you return to the salon where you enjoy a fascinating conversation with a Miss Squires (charming woman, very affable, who you'd spoken to, on the phone, a couple of weeks before).

Just as you'd hoped, a few minutes later, Mhairi nips out back for a quick fag herself, and is astonished to discover …

But you're well on your way home by then.

And the best part of it? You've won yourself some time – some valuable time! Because you didn't remove those unbankable cheques. Nope. You cunningly left them behind. And they'll become a part of the body of evidence, now. It'll be days, weeks, months, even, before you get them back.

You feel like a weight has lifted from your shoulders. In fact you feel so light, so airy, that when Paula Coombes drops by to apologize about the fact that she can't pay for the clock repairs, you tell her it's just fine. And when she confides in you about the prefab, you tell her … How extraordinary! You find yourself telling her to move into the pub. There are three empty bedrooms upstairs. And the older boy can work in the kitchens, in lieu of rent (after his measles have cleared up). And Paula can work behind the bar. She has a barmaid's temperament, you say, with a grin, a kind of crazy optimism – the kind you had yourself once, as a girl, the kind that makes people want to sit down, have a chat, and enjoy a drink.

Later that afternoon, the barman comes upstairs to find you (you're sitting at Duke's desk, in his study, doing the VAT). He passes you a heavy envelope (his finger swaddled in white – the bandage coming loose at the tip). You open it up. Your jaw drops. Three and a half thousand pounds, in used bank notes, and a short message, written on a piece of curiously heavy and porous paper: 'For charity,' it says.
Fin.
The end.

How did I do?
All right?

There are a few things I don't know, obviously: did you keep the money? Did you manage to unblock that toilet successfully? Did the barman need a stitch? Did the VAT add up properly?

There are many things I don't know, in fact, but there are some things I do. I know that Paula Coombes has been a Godsend. I know that business is slowly picking up. I know that Jared has finally found his joy in life (his passion – his true vocation) and that he's training to become a chef. I know Madeline's got a new fiddle, and that sometimes, in the early evening, she climbs up on to the bar and she plays it for a while (to tumultuous applause), then she throws it down, rolls up her sleeve and armpit farts, for an encore.

I know it brings a large tear to your eye, Wincey, every time she does.

And I know you'll never forgive yourself for what happened to poor Rita – that you were the first person (aside from Peter, and from me) to visit her in hospital. I know you talked Peter around. I know you force-fed him on casseroles. I know you were incredibly kind, and generous with your time, same as you always are.

And other things – other things I know? Let's see … I know that pubs are on their way out (hundreds are closing every week), that they're merely a sad reminder of things past (the way we once were, The Good Old Days), just like 'community spirit' is, and communities themselves, and churches, and local bobbies, and pickled walnuts, and brass bands at fetes, and tall hedgerows, and handwritten letters, and home-cooked meals, and sparrows, and boredom, and books, and gob-stoppers, and ladybirds, and innocence …

Yes. All for the high jump. All for the chop. All nearly eclipsed, now (may they rest in peace), by a much bigger, brighter future, in twenty-four-hour digital HD.

Oh, and one last thing; one last thing I know (perhaps the most important thing of all, as far as you're concerned): I know

how to keep schtum. I know when to keep it zipped. I know
how to hold my tongue …

   And I *am* holding it, Wincey. And I will continue to hold it –
for your sake. For mine. For all our sakes.
Fear not.

   Discretion, as they say, is my watchword.

Happy Easter,
God bless you,

PC Roger Topping

PS I quite *like* the new postbox, as it happens.

Dear Mrs Hope,

I won't be in tomorrow morning. A couple of little jobs for you:

1   We need to ring Mrs Lockwood about Sam Lockwood's missing crutch.

2   I see we're almost out of Toilet Duck.

3   There's a pile of letters on my desk, and a list of addresses printed on to a sheet of paper next to them. The letters need to be resealed/re-packaged/readdressed, as specified (whichever method you think preferable), and then returned to the sender as soon as possible. Two exceptions. The letter addressed to a Dr Bonner, please forward it to Nick Endive. And the letter addressed to Nina Springhill: deliver it to her, personally, at her mother's. You're neighbours, aren't you? (Nina's still staying there, I believe, getting some r&r after her unfortunate miscarriage, prior to her imminent move down to Bristol. Or Taunton, is it? Either way … Yes. Thanks.)

4   The ants have returned! It occurs to me that I might have dropped a half-empty (or half-full – depending on how you like to look at it) bag of Revels down the back of the filing cabinet. I fear that's probably what's attracting them. Should we take some kind of decisive action do you think? Or just wait for them to polish the Revels off and then gradually lose interest? I can't quite decide …

5   Have a lovely weekend.

6   I'm sorry about the bullet points (or the numbers), they just keep coming up on the screen whenever I start a new line, no matter how hard I try to …

7   Ridiculous! Quite ridiculous!

8   What a clumsy oaf I am!

9

---

10 Have a lovely weekend.

11

12 Did I say that already?

13 Sorry. Getting a bit flustered …

14

15 I'm off on a jaunt to the L.S. Lowry museum in Salford on Saturday. Never been before. Hired a Zafira (people carrier). I'm actually quite excited …

16 Wish me well!

17 Bye for now.

18

19 Oh yes. Congratulate Lucy on those wonderful accountancy exam results.

20 And best regards to Colin. Hope his tooth is feeling a little better.

21

22 Roger

23

24

25

26

27

28 Dammit.

29

30

31 *Dammit!*

32

33 What's wrong with this stupid thing?!

34

35

36 Why's it always so much easier just doing this stuff by hand?

37 *Eh?*